Mc
Thank you for stopping back.

Ron Hepner

THE BRAVE ONE
STRIKES BACK

By

R.J. Hepner

WCP

World Castle Publishing, LLC
Pensacola, Florida

Copyright © R. J. Hepner 2014
Print ISBN: 9781629890708
eBook ISBN: 9781629890715
First Edition World Castle Publishing, LLC, May 1, 2014
http://www.worldcastlepublishing.com

Licensing Notes

Cover: Select-O-Grafix
Editor: Maxine Bringenberg

Epigraph

*'Men have lost their reason
in nothing so much as their religion,
wherein stones and clouts make martyrs.'*

Sir Thomas Brown

Chapter 1

Los Angeles International Airport
Monday Morning, Early June

Cleared for landing by the LAX control tower, one after the other, British Airways 747s from Nairobi, Kenya, Lufthansa from Islamabad, and Emirates from Cairo, Egypt flew through a cloudy coastal marine layer and arrived at the Bradley International Terminal. Customs and immigration centers would be busy checking hundreds of passengers. Coming through were citizens of the United States and U.S. permanent residents, as well as scores of international visitors from Europe, Africa, and the Middle East. Most were cleared with little difficulty. Passengers receiving additional screening would be turned away or arrested either for insufficient documentation, expired visas, suspicious behavior, seized contraband, and frequently, drug smuggling. Some individuals came in with nothing suspicious, except what their intent may be after arriving.

This morning, each flight had two passengers, all U.S. citizens returning from Somalia, who ignored one another while under security cameras until they exited the departure terminal. Carrying only backpacks or tote bags, the men in their mid-twenties to early thirties, neatly shaved, all dressed casually in jeans, shirts, and light jackets, greeted one another when they reached the roadway median. Shuttle vans and diesel-belching passenger buses from hotels and numerous Southland attraction sites clogged the road. Laughing amid praises of Allah, they mentioned that Immigration and Customs agents didn't inquire about their absences.

A white passenger van approached. All jumped aboard, waved to the young, bearded driver, and settled down as it headed for Century Boulevard. Morning clouds began fading; the sun emerged from behind a hazy sky. The van entered the 405 Santa Monica North Freeway and made its way over to the carpool lane.

***

In a crowded courtroom at the Los Angeles federal courthouse, the bailiff stood and announced for all to rise, Superior Judge Anita Mai Fong presiding. The defendant had to be prodded to stand by one of his two attorneys. The man, tall and slender, youthful looking for a guy in his late twenties with shaggy hair and whiskers, glanced behind him and nodded to a row of Muslim supporters. Two sheriff's deputies surrounded his chair. Reporters hugged the front rows. Murmurs from the spectators grew louder until the judge hit her gavel. Jury members consisting of African-Americans, Latinos, and three Caucasians stared stoically at the defendant, who bounced up and down on his chair.

Judge Fong asked the jury spokesman to rise. Silence enveloped the chamber as every-body anticipated the verdict. In a stern voice, she advised that if there were any angry outbursts, she would order everybody out. She lowered her glasses and began listing the charges:

"Count One: Possession of dangerous components for the purpose of constructing bomb-making materials."

"Guilty."

"Count Two: Detonation of an explosive with intent to kill."

"Guilty."

"Count Three: Conspiracy to commit terrorist acts."

Again, a guilty verdict was declared.

Spectators rustled in their seats. Whispers became louder.

"Count Four: Association with a terrorist organization, the Brothers of Somali Jihad."

"Guilty."

Hearing persons muttering and noticing his supporters shifting around, the judge again warned against any unruliness.

She continued: "Three counts of attempted murder and two counts of murder of police officers."

The spokesman looked down at his notes. No hesitation. "Guilty as charged."

Deputies pushed the standing, shouting Muslims back to their seats.

Fong pounded her gavel harder.

The defendant pushed away the table, brushing aside his lawyers; prosecutors rose to their feet. Voices in the gallery intensified.

More pounding sounded until the judge's words became almost inaudible. Then she ordered the bailiffs to clear all spectators from the chamber. Chants of "shame, shame, unfair" rang out from the men as they were herded out the door and into the corridor. Two court artists flipped page after page, trying to capture the melee.

When the noise subsided, Judge Fong informed the legal teams that there would be a thirty minute recess, after which sentencing would be delivered. Before stepping down from the bench, she ordered the bailiffs to remove the defendant from the courtroom.

Still yelling epithets, he was handcuffed. They had to lock arms around his chest when he resisted being taken to a holding room.

***

Meanwhile, the van exited the 405 and headed east past numerous shopping centers, auto dealerships, fast food outlets, and several commercial complexes. Not until it pulled into a twenty unit, two story motel did the men start speaking again, this time in their native tongue. The driver told them the number fifteen corner unit on the second floor would be their temporary residence. No one from the street or front office would see them.

"Don't use the telephone. Stay there; someone will contact you," he added. "If you need food or water, there's a convenience store and restaurant down the block." Within seconds, the van rumbled onto the boulevard.

Their suite had three beds and a cot, a scratched up plain table and two chairs pushed against one wall, cooking and washing appliances, a dented microwave, a TV, and a clock radio. Carpets were saturated with cigarette burns. One wall painting wobbled when footsteps crossed the floor; greenish stains lined the bathtub, and only one light fixture worked. With the drapes pulled shut, their facial features became shadows.

Two of the men lay on a bed; one closed the drapes, and another splashed cold water on his face. Someone turned on the TV; local stations came up, but no cable channels.

***

When court resumed, only the prosecution members and the defense attorneys, a few reporters, the artists, bailiffs, and five deputy sheriffs, plus court personnel, rose as Judge Fong climbed up to her bench. She ordered the young man to stand, which he did, as slowly as possible. Asked whether he wanted to address the court, at first he shook his head no, but then stepped in front of the defense table. Adjusting his glasses, staring up at the woman who would soon be pronouncing his sentence, he waved his hand, pointing a finger in her direction. What followed was a declaration of innocence, deriding the justice system, how it was in violation of his constitutional rights, reciting sections of law that he had memorized from legal encyclopedias. Then in a raspy voice he recited verses from the Koran, pausing each time on a line that described Islam as the only true law.

Aggravation setting in, Judge Fong advised him to stop. She reassembled some notes, removed her glasses, and spoke in a low voice. "This court finds you guilty on all counts. Mr. Muhamed Dauadi, you have shown no remorse. You have mocked the very system from which you demand rights for your heinous actions, and have left destruction and emotional scars on the citizens of Los Angeles. Your murderous actions took the life of police officers and nearly killed three other law enforcement officers, as well as innocent bystanders."

None of her words brought the slightest stir.

She continued by referring to his former homeland, Somalia, from which he had come to the United States in order to escape tyranny, terrorism, and a lawless society, yet he acted in total disregard of his new home. "You brought your hatred of America and intentionally decided to destroy the fabric of liberty, which our country bestows on its citizens. It is incredible that you became a naturalized citizen of this country, swearing to uphold our laws. If it were in my power, this court would strip you of your citizenship."

He responded by reciting more Koranic verses, declaring that being a martyr for Allah was the highest honor of Islam, and shouting that he regretted not killing more Americans.

She put her glasses back on and leaned forward, pronouncing sentence. "Life imprisonment with no chance of parole on each count of the shootings of the police officers…twenty years concurrent on each of the terrorist related charges."

He started to move closer to the bench. Firm hands of the deputies prevented his approaching any farther. "Infidel, infidel," he yelled. "You're a puppet of your warmongering nation. America will never be safe. Your life has no value."

Judge Fong struck her gavel. "Mr. Dauadi," she concluded, "in prison is where you will end your life."

A slew of curses followed, some in Arabic and bits of nonsensical English.

A bailiff and the deputies tightened their grip and half pulled him into the holding room. While she dismissed the jury, the young man's screaming echoed through the door, words to the effect that *"Inshallah…God willing,"* his Somali brothers would set him free.

Dressed in an orange prison jumpsuit, he was taken outside from the rear of the courthouse to a waiting corrections department van. He said nothing, even ignoring some jabs about his religion. His time in jail would be served at a maximum-security prison in the Midwest. Temporary housing would be at Soledad.

For this trip to the desert, and for security purposes, no other inmates would be allowed onboard; only the driver and a sheriff's officer up front shielded by a wire and steel barricade. An accompanying police car had been planned; however, the Los Angeles County Sheriff's Department couldn't spare an officer.

Heavy traffic downtown slowed the vehicle as it neared the 110 North Freeway. One by one, cars and trucks inched their way into the transition lane. The van driver, behind a pickup, honked several times for it to proceed with the green entrance light. No movement. Confusion set in when the red light returned and didn't change to green.

A Mercedes pulled up behind and touched bumpers with the van. The officers used their rearview mirrors, but were unable to see through the tinted windshield. They gazed back as a Department of Water maintenance truck edged up to the car and parked it horizontally, blocking any vehicle from entering the transition lane.

Minutes passed. Their van was now hemmed in, the shoulder too slim to try and pass the pickup. The deputy decided to check things out. As he faced the Mercedes, a side window lowered and an M-16 automatic rifle burst of bullets threw him against the van and down to the pavement.

The driver had only seconds to react before a passenger in the pickup came charging out and blasted the front window with eight rounds from a .45 mm pistol. Shattered glass and blood splattered across the windshield.

A tall, light skinned Somali in dark clothes leaped into the van and yanked a set of keys from the dead driver's belt. He tossed them to another person, who unlocked the van's rear doors. Muhamed Dauadi, still in restraints, stepped down and hopped into the Mercedes.

Returning to their vehicles, the pickup entered the freeway. Cars in the right hand lane braked and swerved to avoid being struck. At the same time, the DWP truck backed up until the Mercedes had enough clearance to get around the sheriff's van. It too sped onto the 110 Freeway and disappeared, heading north.

Chapter 2

National Security Unit Stake Out
Tuesday Morning, Vancouver, B.C., Canada

Overnight a tremendous wind gust had taken out power lines and knocked over large trees into yards and on roofs. There were bound to be comments that it was rare for Vancouver to get so windy in June. But it happened; gusts continued to blow across streets. If homeowners wanted to know where their garbage containers or parts of awnings had gone, it was best to search down a block or two. This upscale section of the city hadn't escaped the wrath of the windstorm.

Although thick white clouds covered the sun, the two men in flak jackets left sunglasses on to prevent pieces of debris from hitting their eyes. That's why both stood alongside of the dark blue SUV.

Their focus was on a two-story sandstone and brick house half way down the block. Crumpled hedges improved their sightline. Acting on a tip, they waited for a late model Lincoln Town Car to return.

Art Dodek, the lead agent, and his partner, Keith Dawson, were accustomed to surveillance assignments. Last year, joined by an RCMP assault team, they had broken their way in on three Pakistanis planning to become suicide bombers. Remembering the young guy who had slammed a two by four on his shoulder during the raid, Art moved his 180-pound frame as dust and branches flew around his head.

Over two years ago the Canadian prime minister had approved the counter-intelligence agency — the National Security Unit (NSU) — providing it with more flexible investigative methods and power above that of CSIS, the Canadian spy agency. The new team succeeded in eliminating two ruthless assassins from Syria who plotted to kill a visiting Israeli prime minister. Those men weren't terrorists fighting for their Islamic religious beliefs; they were hired Middle Eastern killers who meant to disrupt and destroy as much of the Vancouver area infrastructure as possible. Shootings, murders, an attack at a synagogue, plus a suicide bombing that killed scores of innocent passengers on a commuter train; nothing was sacred to these inhuman characters.

He realized, too, that being Jewish sometimes handicapped his role as an agent: the target of numerous bigoted incidents; hatred and defiance from Muslims he apprehended; even interpersonal relations with his NSU boss, Alistair Burke, often resulted in doubt whether Art could put aside his ethnicity when pursuing Islamic militants. Sometimes, though, the outcome depended on how far they would go.

He had to let those parts slide…otherwise, he would've become too vulnerable in his job. Perhaps that's why, in order to obtain validation, he pushed himself harder. One explanation could be that his early intelligence career started with fighting Fedayeen warriors in Palestine and the Israeli West Bank. In fact, a man who would become his mentor— a Mossad agent named David Tivi—gave him valuable, life-saving tips about pursuing terror suspects. However, he told him, first you must have will, determination, a goal, and, above all, never expect success if you don't seriously believe what you're doing is for the public's benefit. Moreover, never allow trust to cloud your judgment. Friend or associate, trusting someone too closely can blow up in your face. It was unfortunate that Art forgot that fact when his best friend betrayed him for supporting extremists.

Dawson, who joined NSU at the same time as Art, munched on his favorite nuts, cashews…not as a snack, but as a stress-buster. A black ex-cop, both in Canada and the United States, he had experienced his share of discrimination. From other law enforcement members, it ticked him off. You wear the same uniform, you're partners, you share the same dangers. He could've used his size and 270-pound muscular frame to deal with ignorant cops. Instead, his weight—and, on occasion, his mean disposition—easily persuaded criminals not to resist…except one time last fall when he'd shot a nutcase suicide bomber who had put a bullet in his ribcage. Just like his partner would agree, anything can happen; a stake out made no difference.

The wind seemed to seesaw back and forth. Specs of wood, grass, and pieces of twigs continued to whirl around their faces. Lamplights flickered.

Nothing else mattered as they observed the Lincoln turn into the driveway. Two Middle Eastern men, one of medium build, the other, shorter, his choice of clothes almost gaudy in appearance, started unloading the trunk of heavy sacks, cans, and plastic bags.

The two agents drew nearer, both of their hands over side arms. Art's preference was his 9 mm Glock for its lightness and quick action, while Keith wouldn't be without his .45-caliber pistol. The contents of the trunk were all that mattered to them right now. Tips to NSU had mentioned suspicious activity at the house. Now, advancing with guns drawn, they were about to find out. It wasn't until the driver shut the trunk lid that he noticed the two agents springing forward, weapons pointed in their direction.

"Stay where you are," Art shouted.

The surprised driver dropped a bag.

Keith lumbered between them, pushing the shorter guy onto the trunk.

Mr. Tall held his hands mid-level with the car's roof. His eyes circled the space between himself and the man holding the weapon, wondering whether to run.

Art replied for him by spinning him around and pinning his arms back.

"What do you want? Who are you?" he asked.

"NSU. The National Security Unit, if you can't spell."

"I'm a doctor. My name is —"

Keith held the other one's shoulder with his large hand. "We know who you are. Want to explain what you've got here, Doc?" Stooping, Art emptied the bags on the driveway. Spray cans and several bottles of hydro peroxide bounced off the asphalt. He used a knife to cut a slit in a sack. Out poured what could have been mistaken for sawdust, except it was fertilizer.

"We have a big lawn," the doctor rambled off.

"Yeah. And you're gonna spruce it up with beauty supplies," smirked Art, holstering his side arm. "We have a federal warrant to search the premises. FYI: You're busted."

"Cousin," the gaudily dressed one interjected with a slight accent. "Can they…search?"

"Be quiet. We want to contact our lawyer."

"Sure you do," Keith grinned. "Is he a cousin, too?"

A Vancouver Police Department van pulled up. Keith assisted the officers with placing the men in the rear, and explained the bomb making materials were to be held as evidence.

Inside, the house was furnished throughout with Greco-Mediterranean themes, plus obvious signs that the cousins were devout Muslims: prayer mats facing east, large mural paintings of imams blessing crowds of men in mosques; no photographs of families or women were discovered. Two loaded handguns turned up stuffed behind pillows in a downstairs bedroom.

Indeed, the agents knew their names. Background checks came up with their Somali-Canadian dual citizenship records. Mr. Tall may have performed physician procedures in Somalia, although he never graduated

14

from medical school there or from any other country. Provincial medical boards refused to certify him in Canada, ascertaining that documents he presented were fraudulent. As well, he and his cousin had both applied as refugees five years ago.

During the last decade, hundreds of Somali's had entered North America, always claiming asylum; most settled in the U.S. Northeast, Minneapolis, Montreal, and Toronto. It wasn't unusual, either, that some were on U.S. watch lists, despite obtaining citizenship. Interesting, too, that in their applications they described themselves as homeless and impoverished. This three story, 5,000 square foot house wasn't acquired with welfare funds.

Over the next hour the agents discovered a variety of items — air route and airport directional maps; downloaded maps of government buildings, in the U.S. and Canada; numerous Islamic videos and DVDs portraying Muslims as freedom fighters and disciples of Allah; non-stop graphic videos of Rocket Propelled Grenade and Improvised Explosive Devices attacks against American troops, routinely with the backgrounds of chanting and singing. In an upstairs bathroom, a false ceiling valance contained about $350,000 in $100 bills still wound with rubber bands. They could be genuine, maybe counterfeit — it would be up to the Secret Service to verify their authenticity.

Both rolled their tongues. Words weren't necessary. That much money had to be for a purpose. It could buy a lot, too…like parts to make explosives, import illegal weapons, equipment for their roster of militants, or recruit youths across the country.

Most of the afternoon had the agents making reports and filling out endless forms. Shit, they figured, the word *duplicate* should be banned from the English language.

RCMP crime labs would test the materials confiscated, although there was no doubt what their application would be intended for. Once mixed, plus a few other ingredients, those chemicals could've been bomb-ready. Vancouver? Where? Last year the city was hit by several bombings with disastrous results and high death tolls. If this find disrupted another attack, countless lives were spared.

Interrogating the two suspects went nowhere. Both proclaimed their innocence. Explanations for the supplies became more ludicrous the more they…or rather, the "doctor"…talked. Yes, the home belonged to the cousins, purchased only months ago at the original asking price of over $1,200,000; which was odd when real estate markets hadn't rebounded. Cash also paid for property taxes, legal fees, insurance, and six month advanced payments for utility expenses.

Back tracking stores where the products were bought was futile when all items turned out as cash sales. These "cells" often used clandestine financial transactions to prevent paper trails. The so-called doctor was asked where he obtained the money. Naturally, he refused to answer. Not bad for impoverished villagers who applied for refugee status. Another roadblock emerged — this time diplomatically. The Canadian Citizenship and Immigration Department sealed their Canadian asylum records.

Nevertheless, help came from the U.S. Department of Homeland Security, which oversees America's immigrants, and the State Department, who issues visas. Before they were granted Canadian naturalization, apparently they had entered the United States from Kenya as B-2 visitors. After their visas expired, both sought refugee status in Canada. In any event, neither man's name appeared in any criminal database, nor in DMV files. Checks into previous departures and reentries between the U.S. and Canada indicated multiple trips to Mid-Western cities, but never for more than a few days. Where they stayed or whom they met was any body's guess.

Entering the central processing room about an hour later, the Security Unit's major operations center, Art's Blackberry beeped. He picked up on the second ring. "Senior Agent Art Dodek speaking."

"Agent Dodek, this is Consuela Mercado, Special Agent from the U.S. Department of Homeland Security," the caller's crisp, articulate voice said.

"Yes, how can I help you?"

"I'll get right to the point. There's been an alarming number of missing young men in my jurisdiction — Los Angeles."

"Yeah, okay. What's that got to do with me…with NSU? There's a missing persons bureau in Los Angeles, isn't there?"

"Of course. Except, we're security, not the police. These missing men have returned."

He drew back in his chair. "Go on."

"Let me explain. We've noticed that scores of young Somali men, ages eighteen to thirty, all U.S. citizens, head for Kenya, then Somalia, and have been tracked entering Pakistan. Average length away is six months."

"Right. We've heard there's a number in Minneapolis."

"And our area, too, Agent." A short pause. "It's what they may be returning for. Substantiated intelligence has spotted most of them in training camps along the Eastern Afghan-Pakistan border."

"You're suspecting Taliban and al-Qaeda connections?"

"Unfortunately, yes. We believe they're coming back to conduct terrorist activities. At least one in Chicago and another in Seattle have already been arrested for suspicious collaboration with a known Islamic group. When we get reports that entire families can't — or won't — account why their sons are missing…well, you get the picture."

"Definitely. We've had our share of Muslim youths recruited overseas. And on our home soil. Like yours, as you've inferred." He mentioned that earlier that day NSU had apprehended two Somalis for alleged terrorist activities.

"We share more than a common border, Agent Dodek. We know you played an integral part in exposing and terminating militant operations in Vancouver."

Art took a long breath. "I still don't understand why DHS wants —"

"One distinct link we've discovered is that a suspect from Canada, Saleh Ali Nabhat Saleh, an adherent of *Jihadi Salafism*, a fanatical Muslim sect that preaches violence against any non-believer, may be playing a pivotal role. You know that means anyone in the West. Listen, I'm not calling you to discuss religious doctrines. We're sure he's here on the West Coast, maybe right here in Southern California. That's why I'm asking…would you be agreeable in joining us?"

"Well, sure. But it would have to be cleared by the National Security Unit. What about your State Department?"

"Done. Your Public Safety department has already given you clearance. State has agreed."

Art sat up, gazed about the operations center, subconsciously watching other agents at their computers and on telephones. "Agent…Miss Mercado —?"

"Consuela will do. Details are on the way, arrangements made, including a weapons transport permit. Art, listen, we suspect, even anticipate, ugly consequences from Saleh. From what I've heard, you have the smarts to tackle this kind of threat. Be ideal, too; learn first hand what DHS is doing in the war on terrorism. The sooner you get here, you know, we can get underway. It's essential that we find him." Another pause. "By the way, you're meeting us tomorrow." She clicked off.

Los Angeles, he thought for a moment, recalling a few years back when he'd joined an FBI task force to infiltrate an alleged homegrown plot to attack an interfaith Jewish-Muslim peace conference at the Holocaust Museum in Beverly Hills.

Alistair Burke, his boss and director of the NSU, stepped in and out of his office, followed by an assistant taking notes. Since NSU began, he and the director had crossed swords. Friction and disagreements weren't unusual. In the field, Art relied on his wits and intelligence training to prevent dangerous situations. Burke, however, a former army officer, decided that all counter-terrorism missions should possess overtones of a regimented military operation. As the NSU senior agent, Art would never upstage his boss; just keep the military apparatus out of it, that's all. Art respected and admired all the men and women who served in the armed forces. Hearing of a soldier dying in Afghanistan or a cop going down in

17

the line of duty, he thought about their sacrifice, and promised to do more against these radical extremists.

A smile slid across his face as he headed to ordinance to pick up his Glock 9 mm handgun. Would Burke worry that about his absence? Maybe he got his question answered. Returning to central processing, secured faxes arrived from the DHS. He poured over the details, which included a print out of the flight documents, an attachment from Burke approving his reassignment to Southern California, and a signed order from the secretary of Homeland Security.

***

Consuela Mercado sifted through Art Dodek's file.

At thirty-six, she had risen quickly through the ranks in the Los Angeles DHS regional office. Now special agent and supervisor, the Justice Department admired her dedication and the number of successful convictions of terrorism suspects she'd racked up while a member of the FBI. To her, a native-born Angelino from the Barrio, making it through high school and earning a degree in applied computer science outweighed the achievements in civil service. Her mother had died before her graduation from UCLA. The man who she believed was her father was actually an illegal alien from Mexico and got deported.

Before she was even a teenager, Chicano gangsters gunned down her younger brother and a cousin, which led to her choosing a career in law enforcement. She knew that no one could stop the Latino and black gang wars devastating her neighborhood; but perhaps by preventing terrorism from abroad and within the country, she could make a difference. She discovered that in the areas of security and protection, whether for government officials or unearthing some suicide bomber's plot, she had an uncanny investigative mind. Accepting dull, time-consuming assignments, she applied herself, and the hard work paid off.

She bore a striking resemblance to Selena—a popular Mexican *Tejano* singer shot to death in the early nineties. Brownish, red tinged hair drooped over her shoulders. A touch of blue eyeliner brought out the glow of her dark brown eyes. Despite her five foot five slender frame and a body honed by years of sweat-dripping exercise and a vegetarian and seafood diet, she could—and would—deck a guy twice her weight.

Art Dodek's file contained photographs of himself, his wife Lynda, and their only child, Rachel. His complete dossier included other NSU agents with whom he'd worked—even assorted pictures of himself with David Tivi, the Israeli Mossad secret agent—schools, universities attended, and diplomas obtained. His military background included initial training by the Mossad security forces, missions, stints with the Israeli Military Forces (IMF), and assignments engaged on Canadian and American soil, including names, information, and outcome of foreign and

18

native nationals apprehended or eliminated. Near the end of the folder, she gazed at photographs of his longtime friends, Mohammad Abdul Youseff and Zahra Adel, a Muslim couple. She rubbed her chin, and then noted an additional reference; his friend, A.K.A. "Mo," had died when his wife accidentally shot him as they scuffled during a counter intelligence investigation with Dodek. Also included was data on their son, Mohammad Adel Youseff, imprisoned for terrorism conspiracy. An official from the Ministry of Justice had stamped a notice in the file about the young man's conviction that stated "Evidence Sealed for National Security." The final item in his jacket, a letter from Alistair Burke, raised her eyebrows:

Not a real team member. Too independent. Personality ranges from emotional, wired-up to overbearing. Tends to be argumentative. Professional and achievement-minded. Sets high expectations for himself. Effective field operative. Leadership qualities. Strong analytical ability. Firearms specialist. Noteworthy: thinks and acts outside the box."

Her eyes widened at the final notation:

Don't cross him.

"Just work with me; we'll be fine," she whispered, leafing through his references and commendations.

***

Later, during dinner at home in Vancouver's Little Mountain area, Art informed Lynda about the call from Homeland Security. "They're bringing me to California," he announced, sipping a glass of Chardonnay.

She combed her hands through her angular-cut light blond hair. Blue eyes focused on her husband and a smile broke out. "Well, I'm not quite sure what to say."

Half expecting her to reply in an open-ended manner, which she often did, he clasped her hand. For most of last year she had wanted him to leave the National Security Unit, or least be reassigned to Canada's capitol, Ottawa. Her anxiety increased whenever he came home beat up or shot at. No way, though, would he pack it in or take some bureaucratic position back east.

"When are you going? How long? Am I going, too?"

He laughed. "Truth is, Lyndie," he said, calling her by her nickname, "I leave tomorrow. How long, I suppose, depends on when they don't need me. Are you going? No. This is a solo trip. I'll be working for Homeland Security."

"Oh. Like your early days going overseas. What kind of mission are you…?" She didn't finish, knowing he wouldn't divulge classified casework. "Since I only have one home showing tomorrow, I can drive you to the airport."

"Not this time. NSU is providing transportation."

19

"Oh. Where will you be staying?"

"Somewhere in Los Angeles." He paused for a few seconds, topped up her glass, and added, "I'll let you know. I'll miss you."

"Will you?" Moisture appeared around her right eye.

He rose and encircled his arms around her waist. "What do you think?"

"I wish you weren't going. You know how worried I am when you're on a mission. I'll miss you, too, you know that," she said, kissing his temple, running fingers along the stubble of his chin. The closeness felt reassuring. "When are you leaving?"

"In the morning. Early. A seven o'clock flight."

"Sweetie," she smiled, brushing her damp cheek. "Don't you dare stop holding me tonight. Finish your dinner, it's getting cold."

"Copy that."

When they laid together in the soft light from outside the bedroom window, neither wanted to let go or even shift their bodies. The slow moving of his thrusting and her swaying to feel him deep inside continued until there had to be release. He couldn't fight the rush that he sensed overcoming his body, and he came first, as though invisible hands pushed him deeper and deeper inside her.

Lynda's murmuring intensified as the tiny hairs on her skin rippled. Her hands clutched his sides, elbows inward, then her fingers wandered to his face, touching and outlining the grooves along his lips and chin. They rolled back and forth for a few seconds, their mouths pressed close together, and they rollicked in the rapture of their passion. She placed her head on his chest, bobbing her head up and down each time he exhaled, then whispered something that sounded like, "Be careful."

Chapter 3

Los Angeles International Airport
Lower Concourse, Terminal 3, Wednesday
Morning

DHS had authorized Art's customs and security clearances in Vancouver.

Draping a garment bag and carry-on over his shoulder, he passed crowded, noisy baggage areas and stopped near an exit. Sunlight streamed into the expanse of the arrival terminal. He set the tote bag down and removed a beige golf jacket.

"No sense getting comfortable," a female voice rang out.

"You must be Consuela Mercado," he responded.

The DHS officer extended her hand. "And you're Art Dodek. Welcome to Los Angeles. How was the flight?" In a white, button-down long sleeved top and dark knee-length skirt, a trail of sunlight accentuated her slender frame.

"Damn near perfect. Thanks for providing the ride."

A group of tank-topped, chattering teenagers lugging surfboards whizzed by.

"Hungry? We'll grab something downtown. That's where we're heading—transportation is right outside."

He laughed. "You arrange a police escort, too?"

No comment.

Outside by the center median, taxis, shuttle vans, and buses small and large rumbled by, stopping at designated colored posts. A tall, black-suited, sunglasses wearing man opened the rear door of a window tinted blue Ford Victoria, then took Art's luggage and laid it out in the trunk; an attaché case, an M-16 rifle, plus a couple of steel canisters rested nearby.

Within minutes they were on Century Boulevard. A few turns later the driver entered the 405 North Freeway and moved into the third lane. This time of morning his speedometer didn't pass the 40 mph mark.

Agent Mercado slipped on her blazer. Opening a valise, she withdrew a holstered P-34 Reutger pistol. This weapon used by federal law enforcement agencies and some police departments because of its deadly stopping capability could accommodate nineteen bullets in its magazine. After clipping it to her right side, she turned to the NSU agent. "I mentioned Saleh Ali Nabhat Saleh yesterday. What do you know about him?"

"What you told me yesterday. He's a Canadian citizen. We don't have him on any current watch list."

"Well, he should be. He's on *ours* due to the fact that he flies to Canada, travels to Pakistan and Afghanistan from there, then comes back to your country and returns to ours after short absences. You getting the picture?"

"Uh-huh."

"When the Minneapolis FBI office contacted us about numbers of young Somali's leaving—gone missing, actually—we started our investigation. Intelligence indicates he's the numero uno leader of *al-Shabad*, a vicious Islamic extremist organization. DOJ and State has put him on top of Homeland Security's most wanted. There's Intel about Somali activity in L.A. He's my concern. Now, Agent Dodek, he's also your concern."

"When do I start?"

"Soon as you got into this car," she replied. "You'll be meeting my team." She paused, and in a serious voice, asked, "What is it with you Canadians? You seem so reluctant to investigate somebody. Or arrest them."

Art tried to be nonchalant. "I'm not a politician. But we do operate under a different set of practices, like with our security certificates. You have the Patriot Act; we don't."

Mercado didn't respond. Instead, she said, "At least you fought your way through the West Bank and Gaza. No offense, but you and your Jewish Mossad friend, David Tivi, must've witnessed a lot of horrendous terrorist attacks."

He nodded. "No offense taken. Yes…we did."

After repeated stopping and inching its way down the ramp, the Ford transitioned onto the 10 East Freeway, all five lanes increasing in traffic volume. About five miles further along the driver managed to pick up speed. Exiting and then transferring onto another freeway for a few minutes, he angled down a ramp, going by rows of Korean, Vietnamese, and Middle Eastern stores, shops, markets, and restaurants. Almost every

22

block had boarded up windows or For Sale signs dangling off shuttered front doors. Looking entirely out of place, a flower shop and a couple of upscale retail boutiques, their doors behind iron bars scrawled with graffiti, sat next to a gas station. Vehicular traffic clogged the roadways, including diesel buses that chugged by, blaring horns at anyone cutting them off.

"*Asi` es la vida*," she chuckled.

He knew the expression meant "such is life."

Clouds hung low, left over from the morning coastal marine layer. Soon the tops of the downtown skyline edged their way through. Although it had been years since Art visited Los Angeles, familiar buildings appeared, some showing the effects of advanced age, their painted names faded by years of sun and moisture. Several new condominium buildings and office towers had been erected, as well as the odd commercial structure, many still undergoing restoration by work forces almost entirely comprised of Mexicans.

Up until today he had only seen the new Multiplex Staple Center on TV. With its unique Southern California architecture, aquatic tinted glass, vertical and horizontal beams, and huge flashing neon signs, Angelinos had an iconic sports palace to house the NBA Lakers, the city's most popular team. Nearby stood another landmark, the L.A. Convention Center, where thousands of new immigrants clustered for their citizenship swearing-in ceremonies. As they drove alongside, the billboard indicated a home and garden show was underway; below that were red letters announced an upcoming Adult Films Award Extravaganza.

On nearby side streets, older ramshackle homes offered no hint that L.A.'s notorious Latino gangs occupied many, openly selling crack, meth, ecstasy, and other hard line drugs, and intimidating, roughing up, or murdering anyone who dared to tread on their territory.

The Crown Victoria entered a basement parking lot, going down two levels below the downtown federal building and stopping by an elevator marked Authorized Personnel Only. Art stretched out his arms. A two and half hour flight from Vancouver and the long drive had stiffened his limbs.

The driver stowed his belongings in the back of a silver Ford Fusion. "It's yours," he said, tossing the keys to Art, and added, "The GPS will direct you to your apartment in Santa Monica."

Mercado pointed to a ceiling camera near an entrance when they reached the sixth floor. Following her lead, he pulled open his jacket, revealing his Glock automatic and displaying his NSU badge. In seconds they were marching down a long corridor dotted by office doors. The next turn led to two wide glass paneled doors—the Department of Homeland Security.

23

Inside, the Stars and Stripes and the flag of California stood in two corners. Photographic reminders of the 9-11 terrorist attacks lined walls, offering a stark reason why DHS maintained vigilant security over America.

The two agents passed various staff members. Workstations, electronic devices, and multi-communication equipment chattering away made Art Dodek feel as though he had entered the NSU Central Processing Center in Vancouver.

While Homeland Security was the primary governmental office, he noticed that agents from the FBI occupied several of the stations.

Mercado directed him to a counter laden with pastries, buns, assorted cheeses, and two large coffee dispensers. She told him to help himself and smiled when she mentioned there weren't any bagels, finishing by saying that the meeting would get underway in a few minutes. Watching her remove her blazer and disappear into another room, he munched away on muffins and downed two cups of coffee. Up since before five that morning, a clock above a doorway indicated almost half past eleven. Hungry yes; however, he was not the slightest bit tired.

A very refreshed looking Consuela Mercado strolled toward him, her hair dancing over her shoulders as she walked, as if swaying to a Hispanic musical tempo. She moved with cat-like confidence.

"They're waiting," she said.

They entered a larger room sporting polished oak furniture, U.S. themed furnishings, and wide angled, rectangular pictures of Washington, D.C., Los Angeles, and New York landmarks. Photos of the president and vice-president hung on a sidewall. Four men in white shirts and loose ties and one woman stood alongside a long conference table.

Art could feel everybody's eyes focusing on him, as if mentally sizing him up; not so much as the new guy, but rather, for what this Canadian operative could add to their Intel efforts.

***

A black Mercedes and a pickup truck drove to the far end of the motel and four Somali men of assorted ages, including the assailants of the corrections officers, scrambled up the stairs to corner unit fifteen. One pounded on the door, two held large duffel bags.

A curtain slid half open. Two of the young men inside cautiously stood in the doorway, opened up, and embraced the visitors as they entered the darkened room, which resembled a dilapidated homeless shelter. Clothes, food cartons, and water bottles were strewn on chairs, over a table, and on a desk. Most of the bedding lay in a heap on the floor. Assorted prayer mats and a Koran holy book were the only items that remained carefully uncluttered. A CNN program was on TV, although the sound had been muted. One of the new arrivals shut the door.

24

Then rejoicing Arabic voices rang out—"*Allah Bakbar…Salaam…Illahal….*"—extolling God, peace amongst us, divine justice.

One of the men moved around the messy room. Even with the dim lights, his shaggy hair could be seen protruding outside his kufi, the white-meshed cap worn by most Muslim men. His eyes roamed quickly at the trio from overseas. "My name is Muhamed Dauadi," he uttered in one unvarying tone. "Don't forget it."

All those inside nodded yes.

"The stupid Americans, they thought they could convict me. Sentence me to prison." He waved his hands outward in a dismissive gesture. "I stand before you as testament I am above them. The day will come when all Muslim brothers, when the twelve caliphs return to take back what is rightfully ours. The Americans will be the first to bow at our feet."

"And the annihilation of Israel," one of the older men shouted.

"So it shall be," Dauadi intoned. He motioned for the duffel bag to be opened. "You were selected and trained in Pakistan for expressly one purpose: to fight for Allah, to give your lives against the infidels. You may be American citizens who took oaths to be vigilant against its enemies. Americans are your enemies. Forget what you became. Remember who you are—brothers of al-Shabad. And Brothers of Somali Jihad, who swore that you would fight and slay our enemies. Your allegiance is to Islam and only to Islam. Al-Shabad. Say it. Say it!"

"We are al Shabad," they exclaimed.

"What shall you do?"

"We shall slay our enemies."

From the bag he withdrew pistols and revolvers, including .357 Magnums, automatic rifles, bullet clips and large caliber magazines, C-4 explosive bricks, and detonators, handing the items to each of the men who had arrived yesterday. "You were trained for combat. You practiced setting off…." He pointed to the C-4. "Soon you will have the opportunity to commit yourself to Allah. Say it."

"We commit ourselves to Allah the Prophet."

Someone asked, "When? Where?"

Dauadi stood eye to eye to the man and placed his hands on the young man's shoulders. "In time you shall know, my brother," he said in the same unwavering tone. "In time."

***

Mercado placed her hand on Art's arm, motioning him to approach her team.

He gushed. To deny that her touch felt electrifying would be lying.

25

"I'd like you to meet Senior Agent Art Dodek from Vancouver," she began, "from the Canadian National Security Service…NSU, as it's known up north. Art, meet our DHS managing director, Walter McLaughlin."

"Agent Dodek," the man said with a touch of a New York accent. About six feet tall with a rounded chin, he could have been in his early fifties, although forty-four to forty-six would probably be more accurate. Bushy eyebrows sat atop hazel eyes. Receding brown hair growing slimmer near the crown appeared slicked down. An oversized watchband protruded just below his left shirt cuff.

The two men shook hands. Art's smile didn't enlist one from the director.

"I'm with the DHS," a stocky, dark haired man said as he stepped forward. "The name's Tony Lamborghini. Yeah, my name is same as the car. If I were a family member of the namesake, I wouldn't be here meeting with you or worrying whether some Taliban nutcase is gonna blow up Disneyland."

"That's why we must never let our guard down," Art said after shaking hands.

"You sound like The Man," the DHS agent chuckled.

Mercado brought the two remaining persons over to Art's side. Both African-American, they smiled and waited for their supervisor to introduce them.

"This is our FBI team," she announced. "Special Agent Dan Curbside and Agent Aylesha Reeves."

Curbside could pass for an Olympic wrestler: solid physique, agile movements, as if ready to spring at an opponent. Day-old whiskers covered his chin. His partner, Aylesha, appeared to be in her early thirties, and had a lighter skin tone, along with a shorter frame carrying a tad of extra weight. Her dark hair was worn ponytail style. Her only ring was a gold inlaid single diamond worn on the second finger of her right hand. Brassy hoop style earrings shook in circles each time her head shifted.

Introductions over, Mercado told everyone to sit down; she remained standing. Using a remote, she turned on a large TV monitor adjacent to the table. DHS and FBI logos appeared. Two buttons later a Middle Eastern male appeared on the screen. Bearded, he was wearing a *dishdashah*—a long Arabic outer garment—and his eyes seared outward; he appeared to be in his late forties.

"This is Saleh Ali Nabhat Saleh," she told the group. "Take a good look, Art. A real slick-dick, this guy. He's one of your countrymen. Our Intelligence confirms that he's the mastermind behind recruiting young Muslim males from various U.S. cities, bringing them over to Somalia via Kenya, and instructing them in the use of firearms, kidnapping, guerilla warfare, and bomb making. These are the militants he sends back to America to do the dirty work. Need I elaborate any more?"

Lamborghini snickered, "You left out Man of the Year."

"All right, enough," she admonished her team member. "So, Tony, what's the latest?"

"He's on the TSA No-Fly watch list. So it's doubtful he flew into the country."

"Check," Aylesha added. "Agents are maintaining 'round-the-clock checkpoints in the usual Southland transportation hubs."

"Mercado, safe to say that Nabhat Saleh is roaming our neighborhood?" asked the director. "Nobody knows what he's up to?"

"That's our take, Walter. Something else you should be aware of, Art. An offshoot organization has formed here in the Southland—the Somali Brothers of Allah Jihad. We suspect they're the returning Somalis. You know they weren't visiting Pakistan—like the Swat Valley near Islamabad, or showing up in the mountains of Afghanistan—for cricket games. Several of the recent terrorist bombings launched against Western interests in Pakistani business sectors have been connected to Saleh Ali and his militants. Unfortunately, as you hear so many times, it's civilians who endure the worst."

"Agent Dodek, tell me, please," McLaughlin said. "How is it every time you arrest a terrorist in Canada—and you have them in abundance—nine times out of ten your government lets them go? You hardly ever hear about a goddamn conviction up there."

Art turned and faced him. "Well, when we convict the tenth one, we've done our job. Mistakes happen. Problem is, our laws differ drastically, and—"

"Maybe if you had a 9-11 up there, you people would think differently. We go after them here and we sock it to them. And they're locked up for life."

Voices from the group started to get excitable.

Mercado waved her hand. "We also have another problem. A convicted terrorist, Muhamed Dauadi, got sprung from a prison van yesterday. Whoever helped him killed two deputies. He's a real specimen of humanity...cop killer, explosives expert, a terrorist who has already killed and who wouldn't refrain from killing again. Our team went to enormous lengths, spent almost a year tracking Dauadi down and apprehending him. Now he's out there again. He swore that he would make Americans pay for taking him to court. The longer he's out there, the more dangerous he becomes. I shouldn't have to remind you: put him and Saleh Ali together—we don't just have a problem—we have a calamity in the making."

McLaughlin stood. "Any leads on the pricks?"

"Yes, sir," Curbside replied. "We're investigating all leads. We're speaking with people who may have come into contact with them."

Flicking another button, Mercado flashed a blown up photograph of the escaped terrorist. "Take a good look, Art. Don't let his geek-like appearance fool you—this bastard is one hell of a killer."

The NSU agent let out a breath. "You've asked me to join your team. Add me as one who will help you find Dauadi, and, if he's here, Saleh Ali Nabhat Saleh."

"He's here," the others said, although that fact was as yet unconfirmed.

McLaughlin squinted. He turned and faced his team. "Okay then, people. Take your faces out of your asses. Get your task force up and running. Organize your priorities. Dauadi has to show his face somewhere. Mosques. Religious schools. Cafes, stores catering to Muslims. Find him." He paused, and as if for emphasis, added, "Find him...you can bet Saleh Ali won't be far away."

After Lamborghini and the two FBI agents departed, the director motioned Art over.

"Think you can fit in with the unit?"

"I think so."

"He's got the smarts," Mercado assured her boss. "I'll vouch for him."

McLaughlin crossed his arms. "In the event of a fire fight, whose ass you gonna save?"

Art raised his eyebrows.

"Well, yours or your partners?"

"If it's possible...both our asses."

The director clicked his teeth, pondering. "Dodek, I'll say this once: you may be the reincarnation of Jack Bauer. Personally, I could care less. You're here because Mercado figures you're a savvy Intelligence officer. No games. No heroics. Do it my way. Understood?"

"Entirely." McLaughlin's in-your-face manner surprised Art, but he shook it off. The next remark was a different story.

"Read my lips, Agent Dodek. You fuck up and I'll send you back to Canauckistan."

Feeling tension riding up through his chest, he started to clench his lips. *Just forget about it*, he figured, as the DHS director left the room. Never failed. Security directors and their bellicose attitudes.

Smiling, Mercado sashayed toward him. "Don't get your balls in a knot. He can be brash. Get to know Walter—he'll back you unequivocally, let me assure you." She gazed into his eyes until a smile flickered. "You hungry? Like Mexican? Come on, I'll treat you. A *Dos Equis* will lessen the spiciness if you're not used to it." She placed a couple of fingers on his upper arm, indicating to follow her.

Nodding in the affirmative, he followed. *Yeah, a cold beer would be nice about now.*

As they reentered the corridor, she told him there was another staff member to meet afterward, the department's prima donna analyst, Noordine Assad.

Outside, even with the sun not visible, the hazy afternoon sky made the four-block stroll a little uncomfortable. Maybe all the people scouring about were used to it; he sure wasn't. Nor did it matter which direction traffic and Angelinos headed, each block contained Mexican markets, sidewalk vendors selling everything from food to cheap jewelry to wilted flowers, liquor stores, small to medium-sized restaurants, cash exchange shops, and *notarios*, who Hispanics consulted for legal matters, including unreliable immigration information. On one block, kids at an elementary school chased soccer balls on a field shielded by high iron posts interwoven with strands of wire mesh. His ears rang non-stop from the endless roar of diesel buses, produce trucks, blaring horns and screeching tires, and sirens wailing from nearby streets. But none of the clamor or bustle seemed to faze Mercado. Each step was confident, each movement determined.

They entered a Mexican diner, where a few people munched away at small tables. Once in a while someone would nod to Mercado, while others were aloof to her presence. Although the fire arm on her side may have given the impression she was a cop, most knew her as a *federale*, a federal agent of the United States, and not from *immigracion*. Mexican flags and faded photographs covered walls papered with faux brickwork. Strong smells of cooking oils, fried rice, and baked beans permeated through the entire café. Girls behind the counter greeted her with giggles and laughter. The *Gringo* with her, not unexpectedly, didn't rate much attention, until she said, "*El Hombre is me amigo.*"

In Spanish, some of which he followed, ignoring the wallboard menus, she ordered an array of appetizer and luncheon specials, telling him they'd tone down the spices on his order.

Offering to pay, he reached for his wallet.

"Put it away," she said with a gentle tap on his shoulder

In about five minutes they carried trays out to a front patio. Mooching sparrows and pigeons began gathering under their table.

Not often did he eat Mexican dishes. True to her word, his meal of two beef burritos layered with shredded lettuce, pepper sauce, black olives, and tomato slices wasn't that spicy. He sat facing the street, she to his right. An umbrella provided some relief from the hazy sky.

While chatting about pieces of Los Angeles-Hispanic history, she ate slowly, ending each bite with a white tinted fingernail brushing salsa from her lips. Two rings adorned her right hand, an opal birthstone on her third

29

finger and a small diamond cluster on her pinkie. A beer glass on her tray remained unused. This lady preferred to sip from the bottle.

She clinked his glass, and in a soft voice, whispered, "*Salud.*"

He responded with "Shalom."

The way he pronounced it made her laugh. Crossing her legs, she used both her hands to emphasize Los Angeles's history. "Everybody in Los Angeles calls it L.A. The original name of the *ciudad* — city, to you — *El Pueblo de Nuestra Senora de Los Angeles or El Pueblo de la reinada de Los Angeles*, was a take on Queen of Heaven Maria, Village of our Lady, Queen of Angeles."

The corners of his lips turned upward. He had never heard Spanish spoken in such a sexy manner.

"Spanish expeditions first arrived here in 1542," she carried on. "I think occupation basically started about 1769. At least the Spanish explorer, Gaspar de Portola, visited this area around that time. Anyway, Los Angeles was founded on September 4, 1781. How old is that?" she beamed. "At a time, 'Queen of Angels' was the capital of Alta California. This Mexican governor...what was his name? Oh, yes, Felipe de Neve; he ran it as a province...I guess state sounds more modern. Me, I don't think about it much, but to some Hispanics, when Mexico lost the war against the U.S. in 1847, they had their heritage robbed." She munched on a piece of salsa-dipped chip and took a quick sip of her *Dos Equis*. Rolling her tongue on her moistened lips, she continued. "After Mexico ceded California, L.A. was incorporated as a city in 1850. Get this. Right smack between Beverly Hills and Bellaire, among other ritzy places. Like Westwood Village, it's one of the oldest cities in L.A. County. There, you are, Art; every time you see a taco commercial, you can think about us."

Her mouth and eyes widened when he surprised her by applauding.

From his two-o-clock seating position, glancing across the street, flashing neon colored lights over an open sign and blue painted letters with *Dream Girls Body Massage* painted on the front window wouldn't ordinarily hold his interest. Rather, it was who congregated by the front door of the massage parlor that caught his attention.

"Consuela," he said, wiping mayonnaise off his chin. "The building over there, Dream Girls...notice who's wandering around the entrance?"

Squinting, she dropped the remnants of her taco.

Single men entering and leaving the building; nothing unusual there. However, all the men, mostly college aged, appeared to be of African descent.

"Really, Agent Dodek," she grinned. "How observant you are! You ever been in one of those places?"

Laughing, his lips formed the word, "No."

"Perhaps we should take a closer look," she suggested, sliding back her chair.

"Don't you need a warrant if you suspect something's going on? Like criminal activity."

"You're not in Canada, you know. As an officer of the Department of Homeland Security, if I suspect any illegal activity, I can enter without one. That's probable cause. You and I should check what's going on."

Art tossed his burrito aside. That'd be a first for him, entering a massage parlor for Intel purposes. In this business, however, you never lowballed anything. And you kept your hand near your holster.

They both rose together.

Chapter 4

They climbed over a green painted iron railing. Pausing by the curb and giving the street a peripheral glance, they stepped onto the road, dodging traffic and blaring horns. Not until Art and Mercado approached the building did four men notice their presence. Two of them instantly scattered. The agents managed to block the others from running away.

The youngest of the pair kept muttering that he and his friends were just hanging out, not doing anything illegal. This, to an extent, was true; visiting a massage parlor was not a crime, unless the masseuse solicited money for a sexual act. Mercado told them to shut up, that she and her partner weren't vice cops.

Art pushed them inside the building, where Asian artwork lined the walls of the short entrance. Behind a glass partition, a Chinese woman who looked about forty jumped off her office chair. Staring at Mercado's badge and side arm, she turned to the right, grabbed a microphone off the counter, and shouted in Chinese for everybody to get out.

Both agents ordered her to be quiet; twice they told her they weren't the police. Mercado pounded her fist on the counter, sending a bowl of artificial roses spiraling to the floor.

"We're federal agents from Homeland Security," she said, exasperated. "I don't care what your customers are doing. We're going to check out the premises."

"You no have right. Where's warrant?"

"Sit...down...and shut up."

The woman slumped down onto her chair, trying to conceal the fact that she pressed a buzzer beneath her desk.

Within seconds, three scantily clad Mexican girls dashed from private rooms further down the hallway, followed by two middle-aged Asian men. The young women ran into a bathroom while their customers, half dressed and shoeless, headed for the door. Laughing, the agents didn't try to stop anyone.

One of the African men tried to use the commotion as a distraction to run. Art grabbed both his shoulders and pushed him onto a couch. "You move," he glowered, "and I'll handcuff you to that handrail."

"Names. ID," Mercado said, holding the other man's arm.

Wallets came out.

She inspected the contents—both of them Somalis, with U.S. citizenship cards. "Art, see who else is here."

Nodding, he sauntered down the hallway, checking the side rooms. Each contained evidence that not just ordinary massages occurred inside: subdued lighting, low filtered music, towels thrown aside, open oil decanters, a thong bikini lying on a cot, and five twenty dollar bills atop a table.

He opened the bathroom door and was greeted by one nearly naked girl, and another in shorts, yelling at him in Spanish, and he slammed the door shut.

Next door, his ears picked up the sounds of humming electronic equipment. A hand over his holster, he edged his way into a laundry room, reeling at what he spotted. He withdrew his Glock and shouted, "Consuela, down here."

A dark skinned man wearing a Blue Tooth earpiece rose from a table behind a corner desk that held computers, printers, and fax machines. Momentarily stunned to see a gun pointing at him, he reached into a drawer, and Art pushed it shut on the man's fingers. Using a shoulder to block the man from moving, he pulled out a revolver and slid it into his waistband.

Just as the computer programmer stepped sideways to flee, Mercado burst in. Lifting her elbows, she bashed both his ears, sending him groaning to the floor. She grabbed his earpiece and also yanked out a memory stick from a laptop.

A monitor displayed Arabic script, another an interrupted e-mail text. The two agents exchanged glances, sensing that what they'd discovered warranted further investigation.

Mercado opened her cell phone. "Aylesha, get Dan and Tony...Dream Girls Massage on Alameda. Yes, you heard me right. Get over here." Turning it off, she looked back at Art. "Well, now you can say you've been in one of these places."

"Different strokes for curious folks," he chuckled, picking the programmer up from the floor. "I see what you mean—probable cause; suspicious activities."

About an hour later, Art and FBI agent Curbside loaded the computer equipment into a van. Mercado and Aylesha Reeves continued to question the two Somali men, who seemed afraid to talk. The

33

programmer, claiming police brutality, refused to cooperate, insisting he was just checking the Internet while waiting for a friend.

Mercado told the masseuses to get dressed and leave; their presence had no relation to the men. However, accompanying those going to DHS for further questioning, the Chinese proprietor, she theorized, could be a material witness. Before everyone left, she phoned the Los Angeles Department of Licensing and Permits to shut down Dream Girls.

***

A cell phone rang as Muhamed Dauadi's Mercedes skirted North Hollywood. Picking it up, he listened attentively to the caller's message. Bobbing his head up and down, he hung up then dialed the number of the east end Los Angeles motel.

"One of our safe houses has been comprised, brothers arrested," he said to the person who answered. "DHS has confiscated sensitive materials. I think it's time that the infidels know what the Somali Brothers are capable of." He paused for a few seconds. "Yes, of course, I am aware of what it means. That's why I am changing our plans, and what will be targeted. I am the one who decides. Stay where you are." He clicked off.

Making a U-turn at the next light, he headed for the nearest southbound freeway.

***

Mercado shook her head. Nine times out of ten, she figured, none of the suspected Somalis that DHS apprehended had any prior criminal records; not surprising, when they must possess no immoral character behavior when they applied for naturalization. Then a trend materialized: as soon as they were granted their American status, like so many others, they headed for the Middle East, namely Pakistan and Somalia, reentered as Americans, and dropped off the radar. What was disturbing to DHS and the Justice Department, these young men returned fully indoctrinated as charged-up Islamic fundamentalists ready to give their lives for reprisals against the United States.

As citizens they had complete freedom to roam the country and make unusual purchases without any peculiar reaction. Already battle-hardened from skirmishes and attacks in Pakistan's Swat Valley and Peshawar Province, targeting hotels and police stations and killing local civilians and government administrators, when their mentors ordered them to strike in the US, they would do so without question. These young soldiers of Allah viewed death as martyrdom.

Somalis traditionally observed *Sufi Islam*, a relatively moderate form of Islam. Those who sought paths as insurgents—God's warriors—followed a more austere *Wahabi Islam* rooted in Saudi Arabia; Osama bin Laden was an ardent follower. Wahabism was a component of *Jihadi*

34

Salafism, a doctrine that preached spreading a strict interpretation of the Koran through extreme violence.

In Somalia, the Shariah court, run by al-Shabad, enforced its laws through fear, intimidation, corruption, ignorance, and instant execution of any non-believer. Little wonder hundreds of foreign fighters from Pakistan, Yemen, and Saudi Arabia joined al-Shabad to fight and become suicide bombers. This ultra-terrorist group controlled much of Somalia, including lawless Mogadishu, the capital. The U.S. considered them as a terrorist organization that had trained elements of al-Qaeda and the Taliban, providing logistics and weapons training and financing illegal shipments of military equipment. Somalia maintained a safe haven for wanted terrorists.

One in particular, Saleh Ali Nabhat Saleh, was deemed, after bin Laden, the Middle East's mastermind of al-Shabat terrorism emerging in America. No doubt his holding Canadian citizenship allowed him easy access to traverse the Northern Hemisphere. For all of his trips to Africa and the Middle East confirmed by the State Department, never once had he been flagged as entering the U.S. Clever. Cunning. Aligned with Muhamed Dauadi, they posed a threat unseen since 9-11.

Mercado's report to Director Walter McLaughlin at first received less than excited acceptance. He remarked that he would be more inclined to approach the attorney general if that afternoon's bust hadn't uncovered so much circumstantial evidence.

Maybe, she figured, Noordine could extract something of value from the computers.

She signaled for Art to follow her, and told him from now on to wear a vest and carry his side arm, adding that he was not just an observer, but a DHS Intelligence agent, authorized to act according to the threat. A minute later, he accompanied her into the agency's communication center.

He almost felt at home inside NSU's central processing room. Assorted electronic equipment buzzed and hummed. Graphics, maps, and charts adorned walls, as well as portable boards and sliding cubicles. Various colored telephones were no doubt connected to essential departments, agencies, even the upper echelon of state and federal officials. About ten staff members manned computers, mobile, and land phone lines. To his left, Agents Reeves and Lamborghini, examining state department records of the suspects taken into custody, spotted him and waved.

Stepping toward a long desk loaded with monitors, scanners, and printers, he saw a woman in her late twenties with the whitest teeth he had ever seen look up and smile, her hazel eyes inquisitive yet warm and friendly. Sitting cross-legged, curly black hair draped over her white jacket, and a charcoal skirt fit snugly to a hundred and ten pound lithe frame. Her complexion was clear, with only a hint of rouge on rounded cheeks. Long, natural uncolored fingernails tapped both corners of her keyboard. Uncrossing her legs, she removed her headset.

Mercado pressed her lips together, stopping herself from reacting to Art's obvious staring. "Noordine," she said, "this is our new investigator, Art Dodek, from the Canadian National Security Service. He's here to assist us in putting an end to a potentially deadly group of Islamic terrorists. Art, this is Noordine Assad."

He had to clear his throat. "A pleasure to meet you. Shalom."

"Salaam," she laughed, shaking hands, responding in Arabic to his Hebrew greeting. "You knew that I am Arabic, Mr. Dodek?"

"Uh, yes. Art is fine. You're not Persian."

"Of course not. My grandparents and parents are Jordanian; I was born in Virginia."

"How long have you been in California?"

"I earned my masters at UCLA. Los Angeles has been my home since then. Anyway, I heard you single handedly raided a massage parlor."

Consuela and Noordine both lowered their eyes in order to subdue their smiling.

"At least I found out what *doesn't* belong there." He thought his comment would make them blush. It didn't.

"That's why we're here," Mercado said. "Noordine is our translator and expert linguist. She's fluent in Middle Eastern languages—Arabic, Iranian Farsi, Persian, and Afghani, Pakistani dialects."

Noordine tried to take the compliment modestly. A tinge of pink lit up her cheeks.

"We found a number of e-mails and other items, including a memory stick," he said, taking a chair offered to him. Mercado remained standing. "Anything incriminating?"

"Yes. That's what I'll be examining. Some of it's encrypted. I've noticed some lines and passages appear in a kind of Somali short hand, full of Arabic colloquialisms. I should be able to decipher most of it, as well as several of the e-mail exchanges."

He took a short breath. "It's critical that we discover a link with Muhamed Dauadi; he's got connections to Somalia...the Jihad Brothers Brigade."

"Actually, it's known as Somali Brothers of Allah Jihad. They're al-Shabat followers who want to impose Shariah law. They're as dangerous as they are unpredictable. And brutal."

"There's also Saleh Ali to contend with," Mercado added.

For the first time Noordine's expression conveyed concern, as if just the utterance of his name made her skin crawl. "He is...he's the most feared, hated—"

Mercado touched the linguist's shoulder. "Keep us posted on the contents." She stepped away from the monitors.

When Noordine noticed Art reaching for his cell phone, she flipped open the cover, pressed a few characters and digits, scrolled through the menu over to a numerical list, and entered a recall sequence. "There, Art, it's now programmed to network your whereabouts so we can notify you, plus an emergency alert. Kind of like 9-1-1 in reverse."

"Thanks," he smiled, standing, pocketing the iPod. "It's been a real pleasure meeting you. I hope we can work together."

"Awesome. I know we will." She leaned forward and offered her hand. "Consuela, keep your eye on him."

"Absolutely. Come on, Art. We're gonna have another round with our suspects."

As the two agents exited the communication center, he glanced back quickly, and joined his partner in the hallway.

Jeers and whistles from leering inmates—detained immigrant violators—greeted Mercado as she and Art walked past holding cells on the way to the section where DHS suspects were stationed. Most voices wafting through the corridors were Hispanic, with a few foreign accents adding to the excitement. The majority of men, arrested for violation of their nonimmigrant status—those brought there from regional detention centers to eventually appear before judges or Immigration Customs Enforcement (ICE) interviewers—as usual, were Mexican and Central American. Depending on their outcomes, some would continue to be held in cells or relocated to federal centers for deportation. Add to this mix felons of various nationalities, and uproars and occasional fights broke out. DHS had no other option but to detain alleged terrorist conspirators in the same housing unit. Try as they might, overcrowding and an overburdened justice system couldn't move them through fast enough.

In any event, the two men apprehended outside Dream Girls, Walter McLaughlin's legal counsel had advised the agents, had to be either charged within twenty-four hours or released. Their presence outside the parlor, they were told, was irrelevant. Any court would have acquitted them for simply knowing what someone was doing inside.

The Somali computer programmer was different; discovered in the act of alleged terrorist action, such as being caught with e-mails and suspicious online software programs, as well as contacts with sources likely to promote, engage in, or plan terrorist activities, he could be held as complicit. Moreover, under the Patriot and Anti-Terrorist Act, he could be held indefinitely and refused access to an attorney until charged and ordered to trial.

The agents were at the clerk's station when the two men were issued their deportation orders. Although no words were exchanged between either side, searing eyes from the outgoing duo said it all: "*Go to hell.*"

With an ICE officer outside the interview room, a second round with the programmer, Tariq, resulted in the same outcome: denial of any charge; police brutality; false accusations; rights abused; as a U.S. citizen, the right to *habeas corpus*. He denied knowing the name of or being acquainted with Muhamed Dauadi, and had no idea where he would be hiding, referring to him as Muhamed. His eyes blinked and he fidgeted upon being asked about Saleh Ali.

Attribute that to fear, the agents figured. Just a mention of his name brought out an inexplicable mood change.

Mercado explained—during continuous rants about American injustice and the illegal occupation of Muslim lands—that he would be held while background and fingerprinting checks were conducted. She didn't explain, however, that the CIA was also performing a thorough check, as was the DOJ. Plus, the State Department intended to eliminate his name and passport number, barring him from leaving the country or returning to Somalia.

Art gripped the metal bar over the man's hand restraints and pressed down until the man clenched his teeth. "Sure you don't want to tell us something?" Pressing harder brought out a murmur, followed seconds later by a moan. "Help us. Help yourself. Up to you. Tell us about your connection to Muhamed Dauadi and Saleh Ali Nabhat Saleh. Where are they?"

"Y-You're hurting my wrist. Let go." Art maintained pressure for a few seconds more before he removed his hand. "I have nothing to say," the man declared, rubbing a red welt under the hand restraint.

"What you figure—twenty to thirty years in a federal prison?" Mercado injected. "Tack on another twenty if he's connected...and he is...to Dauadi and Saleh Ali."

Tariq looked up, his lips tight, short breaths going to longer breaths. "You Americans," he sneered. "You think all your military might frightens us? By the dozens, hundreds, *Inshallah* God willing, you will bring more body bags back from Muslim countries. Think you are safe under your corporate towers? Do you stay awake nights wondering what a bomb can do to the human flesh? Have you ever seen what we can do with a roadside bomb? How are you going to protect all your women and children?" He clenched his fists. "Look who's questioning me—a woman...a Hebrew. Israelis shall soon find themselves drowning in the ocean as they flee from our warriors."

Art and Mercado flinched as he spoke, despising everything he stood for. His words, terrible as the raspy voice that said them, spoke not just threateningly, but as a pledge that radical Muslims would never stop attacking American interests, or its people.

Mercado approached the table, leaned over, and stared him in the eyes. "It's a given. I'll make sure the judge who sentences you is a woman and Jewish." She straightened up. "We're finished here," she said, preceding her partner from the interview room. "Arrogant S.O.B."

He nodded. Passing a clock at the end of the corridor, it dawned on him that twenty-four hours ago he had been at Vancouver International Airport waiting for the DHS charter flight to Los Angeles. Maybe he would sleep tonight through. He wished. Despite being tired numerous nights, he would keep waking. Sleep aids, like prescriptions, were not an option, and frowned upon; they could've dulled his reactions to early morning emergency calls.

As she headed for McLaughlin's office, Mercado suggested that he check with Noordine about the confiscated messages. On the way to her desk, two ICE agents were escorting a young, bearded Middle Eastern man down another hallway. Immigration infraction? Terrorist allegation? He wondered.

Chapter 5

Noordine spotted him entering the analysis center and, smiling, waved him over. "Agent Dodek, some of these exchanges are extremely disturbing. I managed to break through the encryptions and get this. Your suspect, Dauadi, received data from a single IPO server in Paris, relayed through a network in Tel Aviv, if you can believe it, which transferred to a link in Mogadishu. I'm not surprised where it went next—Tehran, so forget about authenticating the source. Then it was routed back to the U.S.—Los Angeles, to be exact. Whoever did the keying masked passwords. Nevertheless, look on the screen...." She clicked, sending the browser arrow to both top and middle passages. "....Where it begins...."

Hitting a corporate target should be considered a viable option.
Doing exactly as planned will result in massive damage and personal loss....

"Where? Did he say?"
"Wait. Read on. Especially there. Follow me."

We sing the praises of Allah our God because He has shown us the Right Path. It shall be our sacrifice, the festival of 'Idu l Adha. Heed the words of Muhammad, the Prophet, who has said to His followers: He has fulfilled His promise, and made victorious His mighty soldiers and defeated the confederates, even though the infidels hate it. Ciidwayneey, Brothers of Somalia.

Jihad, the time is nigh; gather up, prepare to strike; those of the 10th shall be Victorious....

A series of numerals followed. She continued, keying the numbers onto the monitor. "I thought the sequence was odd until I mapped in a section of Los Angeles. Art, look. They're satellite coordinates. When I ran a search engine, up came the city registration numbers, including the building roll number for the Bank of America Tower at 5th and Hope

Street, downtown. Art, you must've seen the building; it's the black glass tower next to a major hotel."

He stared at the screen's contents for a few seconds. "Good work, Noordine. I gotta ask…does it say when…with what type of device?"

Swiveling her chair so that she faced him, her fingers just above the keyboard, she said in a soft voice, "Only indication is daytime."

"Yeah. Inflict maximum damage. The bastard who sent this—no indication of who it's from?"

"I wish I could tell you. With all the re-routing, no passwords, an unidentifiable IPO, this person has deliberately prevented detection." She glanced up at him, her eyes and mouth widened, bordering on fearfulness. "The only one, the only name I can think of is…Saleh Ali."

Grinding his teeth together prevented an expletive from bursting out. "You could be right. Great job, Noordine. Have you sent—?"

She nodded. Consuela and Mr. McLaughlin would be viewing it at that moment.

Art pulled up a chair and peered across the passages, two fingers of his right hand pointing to certain words, studying how sentence composition seemed to hook phrases. He shook his finger at the monitor, as if something streamed in and out of his brain, something he recognized. It was there. Why couldn't he say it?

Noordine glanced over, noticing his steep mental anxiety. "Agent Dodek…Agent Dodek?"

He stared at her, still in a trance-like state.

"Art Dodek…are you on a holiday?"

"Holiday!" he blurted, jumping off the chair, his finger tapping over the expression *'Idu l Adha*. "Noordine, that's it. Isn't that Arabic for Eid al-Adha, the Festival of Sacrifice?"

She gazed at the words, then back at Art. "It is…or literally, 'Greater Eid,' the Islamic holiday celebrated by Muslims worldwide to commemorate the willingness of Ibrahim to sacrifice his son Ishmael as an act of obedience to God."

He raised his hand as if to high-five, but she declined to return the gesture. Although she wasn't a devout Muslim, there were still certain male-female interactions she wouldn't share, such as touching a man not related to her.

Eid al-Adha, the Sacrifice Feast, marked the end of the Pilgrimage, or Hajj, for the millions of Muslims who traveled to Mecca, their holiest place on earth, each year. According to the Islamic lunar calendar, it traditionally fell on the tenth day (*Dhu al-Hijjah*) and ended on the thirteenth day. The Koran stated the festivities were to last for three days or more, depending on the country. However, observances were strict that prayer and sacrificing of a goat or sheep be done so that meat could be given to poor people as a donation. Dress code also must be adhered to, such as *Salwar kameez* and *Thawb*—outer wear and head covering—for men; *Chador* and *Hijab*—the long floor-length gown and head cover—for women. It was also related to another reverent major Islamic festival—*Eid ul-Fitr*, or day of repentance, ninth Dhu al-Hijjah—when Muslims fasted from sunrise to sundown. Westerners would be familiar with *Ramadan*, which was an annual festival when pilgrims converged at Mecca in Saudi Arabia to celebrate their history, rituals, and traditions.

Another Arabic word for sacrifice, Noordine explained, was *Qurban*, which was adapted into the Dari Persian-Iranian dialect. Other Muslim occupied countries had their own adaptation, of course. Id *al-Kabir*, meaning "Greater Eid/Festival," was used in Yemen and Syria, as well as spoken in North African nations—Algeria, Tunisia, Libya, and Egypt. Even Russian Muslims and those in Hindi India had their specific expressions.

Art nodded, following her explanation of the festivals, and pointed to the screen. "That, that word—*Ciidwayneey*—whose dialect is it?"

"Ciidwayneey? Somali."

"Uh-huh. Whom have we been dealing with?"

"Somalis. Art, I think you've—"

"Look again at where the...you know, where it's almost like a soliloquy. Tell me, what is the Arabic word for ritual?"

"Oh. Why, it's *Takbir*. A recital. It goes 'Ordered by the Prophet Muhammad that people of the faithful should recite Takbir from the dawn of the tenth of Dhu al-Hijjah, beginning, until the thirteenth of it, when the religious pilgrimage subsides.' I know it as the praising of God—*Allaahu Akbar*—God is the Greatest, which you so often—"

"Hear Islamic suicide bombers yell when they detonate their vests," he said, concluding her sentence.

Noordine agreed how that abhorrent phrase had become a rallying cry for Jihadi extremists. "Yet, Jihad," she explained, "literally means 'striving' for good in Arabic. Those with a warped sense of struggling, unfortunately, don't strive for anything except enemies of Islam, and see it as a duty to act out Holy War. Muslims are by and large peaceful. Anything to do with tolerance has also been blown out of proportion. Perhaps extremist elements blathering about the evil West have propagated the myth that all are bad, not trustworthy, and dangerous. It makes me heartsick to witness what occurs in the Middle East. Subversion, you know, can happen in any society, especially one dominated by religious fanatics. What's worse, we're seeing that it's gone from ordinary struggle to oppression and destabilization of moderate Muslim lands." She hoped that Art understood, not just because he was trained to interdict terrorists, but that he observed the good in some people. After all, ancient Israeli and Islamic texts contained many similarities in their teachings.

Being born in America, Noordine had not grown up with fractious elements of Islamic ideology. While her Jordanian parents had an influence over her devotion to Islam, they didn't interfere with her independence as a female, such as forcing her to wear the chador and hijab, dining with other women while males ate together, or forbidding her from dating members of the opposite sex. The only separation of men and women she encountered were prayer days at local mosques. Her father, formerly the *charge d'affaires* at the Jordanian Embassy in Washington, D.C., sent her to private school in West Virginia. She and her Muslim girlfriends interacted and never had a problem with students from other backgrounds. Her home often became the entertainment center for Christian, Jewish, Asian, Hispanic, Hindu, and Sikh students. Special events that she enjoyed as a teen were when she would prance amongst visiting foreign dignitaries with their stories of distant lands. Alternatively, she found most politicians stuffy and boring, and thought they made appearances only for their own gain. When her father became a citizen, he accepted a posting with the State Department. Now, Middle Eastern political adviser to the executive branch, she and her parents, who remained in Virginia, were lucky if they got together once a year.

Seeking further independence after graduating from university, she relocated to Southern California and worked as an Arabic translator/interpreter for the U.S. Citizenship & Immigration Services while earning her masters in Arabic studies and languages at UCLA. Not long after she returned to Washington, she landed a position within the State Department. This led to her interest in joining the FBI, which was in need of Middle Eastern linguists. However, the newly formed Department of Homeland Security approached her about her expertise, hired her, and assigned her to the anti-terrorist section in Los Angeles. Soon, she was tapping communication devices, entering online websites, intercepting e-mail, identifying and correlating words, expressions, phrases, breaking through encryption codes, and hacking into computers of suspected terrorists, at home and abroad. In addition, she instructed police and military intelligence officers to look out for certain words, like nicknames, slang, animate/inanimate objects, and references to U.S. edifices. She came across scary stuff, such as messages and exchanges between individuals or groups either discussing, planning, or preparing attacks on American soil or against U.S. infrastructures with its allies. A disturbing trend that she noticed was that many alleged terrorists inside the country weren't reticent about their willingness to die for Islam. After a while, she thought one became thick-skinned about what was posted online or shown on videos, but she found that this was not entirely true. Viewing and interpreting the last words of young men bent on their desire for martyrdom depressed her. Nonetheless, she couldn't personalize with them. If she intercepted a known target, enabling law enforcement agencies to thwart and arrest those responsible, it more than made up for the misses.

Sitting back down, Art again waved his finger near the monitor. He searched the screen, focusing on the Eid al-Adha festival contents. Zeroing in on certain characters, his brain scrambling and reconnecting dots like a puzzle, he turned to Noordine.

"The Takbir recital. That's where the sender has indicated when the next attack will be. You found the coordinates, etcetera, and etcetera. To him, it represents destroying a corporate giant while simultaneously taking out a large segment of the population inside." He stood up and circled her chair. Rubbing the whiskers on his chin, he added, "Can you — do you know the verses of the Takbir?"

"Well, yes, most of it. In Arabic, I can recite without having to stop and think what the English word would be. Remember, too, just like most languages, there are big differences in syllables, accents, expressions, sounds, pronunciation, and names. Did you know that the Arabic spelling for Muhammad has two different versions when translated into English? And there are two variations when it's —"

"Noordine," he said, just about sputtering, his heart racing. "Whatever version, what we're looking for is in the recital. It matches up with what I'm sure is the potential date."

His growing excitement floated over her head like a balloon.

Rising to her feet, she commenced reciting in Arabic, first selecting words, repeating a section. She knew each stanza began Allaahu Akbar — God is the Greatest — and was followed by further praises of His words and deeds and His proclamations.

Each time she converted a line into English, Art would lean his head back then tilt it forward, waiting, waiting. He cursed himself for not knowing the Hebrew interpretation. Then he may have understood the sequence of particular words.

Now they stood face to face, she reciting as if a chant, he rolling his tongue back and forth, anticipating the translation.

She paused for a couple of minutes. Slowly, her index finger moved to the monitor. "Art, what you wanted to hear again is the verse —"

"Yes. Yes. Say it."

"'...He has fulfilled his promise, and made victorious His servant, and made mighty His soldiers and defeated the confederates.'"

"Go on. After that part, it's...."

"'...even though the infidels hate it.'"

"Interpretation?"

44

"Soldiers are the faithful and devout who have defeated the military of the non-believers who stand opposed to Islam."

"Thank you, thank you. Scroll up, please. Little more. You don't see it? When is Eid al-Adha celebrated...and ended?"

Without the slightest hesitation, both their hands, flat-out, reached for the screen.

***

Muhamed Dauadi pounded on the motel door. He brushed by the person who let him in and told those inside Allah had given him the signal. He waved his arms to stifle their chattering, pulling sheets of paper from his pants pocket and, like a robot, wandering around the dimly lit room. "My brothers, who among you are ready?"

"We are! We are!" they chanted.

"Who among you are the faithful? The pilgrims of Allah, our supreme God?"

"All of us."

"Then listen. The festival of Eid al-Adha," he pronounced in Arabic, then uttered the Somali version again. "*Ciidwayneey*. Do you understand why you were chosen to return from your Homeland?"

Everyone affirmed by nodding their heads.

He spread out the papers on the floor. His finger flew into the center of the first page. Some of the group fell to their knees, slavering at the schematics.

***

One after the other, Art and Noordine shouted at the line that read, "Starting the tenth day of the month and ending on the third day."

He slid his right palm toward hers. This time, smiling broadly, she obliged and high-fived.

Exhaling, he sat down beside her. "Today's the eighth of June. The attack will take place on the tenth."

"Yes," she agreed.

"Starting the tenth and ending the thirteenth." Seriousness now crowded the lines on his forehead until they resembled unwound yarn. "The bastard," he swore, surprised that she didn't react to his swearing. "There will be *three consecutive* attacks."

This time she squirmed at how chilling his statement sounded.

His cell phone beeped. Short on words, the text from Consuela read: "Conference room — now."

"They have copies I downloaded," she said as Art showed her the message, and added, "I'm coming with you."

"They'll be glad you do," he said. "After you." A grinding machine could have cut through the tension as each of the team members filed into the room. McLaughlin had already taken a seat. The others followed;

45

Mercado to his left, Art beside her, then Noordine. The DHS and FBI agents sat on opposite sides.

No one had to count to sixty, as that's exactly how many seconds passed before McLaughlin leaned back on his high-backed chair, his eyes fanning over the group. Silence came to an end when he snapped a pencil in half. Both hands on the desk, he seemed to be waiting for someone to start explaining what the hell was going on.

When his cell phone rang, the sudden ringing tore through the silence like a blade. He listened for about a half a minute. Closing the cover, he said quietly, "LAPD has found Dauadi's prison coveralls…in a trash bin near Century Boulevard. Where do you think he is?"

No one could provide an accurate answer to his query.

"APBs are out, any lead checked over," Aylesha replied for the group.

Consuela Mercado, being the agent in charge, felt the heat of his gaze. She knew the director wanted more than "just looking" information. "According to the info deciphered by Noordine," she said, "there's an eminent attack planned this week. We know where. Good chance we know when, but not the exact time."

"What are you doing about it?" he asked, scattering pieces of the pencil slivers and ruffling through the e-mail messages.

"I'll answer that," Lamborghini said. "The LAPD and sheriff's department have been notified. I also alerted the B/A security people. Officers are also adding extra patrols to the area."

"I think we should arrange an FBI SWAT team," Agent Curbside suggested.

"Absolutely," Mercado followed. "A show of force surrounding the B/A building could just make Dauadi think twice."

McLaughlin turned and faced Art. "What do you think, Agent Dodek? Could he get away with it?"

"Very possible. A show of force, whatever blockade we might place in his way, won't necessarily keep him from acting. Terrorists don't care. You could also be endangering not only the lives of cops but civilians as well."

"What do you propose?"

Mercado held up her hand. "Hold on a minute. He's indicated the place, the day. Do we know how?"

"Yeah, Art," Curbside inquired. "You viewed the messages. Did he indicate explosives?"

"It was never revealed," Noordine said.

"Unfortunately, that gives the bastard the advantage over how we respond," the director said. "You forget, too, there's a large hotel adjacent to the bank. That means a lot of people."

Glum faces stared out after his remarks. Civilians nearby could pose a problem.

"What about the National Guard?" asked Aylesha.

Art straightened up. "Not a bad idea. But troops rolling up to a hotel and bank would cause an immediate panic. I think that's what we all want to avoid. Dealing with terrorists is one thing; panicky civilians in harm's way is another."

Heads shook in agreement.

"Uh, Noordine, show us the schematics of both buildings," he requested.

The translator-analyst opened a laptop and went to Google and two satellite imaginers—Digital World and GeoSky—then clicked on another machine, which accessed the blueprints for the Bank of America. She projected the images onto two 36" TV wall monitors behind McLaughlin.

Everyone turned and faced the screens. One concentrated on the B/A, the other overlaid side-by-side ground site satellite map tracking images.

Art got up. Part of the upper portion of his torso and face reflected onto the monitors as he stood beside them. Noordine easily followed his moving index finger with the computer arrows. Where he wandered, she expanded the pictures, more so when he pointed to street level images. To the north of the bank tower, a doublewide sidewalk ended at the old Los Angeles library building. From the sidewalk, inclined walkways headed to at least four bank door entrances. Neither door had security guard or curbside parking. *That restriction may be a plus*, Art thought, now sliding his finger downward, going south, next door to the corner of the hotel, with its upper level valet parking driveway entrance and partial circular staircase to the front large glass doors facing Hope Street. Temporary vehicle unloading could be a negative. Extra pluses were Consuela's remarks that both structures had closed circuit and surveillance cameras placed overhead at entrances, as well as two smaller digital cameras attached to the hotels outside pillars.

He concentrated on the bank's interior...standard fixtures, furnishings and counters. Several offices and cubicles lined various hallways. Outside were two or three ATM's, and one section inside the entrance held six automatic teller machines.

The B/A also contained offices within its tower, many commercial and corporate businesses and companies, international subsidiaries, consulates and commissions Noordine zeroed in next to the elevators, moving her arrow to the building's floor and name informational wall and marble counter charts. One particular floor, he remembered, housed the Canadian Consulate General offices. During his previous mission in Los Angeles, he had assisted in combating and dismantling a group of illegal gunrunners smuggling firearms into Canada in trade for marijuana (B.C. Bud) where possession of handguns was essentially barred. Other consulates or foreign business agencies would be interspersed throughout the tower as well.

He stepped a couple of feet away from the monitors and enquired whether any levels contained U.S. military contractors or were occupied by affiliated defense suppliers. "Terrorists," he explained, "target not only the private sector; anyone connected to the armed forces would be a likely source for Islamic extremists."

After no immediate response from the group, the director instructed Lamborghini to find out. Then, standing, he advised Mercado to devise a counter-action plan for the tenth, a day and a half away, and added that a show of force, extra manpower, wasn't just a good idea, it was a necessity.

The agents stepped away from the desk.

"Where do you think you're going?" shouted the director. "I don't remember saying this meeting was over."

Unit members stayed by their chairs.

"You're supposed to be the unit the DHS put together for occasions like this. Are you hamstrung? Everybody has a theory. Nobody has given me one goddamn useful suggestion. I want you to come up with a strategy that we can use against Dauadi." He scoped the group. Unhappy with their blank expressions, he walked slowly to the other end of the desk. "You waiting for me to give you instructions? Get out and do something."

After everybody shuffled out of the conference room, McLaughlin flipped through a Rolodex. Sliding out a card, he opened his cell phone and began punching numbers. "We have a dilemma," he said to the person who answered. "Tonight. Yeah, same place. Text me. I don't care how you do it." He shut the cover and circled his chair, peering up at the monitors.

***

Art poured a coffee in the staff lounge as Mercado entered.

Hours earlier she had looked refreshed, enthusiastic. Now her eyes showed nothing but concern; even a few extra lines had popped out on her forehead. Granted, as the team supervisor, she carried a full plate. A potential terrorist attack in the midst of Los Angeles's downtown area would freak anyone out.

She began pouring coffee, put the cup down, and returned the pot to the machine. In a quiet voice she announced that they were heading for a conference at police headquarters, followed by a closed-door meeting with the city's emergency response directorate. "Don't count on seeing your apartment anytime soon," she quipped as they neared an elevator.

When the doors opened, he had time for a quick swig, and then tossed the foam container into a wastebasket. Going down, he rubbed his tongue over his gums, trying to cool the burning sensation in his mouth.

***

A pickup truck parked alongside Dauadi's Mercedes. Lugging heavy canvas bags in both hands, the Arab driver ascended the stairs and sauntered down the corridor to Room 215. A corner of a window drape slid back. Once inside, the man and Dauadi embraced and uttered a few phrases in Arabic and the Somali dialect. This person was one of the deadly shooters at the freeway on ramp. He dipped his hand into the bags and withdrew pistols and magazine clips, which he handed to each man. Real excitement developed when he withdrew a bundle of AK-47 automatic carbines. The group could hardly wait to fondle the rifles.

Then he brought out what the group was hungering for—bricks of C-4 plastics explosives and detonators; again, each man received the items.

Dauadi got everyone to sit cross-legged on the floor. Like before, he spread out a series of blueprints of the bank tower. Colored circles, square boxes, red check marks, and several letters dotted entire sections of the computer printouts. One by one, he pointed his weapon at his comrades, indicating that person's location.

Then a string of black and brown prayer beads was passed around from person to person. Each man wound the Tasbeeh around his fingers and held it to his mouth.

"God is great," they sang. "We, the Brothers of Somali Jihad, your servants, continue your prophecy to darken the skies of the Great Satan."

As though they were instructing Boy Scouts on how to tie knots, the driver and Dauadi, using pocketknives, began peeling back strips of the C-4, inserting green, red, and blue wires, twisting the ends, and covering them with small plastic caps. Through pre-drilled holes, skilled, slow fingers pushed in the detonators.

Dauadi removed a cell phone-like device from his shirt pocket. Lips narrowing, his lower eyelids tightening, he waved it in front of the young Somalis, moving his thumb over certain numbers.

The exhibition ended with rings of cheers and the smacking of applause.

Chapter 6

Following the voice-activated GPS in the Ford Focus, Art managed to arrive at his temporary home in Santa Monica. He didn't have to check his watch…the setting sun had provided an idea of the time. An ocean breeze drifted inland; this would have placed him near the stretch of beaches along Ocean Boulevard. Once parked in a secured garage, riding the elevator to the fifth floor and getting to his apartment, he realized it was after 10 p.m. Still reeling from the night's back-to-back meetings, the first place he headed was the refrigerator. No alcoholic spirits, not even beer; fine, he could get along without them. Shelves held assorted condiments, a bag of bagels, a quart of milk, and two different fruit cans. He reached for the pitcher of OJ, found a tall glass, and poured. The tangy, cold liquid was likely the best drink he'd had all day.

Undoing his vest, unhooking his holster as he topped up his glass, he gazed around the furnished apartment. A patio faced northwest. Some of the Santa Monica pier lights shone in the distance. The furniture appeared new and functional—one tan sofa, a love seat, and two leather chairs around an octagon table, and commode and coffee tables filled the living room area. A short hallway to the left of the kitchen contained the bathroom and sleeping quarters. An HDTV sat above a wide four-drawer dresser. Wall artwork depicted palm trees, beach activities, and the commercial and entertainment promenades nearby.

He switched on a bedside lamp and lay down on the bed, propping himself up with pillows. After exhaling for a few seconds, he punched in his cell phone home number.

Two rings and Lynda's hello brought out a wide smile. "Hey, Lyndie, glad to hear your voice. How's my girl?"

"Hi…sweetie. I was waiting for your call. How are you doing? What's happening?"

He pressed fingers against his mouth to stifle a yawn. "Getting around, familiarizing myself with Homeland Security. Some of their techniques are more advanced than NSU."

"Having fun in the sun?" she chuckled.

"I wish."

"Guess what? I might have a sale tomorrow. The seller sounded like she'll take the counter-offer I suggested."

"Terrific. Who could resist you?"

She laughed. "Who's your new partner? What's his name?"

"Her name is Consuela Mercado."

"Oh." A pause. "Your partner is a woman?"

"Well, yeah. She sure knows her way around the block. Nothing passes by her."

Another pause. "I–I miss you, Art."

"Same here, Lyndie. You take care. Okay?"

"Call me soon...tomorrow."

"10-4," he chuckled, turned off the phone, and kicked off his shoes.

Seconds after talking with his wife, his mind's eye found itself remembering how stunning Mercado had appeared that morning at LAX. He blinked. *Okay, she's nice looking. She's my partner, nothing else.*

He was about to get up when his phone beeped.

"Agent Dodek, you like the apartment?" a crisp, articulate female voice asked when he answered.

He felt that momentary lapse, like when a word gets stuck in the throat. Then, sitting up, he said, "Consuela...your calling kind of surprised me."

She had a deep laugh, the kind that made you smile instantly; although he didn't want to admit it, it was the sexiest laugh he had ever heard.

"Are you checking up on me?" he asked.

"You think I should? Anyway, the team thinks you handled yourself very professionally today. Walter may not come out and say it, but he thought you acted according to DHS policy."

A few seconds went by on his end, thinking that she could have mentioned this in the morning. "Yeah, well...."

"We all want to accomplish the same thing, don't we?" she asked.

"Isn't that the whole point of why we're out there?"

Soft laughter filtered through the phone. "Well, see you tomorrow, then."

"Sure. Count on it."

"Good night, Art."

"Good night," he repeated, clicking off. Resting his head on a pillow, he recalled again how stunning she'd looked at LAX.

Chapter 7

Walter McLaughlin, entering the prisoner detention area, summoned a guard to bring the programmer to the interior hallway. For security, two separate electronic floor-to-ceiling bulletproof glass doors had been erected to prevent someone from leaving the holding section and trying to escape. Even if the officer figured it odd that this late at night a prisoner would be brought out, it was doubtful he would question the director's request.

A tired looking, shackled Somali, guards on either side, appeared behind the inner door. After being buzzed through both doors, a stern looking McLaughlin took hold of an arm and led him past the outer holding section and over to an elevator. Once downstairs in the garage, he led his charge to a Chevy van, slid open a side door, and wound leg restraints anchored to the floor around his legs. He then leaned over and slid a dark hood over the surprised man's eyes. Protests went ignored as the director fired up the motor and peeled out of the parking lot.

Traffic volume was low in this section of downtown at night; in fact, it was almost deserted. The van made a couple of turns then headed straight on Olympic to an industrial and commercial area. Here, grocer distributors and numerous suppliers wouldn't be opening until dawn. Several tractor-trailer rigs were parked by loading platforms or had lined up out on the street.

The van's headlights picked out a long steel mesh fence. Flashing its high beams, a person obscured by the reflecting lights opened a padlock for the driver. Once inside the lot he angled toward an abandoned packinghouse. This building, about three stories tall, had long ago shut down; its exterior of steel sheets had rusted, and debris left over from the structure's days as a shipper lay scattered around the yard.

McLaughlin and the other person dragged the Somali from the vehicle and strong-armed the blubbering prisoner to a side door. A flashlight found a switch panel. Just one dim overhanging fixture and a wall light were flipped on. Footsteps on the concrete floor echoed inside the vast, empty carcass of the building. Somewhere, water dripped and bounced off the floor.

Two pairs of hands pushed the man onto a chair. Unable to see, not knowing where he was, fear seemed to grip the young man. Again and again he asked where he was, who was there. He didn't know if McLaughlin had put him in the van, or whether the DHS director was still there. The silence just added to his obvious confusion.

Circling the chair, the dim light picked out a tall, light haired man in a dark shirt and khaki pants, who slammed the back of his hand against the prisoner's face, sending him and the chair crashing to the floor. A muffled cry sputtered from his lips under the hood. Then he was reseated. Within five seconds he was knocked down again. This time a boot ground into his chest, the heel turning and digging inward. Only after the foot was removed did he let out an anguished moan. As he tried to raise his back, another foot came down, stomping just below his collarbone.

McLaughlin got another chair and seated himself about six feet away. "Your name is Tariq?" he asked, leaning sideways.

The prisoner coughed and drooled, his orange jumpsuit wet from pools of floor water.

"Your name is Tariq?" a gruffer voice asked.

"I–I…yes, that is my name," he said, sucking in air.

"Well, Tariq, we're going to ask you some questions, and you will answer us truthfully, won't you?"

Hesitating, he coughed as the boot inched deeper into his chest. "Y-yes. Answer what? Where am I? Who are you?"

"Shut up and listen. You're an intelligent young man," the director continued. "This afternoon you were communicating with someone about preparing an attack on Los Angeles. Who was it? Where in Los Angeles? Tell me."

Heavy breathing. Gurgling. "I don't…I can't breathe."

McLaughlin nodded to the other man to reduce the pressure. "It was your friend Muhamed Dauadi, wasn't it?" With no answer forthcoming, this time the gruff voice intensified as he asked, "Wasn't it? He was planning an attack, a terrorist attack, against this city, against the United States of America. This week, right?" Hands in pockets, he rose. "Where is Dauadi? Where…is…Dauadi?"

"I–I don't know. I don't know."

McLaughlin nodded to his accomplice.

The whir of metal hovered nearby, accompanied by the sound of a steel wire pulley lowering.

The other man grabbed the prisoner's arms, yanking his body so erect that it made him groan. The whirring of the pulley came closer, then hemp cord cuffed his wrists. His body flexed as he was pulled up until his shoes were a few inches off the floor.

"What are you doing?" he shouted. "You're hurting me. Let me down."

Tariq's dangling body was spun around, and he cried out as the cords on his wrists dug into his skin like slivers. His jumpsuit zipper was quickly pulled down to his waist, and McLaughlin's associate grabbed at Tariq's white T-shirt and tore it open, exposing bare skin. He winced when metal clips were affixed to his nipples and to the loose skin under his Adam's apple. Then the man moved away, his footsteps decreasing in sound and creating an unnerving silence.

"Tariq, do you really want us to do this? McLaughlin asked. "Be reasonable. Tell us where Dauadi is."

"Please believe me. I don't know."

A sudden electric jolt shot through Tariq's body. A cry, muffled at first, burst out from his lips.

"Tariq, Jesus Christ. Answer the question."

"I-I told you, I don't—"

The next jolt slammed into his body, spinning him 360 degrees. The men could hear him sobbing as monosyllabic half words flowed between his quivering lips. All his fingers flexed upward. The next shock was so intense that he screamed and cried as his body dipped, lurched, and twisted. His grinding teeth sent specks of blood oozing through the hood.

"If you receive another blast, Tariq, it may kill you. Think about it, you dumb fuck. Do you want to die?" The question, meant to generate a stronger threat, was really all that McLaughlin could do. Killing the Somali wasn't an option. A dead prisoner couldn't be dragged back to a cell. He knew that his partner, however, had no such constraints. If Tariq died, who cared? He didn't.

The director waved his hands in a time-out gesture as the electrical panel switch was increased to its highest level, which would most likely prove fatal if released.

Leaving Tariq dangling and crying, he strode over to his accomplice and they exchanged a few heated words. A minute later they lowered the Somali's shaking body, removed the cords, and placed him back on the chair. The director picked up a half-filled water bucket and dumped the contents over the man's head. His soaking wet jumpsuit rezipped, both men lugged him outside and into the van. Shackles anchored his legs to floor locks. Dazed and sobbing, Tariq slumped sideways onto the seat.

"He knows the location of that fucker Dauadi," were the only words uttered by McLaughlin to his partner as he backed up the van and sped out onto the road. The episode in the packinghouse had left him frustrated and cursing. Used to getting his way or obtaining what he wanted, the prisoner's refusal to answer his questions, even under duress, made him angrier as he swerved in and out of lanes heading back downtown. This wasn't the outcome he desired. *Not after busting my ass for the government*, he scowled.

He had spent years as a senior bureaucrat with the Justice Department. Gradually, through political and personal connections, he joined the internal division of the CIA as an anti-domestic terrorist investigator. He remembered the times before 9-11, when most operations he investigated involved American fanatics blowing up government buildings, or burning down churches and large condominium developments. He had participated in the first New York Twin Towers explosion investigation, and the terrorists responsible were arrested, convicted, and imprisoned. Convictions impressed his superiors. The taste of outside foreigners attacking America also whetted his appetite to personally go after extremists, now identified as Islamic terrorists. His big opportunity came after Osama bin Laden's al-Qaeda organization orchestrated the 2001 mass killing of thousands of people on American soil. When the White House created the Department of Homeland Security, he was appointed a senior offshore CIA counter-terrorism supervisor in the Middle East. His methods in acquiring information beneficial to U.S. military interests were often overlooked by senior advisors. In the early days of the Afghan and Iraqi invasions, American politicians were more interested in results than apologies.

Opportunity continued to follow...perhaps some political influence helped. When DHS established a West Coast regional office in Los Angeles, his appointment as director and manager of a combined FBI and DHS taskforce to investigate onshore terrorist attacks from radical extremists came as no surprise, nor was it opposed. At last, after seeking a position with clout in the country's war on terrorism, he had found unfettered access to high-level government officials in CIA and DOJ boardrooms. McLaughlin didn't end his sights on Los Angeles—not when appointment as the assistant secretary of Homeland Security loomed in the future, a position he believed he deserved.

Also, he decided what agents would work for him, enlisting individuals who not only supported his administrative powers but also could assist him by stepping outside normal boundaries and push the right buttons...individuals like Aylesha Reeves, Tony Lamborghini, and Dan Curbside. Feisty, smart Consuela Mercado he brought in as lead unit member.

Plus a trusted ally, his interrogation accomplice tonight. The two worked together as CIA field investigators in Kabul, Afghanistan, and the Peshawar region of Northwest Pakistan, homeland of the Taliban insurgents. If tactics used were unorthodox, so be it. When it came to preventing American casualties, the lives of Taliban militants were irrelevant. If civilians got in the way of counter-intelligence, hell, they were collateral damage.

The federal building came into view as he rounded Alameda Avenue. Still cursing, all he wanted to do was dump off Tariq and head home for a stiff drink.

Chapter 8

Art Dodek sat up in bed. He had dozed off, forgetting to kill the light in the bedroom. The trouble was, he had not enjoyed a sound sleep. The years of forcing himself to stay awake during missions came back to haunt him. Sleepless nights. Broken sleep. REM sleep meant dreams, sometimes horrific, violent episodes, some of which repeated themselves night after night. Scenes and characters varied; danger didn't. Some men dreamt of always falling, without ever knowing whether they hit the ground, or saw peculiar out of character images.

Overtiredness stole his strength as he staggered into the bathroom and took a leak.

Rubbing his tongue over dry lips, he gulped down a small bottle of water from the refrigerator. He got a surprise as to how late it was. Gazing out the patio window, the first yellowish light mixed with the final purple coat of the night locked in his eyes. Back in bed, he opened and closed his eyes and buried his face in the pillow, until sometime later – he had no idea when – he drifted off.

***

Crouching by a fence, Art released the safety lock on his Glock. Darkness and the stillness of the night forced breaths of air non-stop from his mouth. Even if situations like this had occurred before, a gunman approaching never lessened the tension. Any sound made him tense up. *Were those footsteps? How close is he? This is insane; I'm the one who should be doing the chasing.* Now he was the hunted. No backup either this night – his NSU partner, Keith Dawson, was nowhere in sight.

In a kneeling position, he raised his head level with the fence post. At that instant, a bullet slammed into the wood, sending fragments over his hair. A second shell whizzed over the fence.

Then a figure appeared almost out of nowhere. The shadow of a pistol waved along the grass. Now, hunched over, he jumped up, firing twice alongside the shadow. A bullet flew over its shoulder. The shadow grew and became a figure. He recognized his assailant – Siad Asghar

57

Abbas, the Syrian gunman who had bloodied him in a fight in Vancouver and damn near killed him. And he couldn't understand why the figure continued to expand in size or why the ground kept shaking and opening, as if his body was being swallowed.

Both men, standing mere feet from one another, blasted away. Orange flames from bullets discharging and columns of smoke seemed to be all that was separating them.

Art's body lurched. Searing pain made him grit his teeth. Something wasn't right. He couldn't distinguish where the pain came from. He couldn't fathom why his wife's face faded in and out before his eyes.

The Syrian had another weapon—an M-16. A finger pressed back the trigger. The bullet flew toward Art's head.

***

Sweating, mouth wide open, sheets clenched between his fingers, his body jerked until he sat up in the semi-darkness of his apartment. At first, confusion set in, then realizing a nightmare had awoken him, his head fell back down on the pillow. Breathing heavily, he experienced a feeling of floating; his eyes opened, then closed. Misty shadows floated nearby.

***

Wine glass in hand, Art strolled through various rooms, none of which resembled his apartment or even his home in Vancouver. This place had windows, lots of them. Weird, though, one minute they were two-way, the next, frosted ripples covered the glass. Furniture, furnishings, fabric, color, or material, whatever appeared around him gave him a strange, compelling urge to continue wandering.

He sensed that he wasn't alone. The feeling of another person in the room drifted around him, someone whose skin emitted a sweet, peach-like fragrance. A woman's breathing piqued his curiosity. A hand, soft and silky, touched his arm, beckoning. Turning, he faced her, yet her features remained indistinguishable. Another hand brushed along the side of his neck. *Is this apparition a dream? Some sort of a devilish trick? Is it real? If it is, show who you are.*

Consuela Mercado, in a strapless white gown, smiled, her dark eyes inviting rapture.

Both stood inches apart, eyes locked, lips approaching. The sensation he felt in his loins…. The harder he resisted, the more he yearned to sweep her up in his arms. They embraced….

***

A burning light enveloped his face. He sprang upward, blinking, trying to see through the flashes of bright light. It was the early morning sun filtering between the curtains. He rubbed his forehead and settled back down. Now lying on his side, he stared at the window, his mind repeating: get up…get up.

A ringing cell phone echoed in the background, ending any chance of more sleep. Instinctively, he eyed his watch—6:07 a.m.—picked up on the third ring, and muttered a sleepy "hello" to the caller.

"Art, it's Consuela. Are you awake?"

He let out a yawn away from the mouthpiece. "Yeah, yeah. You're my wake up service, too?"

There wasn't any humor in the voice that said, "Hurry, get downtown. We've got a problem…it's serious." She clicked off.

The sound of the phone signal cutting off jarred his head.

What now? his brain asked. Stretching, he ran into the bathroom and banged the door shut.

Chapter 9

June 9, Eve of Eid al-Adha, The Festival of Sacrifice

As soon he passed the security kiosk on the sixth floor, Dan Curbside told him people were waiting for him in detention.

ICE agents and L.A. paramedics milled about in the holding cells section. Mercado, a blank expression clouding her face, made a U-turn when she spotted her partner.

He could sense concern in the faces of those strolling through the corridor; their silence said it all. Reaching the third cell, his head jerked back when she pushed open the door.

A rolled up, ripped T-shirt wound around his neck, an overturned stool nearby, Tariq's lifeless body dangled from the cell's ceiling light fixture. From the height, it must've taken hours until he strangled himself to death. His eyes bulged outward, and part of his tongue protruded from his mouth. The paramedics confirmed he had bitten through it.

Mercado and Art stood outside the cell, speechless; not from the gruesome sight, but that they had lost their link to Muhamed Dauadi. If Tariq had lived, they wondered, would he have given up the escaped Somali's location?

Frustrated and upset, Mercado banged a fist at the steel door. She blasted the two marshals who had patrolled the cellblock.

One officer remarked that they had no reason to suspect the prisoner had suicidal tendencies; he was sleeping on the cot when they had last checked him a few hours ago.

While an ERT member called for the coroner, the agents wandered down the corridor.

Just before reentering the DHS offices, a detainee at the last holding cell hooted as Mercado strolled by. Without stopping, she told the man to go play with himself.

***

About 8 a.m., both the Mercedes and the pickup truck headed west, destination Beverly Hills. None of the Somali's, including Muhamed Dauadi, dressed in casual clothing and black bandanas tied below their chins, spoke. On the floor of each vehicle rested AK-47 rifles, equipped with fully loaded magazine clips, wrapped in towels. Cold, blank eyes stared at what they believed was western decadence—upscale stores selling indecent women's apparel, corporate offices, some with links to the Middle East, entertainment centers, movie theaters, an abundance of alcohol establishments, Christian houses of worship. No one felt any reservation about what was expected of him today.

The lead car made several sweeps along Wilshire Boulevard, the driver focusing on intersections, particularly those with No Left and One Way lanes, slowing down when passing underground parking lots. Heavy traffic flow and pedestrians ignoring Do Not Walk signs neither bothered nor affected his relaxed mood. At one corner, he even apologized when a group of young women darted in front of him. Turning at the next street, he waved at a traffic officer. Then he leaned forward and glanced left, his attention affixed to the next street.

***

Agents shuffled into the conference room, and McLaughlin indicated for them to sit down. A phone rang to his left, which he passed on to Mercado. She listened to the call for a moment, hung up, and explained to those in the room that the LAPD had received a call from a motel manager about a trashed room and unpaid lodging. Odd as it sounded, she said she and Art would check it out.

As she pulled into the motel parking lot, two officers and the manager greeted her.

"We wouldn't have called," one officer stated, "except the room had been rented to a group of Muslim men who refused anyone entry...even forbade the maid from cleaning up."

Art switched on a lamp, and Mercado propped open the door for extra daylight. Both slipped on plastic gloves before they touched bedding, moved chairs around, or pushed over countless fly-ridden, open food containers. As the agents wandered through the third floor corner suite, they saw that the term pigsty would've been an understatement. As well as reeking of body odor and stale food, bed sheets had been used as rags to mop up the overflowed sink. Verses from the Koran were scrawled on walls. Dresser drawers were left hanging open, but not one item of clothing was found inside them.

Art knelt by a table. Thinking at first that a piece of yellow cheese had fallen below it, he was about to rise when he grabbed it and held it to the light. "Consuela, take a look at this."

61

"What is it?" she asked, peering at the half-inch object between his thumb and forefinger.

He chipped off a sliver and rubbed it for a few seconds. His eyebrows rose. "It's not cheese...it's C-4."

"You're not kidding, are you?"

"Would you?" he asked, checking items on the floor a lot closer.

Mercado used a pen-size flashlight beam to check any piece of debris left on the torn, soiled carpet. Something piqued her interest. What looked like threads turned out to be plastic shavings from colored electrical wires.

Both nodded, agreeing someone had been fabricating an explosive device. Their eyes asked the same question: did Dauadi and his accomplices stay there?

"I'll get a bag from the truck," she said, wrenching her nose from the smell.

***

As soon as a bus pulled out, the Mercedes and the truck stopped at the curb. Leaving drivers in each vehicle, four men bailed out onto the sidewalk. Their waist length jackets partially concealed the weapons. Passers-by, too busy in their own daily rituals, paid little attention to men forming a square.

In front of them were a fast food restaurant and a coffee shop filled with customers, a travel agency displaying trips to the Holy Land, and next door a Christian bookstore. Racing to beat a traffic light, four young office workers, laughing, engrossed in their morning chatter, stopped near the corner. Others either filtered out of the stores or gathered along the sidewalk; the men were almost hidden in the crowd.

"*Allah Bakbar...Allah Bakbar!*" they screamed in unison, sliding the bandanas marked with Arabic characters over their faces and turning toward the storefronts so that they formed the shape of a diamond.

AK-47 automatic weapons whipped from behind their jackets started firing indiscriminately. As though encased in an iceberg, those persons nearest them froze, while those heading toward the corner were totally unaware, unable to hear the clatter from the noise of street traffic.

Gunfire ripped through bodies, sending some to the ground and some toppling over one another or onto braking cars. Sheet glass shattered by bullets flew and sliced through others. Those escaping the shower of bullets by jumping outside onto the street were cut down before they reached the sidewalk. Scream after blood-curdling scream echoed down the block. One gunman wheeled around and fired a perfect score at the four women, all of them jerking out of their shoes and stumbling into the road. The youngest got squashed by a delivery truck that was unable to stop and plowed through the doorway of the travel agency. Pedestrians trying to take cover by running into the street were hit either by

62

ricocheting bullets or vehicles bashing against each other. Sounds of screaming and smashing steel rained down in every direction. Some people strangely avoided a strike by being engulfed in smoke and dust.

No one attempted to charge a gunman. Who would with powerful bullets ripping through flesh and the ugly bloodletting? Despite the carnage, an inexplicable sense of disbelief seemed to hover over those fortunate enough to have evaded death.

The traffic officer who had gotten a wave minutes earlier lay dead alongside a curb.

Flames blasted through the bookstore windows, stoked by the volumes of paper products. Bullets ripped through a marquee glass cover, sending shards down onto a couple that had tried to take refuge under the theater's arched beam. Streams of blood flowed into a corner culvert.

The four gunmen backed themselves up toward their vehicles. Loading, firing, reloading, shooting into the buildings and at persons begging for help, they scrambled inside. Brakes squealing, they sped through the intersection, sending metal fragments, chromed parts, pieces of plastic, and glass flying throughout the street.

Sirens mingled with the cries of the wounded and bleeding. For a few seconds those able to stand remained still, silent, fearful of the gunmen returning. A few coughed up blood from the stinking thick smoke of the AK-47's. As if in trances, one or two men knelt over someone who showed signs of life.

ER teams and scores of police officers descended on the streets and sidewalks. Blades from circling helicopters stirred up dozens of dust bowls. At first, paramedics and firefighters raced between injured pedestrians, unsure of whom to offer aid to first. Police officers attempted to hold back people who screamed that their relatives or friends lay wounded or dead. An LAFD pumper truck, unable to approach the corner, laid out a hundred foot hose to spray the burning structure. Adding to the confusion and panic, dozens of people from nearby offices and looky-loos descended into the streets. Several witnesses disagreed about the gunmen's descriptions. A bicyclist leaned down and filled his hands with spent bullet cartridges; to his horror, some were hot enough to burn his fingers.

Crews from TV news trucks laying out cables got pushed back, scrambling to find another opening in order to interview eyewitnesses.

***

At the motel, both Art and Consuela's phones beeped. On hers, Aylesha Reeves said the unit agents—herself, Dan Curbside, and Tony Lamborghini—were on their way to a mass shooting in Beverly Hills.

"Better get going," the agent said, texting the location.

63

They raced down the stairs of the motel and jumped into their vehicle. Art, behind the wheel, switched on the police channel, and his partner texted the FBI and DHS offices for current information. He sped out of the lot—a bus had to swerve to avoid a collision. This SUV had lights and a siren. Best estimation, twenty, twenty-five minutes.

McLaughlin came on the line and said all available agents were streaming to the shooting site. There were no solid descriptions of the gunmen, he added, just four guys taking off in two cars...not even license plate numbers. He told them he would meet up ASAP. Mercado implored him to retrieve all the surveillance cameras in the vicinity.

***

Peeling off his bandana in the Mercedes, Dauadi punched numbers on his cell phone. "Watch CNN if you want to know how many," he chuckled to the person on the phone. "We're heading to Hollywood. One guy squealed like a pig—I shot him in both eyes."

Laughter broke out from the back seat passengers.

***

The closest Art and Consuela could get to the site was about two blocks away. Ambulances sped in and out with wounded bystanders. A half dozen drape-covered corpses, some gender unknown, were placed further up the street for later identification. Gray smoke settled over the sidewalk while firefighters mopped up water and bloodstains. A cop figured that over a hundred shells littered the pavement and roadway. One woman in bandages, still dazed from the shooting, clung to a paramedic, sobbing that she couldn't see her mother. A young boy nearby with blood oozing through his yellow hair cried out for a parent who didn't answer. Women's purses lay where they'd fallen. Too early to confirm those killed, ER crews had their hands full tending to the injured. One cop and a cameraman tussled when the guy buzzed too close to a dead woman lying halfway inside the travel agency.

There wasn't much the agents could do. Initial shock subsiding, they collected notes from a couple of cops who were too busy to talk. Agents Reeves and Curbside, interviewing a handful of onlookers, nodded at their presence. McLaughlin arrived minutes later, barking out orders, most of which were unheeded in the commotion. Nearby, Lamborghini, standing by a police car, relayed details to emergency agencies. Rushing past the director, he remarked that videotapes were en route to DHS for analysis.

LAPD investigators continued to search the streets for any signs of the get-away vehicles. Shooter descriptions, though sketchy, were being broadcast throughout the city.

Only a few restaurant patrons with non-severe wounds remained as the four agents met up to compare notes. Suspicions of a terrorist attack highlighted their discussions. What other motive could there be?

Quietly walking away from the group, Art took a long breath and gazed around the area. Nine months ago in Vancouver, Canada, two Syrian extremists had almost succeeded in assassinating the Israeli and Canadian prime ministers, who were attending Yom Kippur ceremonies. Besides the Israeli ambassador, two Israeli bodyguards, and an RCMP officer gunned down, nine innocent spectators were also killed and over a dozen people wounded. At that time Canadian security agents from the NSU, he included, were on the scene prior to the shootings in order to prevent such a tragedy. A lot of good it did. Plus, as senior agent he received the bulk of criticism for not doing enough. Vivid as ever, that afternoon continued to haunt his mind. And just like today, he knew this shooting had the signature of a pre-planned terrorist attack.

Standing in the roadway, McLaughlin, accompanied by a police captain, growled at a reporter who placed a microphone too close to his face. The senior cop had to use both arms to lead the director away.

Mercado called his name, but it didn't register. She shouted a second time, and this time tapped his shoulder. He faced her, his eyes steaming. Sure, he'd be upset. Everybody was. Shaking her head as she glanced once more at the carnage, they walked back to her SUV. Going past a row of coroner vans, the shrill voices of 9-1-1 operators dispatching emergency crews blared from fire engine microphones and radios.

Chapter 10

About an hour later, a somber, quiet Noordine Assad greeted Dodek and Mercado in the communications center. She had three monitors going. Two showed the buildings under attack, the other replayed images of persons cut down on the sidewalk. Below her desk a wastebasket containing rolled up wet tissues indicated how the mass shooting had hit her emotionally.

Mercado sympathized with her, adding, "Don't take events personally. That's something we have drummed into us during our training. However, we're human; it does get to you. And that can come with a cost if an agent lost his edge. The one thing we can't become is *vulnerable.*"

Noordine's eyes opened and closed as the shooting rampage continued on screen.

Both agents placed comforting hands on her shoulders.

"Easy, easy," Mercado whispered. "Yes, it's grotesque to watch. I know it's hard not to personalize with the victims. Try to focus on the shooters."

"Yes, I am trying. I'm a linguist. I shouldn't be watching this, but Mr. McLaughlin wants me to review it with you."

Art concentrated on the part where the shooters broke out of their diamond shaped formation. He had a flurry of questions buzzing around in his head. "The headbands. The script. What does it say?"

"It's not really Arabic script. Loosely, it translates to 'Brothers of Somali Jihad.' Is that who they are?"

"Most likely," he replied.

All three cringed, repulsed at the sight of bystanders collapsing onto the sidewalk from bullets tearing through their bodies.

"Can you zoom onto their faces?" he asked, grabbing a chair.

Noordine used the middle monitor to expand the men's features. Other than the bandanas and their foreheads, skin tone, their similarity in height, slim builds, casual clothes, nothing special marked one from another.

Art turned to his partner standing next to him. "Consuela…I think there's…."

"What are you looking at?"

"That guy, the taller one in the checkered shirt, the one just reloading his rifle."

"What…what?" She stared at the screen.

"Noordine, zoom closer. Slow down. Stop. The bottom corner."

"I see it," the linguist said. "Looks like an earring."

"Christ almighty. He's got a fish hook in his earlobe." He pressed his finger over the monitor. "Consuela, you have a photo of Muhamed Dauadi. Let me see it."

She pulled it out of her shoulder purse.

All three scanned the picture, and snapped their faces back to the screen. Visible in the photograph, a thin wire, curled and bent, about the diameter of a penny and a half inch long, hung from the man's ear.

Which one shouted the name "Mohamed Dauadi,"—despite the bandana covering the gunman's face on the monitor and his wildly spraying an AK-47 at restaurant patrons—didn't matter. His ID had been confirmed.

Art rose and swatted his thigh. "That's the prick we're looking for." His off-color word didn't garnish much of a reaction.

"How merciless can a man be?" sighed Noordine, her cheeks encased in her hands.

"That's why we've got to take him down."

"When we find the prick," Mercado scowled.

"Can I turn these off?" asked Noordine, her finger already crawling to an exit button.

Mercado nodded yes. Arms crossed, lips pinched outward, she looked as though she could strangle someone. As the monitors shut down, she quietly asked, "Have any web sites acknowledged this morning? I just boil over when some self-righteous cleric rationalizes the carnage in the name of a prophet."

"Yes, they think their glorification is God's way," she said, opening another screen. "Take your pick. I've given up counting. Some claim they commanded the gunmen. What's pathetic, though, is that they use these videos to attract Muslim youths. I'm a Muslim. I believe in my faith. This makes me so ashamed."

"You have nothing to feel ashamed of," Mercado said sympathetically. "We all have to …we'll deal with those creeps someday."

Her BlackBerry beeped—a text from McLaughlin.

Art cleared his throat. "We still have the threat of a major attack tomorrow," he said near the doorway."

His partner almost let out the f-word. In this charged atmosphere, it was doubtful any one would've been offended.

"Noordine," she said, "please keep looking at the Arabic web sites…militants are fanatics at claiming responsibility for mass attacks and boasting that they're invincible. Check for FBI intelligence reports, too." Despite agents being cautioned about expressing their views publicly, she shook her fist and glowered, "God, I could ring Dauadi's neck. Hanging him would be too merciful. Let's go, Art. We've got work to do."

Noordine watched them leave. As if to add her own declaration, the linguist tightened her lips and hit a new set of commands on her keyboard. As she brought up the home page for Homeland Security and started opening links to secured sites, her fax machine beeped, spitting out pages of new Intel information.

Chapter 11

Parked in a driveway of an older one story house clustered behind gnarled maple trees, the Mercedes driver waited until the front door opened and two middle aged men beckoned for them to enter. Passengers from the car and pickup truck, their AK-47s wrapped in towels, walked across a burnt-yellow lawn, went inside, and leaned their weapons against the wall. Their clothes still reeked of gun smoke.

Muhamed Dauadi had found another safe house, this one in South Pasadena about ten miles north of downtown Los Angeles. There was always someone who allowed him safe haven.

Inside, mismatched furnishings dotted the living and dining rooms; two other midsize rooms held sofas, sagging beds, and chairs. Flooring creaked or tiles had come unglued, and most of the walls were lacking paint. An unpainted, wooden-framed tool shed stood outside, plus a northeast facing patio had been added to the back, although assorted planks and siding attested to a renovation left uncompleted. Not one room in the house contained a mirror.

The double sink in the kitchen was full of leftover dishes, and pungent odors of spices filled the air. A crockpot of lamb stew simmered on the counter; a large pot of rice on the stove steamed beneath a dinner plate used as a cover. Most noticeable was the abundance of chairs, suggesting that many meetings were held there on the floor in relation to the three occupants who lived there.

The man who greeted their guests was Iraqi, with a thick moustache and short gray hair. He wore a long sleeved shirt draped over dark pants. Two dark-skinned younger men hung around the living room. Everyone made eye contact, nodding casually; however, no one exchanged a word. No one mentioned the day's shooting incident. Only Dauadi and his host buzzed cheeks.

Minutes later, when the stew and rice piled on yellow trimmed plates was served in the living room, some of the group sat down on the sofa while a couple preferred the carpet. Conversation began. Cheerful voices rang out. Today they could consume *halal* food—which was prepared to strict Islamic rules—while tomorrow, Eid al-Adah Day of Sacrifice, they would have to fast until sunset.

Everybody ate contentedly and bantered about their homelands and villages where they grew up, of fathers and brothers, some of whom who became martyrs, and their favorite weapons, plus militants and comrades they hadn't seen since their training days in Pakistan. Food wasn't the only topic of interest.

Licking his fingers and sliding his unfinished meal aside, Dauadi, in his raspy voice, smiled, and said, "What Allah bestowed on us today, tomorrow, with his blessing, we shall bring greater honor to His name. If our enemy thought our actions today were catastrophic, from the rising and setting of the sun tomorrow, we will rip every ounce, every breath of their being. They are the non-believers. They insult Islam. They condemn us. They murder our brothers in our homelands and refuse to retreat back to their Godless empire. It is our duty to avenge what they have wrought on our holy soil." He removed his eyeglasses and pushed them into a shirt pocket. "My brothers," he resumed, pointing a finger at each person in the room. "What are you going to do?"

"Avenge! Avenge!" the group chanted.

"So it shall be done," he went on, his dark eyes and mouth wide open. "Any soldier who has shot at us; any man or woman who scoffs at us; whoever follows the puppets in Washington, they are our enemy." He jumped up and shouted even louder. "We will strike at their hearts. Never has this land seen what is to come. The wrath of Allah, the true God, shall darken the skies. Brothers of Somali Jihad, the day America cowers and bleeds…is tomorrow. *Inshallah*. God wills it."

"God wills it," they shouted.

Everyone rose and waved their Korans in the air, yelling together as one, "They will bleed…they will bleed…they will bleed."

The Iraqi brought a serving plate laden with a ceramic teapot and small white demitasse cups. After they were passed around, the hot tea served, eating resumed.

Breaking into laughter, raising his arm to delay a toast, Dauadi blew at the steam rising from his cup. In a sharp, grinding voice that filled the room, he systematically described how bystanders fell to his bullets.

When everyone finished, he strolled outside with the homeowner. Voices were low, conversation casual and lighthearted. Minutes later, on his own, he used his foot to dig a small trench in a pile of dirt near the shed, sliding his shoe from side to side as a marker, which he used to draw a series of vertical lines. The formations soon outlined a building. Glancing to his left, he spotted a spider racing up the side of the shed. *Looking for your prey?* he thought, watching it climb toward a fly caught in its web. It sprang across the threads and attacked. *Like you*, he added, *we will strike.*

He dug a key out of his pocket, unlocked the shed door, and sauntered inside. Within seconds he fished through a cardboard carton.

Chapter 12

Noordine's eyes raced from one screen to another—a sudden influx of pictures, messages, and videos flashed on all three monitors. Arabic, English, and French postings seemed to emanate from different web sites. Most appeared as blogs. Innocent ones reminded the faithful to fast on Thursday's Islamic holiday, do kind deeds, and help their fellow Muslims. Some, as usual, lambasted Western governments, denounced any support of Palestinian-Israeli peace accords, and encouraged the continued struggle to retake the West Bank. No peace. Victory for Hamas. No Israel. Hezbollah video commercials recruited suicide bombers, including teenage girls, to strap on vests. There were sites that called for Arabic nations allied with America to be denounced as traitors of Allah. Another showed protests and screaming demonstrators. Some, as usual, depicted more violent situations in Iraq, Afghanistan, Egypt, and Pakistan; producers of these videos weren't shy about identifying their Taliban and al-Qaeda connections. Scenes also showed jubilant Somali pirates overtaking and boarding a Greek cargo ship off the coast of East Africa. Then there were the ones that made her blood run cold: images of rocket propelled grenades and improvised explosive devices blowing up U.S. military vehicles, dead soldiers, and writhing, injured Marines lying beside their burning trucks.

She leaned forward to her left side monitor. In Arabic, a satellite TV channel announced that a spokesman would make a speech. Seconds later, an al-Qaeda mullah identifying himself as the organization's chief cleric, allegedly hiding in the Bora-Bora mountainous region of Pakistan, appeared in a plain white *Gutrah* head covering and long brown cloak, his face old, worn and lined from the sun, his bony hands together, pointing outward in the shape of a minuet; his words, slow yet audible. She typed furiously, translating as he warbled off a series of sentences.

"Muslims of the world, faithful of our Prophet, victory is near.
Keep up the fight, oh my brothers, go after them

In the streets; their homes; on the roads.
In their work places; their place of worship.
Strike down all whom defile Islam."

Behind him, a map of the United States and scores of burning American flags illuminated satellite images.

Enormous amounts of chatter from the Middle East kept flashing on the monitors, some flipping by in such rapid sequences she couldn't keep up with pinpointing their sources. Arabic captions then trailed along the bottom of the screens.

She persisted, relying on her memory and speed typing skills. Noordine speculated that many might affect national security; she made it her duty to keep up and capture the major Arabic communications in order to translate on screen. Like most languages, meanings could be misunderstood, varied as much by their interpretation as their meaning.

Taking a deep breath, she inserted a new non-readable disc, opened a secured software program, and sent a copy to the Quantico FBI analysis center, a second edition to national Homeland Security headquarters in Washington, D.C., plus one directly to Walter McLaughlin's computer.

She shook her head for a few seconds. These weren't the messages of tolerance she had known as a young Muslim growing up in West Virginia. Even her father, devoted to his faith yet proud of becoming an American citizen, would visit Mecca in Saudi Arabia for the annual Hajj ceremony after Ramadan. When he returned and swept up his daughter in his arms, it wasn't to extol Islam; rather, it was to praise the United States, its freedoms and liberties. You can be a Muslim, he told her, but you are an American first.

Noordine kept two mementos in her purse that only Consuela Mercado knew about—the Pledge of Allegiance she had written on a card as a child, and, although American-born, a copy of the citizenship oath.

Her monitor clicked out a text that classified messages were coming.

The first, from Interpol's Office of Strategic Counter-terrorism Agency, announced that four Algerian-American men in Madrid and two Iranians had been arrested for allegedly funding the al-Qaeda insurgents who had killed fifty-four European tourists at upscale hotels in Lahore, Pakistan and Mumbai, India. In addition, Italy's Intelligence Service had apprehended the extremists who planned and firebombed a girl's day care center in Pakistan's capital, Islamabad, plus destroyed a Christian school in Nairobi, Kenya. A footnote read "unknown number of adults and children killed." Two suspects were found in Rome, a third in Florence, Italy, and three disguised as fishermen in a remote village on an inlet off the Sardinian coast.

Instantaneous messages followed from the Central Intelligence Agency and the Department of Homeland Security. She focused on the first one, enlarging the screen. She pounded in her password in order to access the encrypted codes, eye-balling the message from left to right.

Date: 10 June, 12:47:26 p.m.
From: CIA Operations ****
To: ****Admin.
CC: Q2RT75T5
Subject: "Money Laundering"

REPORT: CIA yesterday apprehended a Somali father and son at **** in **** who allegedly spent over $300,000 to set up untraceable phone networks in the U.S. and Middle East then sent sums of U.S. dollars to a non-existing company in Minneapolis, MN.

PURPOSE: Detainees used stolen phone numbers from European Internet Service Provider accounts; possessed five Internet lines (unable to trace) at time of arrest. FBI also conducting internal investigation. Money transfers received at cash advance stores in Hollywood, Long Beach, and Pasadena, California.

ACTION: Money laundering (wire transfers) to the U.S. transacted from unknown/suspicious sources must undergo additional checks; almost impossible to trace or identify sender/payee, thereby providing terrorist organizations an illicit route of funding militants in the U.S. Funds used to buy weapons. Strongly urge more thorough screening.

Once more using her password, she worked her way through the secured sequence. Because this one originated from the office of the assistant secretary of Homeland Security, she kept her eyes riveted to each word as it keyed onto her monitor.

Date: 10 June, 12:46:48 p.m.
From: **** DHS Admin. W/DC
To: DHS ****
CC: Q2RT75T5
Subject: Urgent Notice
Intel O/P No. ****

Countrywide terrorist notification.
Area most affected: County of Los Angeles.
Threat level: Color Code Orange / Possible Code Red.

URGENT: ALERT LAW ENFORCEMENT AGENCIES / CODE****

ENACT SECURITY ALERT, PROVISION NO.****
(Un) confirmed risk to civilian targets…L.A. Unit Team, stand by.

Breathing hard, she studied the final message. Code Orange was the United States' second highest threat level. If DHS directive announced a Code Red alert, an imminent, massive terrorist attack could strike at any time.

Noordine leaned away from her monitors. Rolling her tongue, she hoped that Code Red never flashed on her screen.

A series of encrypted passwords followed. This ensured that hackers couldn't identify names or locations of transmitting operatives.

She scanned several other websites. Not only Arabic messages continued. Blogs from European and so-called allies of the U.S. popped up in support of worldwide Islamic extremists.

A text message entirely in English caught her attention. She had no trouble identifying the sender and IPS number.

We applaud our Brothers of Somali Jihad for their brave defiance of Western corruption. What action was taken today will carry on unabated. They fear us.

They cannot defend against us. We can and will strike wherever and whenever we choose.

Praise Allah the Prophet!

Then in an Arabic online chat room she translated into English the sender's closing salutation. The name made the hairs on the back of her neck tingle.

Saleh Ali Nabhat Saleh.

Followed by the Somali war cry, *Jihadi Salfah*.

That was the violent Muslim organization that overthrew the government of Mogadishu, Somalia and promised to forcefully turn the entire Middle East into an ultra-fanatical Islamic state.

It wasn't just giving her eyes a rest; she couldn't take anymore. After pressing Save and Forward to Walter McLaughlin, Noordine logged off, changing her pass codes as the computer shut down.

Liken to a knot in her stomach, she felt uneasy, strangely uneasy: DHS HQ ordered a national security alert bulletin; FBI and the CIA reported illegal financial transactions and unusual foreign activities. All these sudden alarm bells…coincidence?

Although never trained as a field operative, she sensed that feeling of inadequacy, unable to help when danger could be looming over the

75

horizon. A scary thought sailed through her brain; *please let the notices be cautionary, not conclusive.*

Wheeling around on her chair, she watched several agents, including Lamborghini and Reeves, scurry down the hallway.

Chapter 13

The agents flooded into McLaughlin's office. By now, all the e-mails and warnings had been reviewed. Hushed voices offered ideas. However, comments strayed from that morning's massacre in Beverly Hills to alluding where another strike would hit Los Angeles. Everyone had thoughts…no one had hardcore resolutions. Their only hope of discovering what the Jihadi Brotherhood had planned died when Tariq committed suicide.

The director, shuffling back and forth, observing his team buzzing one another, reflected whether they could even scrape bottom without some assistance, some positive Intel in order to combat an attack within their vicinity. His face matched the mental frustration felt by those he looked to for answers.

Neither the government nor anyone else wanted a repeat of 9-11. Americans were weary of two wars. Although most supported the military, armed intervention in Afghanistan wasn't working. Five years in Iraq fizzled into a quagmire. Moreover, they wanted out from under the umbrella of fearfulness; exactly what the terrorists intended them to feel…disillusionment with their own government. Sure, major plots had been stopped before militants acted. But, whether individuals or groups were involved, almost all emanated from al-Qaeda, which was determined to cause more American casualties. Whatever name these people called themselves, there would be more attacks.

McLaughlin sat down, leaned forward, and cradled a pencil between his fingers, knowing full well that his abusive treatment of Tariq had destroyed any chance of the DHS and FBI countering with a realistic defense. His interrogation had backfired miserably.

Scratching his chin, Lamborghini started the conversation. "For Christ's sake, Chief, we can't let ourselves be bullied by these thugs who—"

"We're sure it's coming, the attack?" asked Reeves.

"Every indication is there," Mercado said, her first words since joining the circle. She slid her chair closer to the desk. "Too many coincidences to be idle threats."

"Dodek," the director said, staring at the Canadian agent, "if you were Muhamed Dauadi, where would you strike?"

"Where he gets the best publicity, what else? No pun intended; he wants the biggest bang for his buck."

"That's why the Internet is their most valuable weapon," Curbside said. "No matter how many times the FBI shuts down their sites, more pop up, more visceral than the previous ones."

"Yeah, and what happens?" Lamborghini chimed back. "More nutcases recruited and willing to die, as long as they take Americans with them."

Art nodded. "Let me tell you something. You may not remember what Margaret Thatcher said when she was prime minister of England; 'We must find a way to starve the terrorists of the oxygen of publicity on which they depend.' Two decades later, we can't stop it. We can fight them. We can arrest a few fanatics. Believe me, the most dangerous ones are those in your own country who rationalize that martyrdom is more important than living. Maybe we should be asking how to better stem young Muslims from becoming insurgents and martyrs."

"What's the point, Dodek?" asked Curbside. "You suggesting that the government shut down mosques?"

"No, of course not, Dan. Days from now, unfortunately, names of those people gunned down in Beverly Hills will be forgotten. The one who carried out that bloodbath—Dauadi—whenever his name is mentioned, he's the asshole who people will remember, the one who's revered."

"You mean infamously, don't you?" Lamborghini quipped.

"So let's think of something," Mercado said, shifting around on her chair.

"I think today was a rehearsal of what to expect tomorrow," Art said. "And...we should all be worried what may happen."

Reeves waved her hand. "Yeah. I think all of us should be—"

"I didn't join the FBI to be frightened; I joined to fight back," her FBI partner interrupted. His remark started all of them speaking at once, each voice trying to out shout the other.

McLaughlin banged the pencil on his desk. "For fuck's sake, people, you're federal agents for the Department of Homeland Security. The president approved creation of the Unit to preempt attacks. You're carrying on like a bunch of fishwives. Knock it off. We know what that lunatic is capable of. If we're gonna try to prevent another of his assaults, we must know where, when…and how. I want to hear how you intend to stop him, and where he —"

Art cut in before anyone else spoke. "Right now we're only aware of the B/A. If he's serious about attacking Los Angeles where there's the largest accumulation of civilians — and it appears definite — you do the math."

"That's my impression, too, Walter," Mercado added. "Thursday, the Muslim holiday, just like every day in L.A. County, everything's wide open — games, sports, malls, theaters, commercial businesses, transportation corridors."

"When isn't L.A. wide open?" Lamborghini asked. "How are we supposed to protect these places when we don't even know what places? You saw the message — Code Orange." He wandered around the table. "Dan, Aylesha, help me out here."

"New York has experienced Code Oranges," agent Reeves reminded them, "and they've reacted pro-actively."

"Aylesha's got a point," Mercado said. "Bringing in extra FBI units, complimenting them with the National Guard at key areas, I think would make a difference."

"Perhaps, but where's the deterrence?" McLaughlin asked, straddling his desk.

Everybody started talking at once again. The director banged the desk, sending papers and pens flying across the floor.

Art managed to inject his voice over the noise. "We're doing exactly what Dauadi wants us to do…running around like cats and dogs after tossed out scraps. It's how they operate. Create fear, panic. Plan where, and then they figure out how to exploit it to their advantage. And how to…." Wondering whether the group digested his comment, he added, "Tomorrow is Eid al-Adha. To Muslims, it's an important holiday. To the extremists, an opportunity for them to show they're unstoppable. What better place than Los Angeles, the sin-shine capitol of America?"

A couple of snickers, hums, and haws greeted that expression.

"Quiet! Quiet!" McLaughlin roared, walking to the other side, positioning himself behind the agents. Now they had to turn his way. "Before you dither heads got here, I contacted the governor; the National Guard is on stand-by, to be mobilized on his order. LAPD SWAT teams and the bomb squads are prepared to move at a moment's notice." He walked between his unit members. "Extra L.A. and Orange County Sheriff's helicopters can also be made available. Plus, I got the mayor's assurance that the city's Emergency Services apparatus can respond immediately, if there's a city-wide crisis."

"Hell, we've experienced earthquakes, survived riots," Lamborghini said. "We can kick ass just as hard."

The group echoed their approval by cheering.

Hands in and out of his pockets, the director walked by each person and returned to his chair. "America is not a police state, you know. I don't want armed cops and soldiers wandering around Los Angeles with automatic weapons. Somebody could get hurt. We could start an unwanted panic. On the other hand, if we don't do enough the media will be the first ones to lynch us as incompetent bastards. We overreact and the sob sisters nail us. Well, I'll tell you something...." He shook his hand at them before they could interrupt, and rose. "I would okay tanks rumbling around town if it stopped one freaking terrorist."

Silence greeted his remarks; they also knew he wasn't finished. To a person, though, any heavy artillery would've been welcome.

"The Bank of America is your major concern. Most likely it's their top target, if that's what Noordine determined. That's where I've decided to pinpoint our resources. Consuela, you and Dodek are primary surveillance at 5th and Hope. Aylesha, Dan, Tony, take up positions nearby. I'll coordinate here. Noordine handles communication. Anything suspicious, you—"

"Shoot it?" Lamborghini asked sardonically.

"Report it," his superior replied. "Think, people. Think. If it buzzes like a fly, you know what to do. I expect you not to bring civilians into this." He paused as the group climbed to their feet. "At last count, thirteen dead, twenty-one wounded in the Beverly Hills massacre."

"Jesus Murphy," Curbside exclaimed.

Noordine Assad entered the room. She had a disk in her hands, and a worried look on her face. "Mr. McLaughlin, you have to see this," she said, going to a desktop computer. In seconds, the monitor fired up a video. "This is a tape from the Transportation Safety Administration relayed moments ago from LAX, Terminal 5. Two flights arrived from Minneapolis and Chicago. I'll speed ahead. The passengers coming off the planes...I'm zooming in." She sent the cursor bouncing across the lower right middle of the screen. "Count them. Two, four, six, eight, all identified as Somali-Americans on the passengers' manifest. Coincidence? Not this close to the Muslim holiday."

"What have we got here—a convention?" Lamborghini commented wryly.

"I've printed out their faces and specs; you'll receive copies." Noordine removed the disk and turned toward her boss. "Mr. McLaughlin, I wouldn't have placed such importance on eight men flying to Los Angeles...but they all arrived from Kenya at the same time in Minneapolis, and all boarded the same flight to California."

"Great interpretation, Noordine," he said.

"Extra gunslingers," Lamborghini said. "That's all we need."

"Noordine, what about surveillance?" asked Mercado. "Inside and outside the airport, were they kept on radar?"

"I notified the FBI for copies. However, two or three different vehicles were used to pick them up. Apparently, they all evaded the agents who tried to follow them. Nobody knows where they are now."

The director thanked her as the group began dispersing. Unlike the boisterous start to the meeting, a more subdued and quiet team entered the corridor. No one could've added much to the discussion. The thought didn't take long to sink in, either…if these men were home-grown Somalis who disappeared, mysteriously turned up in al-Qaeda training camps in Pakistan, then returned, the number of potential hostiles to contend with boggled the mind. For this unit, it sure did.

Art and Consuela stopped in the hallway. Their momentary eye contact spoke volumes. Reuniting these new Somali militants wasn't just meant to target one location. This had all the hallmarks of a hit on Los Angeles with carefully chosen multi-planned attacks. The memos that Noordine had received from the DHS had confirmed a pending attack. Plus, the e-mails had stated the attacks would start June tenth.

If ever a helpless feeling had enveloped them, it was now. Helpless because they saw themselves rummaging through the remains of a firebombed building they had been powerless to protect, and worse; the human remnants of people dismembered by the blast.

Muhamed Dauadi and his Brothers of Somali Jihad weren't directing this scale of an operation by themselves. Organizing, recruiting, logistics, weapons…those were his specialties. The funding and selection of actual targets had to come from Saleh Ali Nabhat Saleh, the mastermind and reputed leader of the Somali al-Shabad extremists. It may be one of many extremist organizations; orders, though, for striking America or European cities came from Taliban and al-Qaeda leaders.

The two agents continued walking, perhaps not keen to speculate the destructive capabilities of these two groups joining forces.

For the next three hours they poured through e-mails and examined more online portals or any information about the Jihadi brotherhood, searching for clues about their planning. Again and again Art browsed his way through pages looking for telltale signs. Noordine brought more translated documents to their desk. This was the phase of Intel that became mundane. Necessary, but hard on the eyes reviewing each word and catchphrase. As usual, Art consumed five cups of coffee during this session. Edginess crept into his system as the evening wore on. Being fueled by frustration didn't help. Once in awhile they backed away from their computers and tried to make casual conversation, but Mercado, dealing with her own stress, wasn't in much of a talkative mood. If the opportunity arose to digress for a moment, invariably it resulted in tackling another round of search engines.

***

Agents Reeves and her partner, Lamborghini, scoured sites around Los Angeles, checking places they knew to be frequented by young Somali Muslim men. Like most ethnic groups, they congregated in neighborhoods that catered to their culture, where Western influences were few. Any Westerners entering their domain brought instant mistrust and the feeling that their private space had been invaded. Silence enveloped when photographs of Dauadi and other militant suspects were passed around, or enquiries about their whereabouts were made. Shoulders shrugged, eyes turned away. Maybe most had no idea where Dauadi lived, but they all knew about him. Even if there were the slightest chance someone did know his location, there was no way he would tell federal law enforcement officers anything.

About fifteen minutes later they passed a mosque on El Segundo Boulevard. Pulling over about thirty feet up the street into a taxi stand, they debated whether entering the building would be worthwhile. Heads nodded, agreeing, and both sauntered near the front steps of the building. Small in comparison to some of the mosques in Los Angeles, nonetheless, it served the nearby Muslim community. A Persian themed coffee shop stood next door.

Passers-by gave the couple odd looks. As worshipers descended the steps, Reeves politely asked them if they'd look at some photos. With quick glances and blank expressions, they rushed away. If they thought indifference from the male worshipers was on tap, they got a rude culture clash wakening.

Lamborghini approached three women going up the steps. All wore the traditional black chador full-length garments; one—he surmised a younger woman by her slim figure—had a Niqab that covered her entire face except for the eyes. He stopped them on the landing by the entrance. He identified himself and mentioned that he was a Homeland Security agent. Frightened expressions greeted his introduction, but before they had a chance to answer, four men roared out of the coffee bar and surrounded the women.

Reeves tapped his arm. While not intimidated by their scowls and jeering, she pulled her partner aside, nodded her head back and forth, and led him back to their vehicle. Once inside, she remarked that strange men didn't walk up to non-chaperoned Muslim women and accost them.

***

Around nine-thirty Art and Consuela turned off their computers. Other members of the analysis center could dabble online. McLaughlin and Curbside had long gone. The last time he'd spotted Mercado she was

82

taking a phone call near Noordine's cubicle. Grabbing his blazer, he tossed a Styrofoam coffee container in the trash bin beside the elevator. He blew a long breath of air, hoping that he'd seen the last of DHS tonight.

His first few minutes on the road, he squinted as he adjusted his eyesight between the darkness and bright neon signs. A couple of blocks from his apartment he ordered Chinese food, selecting noodles with beef and shrimp, a mixture of vegetables, and honey-sauced chicken strips. All of it was devoured within minutes after arriving at his apartment. Quenching his thirst, he downed the remainder of the OJ and a third of a bottle of water.

He stretched out on the sofa and rubbed his eyes with bruised knuckles that never seemed to heal, stroking across the front, careful not to scratch the retinas. Then he thumbed in a number on his cell phone. Just as the person answered, he muted the TV remote; he'd had enough news accounts of the Beverly Hills shootings.

"Hello, is that you, Art?" Lynda asked. His number wouldn't show up on her caller ID.

"Hi, Lyndie. What's happening? How are you doing?"

"Quiet around here. How are…you?"

"You know how it goes; we have our moments."

She paused for a few seconds, and then resumed, her voice wavering. "Such terrible news today. How awful…those poor people. Doesn't it ever end?'

"Perhaps one day," he said, trying to sound reassuring.

"I suppose you and your partner stay pretty much together." Her statement sounded more rhetorical than questioning.

"When we're on the road, working evenings, the office, you know."

"Oh. You're alone with her often?" Another rhetorically asked statement.

He did the pausing this time. "Lyndie, don't even go there. That's not like you. I miss you."

"Really? I-I'm missing you. I'm on my way to bed. Call me soon…when you're not…with your partner."

She ended the call. Tossing the BlackBerry onto the bed and stretching, he re-clicked the mute button, surfing through five channels before shutting down the TV.

What's with Lynda? he asked himself seconds later at the curt sound of her voice. She'd never made such a ripple before about his partners. *For crying out loud, big deal, my new partner is a woman. We're partners. What else do you think we are?*

83

Chapter 14

Thursday, June 10, Downtown Los Angeles
"Day of Sacrifice"

No sooner had Art pulled into his parking spot at the federal building than Consuela Mercado strode his way from the elevator. His greeting was acknowledged by her waving her hand toward the Crown Victoria. Not much of a smile was on her face as they got into the car—he behind the wheel, she alongside.

Regardless of how concerned or business-like her demeanor, her appearance always stood out—a teal colored, button down, long sleeved shirt was tucked into her dark pants. Other than her velour vest, along with a badge and P-35 attached to her belt, she could've passed for any professional woman about to start her business workday at a corporate office.

As the Ford entered Alameda Street, both began speaking, although mostly small talk; this only coated the uneasiness they both felt.

She switched between the LAPD and FBI channels, listening to the chatter of dispatchers, officers, and agents. The dashboard digital clock showed exactly 8 a.m. Rolling down her side window, one arm resting on the door, the other behind his headrest, she tapped once on her teeth. "Sleep much last night?"

"Not much. You?"

Her answer was a long sigh. "Make a right at the next corner. Saves a couple of minutes. So what's your wife like?"

"Hmm?"

"Your wife—you have one, remember?—tell me about her. You must be subconsciously thinking about her…I notice you nudge your ring quite often."

"Lynda? She's terrific, smart, and compassionate. She even won Miss Congeniality in college."

"So...is she happy with what you do, chasing terrorists?"

"Truthfully, no. Realistically, yes, it can —"

"Go ahead and say it, man."

"Pisses her off. It's something we talk about a lot. I understand where she's coming from, but I try, perhaps too much, to stop worrying. Consuela, you know what it's like — you do your job, dangerous as it can be sometimes, do your best to play it safe — then move on."

"Gotcha'," she smiled, lowering the scanner volume. Lifting her left arm, her hand brushed against his shoulder. "Uh, sorry. I was —"

Two instantaneous glances; two quick eye contact U-turns.

At the next signal light he asked her, "What about you? You must have a personal life. Ignore me if you think I'm getting too personal."

"You're not. Not much to say. I grew up here. Being a teenage Latina in L.A. had some drawbacks. I watched my parents struggle. Hell, though, I've got a great job. I like the challenge. Nailing some extremist creep who wants to blow my head off, that's satisfying."

"You ever been married? I noticed, too...no ring."

She hesitated for a few seconds, as though his question hit a nerve. After a long sigh, she said, "Once. Just once to an LAPD detective. Our being on different shifts, following our own jobs, it had to happen. He had an affair with his partner. Took me a while to catch on. Hate to admit it; I even tailed the S.O.B."

"It must've really shaken you up."

"Shit, man, no. My ex, that schmuck, was gay, bisexual, whatever. Two of them...in their car, on duty." She tilted her head. Recounting her marriage breakdown didn't seem to bother her. "Anyway, I never suspected it. Our affection for one another wasn't that hot, either. He's the one who admitted it. His own squad ignored him after that. I heard that he resigned. I couldn't get divorced fast enough...and checked over."

"Consuela, okay, okay. I won't ask, and you don't have to tell."

A slight smile started on her face. She laughed. "Art, there's the turn. Ease your way over. It'll give us a good vantage point. Agent Dodek, call me Connie, okay?"

He rolled to a stop and turned off the motor. They were on Hope Street, facing Fifth Avenue, with the Bank of America tower across the street and the large hotel adjacent. Valets and guests scurried up and down the sloping entrance. Although the bank's lower floor had its lights on, there wouldn't be any customers entering until 9 a.m., in about forty minutes.

Mercado spotted her partners' vehicles. FBI agents Aylesha Reeves and Dan Curbside were facing east, and DHS agent Tony Lamborghini was parked about a block further.

She picked up the microphone. "This is Lead Unit One. Check in."

"We see you," Reeves responded. "Check."

"Hi guys. Got any more coffee?" Lamborghini acknowledged. "Hey, Consuela, say 10-4. I love the way you pronounce it."

"Stay focused, Tony. Anything suspicious let us know."

"You got it."

Art clicked the car key once to the right, allowing enough juice to roll down his window. His hand swept over the butt of his Glock. He had fully loaded it before leaving his apartment, never knowing what to expect. He'd prefer no trouble, but if armed force became necessary, there would be no hesitation; he would use his weapon.

What also ran through his mind was Consuela's reaction if gunfire erupted. Since his Canadian security team had begun operations, Keith Dawson, an ex-cop, had been his partner. Both relied on the other. Doubting either's role or backup never entered the picture. Taking someone down, returning fire — deadly fire — to protect one another, you counted on your partner. Anticipate. React. That's how you were trained. That's what he also expected of her. Nothing less.

He gave her a casual glance. If she felt apprehensive, it didn't show. Rather, it was confidence she exuded. *This in-your-face agent, she's had field experience. She'll know what to do.* His thoughts trailing off, he resumed placing his hands over the steering wheel.

Mercado asked about his counter-terrorist soirees in the Middle East, what places in particular were troublesome, and dangerous. Pakistan, he told her. Not only from Taliban insurgents, but its government, especially the Intelligence service...unreliable, at times even untrustworthy, and easily corrupted. When working with CIA operatives, he added, uncovering evidence of collusion and ties to Taliban fighters on the Afghan border was routine. Even today, despite so-called affable relations between Pakistan and the U.S., interference and instability from top levels still plagued the country's government. Add to that the fact its army was pro-Islamic. Our military could make advances, like flushing out Taliban training camps in Peshawar, and their army would prohibit us from interrogating prisoners; that made the danger worse. And, unless the White House cajoled them or made the odd threat, their refusal to hand over alleged terrorists to us lessened our resistance.

When she asked him a personal question, he didn't hedge; the answer came naturally.

"Art, weren't you ever worried, you being Jewish over there? You could've been — "

"Number one...you don't tell anyone. Most of my cases rarely involved interaction with suspect groups. You played low key; you had to. Yeah, sometimes it got a little hairy. You deal with what you can."

He made a wide scan of the bank and hotel, then up and down the roadway. Above, three airplane vapor trails streamed through an almost cloudless sky.

"God, Art, you could've suffered the same fate as Ron Pearlman."

"Shows to Goya," he smiled, masking his true feelings by joking. Nevertheless, he had managed to leave Pakistan without a scratch. Memories of what he'd witnessed, though, stayed etched in his mind: the total destruction and annihilation of entire villages; the shooting of teachers and young Muslim girls for attending school; the hanging of town elders for aiding NATO soldiers; extremist Mullahs ordering young women stoned to death for not wearing full-covered *burkas*, a head to foot garment. Teenaged suicide bombers were forced to set off explosives in markets, outside mosques, at police stations. Time and time after returning, he had asked the foreign affairs department to never station him there again.

"What about you, Connie? Where did you serve?"

She blew air from the corner of her mouth. "The U.A.E. mostly, a stint in Egypt—I liked Cairo, kind of. Believe it or not, I was assigned to the Kandahar airport to advise Afghan police officers on intelligence and security methods. All men. Let me tell you, they were not amused with a woman telling them what to do. Though, I've been with the FBI and DHS here on the West Coast mostly. You worked with the CIA, trained with the Mossad in Israel. Maybe foreign hotspot exposure gave you an advantage as an intelligence officer."

A voice crackled over the radio. "Hey, Consuela, your secret admirer checking in," Lamborghini chuckled. "All quiet on the Western Front."

"Copy that."

"All quiet here, too," Aylesha Reeves reported.

Art and Consuela resumed their observation. More pedestrians occupied the sidewalk below the hotel. Several customers lined up for the 9 a.m. bank opening.

Since this short roadway had no through exit, when a vehicle did enter the street, it would turn around and leave. Making a wide-angle turn at the corner, a white and blue trimmed armored truck eased alongside the bank. No one emerged from the passenger side or rear doors.

The bank doors opened. A Hispanic security guard stepped aside as customers streamed into the lobby.

Across the street the two agents peered at what seemed to be a regular bank pickup and delivery. They did notice the truck's engine hadn't shut down.

Art gazed at the truck's name. Neither he nor his partner recognized its call letters, "U.S. Armoured Bank Transfer."

A tall, lanky person in a blue uniform came around from the passenger side and unlocked the rear doors, and three young men jumped out. Two hand push dollies were yanked out and placed on the sidewalk. One by one, three sacks were piled on. Glancing back and forth, the quartet headed for the door of the bank and were escorted inside by the guard. A few seconds later, another man disembarked. This one, gripping a sack, walked slowly up the ramp leading to the hotel entrance. While all five wore side arms, he carried a pump action shot gun arched over his shoulder.

For the first time, Art and Mercado, observing the truck and its passengers, felt uneasy. Their eyes followed every movement made by the truck's occupants. Nothing really stood out, yet everything stood out. They gave themselves a brief glance and got out of the Crown Victoria. Standing by the driver's door, the peculiar activity across the street now had their full attention.

All five men were in the young to mid-twenties range, wearing ball caps and sunglasses and untrimmed beards, and were dark skinned but not African-Americans. Call it like it was. They had the swagger of East Africans. Somalis? Kenyans?

The two agents strolled over to the truck. Two more anomalies hit them. First, the vehicle's name…U.S. companies didn't spell "armoured" with a "u." Plus, the misspelled lettering painted on the side was sloppy, as though the uneven stenciling had been hurriedly applied.

While Art stepped to the corner of the driver's window, fingers touching his Glock, Mercado, using a wrist-sized microphone, called her partners. She also contacted the LAPD SWAT team parked about two blocks away.

He tapped the tinted window. Tensing up, unable to see who was behind the wheel, he knocked again. No response. This time he grabbed the door handle. "Come on out," he ordered, realizing it was locked.

Without warning, the explosion of a pistol rang out as a bullet blasted out the bottom part of the shaded window and whizzed a foot past his head, striking the rear panel of the DHS vehicle.

He sprang upward to the door and fired twice into the cab. He had to step back quickly as tinted glass pieces sailed out onto the pavement.

Mercado, hearing the gunfire, un-holstered her P-35 and rushed alongside the truck. Her hand fully extended, she checked the rear of the armored car, which now was empty.

Using his gun butt, Art hammered against the window until it cracked, then shattered inward over the East African driver half slumped over the steering wheel. Both bullets had struck the man in the upper right temple.

She seemed about to ask him what had happened, but refrained. He wasn't in a mood to explain.

Car tires squealed near the corner. FBI agents Reeves and Curbside, their weapons drawn, followed by DHS agent Lamborghini, bounded toward their senior partner. An LAPD van roared to a stop outside the hotel, its flashing red and blue lights cascading over pillars outside the building. A contingent of heavily armed SWAT officers jumped out.

Although about three hundred feet overhead, vibrating blades from news and police helicopters drowned out anyone trying to speak. Additional police cars and two paramedic trucks lined up at the intersection. With all the emergency personnel milling around, pedestrians and vehicles found themselves blocked from exiting all four street corners.

With only seconds to assess the situation, Art, Mercado, and Curbside headed to the bank. Agents Reeves and Lamborghini rushed over to the hotel. Each group had a squad of ERT armed cops accompanying them. After receiving brief assessments from the agents, squad leaders sent a team to cover lanes, driveways, and parking lots behind the buildings.

Take down any suspects attempting to escape, they were instructed by Mercado.

While the bank windows were tinted, Art's group could peer inside. Normal looking. Customers waiting for service, staff transactions at the counters, several lined up at the ATM machines, individuals chatting together, going about bank business.

A surprised security guard, seeing the agents and cops outside, opened the front doors. Questioned by a police sergeant, he couldn't confirm where the armored guards had taken their dollies. Shocked customers froze as armed cops charged into the lobby, ordering them to disperse and gather at the end of the street. The unarmed security guard marshaled them outside. Some became frantic and had to be reassured they were safe.

A second tactical unit arrived. The team leader split his force between the bank and the hotel next door. This time an officer led a bomb-sniffing Labrador into the lobby.

Two more police units swarmed, stationing themselves along the entire block. A sweep of the main floor offices didn't turn up anything suspicious, nor any sign of the disguised armored guards.

The bank manager was the last civilian remaining; she, too, hadn't noted their location, only that she'd watched a routine bank service pushing loaded dollies inside. No one replied to her enquiry of whether this meant a bank robbery. She led the way to the elevators on the other side of a large partition off the main lobby. She explained that both sides rose to the tower suites, with connections to the second and third floor hotel lobbies via escalator. At that point, she was requested to rejoin her staff outside.

Art and the sergeant didn't have to confer for long. They knew they had a dilemma. Where exactly would the quartet go? What floor? Particular offices? What was in the bags? Currency? Doubtful, they surmised; extra weapons and improvised explosive devices (IEDs), most likely. He wondered whether Muhamed Dauadi was among the group. If the Somali arranged the assault, whom would he target? The expressionless looks he got from Mercado and Curbside didn't ease his tension.

A team of officers, along with another canine handler, was instructed to check the hallways and corridors leading to the bank and hotel's lower floors.

Checking the building directory situated on a marble pedestal between the elevators, he scanned the business names, corporations, branch and subsidiary offices, rolling his eyes at the numbers of attorneys, law firms, magazine publishers, financial and commercial advisers, sports and entertainment agencies, and development companies housed in the towers.

Yesterday DHS had obtained a list of companies with possible military links. He pulled out a small scrap of notepaper and studied the three names stenciled in the directory. Two names looked familiar; the other had slightly different spelling, but could be accurate; all located on the eighth, eleventh, and thirteenth floors. Accurate or not, he had no time to just stand there and speculate. *Who knows what's happening up there?*

The building engineer, who had been summoned by the police, entered the lobby. They ordered him to bring both elevators to the ground floor and shut them down, in addition to the electronic doors dividing bank and hotel foyer and lobby connections.

"Plus," Art ordered, "lock all rear exits, as well as the walkway doors to the rear car park. No one is gonna leave this structure." If the others presumed he meant dead or alive, they hadn't misread the rush in his eyes.

Mercado picked up his tension immediately; mouth taut, eyes riveted straight ahead, skin on the face flushed…no holding back. The brain had already made its decision. Awash with nervousness snapping at her heels, her hand skipped non-stop over her side arm.

Chapter 15

It felt like an eternity, although just minutes passed as the elevators descended. Flashing buttons stopping on various floors made the wait nerve-wracking. Would the Somalis be in one of them, ready to blast away as the door opened?

The agents, along with the tactical unit, guns pointed straight ahead, watched the lights reach closer to the bottom. Heavy breathing likely obscured pounding heartbeats. Try as he might, the canine cop couldn't tone down his dog's excitement. Then, like clockwork, both doors slid open. Screams from office workers, bodies frozen like ice statuettes, arms stretched above their heads, greeted the law officers.

Fingers loosened on triggers. The sigh of relief from those holding automatic rifles could've bowled someone over. Without explaining their presence, a cop hurriedly escorted the group out of the building.

Civilians gone, everybody marched down the hallway to a sign indicating a stairway.

Art waved off a cop who grabbed the door handle. "Hold on," he cautioned. "The elevators may be secured, but we don't want anyone taking a risk running up the stairs."

He took Mercado aside. Both pulled out their phones.

She got hold of Noordine Assad in seconds. "Can you hack into the closed circuit cameras on the eighth, eleventh, and thirteenth floors?"

"In a heartbeat. I'm overriding the pre-programmed video. Should be coming up. What do you specifically — ?"

"On those floors, send me video of the hallways. And scan these suite names: ACR-Tech Products, Ltd.; American Ballistic Communication; Encada Engineering, Inc." The transmission took less than a minute. "I have them. Thanks."

"Noordine, this is Art Dodek. I want you to continue focusing on those sites. Something else. On my phone, can you send thermal images?"

"Body heat images? Yes. May take a while."

"Noordine, we don't have a while."

"I'll do it as quickly as I can."

He almost shouted into his phone. "Please hurry up. We don't know what the threat is. They might keep us alive."

"Understood, Agent Dodek. Those circuit cameras may not be exactly electronic wonders, but you should be receiving now. Video may be a bit grainy looking."

"I owe you, Noordine. Thanks."

"Big time, Agent Dodek." A pause. "Art...be careful."

The two agents passed around their phones, which showed assorted videos of the three floors. Whatever arsenal waited for them upstairs, at least they were equipped with visuals. Moreover, obvious escape routes for the Somalis were becoming few and far between. A cop quipped that it was too quiet. No one had to respond; they felt it.

***

Across the hallway on the hotel lobby side, agents Reeves and Lamborghini explained to the manager to carefully guide guests outside and to keep staff locked in their offices. To minimize alarm, they gave a second order—notify your guests in their rooms not to open their doors unless advised by the police. A few people lingered. It took extra persuasion to clear them out. Perhaps the sight of machine gun-toting officers convinced them to leave.

Now they had to figure out where the two men could be hiding. Nothing appeared out of line in the foyer and lobby except chairs pushed askew when the police arrived. Empty bar stools and drinks left in the nearby lounge indicated a quick departure of imbibers. Armed and unpredictable, the duo could've entered any of the hundreds of rooms or concealed themselves anywhere in the hotel.

Reeves and her partner notified Mercado of their situation, and that with their team of SWAT officers, they would begin a ground search. Other entrances and rear exits had to be blocked off, she heard her supervisor say. Nevertheless, they were worried that the Somalis had the advantage of surprise.

Two restaurants occupied the main floor nearest the check-in counters. One, a smaller coffee shop, remained open; the other, a larger dining room which had evidently served an early breakfast, was closed, an "Open at Noon For Lunch" sign outside its gates. Computers hummed. Reservation printers clacked away. Reams of paper had piled up on fax machine trays. Unanswered telephones rang non-stop. The absence of hotel staff had the agents and cops on edge. Guns were aimed at every turn, at corners and corridors; huge potted plants were pushed aside, sofas and tables tipped over. Any noise, however immaterial, emitted an eerie echo in the empty mammoth lobby.

92

Footsteps creaked behind a wall, becoming louder as they neared the armed group. A man's shoe and pant leg emerged. Reeves rounded the corner, her .45 gun hand stretched out as far as she could reach, while Lamborghini pounced on the figure. Not much of a struggle ensued. The surprised cleaning attendant just about fell over from shock. A cop marshaled him out the front door, which was then locked from the inside.

Then the last sound the agents thought they would hear came from the lobby office. A scream like a wounded animal struck by a car vibrated against a glass window, followed by the loud blast of a shotgun.

Heads turned, then feet, at first frozen to the floor, ran to the office door. A shot blasted through the door, hitting one officer in the upper shoulder, throwing him against a couch. One of the tactical members dragged him backward, quickly applying a bandage from an emergency medical pack to stop the bleeding.

Through the shredded door, the group could spot one of the Somalis, still wearing sunglasses and the cap.

More screams echoed, followed by voices pleading. The next chilling sound was the clank of the shotgun barrel being pulled back in preparation to fire again.

Two cops and Lamborghini tried to break down the door, which resulted in its thick construction shaking against the frame. The insurgent didn't hesitate to fire. His shell ripped outward, narrowly missing agent Reeves's left arm. This gave her a chance to return fire between the dismembered door panels. Her aim wasn't accurate, however. Her two quick shots whizzed by the gunman's ball cap. In mere seconds, her partner and a tactical officer sent bullets flying into the office. They knew their sudden firing could imperil staff members; however, they had to disable the shooter, and fast. Bullets bounced off walls and shattered glass picture frames, while ringing telephones and people screaming added to the bedlam.

Reeves had a choice…to either hold back or fire at the Somali holding a woman employee. She winced and pulled her trigger. At the same time Lamborghini knelt and aimed his .45 through a two-inch hole in the door.

Her shot skipped across the crown of the man's cap. His bullet ripped into the Somali's right thigh. Although their shots brought him to his knees, he didn't let go of the woman, who couldn't stop screaming. Despite the pain, and blood oozing through his pants, he tried to raise the shotgun.

At last, the cops managed to push back the door. Four M-16 assault rifles, inches from his head, dared him to keep moving. They yelled over and over to drop the weapon.

Slowly, he released the crying employee, who crawled forward to a desk and Reeves's waiting arms. Without flinching, the gunman shoved the short-barreled gun under his chin and fired. Massive blood, pieces of his mouth, teeth and chin, skin and bone fragments, splattered over one cop's legs and the carpeting. With a slight exhale of air, he sank to the floor.

Only then did scared staff members, cowering behind chairs and the photocopier, begin to emerge. Near a desk lay an older man, drenched in a pool of blood, his upper torso blown apart, the victim of the first shotgun blast. Hardly discernable on the suit coat lapel was his name and title pin: Hotel Manager.

Another officer pulled a .38 caliber revolver from the Somali's holster, surprised to discover the gun contained no bullets. Also, they all shared a sigh of relief when opening the man's shirt revealed no body-wrapped explosive device. As quickly as possible, the cops walked beside the other employees toward the front door, where ambulances and paramedics converged outside. Getting the wounded officer to a stretcher was top priority.

While Reeves contacted Mercado, then made a hurried report to Director McLaughlin,

Lamborghini searched the office for other weapons. Overturning fixtures, pushing aside electronic devices, rifling through drawers and boxes, he found nothing out of the ordinary, or anything to suggest an accomplice had been in the room.

As Reeves rejoined him, both agents now faced the task of locating the second insurgent.

Three more armed SWAT officers and a duet of FBI agents rushed past her before she could give them a heads-up and headed to the third floor check-in lobby. She checked her watch, wondering what was happening next door. Also, noticing her partner wincing, she caught on. *Why didn't we check the managers' offices before we ordered everyone inside?*

94

Chapter 16

Carefully, Art Dodek, Consuela Mercado, and Dan Curbside followed two tactical cops up the first flight of stairs of the B/A building with guns drawn. Ascending behind them were three other armed officers, along with a bomb sniffing canine and its handler. Each staircase, each hallway had to be screened.

The Labrador scampered full circle ahead of the team. Nobody knew if someone lurked or hid around a corner. Everybody held their breath as they strode each step. Right now, they were on their way to the eighth floor, occupied by ACR-Tech Products, Ltd., one of the American military suppliers, and potentially a Somali target. As they reached a new floor, everyone stopped, aiming weapons into the hallway. They noticed that alternating levels had wider expansions with longer corridors. Even though the power to the elevators had been discontinued, panel buttons still flashed, mostly from the tower floors. Return to your offices, the group pleaded mentally. Civilians confronting either the insurgents or the officers was the last thing they wanted. Their only allies at this moment were the ceiling lights and the attached high-level cameras.

On the sixth floor they found the dolly the Somalis had used to carry sacks into the bank. More than anything, it was probably discarded when the elevators shut down, or left so they could walk up the two floors.

Yet, a burning sensation ate away at Art's stomach. He counted heads, then whispered for teams to knock on office suite doors and shout, "'Identify yourself.' We don't enter unless people inside say they're okay. Repeat this on the next level."

Five units were checked. Persons who answered were told to stay inside, no ifs or buts, and to keep doors locked.

Officers in their heavy tactical outfits sweated, the others crouched slowly as the door to the seventh level pushed open. Guns waved as, eyes squinted along the walls, they moved down the hallway. Doors were pounded upon, questions were asked whether everyone was okay, and

95

everyone was ordered not to admit anyone unless advised by a law enforcement officer.

The dog almost broke free from his handler's leash as it pawed on the next door, the one to the eighth floor. All doors had a large red number indicating its level, plus a 2' x 2' window at its mid-section. Each person glanced at the other, yet no one spoke. Each person's expression asked the same question: What now? The sight of nine officers gritting their teeth may have appeared funny to an onlooker; it wasn't. Neither was the thought of busting out all together onto the stairs. And, who exactly had the final word as team leader—Agent Dodek or DHS Unit Supervisor Mercado? Minutes away from striking, neither one, nor the back-up team, cared, as long as their coordinated efforts worked.

Barking, the Lab jumped at the door, evidently picking up a scent of something…or someone.

Art and Consuela's phones came out and were turned on, her camera picking up the eighth floor corridor, although the picture shook. His started its thermal imagery. As Noordine had mentioned, images appeared grainy-looking.

Pulling the door open and tossing a smoke bomb down the corridor was ruled out. Air conditioning fans could blow the smoke backward, impeding the group's vision by providing an adversary with advantageous cover.

There didn't seem to be anything simple about this operation.

Mercado raised her P-35, nodded, and stood to the right of the door.

Art took a deep breath, stuck out his left hand, counted down five to one, then pointed his Glock 9 straight ahead. He braced himself on the opposite side. Not a word was uttered as the group used his signal to go for it.

Unleashed, the dog barked louder than ever. Once the door opened, it raced down the hall, stopping only when it reached the other side of the right elevator.

"Aw, shit!" Mercado blurted as her camera phone dimmed, eroding the visual.

Standing abreast of the first two SWAT officers advancing forward, Art murmured, "Careful."

Mercado, Curbside, and the others followed, swinging their gun hands from side to side. They could make out the letters of the ACR-Tech suite, adjacent to the spot where the animal continued barking. His handler caught up to him, but it took a full minute before he finished reconnecting the leash to the dog's collar.

Two large outer doors appeared to separate the suite from its interior offices.

The group slowed their advance, on edge from the dog's behavior. He wouldn't act like this for nothing. Was he detecting an explosive component? Or gun powder?

Another cop pushed open the door. The Lab jumped about five feet off the floor as he pressed his paws against the wooden inner door, using all his weight to force the shaking door to slide open.

No one broke rank...yet.

The handler looked at his colleagues. He knew what they were thinking: *Sorry, man. Sacrificing the dog's life may keep us alive.* He knelt down, hugged, and unleashed him. Somehow it felt its action was necessary. Anxiously waiting for the command, ears erect, its tail straight up like a bamboo branch, he licked his master's chin.

The officer stood back up and shouted, "Jet...go!"

With a series of long, loud barks, the well-trained animal responded to his master's voice and charged into the reception area.

Gritting their teeth, both Art and Mercado, gun hands stretched straight out, cautiously entered. Except for the barking, everything seemed normal. Too normal, they thought. They peered around the offices; nothing out of the ordinary, if an empty office at ten in the morning was the norm. No receptionist; telephones silent; communication equipment shut down. Not one employee was at their desk, nor were there any sights and sounds of a busy office.

Then what had the Lab picked up? Why was he racing around the empty rooms?

Officers strode in and out of various offices, returning to reception with guns lowered.

Art trailed the Lab, watching its reaction as it circled the room with its nose low to the floor. The dog came to sudden stop behind a bank of desktop computers. Sitting on its haunches, he barked and looked up at his handler. The officer and Art leaned over to where he indicated several cables attached to PCs, printers, a fax machine, a scanner, and a wireless router. They examined the wiring, even pulled a couple apart, puzzled as to why the dog kept rubbing its paws along the cables.

Mercado joined them. She, too, couldn't figure out its behavior.

Art grabbed some of the wires. If the Lab had discovered something in particular, damned if he would ignore it. Starting from the backs of the electronic devices, he slid his fingers along the wires to where they were plugged into a six-pronged surge bar. Pushing a printer aside, running a finger along a cable, he spied a single light blue wire, barely visible, winding its way down to the surge protector with the switch in the Off position.

Affixed to the bar was a small black plastic device with a short wire connected to the button, plus a fuse taped to what looked like a molded, rolled up portion of plasticine…only it was C-4 explosive putty. "Oh, shit," he muttered. If someone had switched the power button back on it would have detonated an IED—killing every occupant in the office. This proved the insurgents had been there. So where were they, and all of the employees?

No time to squander. He waved everybody back, and advised the tactical team sergeant to notify the bomb squad. This wasn't the end of their investigation; two more suites had to be checked out. With an officer stationed outside, they headed for the next staircase.

He didn't have to remind them to be cautious.

The frisky Lab got a pat from his handler and the leash reconnected. Gnawing down a treat, it rushed toward the fire door.

Mercado contacted Reeves, or tried. No answer. Her phone worked. She called a second time; still no ringing. Her face dropped. Art could see her concern, although there wasn't much anyone could do.

Reluctantly, she agreed. *We've gone this far*, she realized. The agents next door had to fend for themselves.

Chapter 17

Reeves and Lamborghini had reached the third floor check-in area without incident. Their police reinforcements were searching other sections of the hotel...they were on their own. Now they faced a threat unthinkable only moments ago.

As soon as they got to the top of the stairs, one of the militants, hiding behind a pillar, opened fire with an AK-47, pinning them down by the concierge's desk. Lying on the floor, Reeves could just return fire intermittently. Bullets flew over them, shattering mirrors, piercing walls, sending particleboard dust and pieces of wall fixtures over their clothes. Her partner, crouching alongside, wasn't about to raise his head. He could make out his surroundings and saw some movement, and was sure that he'd spotted the other Somali darting past the nearby elevators. Unlike at the bank, power hadn't been disconnected. He noticed a knee-high ledge that led to several divided counters all the way to the elevator lobby.

On hands and knees, Lamborghini managed to make it to where the glass ledge ended at a walkway. Literally squeezing his weapon, he thought that if he could get off a couple of rounds, the AK-47 shooter would redirect fire his way. The idea was to provide Reeves with a chance to take the guy out. Easier said than done. The speed at which the shooter could reload and continue to rain automatic fire toward the agents' hiding place was unbelievable. A quick glance to the lobby brought beads of sweat rolling off his forehead as he thought his track of floor was the scariest place on earth. And where had the other guy gone?

He observed Reeves, almost in tears, unable to move. Jesus Christ, he had to do something. Rising like a bear, he fired at Mr. AK-47 until his gun ran out of ammunition. That gave her a window of opportunity. Using her elbows as a brace, she got off two quick shots, looking doubtful that her bullets hit their mark. No matter. Automatic gunfire ceased for a few seconds.

Something hit the side of Lamborghini's head. As he turned, a dark skinned guy in a ball cap and sunglasses toppled over him, sending both of them rolling into the walkway.

Reeves rose to her knees. "Tony!" was the only word she got out as she watched them fighting on the floor.

Funny what ran through his mind in the face of danger. *What the hell am I doing here?* he mused, recalling why he'd joined Homeland Security; to pursue and arrest domestic terrorists. Two former FBI partners, along with his girlfriend working in the revenue department of the downtown Oklahoma City, Oklahoma federal building, were among victims killed by local extremists. He wanted to even the score, and not out of revenge. He believed that by being a part of DHS, he could try to prevent future attacks.

Reeves's stint with the Federal Bureau of Investigation came about under different circumstances. She had spent several years at various Midwest branches before being handed assistant special agent status in California, first up north in San Jose, then in Los Angeles in partnership with Dan Curbside. Her father was a former Alcohol, Tobacco & Firearms (ATF) agent stationed along Southwest border towns with Mexico. Sucked up in cross-country drug corruption and a sudden fractious split with her mother, he eventually drank himself to death.

Despite her turbulent family history, she still dreamt of entering law enforcement. Her first choice, the LAPD, turned her down, for reasons she never fully explained to her future partners. Nevertheless, graduating with high marks from Iowa State University, she applied for a position with the FBI. While waiting for admission to the Quantico, Virginia training academy, she worked in the state attorney general's office and criminal investigation department. Years later, when she started with Walter McLaughlin's combined DHS-FBI counter terrorist intervention division, standard practice teamed a member from both departments, and she and Tony had become partners. Good call. Although from different backgrounds, the two forged a cohesive, working relationship.

Now here he was on the floor with an alleged terrorist flailing away at him.

His hands and arms blocked some of the blows. Sweat dripping into his eyes made it difficult to see the face of his attacker. Damn, a stun gun would've come in handy. He still held his .45, but it was useless since he had emptied it just moments earlier. But his attacker didn't know that.

He jammed the gunpoint to the man's temple. Thinking he might get shot, the Somali lessened his assault on the agent. A twenty-five pound weight difference gave Lamborghini leverage. Striking non-stop against the side of the attacker's head, he managed to push him aside with a free hand and, as hard as he could, punched his assailant's temple. "Christ

Almighty," he swore, shaking his bruised knuckles as blood dripped from the young man's lacerated skin.

It didn't dawn on him that the AK-47 gunfire had ceased until Reeves crawled over. Visibly shaken, face flushed, though relieved he was all right, she clutched at his arm.

Their valuable partnership superseded any words that they could've uttered. What concerned them was that the shooter had disappeared. Angry that they couldn't apprehend him, Lamborghini let loose a salvo of expletives, including one that referred to the female anatomy. Another time or place Reeves might have slapped his face.

He bent down, using his arms to raise the young assailant. When he removed the ball cap and dark glasses, they were astonished that he had fought with a teenager who couldn't have been more than eighteen, and looked scared. He also had a side arm, a .45, just like all the other disguised armored guards, which he hadn't used. Maybe he didn't know how, the agent suspected. Lamborghini slid out the weapon, and was not surprised to find that it had a full bullet clip. He put the magazine in his back pocket.

Reloading their own weapons, they carefully resumed strolling through the lobby.

Two SWAT officers entered the foyer. Reeves instructed one to cuff the Somali teen and take him straight away to the DHS lock up.

She pulled out her cell phone from beneath her vest pocket. "Holy shit, Tony!" she said, and stared wide-eyed at her left shoulder and down at the phone, where an AK-47 bullet had struck it and deflected off the thick fabric.

"Aylesha, you're one lucky son of a bitch!" he said, grinning.

***

About three blocks west, sipping tea in a Persian restaurant, Muhamed Dauadi flipped open his cell phone and hit redial. When someone answered, he asked if the Brothers of Somali Jihad would be feasting tonight after sunset. After hearing an elated "Yes, *Inshalla*...God wills it," he snapped down the cover, pleased that the IEDs had been installed, and then ordered more tea. The waiter also brought him a Blackberry.

Quickly hitting a pre-programmed number, he texted first a reference to today's Festival of Sacrifice Muslim holiday, Eid al Adha, followed by the equivalent expression in Arabic: *Idu l-'Adha*

He ended his text with the notation, Rejoice this day!

Within thirty seconds, a reply scrolled across the screen: *I shall.* Signed *Saleh Ali Nabhat Saleh.*

He withdrew another device from his jacket. Checking his watch, he moved a switch from the off position to arming, then set. As a small red light flashed, he closed his eyes and envisioned the sun ablaze like a fireball.

Chapter 18

Guns at the ready, Art and Consuela's group began their ascent to the eleventh floor. The Lab kept its nose to the ground, relying on its keen senses to pick up anything suspicious. Still, no one was about to let his guard down. It was anybody's guess what could be waiting in the next stairwell.

Slowly opening the fire door, the handler unleashed the dog and let him scurry through the corridor. Sure enough, it started barking as it darted past the elevators and stopped at the office of American Ballistic Communications, a designer and supplier of rocket guidance systems, and brushed his paws on the door frame, alerting his master that something in there must be checked.

With the two agents on each side of the door, the tactical cops threw it open, rushing past the reception desk, slicing M-16's through the air. Just like downstairs, silence and no employees greeted them. Officers ran in and out of the offices, exclaiming "All clear."

This time the dog lurched up at a wall near a row of filing cabinets. Standing as high as Jet could, he let loose with a series of yelps and growls.

"What is it, boy?" asked the dog's master. "What did you find?" He motioned for Art to take a closer look.

At first they couldn't discern what caused the noisy outburst. Even pushing aside a cabinet didn't lessen its high-pitched barking. They slid open drawers, rummaged through folders, felt underneath desks. Agent Curbside joined the search, even patting the wall for irregular sounds. Then all three glanced upward. The air vent below the ceiling…could that be it?

Art grabbed a stool. At six feet and with outstretched arms, he managed to peek through the metal slots, and then jumped down. "Up there," he pointed. "Fused, wired, and charged. Hidden a few inches down the metal channel, another—"

"C-4 explosive package," injected Mercado. "The Somalis are systematically setting bombs in—"

This time he interrupted. "In the military hardware R & D offices." He cautioned everybody to step back. "Take my word...it's ready to blow."

"So, what's hidden on the thirteenth?" Curbside asked, eyes skyward.

"Let's check it out," Art said.

"In a rush, are we, Captain Courageous?" Mercado said, and turned to the SWAT leader. "Let the bomb squad know we've found another explosive device. Tell them to hurry—we've now got two live bombs around us, and there could be another."

Nodding, he lifted off his shoulder microphone.

"The sooner someone dismantles them, the safer we can carry on with our business," she added, joining her group at the door.

Curbside inquired what they were all wondering. He received abundant stares, no answers.

Just an observation of the facilities reflected what must have been a fast intrusion and exit by the militants. All the telephone lines had been cut or yanked out. The switchboard was smashed, rendering it useless. Papers, journals, and files were torn apart. CDs and DVDs were bent out of shape. File drawers were opened. Equipment quotation printouts had been ripped or shredded. Every wall and ceiling fixture was broken and disassembled. Computer cables were cut in half, and rooms ransacked. Chairs had been scattered, and shelves dislodged from wall brackets. Coats, purses and jackets were emptied, cell phones smashed. There were obvious signs the Somalis had disabled the staff from communicating with anyone outside the office.

It burned the agents just imagining the terror employees must've been subjected to. Equally upsetting, four unaccounted for, armed Somalis.

With another cop guarding the hallway, the search party numbers continued dwindling. If anyone felt worried, they didn't show it.

The assault team, once again led by the Lab, proceeded to the next staircase.

Mercado's phone buzzed. McLaughlin had received word from Aylesha Reeves about the confrontation with one shooter, whereabouts still unknown, and one in custody, both agents unharmed. She updated him with details of investigating the two armament suppliers, and pleaded for the demolition team. Their vehicle, he informed, was snarled downtown by emergency road closures and heavy traffic.

"Hurry up. There's live explosives in the B of A," she added before he terminated the call. The twelfth floor cleared, the group cautiously climbed the stairs to level thirteen.

Well-trained to detect movement as well as combustibles, the attentive canine tore down the hall, bypassing the first two suites, barking and howling as it reached the elevators and ran into an L-shaped corridor. Growling fiercely, his handler, the agents and cops trailing behind, he reacted to a scent, possibly human, which triggered an aggressive instinct to protect his master. This unexpected aggressiveness also heightened alarm buttons in everyone near him.

Before the group caught a breath, the Lab spotted the figure.

***

Several blocks away, Dauadi finished his tea. Leaning back, he removed his glasses and inhaled, holding his breath for a few seconds. As though he were gripping a priceless artifact, he slid his finger over to the on button. Silently, he quoted verses from the Koran, and whispered, "*Allah Bakbar*...God is Great."

Chapter 19

The dog jumped at a man coming at him holding an AK-47. At first, it sounded like hail, but it was semi-automatic gunfire tearing into the Lab's flesh. It hit the floor with a loud thump. Jerking sideways, it let out a wail—as though another animal had attacked its throat—that pierced everybody's eardrums, and then bounced onto its back. The smell of burnt fur permeated throughout the corridor.

All five law enforcement officers let loose with their weapons—M-16s, pistols—slamming bullets into the uniformed armored guard's torso, throwing him against both sides of the wall before he crashed head first to the ground.

Ignoring the bullets showering him from another weapon, the canine cop crawled toward his dog, yelling "Jet...Jet...!" All he could do was soothe it and rub the bleeding underside of its neck, hoping to feel a pulse. The dog's moaning grew fainter, and his handler felt the final beats of its heart. His hand dripping in blood, the officer fired a shot at the corpse of the dead man.

Art tapped the cop's shoulder. The group gritted their teeth. Jet was not just a four-footed crime fighter, but also most likely a longtime friend of the officer.

Footsteps thudded in the hallway, and the second gunman appeared from around the corner. Through a cloud of dense gun smoke, he aimed his carbine, lining up Mercado and the SWAT sergeant standing just inches apart.

Art focused on the man's trigger finger. "Consuela, look out! Sergeant, get down!"

Flinging himself forward, he fired off his Glock, twice. Bullet number one whizzed past the Somali's hand. His second shot entered and bored through the man's upper right arm and took out a strip of wall molding.

Bleeding and in pain, the gunman raised and fired his AK-47, which was apparently set to full automatic power. Bullet after bullet rained through the hallway. Rapid fire, though, didn't mean shots scored a hit every time. This shooter was no marksman. Some bullets flew over the agents and officers. Some hit the floor, some pierced walls, right up to the acoustic ceiling tiles and light fixtures. Others ricocheted against the elevator's metal doors. Any one of them could've been deadly.

Hugging a corner, Curbside fired off a salvo from his .45, astonished that his shells only stunned the guy.

Mercado, going down to her ass on the floor, fired three times at the assailant, hitting him in the ribs and under his armpit, and kept shooting non-stop until she emptied her P-35. "Go down, you asshole!" she yelled, watching him twitch and yet somehow remain on his feet.

On his knees, Art fired again. One or two of his bullets creased the gunman's cheek. Another ripped through skin and sliced an artery in his neck. His face and upper chest covered in blood, he just wouldn't go down.

A SWAT officer blasted his M-16 at the Somali's legs, sending blood trails spiraling over the walls. The assailant groaned and muttered something in Arabic. Then his body jerked and he fell to his knees. Somehow, he still possessed the strength to continue firing. Most shells landed harmlessly, but he found a soft target. The sergeant's carbine jammed, and as he lowered his eyes to loosen the firing lever, a couple of rounds hit his vest, then both of his unprotected arms. The assault rifle, now too heavy to hold, slipped from the Somali's grasp and banged onto the floor.

Shifting his body toward the cop, Art acted as a shield in case of another bullet.

Eventually, the gunman's many wounds and loss of blood took their toll, sapping not only his strength but also his balance. His rubbery legs gave out, unable to keep him upright. He slid backward along the wall, collapsing near his dead comrade.

Reloading her pistol, Mercado pointed her weapon as she stopped a few feet short of the two militants. "Is that sucker dead?" she asked, waiting for Art to join her as she flinched at the massive pool of blood.

No one could escape stepping on the countless number of rifle and pistol shells that littered the floor, or the stench of smoke combined with that of one of the gunmen's bowels that had ruptured.

"Aw, shit." Art covered his mouth with the back of his hand. "There's enough bullets in him, he should be." He was just about to lean over. Instead, he bent down next to the LAPD supervisor, who was being administered some temporary first-aid from his partner. Assured that he would be okay, Art turned to check on the Somalis.

Mercado holstered her gun and exchanged a brief glance with Dan Curbside. The look mirrored his thought: we survived all the shooting. The lull also gave them a moment to observe Jet's handler, who had pulled the Lab away from the bloodied carpet and draped his vest over the dog's body. They also propped the AK-47s against a wall.

Curbside dialed 9-1-1 and told the dispatcher that an injured officer needed emergency medical attention, plus to send over animal services to attend to a downed police dog. He was about to declare that the thirteenth floor had been secured when Mercado, overhearing, waved off his premature declaration.

Still holding his Glock 9 mm pistol, Art, now standing angled to Mercado and Curbside, caught the glint of a gun barrel, and spotted fingers sliding a Smith & Wesson .357 Magnum revolver out of its holster. A shaking hand aimed the weapon at Mercado's head.

"Watch out!" he shouted, brushing past Curbside, almost knocking him over. He grabbed Mercado by the waist and pushed her up against the wall. As he raised his weapon, he kicked several empty shell casings off the floor straight at the man's visual sightline, and then fired off two shots dead-on, striking both sides of his head.

The Somali moaned. His body jerked for a couple of seconds before sinking lifelessly to the floor.

Art just stood there, silent, and lowered his gun, taking in what had unfolded. His face flushed; it hit him that he'd killed a wounded man, but he had no regrets. After all, that's what he was trained to do: shoot to kill in order to defend himself, or when his partner was in a life threatening situation. A life for a life, he figured. And damned if it was going to be Consuela's.

The others didn't say anything. They had their own jobs to look after.

She waited until he loosened his grip on her arms and caught his breath. She held back making any comment, realizing that agents at some point had to make a life altering decision; he chose his. As far as she was concerned, get over it. Move on.

"I...I guess I should say thanks," she smiled, letting go of his hands.

"Why? No big deal. You'd do the same."

Eye to eye, inches apart, they remained standing, close enough that she observed sweat trickling down his cheeks. Close enough that he could see the glow in her eyes; lips, not opened, not closed, yet at that instant expecting her mouth to touch his.

Say something, her brain buzzed. She never got the chance.

Everyone looked baffled. Had the walls moved? Had the floors vibrated? Then uncertainty kicked into disbelief, if not outright shock. There was no mistaking, even this far up, the reverberation of an explosion that echoed in their ears.

Collectively, the name Dauadi rang through their heads. Just like he'd promised, on June tenth, the Somalia Brotherhood of Jihad had struck on the Day of Sacrifice. The Somali terrorist had activated the IED two levels below, which shook the entire floor and loosened light fixtures, jarring a florescent tube out of its sockets.

What they feared had become reality — the bomb linked to the computer surge bar detonated. All they could do was wait out the thump-thump of muffled waves seeming to jump from wall to wall. No one suggested it. Instinct told them to move closer together, counting out the seconds, waiting helplessly for another blast, praying it wasn't under their feet.

Mercado and Curbside may have likened the shaking to an earthquake, while Art, unfamiliar with Southern Californian fault lines, knew firsthand the sound and the rumbling sensation emanated from a bomb. He'd witnessed it many years ago in Israel as a counter terrorist operative training with its secret service Mossad organization. That stifling hot afternoon on the West bank still burned in his mind, when he'd killed a teenage boy just as the lad detonated explosives strapped to his chest. Years later, in the Canadian Intelligence Service, he'd experienced no shortage of IEDs going off in Afghanistan, many of which had killed or maimed American, Canadian, and other NATO soldiers, as well as hundreds of civilians. No matter what name terrorists called themselves — al Qaeda, Taliban, Fedayeen, Hamas, Hezbolla — they were all experts in constructing explosive devices.

Mercado flipped open her phone, informing the director that the team had engaged in a gun battle, and an incendiary device had exploded. She added that they had two wounded police officers, two dead terrorists, and they didn't know what or who was inside the Encada suite.

"Where's the damn demolition team?" she shouted.

After she heard "on the way," she hung up, furious, facing the opposite way so that others wouldn't see her mouthing a sling of profanities.

Curbside placed his hand on the fire door, drawing back at its warmth, even though the blasts occurred on lower sections.

"Don't open the friggin' door," the SWAT sergeant yelled, despite the pain in his arms and blood seeping through temporary bandages over the wound. "If the door's that hot, you open it, we'll be incinerated."

Tension mounted. Everybody braced for the next explosion.

Standing beside the Encada Engineering Ltd. Office, Art noticed whitish smoke filtering through the bottom of the fire door.

***

Next door at the hotel, Reeves and Lamborghini, making a methodical search for the lone gunman, stopped in their tracks, thinking the two detonations were mild earthquakes since tremors occurred all the time in Los Angeles. They felt no shaking, furnishing stayed upright, and there were no flickering lights. But their task was to locate the Somali

109

shooter, so they ignored the sounds at the Bank of America building and started checking conference rooms.

Chapter 20

The bomb had ignited a fire large enough to send smoke up two levels. Art tried to keep his anxiety from the others; he wasn't succeeding.

Joining Art, Mercado wondered if Encada had its own timing mechanism rigged to go off. Consensus pointed to yes. Frightening also was the thought that the other two gunmen could have lashed suicide vests to their bodies. A death trap could be waiting. Faces paled at the thought of confronting them, but no one showed the slightest unwillingness to enter the suite.

Of the three suites selected by Saleh Ali Nabhat Saleh and Muhamed Dauadi, Encada Engineering had to be the most offensive to the Somali Brotherhood. After all, they were a multi-million dollar military contractor that manufactured components for specialized weaponry and accessories for combat firearms. Their inventory included night vision goggles, silencers attachable to SAUER automatic carbines, anti-RPG busters, wireless sound-wave mine detectors, and steel cased coatings for bullets that expanded on impact, inflicting more severe lacerations of the flesh than regular dumdum shells.

Although classified as top secret, radical terrorist organizations such as the Somali Brotherhood had discovered that Encada had developed Advanced Combat Optical Gun Sights that attached to U.S. army snipers' weapons using a tritium composite—a radioactive form of hydrogen—which created light and helped soldiers hit what they were aiming at more accurately...namely insurgents. Incensed that Muslim fighters would die, Nabhat Saleh was determined to destroy the corporation and prevent it from profiting from that insidious device.

Increasing white smoke, mostly concentrated along the walls, didn't alarm Mercado's group...not yet, anyway. The corridor was about twenty feet long, maybe twelve feet wide, and at least eleven to twelve feet to the ceiling. Even with no functioning air conditioning, it would take some time before smoke choked off enough oxygen to imperil anyone.

111

Common to all B/A floor plans, commercial suites contained two outer doors and short entrances to reception and inner offices. If they were to breach Encada, they needed an extra edge, like an additional assault weapon. Depending on what firepower hid behind the door, pistols and M-16s would likely be inadequate.

Art looked at the two SWAT officers. Strapped to the backs of their armored vests, pouches held smoke grenades and lasers. These would help them going in, providing the employees weren't held hostage. Dealing with the gunmen was preferable to watching civilians drawn into crossfire.

Mercado's phone buzzed. Shaking her head and swearing under her breath, she heard McLaughlin announce that the bomb squad officers had arrived outside. What did he want—thanks?

Determined not to let precious time slide by, Art pulled out the paper with the military contractors' names and decided to take a different course. He dialed Encada's number, figuring that someone had to answer. Two, three, four rings, no answer. Then half way through the fifth, a shaking voice said, "H-Hello? Help us, please."

"Who's speaking?"

"Jim Pawluk. I-I'm the general manager. We need help…they put a bomb in our office."

"Are you able to say where?"

"No."

"Okay. The bomb squad is on the way. We're from the DHS and the FBI. We'll do our best to get you out. Jim, who else is with you?"

"My staff, plus people from American Ballistics and ACR-Tech. I think there's about twenty-eight of us."

"All right. We're outside the door. Who else is with you? Are you being held hostage? Anyone hurt?"

Quiet. Seconds later, a scared voice whispered, "They're here."

Art knew whom he meant by *they*.

"Two men with guns," Pawluk continued. "Two women are in shock. My chief engineer, he's hurt badly. He hasn't moved since…." Another pause.

Art sensed in the manager's voice something was wrong, very wrong. Shuffling feet and muffled voices could be heard in the background. "Jim…hello. Hello. Are you there?" Just the hum of the receiver from a dead line sounded in his ear.

Taking his i-Pod, Mercado pushed redial. Someone picked up on the third ring. "Is this Jim? You don't have to say anything; just listen. I'm Special Agent Consuela Mercado from Homeland Security. The police are with me." Heavy breathing drifted through the phone. "Stay cool, Jim. Follow my instructions exactly as I tell you. I want you to reply like this:

one click for one gunman. Two clicks for two." Her fingers tightened around the phone waiting for his answer.

Two clicks.

"If they're near you…one click. No…two clicks."

One click, followed seconds afterward by one hard depression of a digit from his phone.

"You're doing well, sir. Now, Jim, when we come in, I want everybody to lie on the floor. Press once if understood. Fine, fine. Please don't panic. We'll get you out."

She handed Art his cell phone. Half a minute went by before they lowered their eyes. She had given the go-ahead to those inside. No turning away now, regardless of bombs, terrorists, civilians. Uneasiness coated her face no matter how long he looked at her.

Smoke drifted heavier into the hallway. Everybody flinched as the pungent cloud weaved and began climbing up the walls.

Mercado gazed around at Curbside and the tactical cops and raised her thumb. Everyone replied with the universal thumbs up "let's-do-it" signal.

First, she counted heads…Art, herself, Dan, the canine officer, and one tactical cop—ample hands for an assault. Then what? Watch terrorists crazy enough to kill their hostages and blow themselves up….and her team?

Three feet from the double door, Art drew a finger over his mouth. Not only would silence be essential, their safety depended on it.

The sergeant whispered a few instructions about storming the suite that might provide an edge, or a damn good chance of staying alive.

Art indicated for the cops to lay their pouches on the carpet. One by one, they withdrew smoke concussion bombs. What they lacked was a proper battering ram. Brute strength would have to suffice.

Something else…pistols would be ineffective against powerful automatic weapons. His interest sparked at the two AK-47s lying on the floor. He handed one to Curbside. Relying on what ammo remained in the clips, the two agents stood on both sides of the door.

Armed with the assault devices, the tactical cops pushed open the outer doors. With guns pointed, they formed a semi-circle and cautiously approached the inner entrance. Their gamble had to work; lives depended on it. The door was unlocked. As soon as it opened, the cops activated the concussion grenades and lobbed them into the office. Mercado held her breath, hoping that those inside heeded her instructions to drop once they burst inside.

Automatic gunfire whizzed through the smoke. Bullets rained everywhere. Employees screamed and bodies thudded to the floor.

Holding their fire, the agents and cops fell to their knees to stay below the acrid smell of smoke. They realized that once they fired, their aim had to be accurate — blasting shells into civilians wasn't on the agenda. With employees hugging the floor, the terrorists should stand out like target boards. They were half right.

A tall, ball capped figure jerked upward from a corner desk, raised his rifle, and pulled the trigger. Every one of his bullets struck doorframes, even splintered walls outside the office.

Both SWAT officers unleashed their M-16s. Each of their shells was dead-on, striking the man in the upper torso, neck, and shoulders until he cried out and fell over the desk like a mannequin onto the floor.

Art crawled into the suite. Having several pairs of eyes staring at him was unnerving enough. Curbside, almost pushing him aside, with a carbine in one hand and holding his .45 in the other, inadvertently prevented Art from raising his gun. Art sensed that Mercado was kneeling behind him; in fact, with her sweat mixing with her cologne, he smelled her presence.

Hidden somewhere in the room, another AK-47 blasted a volley at the assault team. This guy was more accurate. Some of his bullets knocked the helmet off one officer and smacked into his vest, hard enough to send him reeling backward. Then only the creepy quiet of silent guns could be heard.

A woman's long, blood curdling wail ended the silence. Agents and the lone cop felt as though icicles had pierced their bodies. Gasping and coughing seemed to emanate from everywhere in the room. The smoke now turned bright orange, creeping into eyes and noses.

Pressing a hand over his mouth and blinking wildly, Art thought he spotted a figure rising. Shit. As his vision cleared slightly, he could see that two persons, partly shrouded in a cloud of smoke, had risen. Their silhouettes became clearer, revealing a middle-aged woman and a burly man in an armored guard uniform backing up, the soles of their shoes rubbing along the floor.

A nervous, accented voice shouted, "I'll kill her...I'll kill her...you will all die."

Oh shit, Art swore again. *Now it's a hostage situation. I'm an Intel agent, not a hostage negotiator.* He inched closer, let the AK-47 slip to the floor, and aimed his Glock upward.

The woman's eyes bulged, exposing stark-naked terror. Tears soaked her cheeks. A large metallic gun neared her head.

Mr. Burly waved the revolver back and forth. "Go back, go back!" he yelled, pressing the gun harder against her temple and winding his arm tightly around her neck.

"Let her go," ordered Art, rising to his feet.

"Put the gun down," Curbside said, also inching his way forward.

The insurgent wasn't in the mood to comply. He swung the revolver forward. Everyone jumped as a bullet slammed into a computer monitor a foot away from the FBI agent.

"I–I warned you. This woman is dead if you don't back up…and put your weapons down." The gun trembled in his hand as he pressed it to the side of her temple.

"Okay, okay," Curbside said, and lowered his gun hand. "Let's talk. How about it, man?"

The Somali stared straight ahead, looking bewildered. Likely he'd never confronted an African American FBI agent before.

Art still held out his pistol. The woman's bobbing head shielded the insurgent's face. From where he stood he was at a poor angle to get a shot off, as were the cops raising their rifles; firing would've hit any number of employees.

The God-awful click of the .357 Magnum's hammer pulling back reverberated off everyone's ears.

A gunshot exploded. The bullet hit the brawny insurgent just above the bridge of his nose. Stunned at first, eyes sagging, the gun dropped from his hand. He rocked back and forth, fell to one knee, and then rolled over onto his back. It seemed to take forever before blood started dripping from his nose.

The woman screamed and flailed her arms into the air. Close to fainting, she slumped to the floor and shrieked upon seeing the body beside her.

Mercado, standing about eight feet to Art's right, had no reservation about where to shoot. Lowering her P-35, she took two long breaths until it registered on her that she had killed the man. It was not the first time she had shot at somebody, but he was her first kill.

She holstered her piece, knelt down beside the sobbing, shaking woman, and cradled her for a moment.

The canine officer and two SWAT members swept through the offices. Seconds later, amid bouts of coughing, the "all clear" signal was given.

"Good shot, Connie," said Art, praising her accuracy.

She refrained from answering.

Let her say something in her own time, he remarked to himself. *She's not the fainthearted type. She'll grasp that her action saved a life…maybe many lives.*

The officers and Curbside spent a few minutes checking on the staff, reassuring them they were safe; evacuation would be next. One cop tended to the injured employee who had multiple bruises and lacerations all over his arms and face.

115

One man in a sweaty white shirt glanced around, and Art inquired if he was Jim Pawluk. The manager rushed over and said yes, furiously shaking hands and gesturing a series of thanks.

Mercado phoned Noordine. "Advise the building manager to restart the elevators."

In about five minutes both elevators reached the thirteenth floor. Despite their trauma, most employees seemed upbeat as they descended in groups to the main level. Paramedics rushed to the injured Encada engineer and the SWAT supervisor, both of whom were wheeled outside on stretchers. Some of the staff needed oxygen masks to combat smoke inhalation.

LAPD commanders conferred with the remaining tactical members from the assault unit. A team of firefighters rode back up to assess the damage from the explosions. Soon large portable fans whirred, sending clouds of billowing smoke rings through the hallways, and clearing the engineering office of the acrid smell left from the smoke grenades.

Still upstairs, Mercado ordered Curbside to join Reeves and Lamborghini at the hotel and help in the search for the lone gunman. "Dead or alive, just get him," she told the agent. Then she and Art scoured the Encada suite, hoping no hidden bomb would go off.

Noticing her sullen face, he placed a hand on her shoulder. Most of her energy zapped, she replied by pushing his fingers away and continued searching.

Extreme rage must've sent the Somali militants on a sea of destruction. Anything not nailed down had been destroyed, broken, and smashed. Computers and other electronic equipment were kicked off desks, files were thrashed, furniture was upended and drawer contents tossed about, and fixtures ripped off the walls. There had even been an attempt to break a window, as evidenced by depressions in the glass, possibly made by rifle butts.

Someone in the office had shredded engineering spec sheets, no doubt scientific and procedural data about the advanced gun sight mechanisms. It was doubtful either terrorist could've interpreted the blueprints, let alone read them, but destroying the confidential defense technology information was better than having them stolen.

Ten minutes of wandering through the offices, even the washroom, prying up floor heater vents, and checking every cable they could find, still revealed no IED. This was the company chosen by Nabhat Saleh for specific revenge. Where was it?

Stepping over dozens of spent cartridges became akin to an obstacle course. Subjected to more bloodshed than asked for, Art and Consuela deliberately circumvented the bodies of the two Somalis. Just then a SWAT member and two suited bomb squad officers entered Encada

Engineering. Toting tools and detection equipment, a couple of crime scene investigators garbed in white coveralls followed. Go for it, they nodded, and went about their tasks. The agents figured emergency workers required space and use of the elevators; there wasn't much their presence could offer anyway. Just glad to leave, they headed for the staircase.

***

Director McLaughlin made a call on his cell phone. "Tonight. Yeah, yeah, I know the other one's dead; you don't have to remind me. Not our problem. Do what you want...he's all yours. Yeah, whatever." After hanging up he watched the live news coverage outside the Bank of America on two TV monitors.

Noordine Assad came into his office, first informing him that all agents had reported in, second to announce massive suicide bombings had taken place in several countries. She switched to another channel. Initial pictures taken from cell cameras zeroed in on a child's shoeless foot buried under the rubble of a collapsed roof.

Announcers showed footage of terrorist attacks, surmising all were coordinated to occur on today's Muslim festival holiday. Three bombs had exploded at a Shi'te shrine in the city of Najaf, eighty miles south of Baghdad, killing fifteen people and injuring scores more. Gunmen firing RPG's and driving explosive-laden cars had killed dozens at a crowded outdoor market in Mosul. Likewise, in the northern sector of Kirkuk, a suicide bomber had blown himself up in a mosque, death toll unknown. Two teenagers had run through a crowded bus in the normally stable district of Dihrawud in Uruzgan Province in Afghanistan, murdering everybody onboard. In Kandahar, Taliban terrorists dressed in *burkas* had entered a girl's high school and beat the female instructors to death. At the same time in Peshawar, Pakistan, Taliban insurgents had set off remote controlled IEDs and launched mortar attacks at police stations, while others had blown up a crowded commuter train near Karachi.

Similar bombings had indiscriminately targeted government offices and tourists in Mumbai, India; casualties could climb over a hundred. The West bank area of Gaza was undergoing clashes between militants and Israeli forces, the militants using homemade bomb parts smuggled in from Syria.

Scenes switched to England, where British Intelligence agents had disrupted a group of Pakistani university students minutes from setting off explosives in several urban centers of London and Birmingham. Attacks had also been reported in Madrid and rural areas of Uzbekistan, which bordered Iraq.

When a report of U.S. military fatalities came on, McLaughlin ordered her to turn off the TVs. He punched his desk, cursing and disappearing into an adjacent office.

Noordine left the room, unable to withstand any more scenes of carnage, ashamed and saddened at how cruel these fanatics were against fellow Muslims. She stood outside for a few minutes as tears flowed down her cheeks. This wasn't the peaceful, tolerant sphere of Islam that she had grown up with. Neither of her parents — nor their Muslim acquaintances, from private practice to high level individuals in the U.S. or overseas — had ever aligned or supported the fundamentalists whipped up by the wave of anti-American rhetoric. In fact, they despised the religious zealots who demanded that their cohorts promoted destruction, not peaceful overtones. Her father, regardless of the wrath leveled at him, avoided certain mosques that attracted the malcontents. Almost weaving as she strolled down the hallway, she clutched her stomach as visions of the dead and wounded raced through her mind.

***

If most sane viewers were shocked at the wanton destruction, Muhamed Dauadi, who also caught the news on a TV monitor in the tearoom, applauded as the graphic pictures continued to flash on the screen. The waiter used a remote to switch on a local station on another set to observe the commotion at Sixth and Hope. Dauadi ignored the scenes of paramedics tending to the wounded, preferring to span the coverage from the Middle East. Rocking back and forth, his dark eyes became blacker through the reflection of his glasses. Wherever like-minded Muslims sang the praises of Allah today, the oppressors of their faith had learned a valuable lesson: we will strike, we will attack, we will kill, and you can't stop us.

Chapter 21

As Art and Consuela neared the fire door, a sudden rumbling shook behind them, as if another tremor from the ground below had erupted. The sudden force spun them around in a semi-circle. Their shared glances did not reveal astonishment...it was more like uncertainty. What they had hoped wouldn't happen was about to unfold. They could feel it at the bottom of their shoes. To their horror, an explosion inside Encada flung all the doors into the hallway, followed by ribbons of orange-yellow smoke. Uncontrollably, both agents fell to the floor and rolled over like animals playing.

Crackling flames engulfed the opposite wall, melting the laminated wood paneling. In turn, this sparked a blaze on the carpeting. Smoke mixed with orange sparks blasted open the thirteenth floor windows, and caused support beams to buckle, ceiling tiles to collapse, and singeing the elevator doors. Door trims peeled. An instant later, a second violent outburst from an explosion yards from their feet exploded through the office. Every flammable material in its path sailed into the hallway, roaring flames like dragon's breath up and down the walls.

Everything happened too fast. Unable to breathe, Art felt as though a rockslide had crushed his entire body. This explosion carried with it the hand of death. The bomb squad technicians and the police investigators inside Encada...*God help them*, he muttered, picturing their horror as the bomb exploded.

Art looked for Consuela. On the floor in a fetal position, hands covering her head, she grimaced as she turned toward him, mouthing a combination of Spanish and English phrases. Translation wasn't required; all he had to do was look at her face.

Standing up was not an option....he duck-walked over, reaching out for her hand. Acrid smoke and heat from the flames and debris showering him made it difficult to touch, but he managed to grab her arms. Draping his body over hers, he dragged her toward the fire door.

As he flung it open, another blast above the heavy door blew it off its steel hinged plates, hurtling it to the side and then banging against the walls. Three-inch brass bolts flew by his head like bullets. All around them hell had opened its furious depth.

Mercado tried to scream, but no words or sounds came out of her mouth. Both were reeled backward, then forward, almost sliding over the top stair.

Brown and yellow tinged flames and puffs of smoke trapped in the corridor charged down the staircase, then recoiled and flashed back up the landing. Burning debris flowed along walls, smacking the floor and twirling around as if carried by a tremendous wind. In fact, it felt like a tornado fueled by its own force.

Hugging the floor, they could feel the sting of licking flames mere inches above their heads, scorching the backs of their armored vests. Smoke became dense enough to make them gasp for air, feeling like their lungs would soon burst. Drawing a breath became hard, exhaling even worse from the repercussion of the initial blast.

"Consuela!" he shouted, coughing. "Stay flat. Bite the floor like your life depended on it." His answer was shock expanding in her eyes.

A frantic, gasping voice rang out, "Get me the fuck out of here!"

"You and me both," he muttered to himself, gagging as smoke flowed through his nostrils and down into his lungs. Tears streaming down his cheeks from the smoke stung badly enough that he momentarily lost sight of his partner. Rubbing his eyes didn't clear away the smoke, but he spotted her upper body and began moving toward her. Wood panel splinters hurled over his chest, cutting into the outer fabric of his protective vest

Flames were rolling closer to the staircase, their only escape route. Radiation from the heat bit into his eyes. Squinting only made the stinging worse.

Fire had a sound of its own, and it was scary when the crackling approached. He knew that the path it chose to expand was not up to them, and they would be helpless if it decided to head in their direction. He had no choice but to use force.

Without warning, he pushed Mercado's rear end further into the doorway. "You want to get out of here...then we're going down the stairs."

"Are you nuts, man?"

"Want to be toasted up here? We can make it. You can make it." Staring at flames licking along the concrete walls and dancing near the landing, he may have doubted that thought, but their options were pretty thin. They either burned where they knelt or choked to death.

Depending on how the flames circulated down the corridor, drafts created swirls of weird shapes, at the same time transferring heat from the charred carpets then crawling along the concrete walls.

Art bent over and bored his eyes into hers. He could almost read the words "You're not serious!" written on her forehead.

"Come on, Connie, hold my hand and don't let go," he coughed. "Once we get down a couple of levels, it's bound to be clear. And hold your breath."

He covered his mouth and cupped the other hand over her mouth as she gasped for air, and they started sliding on their butts closer to the edge, now warmer than an electric blanket set on its highest level.

The dumbest feeling whirled through his mind. He looked up at the ceiling. *Goddamn smoke detectors and water sprinklers. Why didn't they go off?*

As he pushed her ass-first over the landing, he withdrew his pistol and fired three times at the overhead tap heads. Reverberations of the gunshots echoed painfully in their ears because of the confined space. The third bullet struck the handle and, in seconds, torrents of water rained over them.

Art laughed, even brushed water down his face. No time to relish the drenching, however.

"Now, Consuela...run like hell. And don't touch the walls."

Three steps down a slab of concrete had cracked and splintered. Fragments, jutting out like sharp, steel fence posts, could've ripped flesh apart. Engulfed in the wet smoke, Mercado started losing her balance as she stepped over the ledge. He caught her before she used her hands to brace herself against the surface of the hot wall. Something in Spanish fluttered from her mouth; he caught the meaning.

He knew this was crazy, but what else could they do? The only way of escaping was down, straight down, or stay and sizzle like hamburger meat.

The sprinklers were unable to snuff out much of the flames. Now moisture created steam showers, which stung their faces. Normally oxygen would've been a Godsend. What he hadn't counted on had happened. Oxygen ignited a back flash below the ceiling. Hesitating would've been disastrous. He knew it. And she knew what he had in mind.

As Mercado screamed, he yanked her hand and they jumped through the smoke and raced down to the twelfth level. Both landed awkwardly on their knees. Frightened, tears blinding her sight yet unwilling to stop, she got up, this time losing her balance, and struck the wall sideways with her legs. Her automatic reaction was to break her fall by grabbing onto something. Reaching for the handrail, her shirt cuff caught a chink in the metal and tore her sleeve off. Her shirt ripped, exposing her left shoulder and chest. Her feet dangled below Art.

In his haste to extend a hand, he tripped and fell down three steps to the next landing. He grimaced as muscles and nerves in his back flared up. The pain stunned him momentarily, blocking out yelling from above him.

"Art, help! I'm stuck."

Shaking off the dizziness, he sluggishly ran up and tried to grab her legs. The force of his grip made her whimper, and he had to let go. "Hold on, Connie. Just hold on."

"Easy for you to say. Get me down."

Weakness in his legs made it difficult for him to stand. "Listen to me. With your other hand, tear off your shirt."

Instead of digesting what he'd suggested, she shouted, "Tear off my what? It's too tight. I...I can't move. I'll fall. You gotta help me."

"I can't reach you from here," he said, ignoring his back pain. "You've got to yank off your shirt."

Almost in hysterics, she stared down at him. "What?" She began spinning. The rocking motion jarred her sideways, and smashed the glass of her wristwatch on the rail. Then the material of her cuff split. "Oh...Christ," she exclaimed, feeling all her weight taking her downward. She choked back a sharp pain when the added weight of her vest pressed against her chest. She didn't want to glance down, but she knew if her shirt ripped, she'd fall at least eight stairs onto the hard concrete landing. At worst, crack her skull; in the least, break a few bones.

Art held up his arms, his fingers unable to grapple the bottom of her legs.

Her shoes slipped off, banging on a step below.

"Connie, let go, I'll catch you."

"Don't let me fall." Her lips pulled back in fear.

"I won't. I promise." He shucked off his protective vest and dropped it beside his feet.

"Oh...shit!" she hollered, watching the curl of a yellow flame near her hair. Her tattered shirt started tearing away from the railing. All she could think of doing was closing her eyes as she toppled.

Watching her legs aiming for his head, he managed to pivot and, holding his arms straight out, caught her front first on his chest, her momentum pushing both of them hard onto the stair edge. The thick vest absorbed some of their weight as he landed on his ass. She wound her arms around his neck. They rolled side to side on the slick, soaked concrete, then straight back up. Coughing and grunting, it felt as though his lungs had collapsed.

When she opened her eyes and glanced upward, the remnants of her shirt caught fire and disintegrated. Then she realized that her partner was stretched out below her. "I'm okay, I'm okay!" she shouted, breathing as hard as she could.

Wincing and panting, he wondered if she would ask about his condition.

For a long time she continued lying on him. As his eyes blinked open, it dawned on her that she was shirtless beneath her vest and the strap of her bra had slipped down her shoulder, exposing her left breast. The situation didn't embarrass her, but at least he wasn't leering.

"Agent Dodek...you can let go of me now." She rested her arms on his elbows.

He relaxed his hold.

She smiled as she got up and adjusted her bra.

Using a handrail to steady himself, almost every part of his body ached when he slowly rose. He felt the most pain near his tailbone, as if somebody had whacked a baseball bat across his spine. All he could do was grunt; repressing a groan intensified painful nerve muscles.

Above them, flames diminished from a lack of combustible materials saturated under the sprinklers. Plumes of white-gray smoke still encircled the landing.

"Ready?" he asked, wiping dust and ash of his pants. "Let's get out of here."

Cautiously, they headed further down the stairs. They were startled when firefighters in masks, lugging hoses, extinguishers, a large fan, and fire suppressing equipment met them coming up on the tenth floor. The five-man crew climbed past him before he could explain what they would find—not just massive damage and dead insurgents, but what may have remained of the bomb squad officers.

Back outside on the street, medics inquired if they needed assistance, but both brushed them aside as the fresh air brightened their spirits. Never had feet on the ground felt so good. Mercado accepted a blanket to drape around her shoulders as she slipped off her vest and tore off the tattered remains of her shirt. Being shoeless was the least of her worries as she patted down strands of singed hair and blew remnants of sawdust out of her mouth.

Dozens of emergency workers tended to the bank employees who had endured hours of being locked in their offices, as well as those from the hotel who had watched the cold-blooded murder of their manager. Two ladder trucks maneuvered upward to the thirteenth story windows of the Encada suite, shooting water into thick smoke banks. Next door, swarms of cops and FBI agents entered the hotel. No one wanted to issue an all-clear sign yet.

Resting against a Medic-One truck, Art brushed flecks of soot from Mercado's hair. "Dauadi must've got his buddies to rig an IED on the fire door's spring loaded door closer," he said. "Set to go off not when it opened inward, but outward. We never saw it coming."

She nodded in agreement.

"Where the hell did they conceal the bomb inside Encada? We looked everywhere." He paused for a few seconds. Lines jutted out on his forehead. "The guys upstairs, they…we…could've prevented their—"

Touching his arm, she nodded again. "You did your best. Look at the number of people you saved."

He clenched his fists and gazed up to the Encada Engineering suite. *Yeah, sure*, he mused. *What about the guys we counted on to prevent another…?* His thought trailed off, partially as a nerve ending in his back flared up, and he heard his partner speak.

"Art, can we leave? I do need some clothes." She tapped his arm and walked toward the Crown Victoria, smiled, and murmured, "You saved my butt twice today. I won't forget it. Thank you."

He shrugged off her compliment. Wiping a speck of ash from her cheeks, he opened the driver's side door. "You gonna get in?"

Chapter 22

Four blocks northeast, Dauadi walked up to his Mercedes and shredded a parking ticket he found affixed to the windshield wiper. Surveying the area for the last time, he jumped in and fired up the engine. People rushing by clamored about the fire at B/A and all the police activities. As if it bothered him. Waiting for a ladder truck to pass, he inched his way forward, only to be blocked by a police van. He stared ahead, but didn't say anything to the officer leaning on the door. A minute ticked by, and the cop reversed to let him pass.

A wide smile crept along his face. He hit redial on his cell phone, and then murmured, "The Brotherhood will feast tonight." Whatever the person replied brought out a look of satisfaction in his eyes. At the next corner he followed the signs to the interstate. Although midday, the traffic flow lights still activated onto the transition lanes. He was angling a bend about four car lengths behind when he edged to the right and, ignoring the indicator signals, roared onto the freeway. With downtown structures lessening in size in his rearview mirror, he knew some of his brothers had died at the hands of the police and Intelligence agents. He was absolutely unsympathetic; other Somali youths would heed Ali Saleh's order and join their Jihadi alliance. What mattered most, three of corporate America's military suppliers had paid a huge toll today for their profiting by manufacturing weapons of mass destruction.

***

By mid-afternoon, the DHS and FBI called off their search of the hotel for the one surviving gunman. Somehow, he had cleverly eluded the dragnet.

His freedom lasted less than half an hour, however. 9-1-1 emergency monitors lit up from motorists and pedestrians frantically calling about a "black guy" in an armored guard uniform running around with an AK-47 assault rifle; last known site, outside the California Plaza Center at 4th Street and Grand Avenue.

Tactical units and dozens of LAPD officers swarmed the south side of the plaza; a police helicopter hovered overhead. Shoppers and bystanders darted for cover. Some actually believed they were watching a TV production. After all, movie and TV shoots sprung up in locations all over Los Angeles. They soon learned that this was not make-believe; those were real cops, and their guns contained live ammunition.

Confronted by cops aiming their weapons and shouting, the Somali froze alongside a curb, but didn't lower his rifle as ordered. In fact, he slid back the lever to activate the firing mechanism. Less than a fraction of a second later he curled a finger near the trigger guard. Eight cops with automatic carbines and pistols surrounded him, but kept about a fifteen-foot distance. Voices intensified as they shouted out orders to drop the gun. When his fingers approached the trigger, every gun around him opened fire. Spinning, jerking, blood flowing from all over his body, he dropped before his AK-47 fell to the pavement.

It was over in a flash. Nothing could've prevented this shooting—he chose not to comply. No connection to the Somali's identity arrived until law agencies throughout the county contacted the FBI and in turn, Homeland Security.

If the Brothers of Somalia Jihad had sought martyrdom today, not one succeeded.

***

About the only voice that could cheer Art up tonight shook with trepidation. "Everywhere you go, a gunfight erupts and people are killed," Lynda said on the phone when she answered, knowing it was his call. "I *knew* you were involved in that shooting in Los Angeles—it's been all over the news all day—as soon as a DHS spokesman mentioned that a special force of agents had entered that bank building. What am I supposed to think, Art? Are you on the receiving end this time? How am I supposed to feel, wondering…? Damn you, Art. I don't know…how I can keep—?"

His fingers tightened around his cell phone. "I've told you before, don't think about it. Besides, I'm with a terrific team. We all watch out for one another." He paused as pain dug into his lower back. "It's something we—"

"What? Take for granted. Spare me, please."

"That's not what I meant."

"Were…were you hurt? You weren't wounded?"

"No." He deliberately declined from mentioning what had happened to him inside the B/A building and upstairs at Encada Engineering.

"You're sure? You're not lying? I had all sorts of awful thoughts that you were…might've been…."

"I wasn't."

126

How many times had he fibbed about what he'd gone through, and played down marks on his body? Flesh wounds, scrapes, and bruises…she'd see them, and ask how he got them. When it got to why Lynda would fall into despair, and then they would argue about his job. Even though he loved her, out of passion for his Intel profession he'd try to deflect the discussion. An overabundance of stress existed in the field; arguing at home shouldn't be on the play list. Yet that was reality. He could fight his way through a lot of situations; fighting with his wife wasn't one of them.

Her next question almost caught him off guard, and the way in which she asked it.

"Was your partner there?"

"Connie…Consuela? Yes." He didn't mention that Mercado saved a lot of lives, including his own, but she wouldn't have been interested, or cared.

"You and your partner…that woman…you're on personal names now? I guess you're close together?"

He sighed. "On the job, yes." He immediately changed course. "When this current posting ends, I'm coming home."

"I hope you mean that." There was a pause on her end, then, "Goodnight, Art…take care."

Her call ended before he had a chance to say anything else.

Art did think about Mercado after he closed the lid on his phone. Like how she may be dealing with her emotions over the shooting of the insurgent. He stared at his BlackBerry. *Call her? Inquire how she's taking it? Comfort her?* Perhaps reassuring her that she performed like a professional agent as she had been trained, taking appropriate, counteractive action. For some reason, he figured "Don't do it."

***

McLaughlin sent a text to all his agents at ten o'clock that evening.

"Your reports, my desk Friday morning. Conference room 9 a.m. sharp."

Half the time he'd scan their summaries, penciling out and circling items or accounts to suit angles that he'd have his secretary revise before sending it to the DHS Assistant Deputy of Homeland Security in Washington, D.C., who directed Special Security Units, such as the team in Los Angeles. Individual agent comments were struck from the record. What the higher ups reviewed was his summary of current counter insurgency actions. What bugged him, however, was that the city of New York received most of the praise for its level of militant arrests and preventive strikes against attacks, whereas, according to them, Los Angeles shared the lion's share of enemy combatants. Most of the persons apprehended back east were former Pakistanis; while they were connected to Taliban planners, the Somalis were more apt to fight than surrender. A West Coast phenomenon, or violence-prone landscape, Washington's view was that New York still remained the hotbed of suspected terrorists. And to top it off, some bureaucratic liberal in the department had the gall to reply that Los Angeles's cult of violence stemmed from racial discourse. *If that's the assumption, when we apprehend more Somalis than those we shoot, we'll ship them to New York.*

At least late that afternoon he received an order for the "City of Angels" to reduce its threat level from imminent to elevated. *Do they think that when the Muslim holiday ends the radical insurgents from Somalia embedded out here will be peaceful?*

Daytime operations turned into evening activities. Counter measures continued, and interdicting overseas communications carried on unabated. Of the hundreds reviewed, several would receive immediate analysis. Since they concentrated on Middle Eastern chatter, as usual, Noordine Assad would have her hands full tomorrow translating those deemed critical. In addition, Intelligence agencies from around the world transmitted vital messages, warnings, and information about unusual activity on the West Coast. The majority were screened through Washington, then relayed through secure channels to McLaughlin, who as director, had to decide which messages would obtain instant action and which agents would be assigned to particular tasks, whether surveillance or "weapon ready" field operations.

Standard night time jobs for him were taking calls and answering e-mails from various civic and state organizations that shared a fundamental necessity to DHS, such as emergency services, local and state police agencies. Some associations outside the security umbrella mainly were sent "we take your concerns seriously and will place them on the list for our next conference." Those who wasted his time he deleted.

Long hours at DHS didn't bother him. Divorced twice and with children he hadn't seen in years, what reason was there to rush home? Fast food dinners at work were the norm. Despite inconsistent dieting and irregular exercise—agents were expected to keep in top shape—he somehow managed to not gain weight. Night shift workers would routinely find the director wandering the hallways. A bottle of Scotch in a locked filing cabinet helped him pass the night. While all federal buildings were non-smoking—his included—he cut down his normal three quarter pack a day to about eight or nine smokes. Yet where smoking was allowed, he over indulged. Stressful conditions sent him reaching for a lighter. Patches or pills weren't in his game plan.

If any, he had few friends, never personalizing with unit members. He preferred the trappings of his private office: mementos from overseas operations, such as pictures, but no family photos, plus a few souvenirs.

Stuffed in a desk drawer was the .45 automatic and holster from his early CIA days. If his agents fraternized with him outside the office, they would likely joke and suggest he kicked back more often. Trouble was, he'd take it as a personal jibe.

Despite the late hour, he had a rendezvous to attend to.

Later that evening he entered detention and ordered the Somali prisoner released into his custody. As usual, the marshals and cellblock officers obliged, no questions asked. When they reached the downstairs parking garage, he pushed the bewildered teen into the van, clamped him in leg shackles, and slipped a hood over his head. The lad's objections were ignored. Within minutes the van sped along Olympic Boulevard. Like the previous trip, he headed toward the wholesale distribution warehouses.

And like before, only a handful of the buildings were open late night hours. Between 5 a.m. and 7 a.m., however, these places were teeming with workers pushing dozens of hand trucks loaded with crates filled with vegetables and fruit and bins of ice, and forklifts scurrying through bays and revved up to empty waiting refrigerated container trucks of produce mainly from Mexico, Central California's agricultural belt, and the U.S. southwest. Distributors were then under deadlines for delivering fresh produce throughout the southland to retail super markets, hotels, and restaurants. Bulk container trailers displaying license plates from dozens of states also trucked produce all the way up the Pacific coast, shipping everything from lettuce, tomatoes, celery, cantaloupe, beans, corn, grapes, oranges, watermelons, grapefruit, and multi varieties of shell-packed berries.

Tonight though, hardly a light shone on any of the warehouses further up Olympic, and traffic was sparse. For their safety, most Angelinos wouldn't venture along these streets at night.

He slowed down and turned into a familiar driveway at a long abandoned building, one of several ramshackle warehouses that he used for his missions. Headlights shone on an SUV parked near a staircase, the driver standing alongside. Above, the illegible frayed name of a once thriving distributor hung clumsily, almost waiting for a wind gust to knock it down.

The director brought his shackled prisoner to a large double steel door. McLaughlin and the stranger forced up the heavy, creaking covering. Three men now entered a warehouse lit by a couple of overhanging light fixtures. Puddles seeped up from cracks in the cement floor. Dingy, smelling of mold, decayed odors of wilted vegetables clung to unpainted walls. Broken pallet boards, bales of torn sackcloth, bands of wire strapping, and shredded cardboard boxes littered most of the interior.

***

Twice the teenager asked where he was, not knowing whose footsteps he heard echoing beneath the high rafters, or whose occasional breathing. The silence inside the huge warehouse intensified his fear.

All of a sudden, a pair of hands gripped his arms and spun him around. When he felt his prison coveralls being pulled down, a voice from the depths of his stomach shouted out in terror. His arms jerked upward and his wrists ached as cords dug into his skin. From somewhere else he heard the clanking of metal and sliding ropes. Wooden pulleys yanked his feet off the ground. His cries of fear were ignored again. He shuddered when cold, metal snaps were attached to his chest. Then he heard chair legs sliding next to his feet. Although hooded, cigarette smoke crept underneath the head covering into his nostrils.

The sound of footsteps approached the teenager, and someone attached something to the snaps on his chest. He could hear the person as they moved away and busied themselves with another task nearby. As the unknown person neared the teen again, his dusty, scuffed brown shoes on the floor were all the boy could see from under the hood.

"I'm going to ask you a series of questions," an unknown, gruff voice said in the semidarkness.

For the teen, unable to discern who was speaking, it added even more trepidation to his anxiety. He wondered if the voice belonged to the one who had dragged him to this location.

"You cooperate, and be truthful," the same deep voice went on, "nothing will happen to you. Do you understand?"

First silence, then, "W–who are you? You're hurting me. Where am I?"

"I do the asking. Understand? Yes or no?"

"Y–yes. What do you want?" he replied, his accented words crackling. "I've...I've done nothing. You have no right to do this. I never hurt anyone. Why am I here? Why is this happening to me?"

"I'll tell you what will happen if you don't cooperate—you're gonna be one fried hunk of crispy beef." The teen heard the man take one long puff and then stamp the butt. "My friend here wants to hurt you. Me? I'm a reasonable man. I can only hold him off for so long. So, I can expect honest answers, right?"

***

What he said was bull-crap. He couldn't care less what happened to the youth. As much as the person at the switch panel enjoyed watching a victim suffer, McLaughlin relished prolonging the fear factor—hooded, hung up, helpless, and scared out of your wits wondering what was coming next.

He continued. "You didn't shoot anybody, I'll give you that. You assaulted a federal agent; that'll cost you major jail time." He nodded to his partner.

The fist sharp jolt sent the youth's body swaying sideways.

"D–don't...don't...please!" he cried out. Before his last words finished, another zap ripped through his chest, his screams echoing through the empty building.

"Now that we agree, let's get started. Nod your head, say yes, wet your pants, I don't give a shit. Just answer me. Your name is Husien Najaif. You're from Minneapolis. You're a Somali refugee who became a U.S. citizen. For Christ's sake, what idiot judge granted you citizenship? You're a piss-poor excuse for an American."

The scared lad wasn't sure how to answer the statements; all he could do was nod. "Why did you leave Minneapolis last October and return to Somalia?"

Silence. Almost stuttering, he finally managed, "What? My family."

"Now that's not all you did, is it?" McLaughlin growled.

Greeted by silence, his hand moved toward his partner at the switch panel.

"School. To a school," a scared voice replied.

"And...?"

"Training school for Somali youths."

"Where?"

"In...Pakistan."

"Where in Pakistan?"

"Peshawar."

McLaughlin knew what he meant by training school. He just wanted to hear Najaif say the names.

About eighty miles northeast of Pakistan's capitol city, Islamabad, Peshawar was a Taliban stronghold as well as a principal training region for extremists and terrorists. Hidden, hard to find, it was still close enough for launching attacks in Afghanistan as well as terrorizing local districts that patronized with NATO soldiers.

"Yes, yes. Then what? And don't lie to me."

"After training...we would join the Brothers, the Brotherhood of Somalia Jihad."

The director rose. "Who ran the school?"

When silence preceded the answer, it took a medium sized jolt until the boy screamed and sobbed, "The Taliban...and al-Qaeda."

"Yeah, yeah. Who organized your group? What's his name?" Again, although not a secret, he wanted him to reveal the name. Whether he did or not, McLaughlin raised his hand.

131

An intense electrical shock flung the boy's legs sideward, followed by a high-pitched scream.

"Stop! Stop! Mercy!" he cried out.

McLaughlin used his foot to steady the shaking legs. "Name, goddamn it."

Hesitation. Then he mumbled, "Saleh Ali...."

"Saleh Ali who?"

"Saleh Ali Nabhat Saleh."

"Good boy. How did he recruit you? You didn't leave the states for a high school reunion. Who in the U.S. sent you? His name."

"A Somali who used to live in Mogadishu — Muhamed Dauadi — he sent me...and others...to California."

His interrogator clicked his teeth and lit up another cigarette. He shoved a silver plated lighter into his suit pocket. "When you came back to the United States — two days ago — what were you told to do?"

Heavy breathing made it tough for the boy to answer. He clenched his teeth, bracing for the next wave of electricity.

"Najaif, I asked you a question," shouted the director, blowing smoke rings at the boy's bare chest.

"Don't hurt me. I'll tell you."

Standing a foot away, McLaughlin had his hand raised for a signal. "I'm waiting."

"To....join other men...Somali American men. Take hostages. Kill westerners. Hide bombs in offices."

"You hate this country that much, you and your lunatic friends would kill innocent people?"

"N–no."

"No what?"

"Saleh told us it's our duty as holy warriors."

The director snapped back. "Do you know how many Americans died in this city because of your belonging to the Taliban? Duty? Fuck you, Najaif." He waved his fingers.

His partner pulled the control switch over the mid-way point, shocking the teen severely enough that he screamed and cried, twisting his body full circle until his head jerked uncontrollably. Gasping, his head flopped down. Blue sparks flashed on his heaving chest. The cords binding his wrists cut into his skin. Still swinging, he shrieked, "Allah...Allah!"

McLaughlin stepped closer. He spit on the floor, incensed at hearing the name of the Muslim prophet. In one way, big deal if the boy died. On the flip side, he wanted more information. And he demanded it now.

Shaking the youth's legs, he continued his questioning, this time in a calmer tone. "Next question I ask you, Najaif, determines whether you live or die. Frankly, I don't care. Understood?"

"Y–yes," he mumbled after a few seconds. "Please don't hurt me any…anymore."

"Tell me, then, where is Muhamed Dauadi?"

Silence. Just heavy breathing filtered from his mouth.

"Turn up the level," he said, motioning to his partner.

"No…no more. Please, no more. I–I don't know."

"Fuck you don't. He arranged to pick you up at the airport. He drove you somewhere. You didn't change into uniforms on the street. You were given weapons. At a house, yes?"

Again, silence.

"I…don't…hear you. Don't play hardball with me, you wimp."

"All I remember is that we were on a freeway."

"Which one? Which direction?"

"I don't know. None of us paid any attention."

"North? East?"

"I think we drove past a big stadium."

"Dodger Stadium. The Rose Bowl."

"Is that's what it's called? Someone mentioned college football games."

"Okay. You're near Pasadena. Where did the driver take you?"

"I don't know," he sobbed, saliva dripping below his hood.

McLaughlin's impatience grew less by the minute. Reluctantly, he had to accept the boy's claim of not knowing. Hurting him anymore was useless.

***

The dead quiet of those inside the building frightened the boy just as much as waiting for another jolt. He began sobbing. Fear engulfed his mind when he heard the distinct click of a pistol chamber sliding open. His heart almost burst when the weapon was pressed against his temple.

"You tell anyone about tonight, I'll blow your fuckin' head off. Understood?"

Just weeping and heavy breathing flowed from the prisoner.

"Say it."

"Y–yes… Yes, I understand," the teen said frantically.

Najaif felt the man pat his legs, and his partner disconnected the wires. The youth slumped to the damp floor after the pulleys lowered his arms. Although relieved to survive this ordeal, he sobbed when the bindings were untied. He felt as if his body whirled around him, and had no idea who zipped up his coveralls. He offered no resistance, either, when someone pushed him into the van.

Secured by leg shackles, he heard the motor start up and the click of the transmission stick shifting into reverse. He had no sense of direction when the van drove out to the street. Between coughing and swallowing for breath, he had little strength to ask anything. Still covered by the hood, his weakened body fell sideways onto the rear seat.

***

With no traffic on Olympic to slow him down, McLaughlin made it back to DHS within minutes. It still pissed him off that the lad hadn't divulged Dauadi's hiding place, but at least he knew the general location.

Years ago as chief CIA officer in Karachi, Pakistan, he had encountered similar instances, although on a larger scale. Corrupt Pakistani government officials consistently blocked the U.S. State Department when it tried to investigate terrorist organizations; he'd encountered their unwillingness to coordinate vital intelligence and their refusal to turn over wanted terrorists to the FBI for questioning. It reached the point that when U.S. forces captured militant Taliban fighters in Afghanistan, they whisked detainees to secret hiding places—sometimes inside the Consulate—for their own interrogations. And it would get rough. While the White House denied it, prisoner abuse, including torture, became common practice. Water boarding and electrical shocking was often employed when ordinary intimidation failed to obtain a confession. Another tactic involved kidnapping suspects and secretly transferring them to the United States. When McLaughlin returned stateside, he and another CIA operative and ex-military associate continued the practice. Obtaining information to safeguard Americans, by whatever means, they reasoned, prevented future 9-11 catastrophes. The occasional pain and suffering his partner injected into interrogations of their prisoners was of little consequence.

Without any words, sometime after midnight he turned Husien Najaif back over to DHS jailers. No one remarked about the boy's disheveled appearance. After washing up he headed to his private office; lighting a cigarette, he unscrewed a bottle of Johnny Walker Scotch.

Chapter 23

DHS Conference Room, Friday June 11

When McLaughlin reviewed his agents' reports, he wanted facts, not conjecture, penciling out immaterial passages, highlighting sections that pinpointed errors or lapses in judgment. Assessing their performances aided in developing new tactics to avoid the same mistake. Also, the more adeptly his agents performed in the field, the more praise from the secretary that he deserved future consideration for higher office in the Homeland Security Department.

Finishing his third coffee, he closed the file reports and tossed the highlighter and pencil aside. For a moment he thought about Tariq, who'd committed suicide, and young Najaif. No apologies for what occurred; he'd do it again.

He heard voices approaching the open door. Slipping on his suit coat, he said, "Hurry up, get in here," as the group strolled in.

Chatting together, Reeves and Lamborghini sat to his left. "My ears are still ringing from that kid who hit me," Lamborghini said, getting comfortable.

"At least he didn't shoot anyone," commented his partner.

Grinning, Curbside shuffled in and took a seat near the end. "Man, I wouldn't want to go through that again."

Last in, Mercado and Art found chairs opposite the director. They sat down quietly, waiting to hear their boss's abrasive criticism.

Reeves and Curbside were the only ones who acknowledged McLaughlin.

The director leaned forward. "You all finished? I'm only going to say this once—it's not what I expected. The situation could've been handled differently. Do you have any idea how many times the mayor has called me? You read the papers this morning. Civilian casualties, damage in the millions, our department blasted for its excessive force."

135

"It wasn't our call, Walter, we did what was necessary," Mercado said, disliking the way he had put down her team for their actions. "Militants aren't known for cooperating. When they decided to fight, we—"

"So it says in your reports. Agents in my organization must take control of the situation. Dodek, Mercado...how thoroughly did you check Encada for that IED?"

"We checked," Art replied.

"According to LAPD bomb experts, the bomb was inside the control panel of a micro-wave. Guess what happened when one of the technicians pressed the open button to check inside?"

The group became somber; a lot of good people had lost their lives.

Just Lamborghini commented. "The prick that organized yesterday's attacks should be locked in a room with one of his own bombs."

The others concurred.

"The other bomb that went off," Art said, "had been installed on our only...." He glanced toward Consuela. "Escape route."

"So you both reported," McLaughlin said, staring at his agents. "Meanwhile, Dauadi is still out there."

No one wanted to reply to an equally explosive statement.

The phone on the conference desk broke the silence. "I told you not to disturb me. Who? Tell the governor I'll get back to him." A pause. "He is? Okay, send him in."

Seconds later, all eyes focused on the stranger who entered the room. Every aspect of his presence spoke military background; short-cropped ginger hair, tanned, square-jawed, gray eyes that never lowered, abdomen as flat as a board, and not one crease in his khaki pants. The sand colored jacket over the opaque polo shirt hung tightly over his taut frame. He walked in military fashion—quick, confident steps—and stood next to McLaughlin, whom he towered over.

From that position, everyone noticed the rosacea covering his nose and the freckles dotting his cheeks. He could have been forty-five to fifty-five, but his obviously regular workouts belied the truth.

McLaughlin shook his hand and turned to the agents. "Another purpose of meeting this morning is to introduce Mack Quintal. He and I worked together in the CIA."

Curbside and Lamborghini were the first to greet him.

Hesitant, Reeves approached. Anything CIA released unpleasant memories. She'd dated a guy in the Central Intelligence Agency who fleeced her out of thousands of dollars before departing for Southeast Asia. Neither he nor the cash ever turned up afterward. She had tracked him to Kuala Lumpur, Malaysia; however, stationed nearby in Singapore, she never bothered pursuing him. She acknowledged Quintal, but refrained from a handshake.

Remaining seated, Mercado smiled. She wore a loose fitting shirt, unbuttoned below her neckline. She felt his eyes peering at the outline of her breasts. Other men would look then turn away, which was normal. His gaze bordered on leering.

As if devoid of a smile, he marched up to Art. "Ah, you're Agent Dodek from Canada. The National Security Police, isn't it?" The voice was deep, Southern accented. Words seemed to rise and lower as he spoke.

"National Security Service. NSU is fine." The two men shook hands.

"Yeah? I've heard your country called *Canauckistan*—all the terrorists we find seem to come from there. What is it with you people? You arrest ten terrorists, and nine are released. That suggests you aren't serious about pursuing them."

"Maybe only the one out of the ten is guilty. And, yes, we take terrorism seriously."

"Yeah? Is that how you ended up with the Mossad—your being Jewish?"

Whatever smile Art possessed disappeared. He didn't answer. It was also the moment he developed an instant distrust of Quintal.

After the agents returned to their chairs, McLaughlin said, "Mack Quintal knows all there is to know about the Somalia Brotherhood. I want you to listen. Mr. Quintal, go ahead."

Quintal picked up a remote control and turned on a wall-mounted monitor. An obviously pre-recorded video opened to a dimensional map of the East African coast, then zeroed in on Somalia.

"For the past week you've witnessed what the Somalia Brotherhood is capable of," he began, revolving the cursor around the country's outline. "It's definitely a group you wouldn't want to see around a shopping mall; to say the State Department has designated the country off limits is an understatement. They're just as ruthless as the Taliban and al-Qaeda. The make-up of the place is almost impossible to comprehend. Its full name is Somalia Republic or Somalia Democratic Republic. The official name: *Jamhuriy adda...Dimugradigaee Sooma...Tariqya*. Don't try to pronounce it; you won't. Everybody has heard of Mogadishu, the capitol city. Basic languages: a Somali dialect, Somali Arabic. Its basic religion is Sunni Muslim."

He paused and eyed the group. "I'm not wasting your time, people. Listen and absorb. Now, the ancient Egyptians called it the Land of Punt. Notice the flag—the blue background stands for the blue sky over Somalia and the United Nations. Go figure that one. Each of the five points of the stars symbolizes the five historic realms of the Somali occupants. Political neighbors: Kenya and Ethiopia to the southwest; a sweetheart of a place named *Djibouti* to the northwest. Surrounded by the Gulf of Aden and the Indian Ocean to its east and southeast, Somalia is typically termed the Horn of Africa.

"To bring you up to date, you have to go back a few decades. Persistent clan wars. Revolts. Dictatorships. Whoever had the most guns led till the next yahoo warlord bought or shot his way into power. Civil wars since 1960. Since the major civil war ended in 1991, Somalia has failed to reinstate any form of a proper national government.

"Most Americans think of Somalia for the U.S. military Black Hawk Down episode in Mogadishu in 1993 and the non-stop pirates capturing, holding, and ransoming freighters from around the world. That's how these militants mostly fund their access to weapons. In turn, this increased their hostility to the west. Just like the predominant terrorist organizations of al-Qaeda and the Taliban, they split into their own cells, some of which equaled them in ruthlessness. *al-Shabaad* is the worst. They're recruiting and training suicide bombers from as far away as Saudi Arabia, Yemen, and Pakistan. Those are the guys who plant IEDs and lob RPGs at our troops in Afghanistan. We kill some, capture some…they keep coming. al-Shabbads are masters at bomb making and domineering whatever place they take over. Hitting civilian populations is where they're the worst."

Quintal squinted and said to Art, "Dodek, Canada is where the top player, Saleh Ali Nabhat Saleh, comes from, and he's responsible for the current influx of Somali-Americans returning to this country trained, armed, ready and willing to kill."

Art knew this. The statement was half true. Any kind of rebuttal wasn't worth the effort.

"You're all running around searching for Muhamed Dauadi," Quintal went on, "when Ali Saleh should be your main target."

Mercado stood up. "If we could get our hands on Dauadi, he'd lead us to Ali Saleh."

"Why haven't you?"

"What do you think we've been doing?"

"We have dead Somali Brothers," agent Reeves piped in.

"Yeah," said Dan Curbside. "What about the kid in lockup? Let us question him."

No one seemed to notice McLaughlin and Quintal exchange glances.

"You are not to question Husien Najaif," the director barked.

"Why not, Walter?" Mercado asked. "Dauadi recruited him; he must know where he is. Let Dodek and me —"

"No!"

Bewildered expressions greeted his remark. DHS had a suspect. What better way to obtain information to stop Dauadi's destructive rampage?

"Right now wouldn't be ideal," McLaughlin said lamely. "I'll handle it. No one is to talk to him until I say so."

"Do we wait for another bomb threat?" Mercado asked.

"Consuela's right," Lamborghini added. "Sir, any lead is —"

"No! Understood?" He turned to Quintal and said, "Another reason for our getting together this morning is to announce that Mr. Quintal will be joining our unit."

Surprised faces looked up.

"You report all investigative data to him."

Surprised faces changed to bits of grumbling. "As of today," continued the director, "he has the authority to act on my behalf. He has the know-how and the experience to give our unit a boost. And, damn it, this group needs a kick in the ass."

"What about Consuela?" asked Aylesha Reeves.

McLaughlin crossed his arms, obviously miffed that anyone would challenge his authority. "Chain of command isn't affected. Do I have to repeat it? You report to Mr. Quintal. That's final. This meeting is over. You're Intel officers…get on with your jobs."

Except for Art and Mercado, the group quietly filed out. She hesitated before leaving. Then nodding, she and her partner departed.

There wasn't anything to say; in fact, remaining silent had likely prevented an argument. In the hallway, however, she shook her head. "What in hell happened in there? Talk about a suck job."

Art nodded.

"I saw it in your eyes," she said. "He ticked you off. You're not too thrilled, either." He shrugged his shoulders in deference to her opinion. Maybe as the newcomer to the unit he wasn't eager to get into office politics.

Just as they reached the outer hallway, Noordine waved at them from the entrance of the processing center.

"There's something you have to see," she said, as they followed her to a row of monitors.

After Art and Consuela crowded around her, Noordine pointed to two split shots of the Bank of America tower and the commotion outside on the street. "These videos are from surrounding buildings," she explained. "Watch when I move the camera angle further up street level. This one was shot about three blocks away…check the figure on the right." She rotated a wheel by her keyboard, which removed grainy shadows overlapping a male in jeans and sport shirt. "Now, when I zoom in on the guy's features, tell me that's not —"

"Dauadi," Art intoned, moving closer to the monitor. "Muhamed Dauadi. When was this taken?"

"Time flashing right bottom, approximately ten minutes before the bomb exploded in the Encada office." She froze the frame.

"How far did the camera catch his picture?"

"Unfortunately, not far enough. It ends with him at Spring Street. He could've gone anywhere."

Mercado studied the enhanced picture until she picked out the earring below the shaggy hair. Clenching her teeth, she rubbed her sides. "Goddamn prick. To think that we risked our butts for that...." Without another word, she turned and left the processing center.

Standing, Noordine watched her disappear into the corridor. The analyst would have run after her if not for what Art said.

"Let her go. Consuela had it rough yesterday. She needs her space."

"She told me what happened. My God, I just don't know how she's holding up. I could never...never shoot another human being."

He tapped her shoulder. *Don't go any further*, he said to himself, choosing not to expand on the subject. Instead, he stepped back. "Thanks for the video."

"Thank the guys in Analysis—they discovered it."

Art gave a thumbs up to the staff nearby at rows of monitors. As he started for the door, Noordine asked, "It's true, then. Walter has put Mr. Quintal in charge of the Unit?"

"Scuttlebutt sure gets around."

"We're Intel, remember," she said, a smile returning to her cheeks.

Back outside, he knew Consuela was going through hell. First kill had a way of scrambling you apart; whether in the line of fire or not, it was still a life. There wasn't any logical trade-off. *But she's a trooper; she'll come out of it.* Add McLaughlin's unexpected news today, and it must've felt like a boot in her stomach.

His BlackBerry buzzed. Surprised by who'd sent the message, he read, "Meet me in the coffee room." It was signed Mack Quintal.

Now what, he mused, heading into another corridor.

As he entered the staff lunchroom, Quintal, gripping a mug in his left hand, was leaning against the sink. The smell of burnt coffee tweaked Art's nose. Up close, he noticed how severe the rosacea had marked Quintal's nose. Although the second left finger was missing up to the knuckle, he wore a large ring with a projecting white stone, which Art recognized as the insignia for the U.S. Army Rangers.

The man never smiled. After a sip of the black coffee, Quintal eyed the Canadian security agent for a few seconds, and then asked, "I have your assurance you'll work with me?"

"If you mean the team, no reason why we wouldn't."

"Your partner, Mercado...she's gotta loosen up."

"She's a great partner."

140

"You fraternizing with her yet?"

Art swallowed a ton of air. Disregarding the remark, he asked, "You wanted to see me?"

"Yeah. I want to hear your perspective about the Unit. Meet me tonight. We can talk shop. Patches, you know it? It's a lounge on Wilshire, near the Ambassador Hotel. I'll expect you." He set the cup down and moved to the doorway. "Eight p.m." Then he strutted down the hallway.

Art rolled his eyes. *Doesn't he say anything without making it sound like an order?*

Chapter 24

Later in the morning, Mercado snapped shut her laptop, still steaming over the meeting. Quintal's arrogance ticked her off the most. *Some guy we don't know a thing about is gonna head our unit,* she pondered, tapping invisible keys on the computer cover. It had nothing to do with her position; she was still the team's senior agent. But to bring on board a guy who didn't have a lick of DHS field experience—they had to be kidding.

Walter's fashion of sometimes going over the top, that she could deal with; he was famous for his inexplicable announcements. If anyone thought that she aspired for management duties in the department, they were dead wrong. She'd witnessed too many Intelligence officers placed in high positions only to either become absurd bureaucrats or chase and hound good agents right out of the department. *No one's perfect, including me, but there's a limit.*

Something else bugged her. The teenager in lock-up, the sole survivor of the insurgents, could lead the team to Dauadi. *And McLaughlin says no. Might as well delete all our Intel files and send us home. Not on my watch,* she fumed.

She marched down the corridor and found her team reviewing notes in an adjacent office. "Art, get off your ass. Come with me."

He stood up, not quite sure what to make of her heated entrance. He didn't need further explanation to understand her determined look.

"Where we going?" he asked, walking beside her down the hallway.

"Husien Najaif. We have questions; he's got answers."

"Didn't Walter just—?"

"We're wasting our time standing here debating. You with me or not?"

Before he could answer she was already buzzing the guards to release the outer security door. Trailing her inside the staging area where agents signed the visitor's log, she almost yanked the pen cord off the register. After signing, a guard buzzed open the inner doors leading to interview rooms, and further down, the cells. They were told to wait until the prisoner was brought forward to a secure room.

In about three minutes the agents came face to face with one of the Somali Jihad Brotherhood members, the teenager who'd grappled with Tony Lamborghini. Shackled to locks on a table, he could move his arms but was unable to stand. The top of his orange jump suit zipped down to his abdomen, he peered apprehensively at the agents as they entered and stood on both sides of the metal table.

Mercado began the conversation. "Husien, we have some questions. Please cooperate, with us, okay?"

"D–don't hurt me," he sputtered.

"No one's going to hurt you," Art said. "Has someone hurt you?"

The teen clamped his lips shut and rolled his hands together in a defensive motion.

"Just answer a few questions and we'll leave," Art said, attempting to allay his fear.

Mercado slid a chair next to the teen and sat down. She said in a calm voice, "My name's Consuela Mercado. This is Art Dodek, my partner. We're with the Department of Homeland Security. It's our job to investigate acts of terrorism. I don't think you're a hard core terrorist." She paused and smiled. "How did you get involved with the Brotherhood?"

"I-I…it is the duty of a true Muslim to oppose oppression."

"Husien, you're an American. Why would you want to hurt innocent people?"

Instead of answering, he said, "I didn't hurt anyone. Will I be sent to prison?"

"You assaulted a federal officer; it's likely you will. However, you can help yourself."

"How?"

"Help us find Muhamed Dauadi," Art said.

"I've told…I don't know where he is." Lowering his head, he fidgeted around on his chair.

"Husien, we know you were met at the airport—we suspect by Dauadi—and you were taken to a safe house. Do yourself a favor and tell us." "Your cooperation could lessen your prison sentence," Mercado explained. "I think you're a reasonable young man caught up in an organization that ordered you to perform violent acts that were contrary to your religious beliefs. You didn't harm that agent, nor hurt anyone. You don't want to see any more innocent people die. Dauadi is the killer, not you."

He looked around the room, as though he expected another person to materialize. Then he gazed up at the agents. "Dauadi said we were Holy

Warriors. People would be afraid of us. We must terrorize Americans. I didn't know he demanded that we also kill them."

Mercado doubted that he wasn't aware of the order to kill, but allowed him the benefit of the doubt. "Then let us know. He's the one who should languish in jail." She clasped her hands on the table. "What city? Los Angeles is full of landmarks. You must remember some that you passed. Anything about the street that caught your attention? The location of the house? Something unusual. Different."

"Come on, Husien, think…think," Art said.

"Just that we saw the Rose Bowl signs."

"Pasadena. Is that—?"

He shook his head. "No. Further."

"Okay. There's South Pasadena. Go on."

"A large house. Other men were inside. They spoke Arabic, but I didn't understand them. Dauadi knew the older man; they drank tea, shared stories. I think he was Iraqi."

"You're doing great," Mercado smiled. "What else?"

"It was yellow, dirty yellow like the paint was fading, and a lot of brown bricks. No palm trees…I mean, like other streets."

Both Art and Consuela's eyes widened, anticipating that the teen would blurt out the street name. A blank expression of a person at a loss for words greeted them.

She tightened her hands over his.

Najaif stared at her wrists. For the first time since the two agents began questioning him, he sat straight up. His eyes beamed. Although cuffed, his hands wandered along the table edge as far as he could stretch his fingers. Something was clicking inside his head.

Art and Mercado couldn't unlock the teen's mind. Either he was confused or unable to put his thought into words. But he seemed transfixed by the floral pattern on the cuffs of her shirt.

His mouth widened. Because of his accent, he yelled out, "Germane."

"Geranium?" Mercado pronounced it for him.

He confirmed by nodding at her.

"Well done," she smiled, releasing her hand and standing. She motioned Art toward the door.

After they cleared the detention area, she told him to round up the team and meet in the parking garage, and then she rushed over to the Analysis center.

Chapter 25

With Art and Consuela leading in the Crown Victoria and her unit following in a GMC Suburban, this late in the afternoon it would take at least an hour to reach South Pasadena. A quick assistance call and the highway patrol provided a flashing-light escort.

A satellite image of street grids, provided by Noordine, appeared on Art's phone. He worked his way through coordinates until the street name Geranium popped up, searched for a match for Hussein's description of the house, the nearest cross street, and the name of the homeowner. He was not at all surprised that it wasn't an Iraqi as Najaif had mentioned. Finished, he entered the information into the GPS. Their adrenaline flowed over the top. Dauadi may finally be within their grasp.

Carefully screening their target area, they turned on Avila Avenue and slowed as they entered Geranium. Sure enough, not exactly as Najaif described it, a yellow one-story house with brownish brick siding and an unkempt front yard loomed. No vehicles were parked outside. In fact, the place looked like it would fit into countless lower middle-class Southland neighborhoods.

A few, if not most, of the homes on the block resembled one another, with brick fronts, tiled or shingled roofs, one level, a couple fenced in and windows barred, worn yards close together. Up and down the street, nobody was out walking. In all likelihood, neighbors kept to themselves, too afraid to venture outside.

The group stopped on both sides of the driveway. There didn't appear to be anything suspicious from the outside. The front curtains were shut, and there were no noticeable sounds. With the Somali Brotherhood lieutenant as a possible occupant, guns were withdrawn as they strode up to the front porch.

This was when law enforcement officers were at their most vulnerable. Danger with a capital D lurked behind a closed door. Their greatest fear was bullets flying at them, or their firing at an innocent person used as a shield. Regardless of the precautions taken, nerves would be sky high, stomachs knotted.

Mercado pressed the bell and banged on the door.

"Homeland Security! FBI!" shouted Curbside and Lamborghini.

A few seconds later, the door crept open. An older man in a white undershirt answered, startled when five armed agents pushed him aside and stormed into the house.

"Who…are you?" a thick accented voice asked.

Two younger men in jeans and T-shirts appeared, but were too scared to speak.

Mercado displayed her ID. "Where's Muhamed Dauadi?"

At first the man played dumb before saying, "Where's your search warrant? I want to see your warrant."

"Be quiet," she ordered. "This is a federal matter. I asked you — where is he?" She directed Aylesha and Tony to check the other rooms.

"I know nobody named Dauadi. Leave my house."

"The lady told you to be quiet," Art said, pushing him onto a sofa. "What's your name?"

"Ahmed Jalbari."

After the all-clear signal was given, she holstered her sidearm and said, "If we find evidence that you are harboring a wanted terrorist, you'll be charged with aiding and abetting as well as obstructing justice. Those are serious felonies. And you can be sent to prison."

The man's lips turned into a sneer as he leaned back against a cushion.

"What about you?" Art asked the younger men, who looked Somali, yet the old man was definitely Arabic.

Their faces were shrouded in fear.

"Let's see some ID," agent Reeves instructed. She checked their driver's licenses. One said they were the man's nephews, which was doubtful. The house address checked out.

Art wandered through the house. Soup bowls sat atop the kitchen table, warm to the touch; dishes and pans were stacked in the sink. The main floor contained three unmade bedrooms and a studio with a pullout couch. In one bedroom he noticed a large basket hamper overloaded with men's jeans and shirts. For the height and weight of the trio in the living room, the contents seemed to contain an abundance of different clothes sizes.

Back in the kitchen, when he stared out of a window he spotted a tool shed in the back yard about twenty-five feet from the house.

"Open it," he said to the older man.

Resistance rooted in his eyes greeted the order.

"Open it!" To reinforce the command, Art gripped his arm and marched him to the back door. Mercado followed them outside.

The old man fumbled with a set of keys; shaking, he removed the padlock on the lop-sided door.

Using a small flashlight and the partial daylight, Art peered through boxes, cardboard cartons filled with items of no importance. An old rusted Enfield WW1 rifle with its bolt missing stood by a shelf stacked with empty five-gallon water jugs. Garden tools and a gas mower, long neglected, leaned together in a corner alongside various lengths of bug-infested lumber. To the left, a workbench covered in sawdust chips, steel shavings, and bits of plastic connecters intrigued him. Shining the light on the bench, he slid back the cover of a carton and rifled through the contents.

Wow, he whistled, finding cell phones, plus parts for circuit breakers, numerous lengths of cut-up colored electrical wires, black tape, and a metal housing, which may have contained a triggering device. A screwdriver and a pair of pliers sat under the other items. He picked up the carton and rejoined his partner, who was clinging to the back of Jalbari's undershirt.

When she gazed at the assorted hardware, she didn't need an explanation. However, she demanded one from the old man. "Mind telling us who this belongs to?"

"Never saw it before," he mumbled.

"Mr. Jalbari," Mercado said, spinning him around and wrapping handcuffs over his wrists, "you're under arrest for providing sanctuary to a wanted terrorist."

He didn't resist, but howled, "I have civil rights. You cannot—"

"Until we investigate further—and under the Patriot Act—we may, and can, hold you for an indefinite period."

They wheeled him through the house. The two "nephews" gaped in surprise.

"What about these two?" asked Aylesha.

"Leave 'em." Mercado looked at them and in a stern voice said, "This house will be placed under a twenty-four-hour watch. Read my lips. You two so much as leave, you'll be arrested. *Comprende?*"

The two men bobbed their heads up and down.

***

As Art and Consuela led Jalbari outside to the SVU, a black Mercedes stopped about ten yards from the house. An unmarked Los Angeles County Sheriff's vehicle was parked nearby. The driver in the German-made sedan lowered his head when the Crown Vic and Suburban drove past. His eyes squeezed together, his mouth curled inward. He banged the dashboard with such force it left bruises on his knuckles.

He made no effort to enter the house...his safe house. Someone would pay for this, he swore, turning the car around, burning rubber as he sped through the intersection.

Chapter 26

Art found Patches, a lounge on Wilshire Boulevard; what wasn't available were parking spaces. He drove up to the valet, a young Mexican wearing a tie and vest. Inside, he was surprised to discover Patches more upscale than first imagined. Dark wood panels and arches, leather backed chairs and wrought iron, glass-topped hexagon tables complemented a curved bar with granite countertops and three high split mirrors which expanded the room occupied by neatly dressed customers, most of whom were couples. The emblems and shoulder patches of NFL teams adorned one wall; a collage of football hall-of-famers hung on another side. Ceiling light fixtures provided adequate yet subdued illumination.

Passing a waitress in a white blouse and dark skirt, he spotted Mack Quintal sitting near a post. At this moment, he still wondered if he should've declined the invitation. Quintal, wearing the short jacket and top from that morning, remained seated as Art approached and pushed out a chair. Two glasses of dark liquid were on the table, one empty and the other half full. He sat cross-legged. Even the minimum lighting didn't hide his dusty, scuffed shoes.

Quintal motioned over the waitress. She strolled over and smiled.

"You look like a guy who drinks vodka," Quintal said. "Right?"

"I'll have a Chardonnay, please, not too dry," Art ordered, loosening the buttons on his blazer.

"For Christ's sake, don't you want a real drink?" Quintal pointed to the empty glass. "Bring me another Cutty Sark—make sure it's with crushed ice."

"Thank you, be right back." She smiled and headed to the bar.

"Kind of young, huh? But they're the best," he smirked, drawing the shape of invisible breasts with his fingers. "Anyway, Dodek, how do you like working with the L.A. unit? More action than you ever encountered in Canada." He finished his drink in one swallow, brushing away a dribble with his left index finger. "Hey, you and me, we can talk straight. You're a sharp guy, not like those yahoos on your team…except for your

Mexican partner." He drew an outline of woman's shapely form by rolling his hands.

"Talk about what?" inquired Art, convinced that he did make a mistake by showing up. And he made no pretense of acting cordial.

"You think I didn't notice their attitude this morning? Wait 'til you know me."

"I don't know you."

The young waitress leaned down to transfer the glasses to the table. Quintal peered over the top outline of her breasts just below the opening of her blouse.

She ignored Quintal. "This is a Californian reserve, sir. Enjoy."

Picking up his glass, Art expected that Quintal would clink glasses or make a toast about something, possibly with a military overture. Instead, he sipped and chewed on some crushed ice, and sloppily reached into a bowl of mixed nuts. "I'm ex-Army. Guess you can tell. Nineteen years in Intel, Special Forces...The Rangers. I could kill a guy easy as just looking in his eyes...especially terrorists. I hate the bastards. The only good Muslim is a dead Muslim. They've killed some good soldiers; top friends. Bloody cowards. You know what they do; hiding in mosques, firing from civilian houses, using kids and women for shields. A dead terrorist is one less jack-off with an RPG. Right? Let's drink to that. Shit, man, you're just like me."

"Nobody could be just like you."

Sarcasm or not, he went on. "This country is too soft on terrorists. Trials? Fuck that noise." He picked up a cigar from the table, slid it around in his mouth, and flicked on a lighter. The smoke immediately wafted through their section.

The waitress rushed over. "Excuse me, sir. There's no smoking allowed."

"Yeah, okay. Another damn liberty taken away," he sneered, grinding it out in the peanut bowl. "Hey, drink up, Dodek. Like I was saying, I also served in CIA Intel— Pakistan. Shit, I hated that country, and everybody in it. You want corruption? Fucked-up intelligence they'd feed us. What's the name of the CIA officer in Karachi? He said he knew you."

If you served with the agency you knew who he was. Everybody did. But Art answered anyway. "Lucky de'Angelo."

"Yeah, Lucky. He had a way with Pakistani officials—when they cooperated. We'd arrest insurgents and they'd release 'em. Corrupt bastards. Sometimes we took matters into our own hands. Shit, man, we had to. And if it meant roughing 'em up...you got the picture? You serve in Iraq? No? You heard about Abu Grarib—al Qaeda and Taliban prisoners being tortured. Army Intel and the CIA, we could be persuasive if push came to shove. They were killing our guys, their own people. Shit, I saw 'em mutilate their own families." He paused and gulped down his Cutty Sark. "Like I said, we went after 'em tooth and nail. Water boarding. Electrical shocks. Sexual humiliation. Threatened their kids. Jeez, this you'll like. This dyke Intel interrogator, she strung some guys up by their pricks. I tell you what, they would've told her the time of day if she had squeezed any tighter."

Patrons glanced at their table because of his loud voice, but it was doubtful he cared.

"What about your commanding officers?" asked Art. "Didn't they?"

"When the generals weren't sucking up to the politicians, damn right they knew."

Art sipped, mentally measuring Quintal's discourse for frankness. He thought the ex-soldier and CIA officer would talk about other subjects; none came.

The hazel eyes glinted, and the hand gestures became more frequent. "Tell you what else, Dodek. We shipped militants back to the States for questioning. Kidnapped the S.O.B's right out of their country. Bet you didn't know there are secret prisons in the States. And if we had to, we improvised locations. When we applied our techniques, they coughed up info that saved American lives…from terrorist attacks they were planning in this country. The White House knew what was going on. Hell, who do you think sanctioned the tactics?"

Art leaned back, motioning with his hand to tone it down,

Instead, Quintal's voice became gruffer, his face redder. "Whas' a matter? Don't like hearing the truth? What about your Canadian soldiers in Afghanistan? They abused Taliban detainees. Do you think it would have happened without government approval? Man, you're either naïve or stupid."

Art's fuse was fading. He balled his hands into fists. Decking the guy would have been an option if he weren't McLaughlin's new man in charge. Even Art's grim expression didn't make a difference to Quintal.

Picking up his cigar, Quintal started to flick his lighter when the bartender appeared at the table.

"Sir, there's no smoking on the premises. Put it out, please."

"For Christ's sake. How about another round?" He squished it out in an empty glass.

"Well, Dodek, whadya' say? You worked for the Mossad in Israel. Do you think they would stand by and let Palestinians get away with murder? What Jew wouldn't fight back? For a Jew, I thought you'd agree with me. Shit, you'd shoot just as much as me."

The waitress dropped another Scotch and Chardonnay; she avoided looking at Quintal.

Art had heard enough. Boss or not, he was seconds from pounding his chin. He stood up and stepped away from the table.

"Hey, Dodek. Where ya' going? C'mon, finish your drink."

"No, thanks. I have to go." Without explaining, he headed for the front, handed the waitress several bills, and left. He thought of a few choice words to describe Quintal's behavior, none of which would've sufficed.

Dusk came early in the Southland, casting its dark shadows between high rises and office towers. And headlights sparked alive, illuminating roadways with their weird colored light patterns.

Before going back to the apartment, he stopped at an Italian restaurant on Santa Monica Boulevard. When he relished pasta, like tonight, he'd choose it over his favorite kosher food. Two waiters tended to about six couples. He ordered linguini with an assortment of seafood — clams, mussels, scallops, and a glass of Verdiccio. While waiting, he munched on warm Kaiser rolls, and sipped the wine when it was served.

While dinner arrived hot and steaming, disappointment began from the first bite: bland rosé sauce and overcooked seafood. Hungry as he was, he forked his way through some edible portions. *Man*, he pondered for a moment, mentally smelling real pastas in Vancouver's "Little Italy" neighborhood on Commercial Drive. *Bella!*

Around 10 p.m., he plopped down on a couch and hit redial. Lynda's voice would cheer him up. After the third ring, an answering machine clicked on.

"I'm unable to take your call. Please leave your name and number so that I can call you."

He shifted himself to the edge, and checked the time. She was normally home at this time. "Lyndie, it's me. If you're home, pick up." No response. "Anyway…I'll try again. Love, cheers. Bye."

Standing on the patio, leaning against the railing, he felt the light breeze coming off the water. From his vantage point, he spotted couples strolling the boulevard. And, for the first time since arriving, an air of emptiness enveloped the deck. He called again twenty minutes later, canceling the connection before he heard her recorded voice. One thought after another kicked through his mind.

Chapter 27

The next morning, Mercado, just leaving the staff lounge, heard the thud-thud of footsteps behind her. Tracking the source wasn't difficult— McLaughlin, anger steaming in his eyes, confronted her.

"Agent Mercado, my office, now."

"Sure, Walter, what…?"

She left her coffee cup on a ledge and followed.

"I want an explanation," he said, banging the door shut.

As the Unit supervisor, she'd often taken heat from her boss, whether about deploying manpower effectively, miscommunication, or missed opportunities. Usually a reasonable clarification would lessen his bite or provide her extra time to resolve an issue. Sometimes it worked. Except when he would throw the phrase "You don't see the big picture" at her and launch a spiel that there was a right way and a wrong way, the latter generally being hers or anybody else's. This frantic behavior signaled something bigger.

They were not alone. She glanced to the right. Quintal, arms crossed, was standing underneath a relief map of Los Angeles. Quintal, not McLaughlin, sent the hairs on the back of her neck sailing. Unsure what he was referring to, she raised her hand as if to ask a question.

McLaughlin pointed a finger at her. "Who told you to question the prisoner in lockup?" He flipped open the jail visitor register. "This is your signature from last night. I gave you a direct order yesterday that the prisoner was to be left alone. Are you now defying my orders?"

"No. I had good reason to interview Husien Najaif. He provided critical information connected to our investigation, and I acted on it."

Both men looked at each other before he said, "What did…he tell you?"

"Where Muhamed Dauadi was hiding out."

Their eyes met again. Quintal dropped his arms and edged away from the desk.

"And you investigated?"

"Of course. Immediately."

"And it required all five members of the Unit?"

"Yes, it did. Dauadi is a wanted terrorist, armed and dangerous. Because of that, I wanted the full unit for back up."

"Did you locate him?" inquired Quintal.

"No." Mercado began to feel hemmed in. "You stay out of this. However, we found evidence that our subject fabricated explosive materials. And we arrested a tenant for harboring a fugitive. What is the big deal, Walter? You've told us to never overlook an opportunity essential to an investigation."

"So you took matters into your own hands. Didn't I say yesterday that you were to first check with Mr. Quintal and me to determine what action may be warranted?"

"While you two make up your minds, we could've lost any advantage we—"

"You don't decide," piped in Quintal. "I do."

"Walter's my boss, not *you*."

"That means you don't disobey my orders. Your foolishness has also caused a major predicament."

"Like what?"

"With the Department of Justice people, that's what. We already have material witnesses whose testimony may be jeopardized by agent screw-ups."

Mercado exploded. "What screw-up? What the hell is going on here? Are you accusing me of something?"

He clutched at his tie, and drew a circle with his forefinger.

"Did Dodek put you up to this?" Quintal asked, stepping closer.

"I authorized the interview. I approved the raid. And I don't appreciate being cross- examined."

"Well, let me put it this way," the director said. "I have the authority to take your badge away for disobeying my direct order."

"Would you?" she countered.

"Get out of my office. I'll deal with this later."

Mercado pursed her lips and departed. Hesitating in the hallway, she exhaled a deep breath of air in order to calm herself. Director and unit leader had argued before, but never to the degree of a few minutes ago. And what was up with Quintal butting in?

She gazed through the frosted window panel, making out the outlines of McLaughlin and Quintal huddling together, their discussion serious enough that fingers pointed at one another. No way were they talking about yesterday. Something else…or someone else…sparked the heated exchange.

Chapter 28

Muhamed Dauadi peered out the window from his second floor room at a hotel on Van

Horne Avenue two miles from downtown Los Angeles. Below, his view consisted of a parking lot between stores and another apartment. Two hookers trying to attract customers loped out to the road whenever cars passed by. A few streets over was bustling Korea Town, and not far away, ramshackle *barrios*. Office towers crowded the skies in the distance. Beyond, shrouded by the remnants of an early morning smog bank, Southland suburbs peeked below the hills to the east. Within minutes the sun swathed over the sidewalks teeming with curbside vendors, pedestrians, and panhandlers. Although the unpaved lot posted No Parking signs, he spotted his Mercedes where he'd parked it alongside a few derelict cars.

Inside, sparse furnishings—a double bed and one dresser with a mirror supported by a 2″ board nailed to the back—had become home for the Somalia Brotherhood recruiter. His location in South Pasadena had been compromised. His co-militants were dead or captured; that didn't worry him. Others would join in his fanatic pursuit of *watanabe* Islam. At this moment he had something more serious to deal with. Betrayal meant death to the betrayer, and he vowed revenge.

Death and revenge weren't strangers. It was a fact of life. More so when everyday became a battlefield, and which side you were on determined your survival.

Years ago as a child in Mogadishu he had witnessed countless terrorist acts. Friends, schoolmates, and some of his family were often victims of the never-ending civil wars and fractioning warlords rampant in Somalia. Association with one group during the day routinely changed to opposing sides by nighttime. Like many youths at the time swept up in the excitement, with easy access to firearms and desensitized to people dying, Muhamed the child became Muhamed the child-soldier, who could

155

strap on a grenade launcher and had no reluctance to fire it at persons who he was told were his enemies.

His parents couldn't control him as long as he remained running amok. Fleeing to America as a refugee became a dream...an expensive dream, but it couldn't come soon enough. The patriarch of the Dauadi family was a political member of the former Mogadishu government security service when it held some legitimacy; reason enough to contemplate leaving. All Muhamed knew about America were the stories of infidels defiling Islam, and scores of CNN newscasts of U.S. soldiers killing Taliban and al-Qaeda insurgents. What really pushed him over the edge was Operation Desert Storm, when the United States and United Nations forces ousted the Iraqi army from Kuwait, and later when the U.S. invaded Iraq, then Afghanistan. From then on his hatred for America intensified to the point it became fanatical. The more he participated with resistance organizations, the more his name spread. Soon members of his mosque recruited him to fight outside of Somalia, such as in neighboring Kenya and further south in Yemen. Taught how to rig electronic devices and assemble bomb making materials, Westerners were his favorite targets — contractors, teachers, store owners, aid workers, engineers, contractors, Blackwater security personnel.

When he returned home, relations with parents and younger siblings grew too hostile. He found better company by staying with his true militant friends.

One day the imam at a local mosque introduced the budding teenage terrorist to the Brotherhood of Somalia Jihad leader, Saleh Ali Nabhat Saleh. Despite the title, Saleh Ali wasn't Somali. Speculation abounded he was Moroccan, or Algerian. No one knew his actual origin.

A Canadian citizen, he traveled to Minneapolis, Buffalo, New York, and Newark, New Jersey, with brief stops in Toronto and Montreal. These trips were for one purpose — to recruit Somali-born American and Canadian citizen youths, and pay for their way to Afghanistan and Pakistan via friendly allies for terrorist schooling. Then six months later, ship them back to North America as indoctrinated Jihad warriors. It was also reported that he held a high position with Saudi combatants who fought against American troops in Iraq, and once sat alongside Osama bin Laden's inner counsel circle. After bin Laden died in a shoot-out with U.S. Navy Seals in a compound outside Islamabad, Pakistan, he turned his alliances to the Taliban insurgents in Afghanistan. In time, he crawled his way up to lead the Somali Brotherhood insurgents. In his circle, you could buy your way in, eliminate your opponents, and take control.

Saleh Ali's orders were simple and direct: plan, coordinate, prepare, and attack. Each firebrand speech concluded with, *"A special place in heaven awaits the Jihadist pledging his life for martyrdom."*

156

With money saved, eventually the day arrived for the Dauadi family to flee Somalia. Leaving Africa was the easy part; bribes paid their way across the continent. Before 9-11 and massive transportation reforms in traveling to Europe and to the United States became restrictive, refugees could enter America from a Third World country and generally encounter no problem when applying for asylum. Depending on your country of origin and a well-founded fear of persecution, you would be granted approval and eventual permanent residency. Of the entire family, a "green card" meant the most to young Muhamed. Five years later, like his entire family intended, they applied for naturalization and became U.S. citizens. And planned for the future.

His plans didn't include his parents working two jobs and saving for the younger Dauadi children's college funds. First settling in New York, then relocating to Minneapolis, which already had an established Somali community, without an education or any professional skills, he discovered employment opportunities were limited, usually low paying and menial. This drove him further into excluding himself from Americans and what he believed were their sinful life styles. Devoutly religious, he was convinced that the U.S. mistreated Muslims. Expanding its military presence in Afghanistan and threatening to chase terrorists into Pakistan couldn't be more sinister or unforgivable. Then on a warm Tuesday morning, al-Qaeda launched the worst terrorist attacks in U.S. history, which claimed over three thousand lives. Joyful, he sent messages to the families of the nineteen terrorists, praising their sons' martyrdom.

On his last visit to his parents' home, Dauadi accused his father of being a traitor to Islam by condemning the terrorists and choosing Western ideals instead of adhering to the sacrifices ordered by the Prophet. It meant nothing to him that he was forbidden to ever again set foot in the family home. More important work lay ahead.

In Minneapolis he became known as the "Agitator" who recruited disenfranchised Somali youths, filled their heads with anti-Western rhetoric, organized protests, and led dozens of anti-American demonstrations. No intention of their being just peaceful marches, he and his cohorts deliberately clashed with police. News of the arrests was often carried on Arabic TV channels in the Middle East. Before the Somalia Brotherhood Association was declared a terrorist organization, it paid for the demonstrators' bail and their fines.

However, these protests were inconsequential to what his mentor and Dauadi had in mind. He decided to apply Saleh Ali militancy with al-Shabad teachings and his guerrilla training to the next level—attacking Americans on their own soil.

Aligned with other naturalized American-Somalis, some headed eastward. Dauadi went west—Los Angeles became his home base—and began recruiting trusted friends who would commit themselves to al-Shabat extremism. What they lacked were weapons and large caches of ammunition. Enter the Russian mob. Handguns to automatic machine guns, C-4 to PETIN explosive materials, the Brotherhood spared no expense. Saleh Ali Nabhat Saleh paid the bills with cash obtained from donations from clandestine charity organizations in Europe, plus benefactors in the United States, and profits from ransoms paid by ocean freighter companies held hostage by Somali pirates. Logistics fell onto Dauadi's lap. He was adept at observing, always alert to people movements, time of day or night for certain events, particularly westernized activities. But to most Angelinos, he was one of hundreds of young Muslim males strolling alone on the streets of Los Angeles.

Chapter 29

Christmas Day,
Seventeen Months Earlier

Before the rampage in Beverly Hills and the bombing of the military contractor offices, Saleh Ali had established plans to hit a target unharmed to date.

Early Christmas Day afternoon, Dauadi and two twenty-something Somalis hot-wired a pickup truck in Hollywood; destination…the University of California Los Angeles campus (UCLA). No one spoke as he drove west. Words played in their heads, not from their lips. Dialogue had ended days ago after exhausting rehearsals. Choosing the day also had significance.

He parked about a half mile from the main UCLA entrance to avoid cameras spotting the vehicle. Each person carried a backpack and gathered at the rear tailgate. Dauadi emptied his bag. While the others watched, he disassembled three cell phones and clipped and taped wires to putty-size packs of C-4. He poured hydrogen peroxide liquid into juice containers, and then transferred them into each person's bag. He set a range of numbers in the phones' circuit boards and snapped everything together. A separate phone device protruded from his jacket.

Although this was Christmas break, many students lived on campus. Three East African young men blended in well with the diverse student population as they strode along pathways lined with lights and bulbs flashing on posts and shrubs. The morning had begun windy and bleak, and now moisture filled the air. Just like most of those they passed, windbreakers and parkas helped to ward off the afternoon chill.

Strolling further onto the grounds and distancing themselves from study halls and classroom huts and the library, a building of interest adjacent to a pond and footbridge came into view. His research included which structure and Christmas-themed event would be occurring today that would attract a fairly large audience.

Ahead stood the campus's highest building, a ten-story co-ed residence. Seasonal banners hung below archways and around the doors. Once inside, they made their way down a long corridor and entered a large recreation room. Christmas lights sparkled on two artificial trees, one on each side of the hall. Ribbons and strings of blinking bulbs were strung along the walls. Papier-mâché decorations lining the ceiling enhanced the festive atmosphere. Between the trees a fifty-inch television was showing *It's a Wonderful Life*, which was being watched intently by about sixty students of various nationalities, thirty on each side sitting in chairs divided by an aisle. Nearby tables contained snacks, mini-sandwiches, a vegetable tray, fruit and cheese plates, two punch bowls, and beers chilling on ice in large metal containers. They had everything handy for a festive afternoon of treats and a movie. Most of the ceiling lights were dimmed for added atmosphere.

Hardly anyone noticed three extra young men joining the crowd. Separating from his comrades, Dauadi strode down the aisle while his co-insurgents marched along the walls and laid down the backpacks. A crease formed along his mouth as he gazed at the students, which included several African and Middle Eastern men and women. Three young Arabic girls huddled and giggled about six rows over; none wore the traditional Muslim chador garment or head coverings. *How could they subject themselves to unholy Western Godliness?* he snarled, returning to the back of the room. Alcohol in their presence made him livid.

Once in a while a student would wander over for a snack or cold drink and hurry back to his seat, passing classmates munching on appetizers and sipping vodka and cranberry-juice punch.

Dauadi signaled the young men by rubbing his hands vertically.

When the movie reached the part where the little girl mentioned that an angel received his wings, all three men reached down and whipped out Sauer military-type machine gun pistols. With super-fast precision, all three started firing at the TV viewers. At first, some thought firecrackers had exploded. Not until bullets slammed into several students did screaming echo in the rows closest to the gunmen. Armor piercing shells ripped apart flesh as clouds of gray smoke began billowing over the hall. Some tried to duck behind chairs, unable to block bullets, or lunged to the floor, falling over persons who fell before them. Flying shells smashed apart the TV screen. Ornaments and light bulbs shattered.

Now they changed to a crisscross firing formation, hitting couples trying to jump clear. Persons in middle rows caught the brunt of the machine gun fire. Dauadi, at the rear, fired point-blank at anyone attempting to breach the entrance. Screaming intensified. Sounds of sobbing and praying filtered between toppled chairs.

Among those cut down were the three Muslim students. *Odd*, he observed, *their faces seemed at peace, not fearful of their fate when death unleashed its fury.*

Discharged shell casings became dangerous objects as students tripped over them in their attempts to crouch along the walls. Cries for mercy went oblivious to the shooters. After dispensing three bullet clips apiece, they rushed to the hallway. A couple running down a staircase adjoining the party room were killed before they neared the landing.

At the doorway, Dauadi ordered his fellow militants to stay inside and shoot anyone trying to escape. The Somali brothers obeyed, taking up positions at each side of the entrance. He shouted at them in Arabic that he would announce the all clear, and when they heard it to run out outside.

He raced outside and tossed his weapon into the pond. Moving quickly as he strode parallel to the library, he pulled out the rigged cell phone. One, two, three number buttons pressed in that order, he detonated the improvised explosives hidden inside the backpacks.

A thunderous roar as the ground shook preceded the first explosion, followed by a snarling yellow fireball that blew apart the entire front of the residence. Bits of wood panels and chunks of bricks landed across the lawn. Mushrooming white and gray smoke drifted skyward. Windows three and four levels up shattered as though a furnace boiler had exploded. Horrified students rushed out from adjoining buildings, helpless, unable to enter the fire-ravaged recreation hall. Seconds later, the third blast ripped through the upper floor residences. Devilish flickering flames curled out of the windows. Ungodly bursts of screaming followed. Except for flying embers and collapsing walls, a strange silence soon followed.

Without glancing around, Dauadi felt the heat of the fires on his shoulders. Emotionless and stone-faced, he even pointed up the bluff to fire engines racing toward the gates. A light shower started, coating the lawn in multi-colored raindrops that reflected from the Christmas bulbs. Little could it do to quell the raging fires.

Within minutes, he throttled the truck's engine and flipped up the cover of his cell phone. His smile increased when he replayed the horror at UCLA.

News reports that followed stated the student death toll exceeded seventeen, and over thirty-six wounded. Police called in the FBI because of alleged terrorism; investigators confirmed that some fatalities were from gunshot wounds. However, authorities were unsure which terrorist group pulled off the "despicable, cowardly" attack. Whether foreign-

161

inspired or domestic, university and city flags were ordered lowered in memory of those who perished.

Ali Saleh and Muhamed Dauadi weren't finished. UCLA proved the Brotherhood could strike without fear or consequences. A second attack would hit the U.S. where it mattered most: the judicial system.

Filling spots vacant from brothers killed in the name of Allah wasn't difficult. Dauadi had fighters lining up at the door — whether local Somalis or recruited from the east — who would join his crusade against the infidels.

Chapter 30

Downtown Los Angeles

The morning after Christmas Dauadi and two young Somali-Americans headed into central Los Angeles. With an extended holiday, government offices were closed. For usually clogged freeways, the trio had an easy drive transitioning freeway to freeway. Similarly, the Toyota Camry stolen at gunpoint earlier had posed no problem either—three guns pointed at the driver's head convinced him to give up the vehicle.

Because of a backup in another current terrorism trial, federal authorities decided to reconvene court for the sentencing phase. Two former Pakistani college students, who had acted independently to blow up a National Guard barracks in Riverside County but belonged to the same al-Qaeda "sleeper cell," would learn that the courts invoked harsh penalties.

Taking up positions on a grassy knoll across the street from the courthouse, Dauadi's group blended in with dozens of Muslim protestors ringing the building and waving banners demanding the defendants be released. Three bicycle officers observed from down the street. Nearby, hidden by TV news vans, police officers in riot gear maintained watch on the demonstrators. Traffic had been redirected away from the surrounding area. And, so far, the chanting was boisterous and noisy, with most of the protestors playing to the TV news cameras. One of the sunniest days this December, most men just wore shirts or light jackets.

Neither Dauadi nor his compatriots watching the procession commented or showed the slightest interest. They moved about ten yards to the left in order to avoid being filmed.

From his perch, he paid keen attention to deputy sheriffs and security guards screening everyone entering the lobby; in particular, the amount of time each person, including women, was subjected to the electronic wand inspection as well as closer body search. He undid his backpack and set it down. Two Muslim women in their long, black outer garments and veils stood in the line, about five persons back from the checkpoint. Their presence aroused no suspicion. Only minutes away from the first deputy, one of the women tilted her head.

That was the sign Dauadi had waited for. He yanked back the zipper.

The women's turn arrived for screening. In a polite voice, the nearest deputy asked them to come forward. His expression spoke volumes: did religious freedom supersede uncovering faces and undergoing a body search, especially for Muslim women?

Across the street, three Somalis reached into the open backpack, withdrew .45 automatics, stepped down from the bluff onto the roadway, and started firing. Bullets struck several people in the line, wedging them between the doorways. With precise aim the women weren't hit, having stepped away from the entrance as instructed.

The bicycle officers dashed up the stairs. One tripped as a civilian pushed him aside. A second officer fell as a bullet ripped through his thigh. Demonstrators ran for cover where none existed. A couple got hit in the line of fire.

One of the Muslim women spun around, facing people waiting to enter. Her partner ran past the security guards. They screamed out the prophet Allah's name, then both lifted up their garments and pressed the red triggers on their suicide vests.

For a few seconds, it seemed time stood still before the ten pounds of dynamite each woman had strapped to their chests exploded. Igniting flames swirled and encircled the two suicide bombers and everyone at the check point, people already cleared who were standing in the lobby, and those in line on the courthouse landing. Deafening roars shook lamp poles on the street, and flames lit tree branches afire. TV crews, attempting to film the demonstrators, dropped their cameras, fleeing a large ball of fire chasing them onto the road.

By now, Dauadi and his confederates were replacing bullet clips to continue firing, hitting anyone rushing toward the knoll.

Shots rang out beside them. The youngest Somali grimaced at Dauadi as he went down, bullets slicing through one cheek and straight out through his neck.

The cops in riot gear shouted at Dauadi and the second shooter to drop their weapons. To reinforce their commands, they fired off M-16 rounds over their heads and feet. This persuaded Dauadi to lower his gun. The other man, though, turned and fired at the nearest cop. A shotgun blast slammed into the man's chest. The force of the shell ripped apart his breastbone, jerking him sideward twice before he fell ass-first onto the sidewalk.

Blood rushing out of the cavity in his chest, he weakly cried out, "Mohamed...help. I...I've been shot," and slowly leaned backward.

Three cops surrounded Dauadi, pistols and a carbine aimed at his head.

"Don't shoot," he bleated like a child about to be slapped. "Don't hurt me. I give up."

Beside him, his partner, writhing and yelling in agony, groaned, "Muhamed...save me, save me."

The cop with the shotgun aimed it inches from Dauadi's forehead. As another officer grabbed his .45, the Somali gripped the shotgun barrel and pushed it downward. The officer was unable to remove his finger from the trigger, and the blast tore apart the face of Dauadi's fellow militant.

"You mother-fucker!" the officer growled.

Pushed to the ground, Dauadi sneered, "You killed a wounded man...Allah condemns you to hell." Regardless of the hate-fueled stares of the cops, he began laughing when they flipped him over and cuffed his wrists. It wasn't an act of kindness that he deliberately killed his injured partner—not with a chance that the Somali might've confessed to the Brotherhood's whereabouts and fingered other cell members.

Infidels arresting him and hauling him into court on terrorist charges never entered his mind. The police didn't scare him; the thought of prison didn't frighten him. Within twenty-four hours he had established that the Brothers of Somali Jihad could attack American institutions at whim, wherever, whenever.

***

Reminiscing ended. Inside the hotel room, Dauadi unpacked a duffel bag. Contents included jeans, a fleece top, a few undergarments, some grooming supplies, a fully loaded .45 automatic, and a screw-on silencer.

Chapter 31

"Stay right there, Agent Dodek," Mercado said, sauntering into the Analysis Center and waved to Noordine translating Twitter boards on her computers. She flipped through several pages in her file folder.

Art looked up from his chair behind a desktop monitor.

In a serious voice, she added, "Have I got news for you. Let me put it this way—it stinks. Our legal team ordered the release of the massage parlor proprietor. Her being on site with alleged criminal activity—I'm not talking about the sex acts—in no way, as they stated, involved her knowledge. Guess what. She contacted the ACLU; she claims we violated her civil rights."

"B.S., Consuela. She was conscious of what the Somalis were up to."

"Can't be legally proven."

"What about the Arab from South Pasadena? When we found—"

"We found squat. A shed full of suspected materials does not a criminal charge make. A sharp attorney would quash everything as inadmissible. We can hold him up to seventy-two hours, hoping he'll admit to something, and then he's gone. The attorney general has to decide whether it's worth pursuing. That's the way it is."

"Sounds as though your Patriot Act has loopholes. Your witness list is getting thin."

She shrugged her shoulders. "We had a witness—Tariq—from Dream Girls; he's history."

"Yeah; convenient, isn't it, his suicide."

"Don't be so sure. I've got the medical examiner's death report. Look here. Strangulation killed him, but the M.E. discovered some injuries pre-mortem. Deep cuts on both wrists, likely due to tight binding, and several searing scars on his chest from electrical burns."

"Tariq was tortured before taking his life."

"Unsubstantiated so far," she closed the folder, "but they sure point to it."

"When?"

"Question is…who?"

"You realize the only witness we have to connect Dauadi as ringleader of the Brother-hood and leading the attacks is Najaif."

"He's isolated and under twenty-four-hour special guard — nobody's getting near him except us. What is it, Art? You look like you're unraveling something in your mind."

"Uh…no."

"Kind of seemed like it. Oh, forgot. I'm going to ask you a question; don't you say no."

"Uh, okay."

"Join me for dinner tonight? I mean, at my place. I'm a good cook, you know." She tapped the folder, anticipating his response.

"Well…."

"I'll text you the address. And I'll be back later." Both Consuela and Noordine waved goodbye as she turned and walked toward the exit.

Mack Quintal brushed past her in the corridor; she kept going and didn't say anything.

Art was shutting down a computer when he strode into the room, marching in as though he was going to have a powwow with his military battalion lieutenants.

"Dodek, stay where you are — I want to talk to you."

Art sighed. Not again.

***

Muhamed Dauadi wasn't alone at the rundown hotel.

Reclining on a titled chair, a beast of a man in his late fifties, pockmarked and square-jawed, just a puff of blond hair on an otherwise bald head, ignored the Somali as he strolled to the washroom. Everything he wore was black, from his suit to his polished and properly laced shoes. Only his royal purple tie and white shirt offset the dark fabrics. Deep-set blue eyes remained fixed to the pages of a Russian newspaper. Where Dauadi was medium height, sinewy, not over one hundred fifty pounds, this guy outweighed him by at least eighty to ninety pounds and looked like he ate nails for breakfast. Prior to the Soviet Union undergoing *Perestroika* in 1990, it was not hard to believe he might have served as some government official's bodyguard or a KGB enforcer.

***

Dauadi took a pair of scissors and hacked off his scraggly hair, then proceeded to snip the beard from his chin. When he got to whiskers and uneven top hair, he flooded the sink with hot water. Using foam from a bar of hand soap, he cleared the chin whiskers with a disposable razor, finishing by trimming his dark hair. Without much of a glance, he checked his appearance. He flushed it all down the toilet — scraps from the beard and locks of hair, as well as the razor.

167

Undressing out of the jeans and shirt, he grabbed a dark suit from a garment bag hanging over the shower bar. The transformation completed, the Somali Brother of Jihad resembled any businessman traversing the hallways of Wilshire Boulevard office towers, with one major difference: a .45 automatic was tucked into his waistband.

When he returned to the living room, the Russian tossed aside the newspaper, jumped up, and joined him at the door. Outside, he aimed the Mercedes CL 450 for the street, glaring at two women, whom he considered whores and sinners of Islam, as they rushed up to his car.

***

Quintal leaned over Art's desk, and was just glad his breath didn't reek of Scotch. "You'd better adhere to department procedures or pack up and go home," he exclaimed.

Art leaned back, waiting for another verbal barrage.

"I re-read your report from Thursday's raid. Are you incompetent or what?"

"What, exactly, are you talking about?"

Quintal stood erect, tapping his crossed arms. Military style crisp creases lined his teal blue shirt. "Senior Agent Mercado is your team leader. There's no mention of your consulting with her prior to your Sergeant Preston of the Yukon escapade forced entry into Encada Engineering. You've been summoned here to assist with locating Ali Saleh, not to take it upon yourself to bust into offices whenever you feel like it."

"With civilian lives in danger, all of us involved decided to conclude the matter, whatever the consequences. Terrorists don't always discuss the situation, you know. Ever hear of them playing nice? We were in the midst of having our asses blown off from the—"

"I could give a rat's ass." Quintal dropped his arms. The more contentious he became, the higher his voice rose and his eyes bulged. "Wherever you go, there are casualties. Haven't you ever heard of minimal reduction of fatalities when you're in a firefight?"

"That wasn't my—or the Unit's—call," Art countered, getting to his feet. "Did you read the complete report? Consuela's? From Dan Curbside? We had no recourse but to respond with deadly fire. It got messy…what did you expect? Minimizing fatalities was our objective. It took a while, but we managed to deploy our assets with the goal of taking control of the situation."

Analysts and other unit staffers strayed from their workstations, focusing their attention on the shouting match.

When Quintal pushed the Jewish button by inferring the Mossad should've kicked him out of Israel, Art brought up his arm and curled a fist, but kept it near his waist.

The gesture infuriated Quintal. His body stiffened, and he held his hands as if he was about to clutch some inanimate object. "I don't like the way you operate, Dodek. In fact, I'd like to throw your Jewish ass out of my department."

Your department? My ass? The button was pushed.

The two men were now within striking distance of each other, just like boxers waiting for the round one bell. Employees stood, anticipating a donnybrook. Across the room, Noordine cringed, worried that their argument would escalate into an all-out fight.

Like crouching tigers, first one then the other extended their hands sideways and spun into martial arts stances. Now it became a staring match. Neither moved an inch or lowered an eyeball. Even their breathing seemed suspended; a church couldn't have been any quieter.

Quintal sneered. A smile creased the corners of his mouth. "We will...we will meet again." He ended the suspension by lowering his arms and, without taking his eyes off Art, nonchalantly departed.

Art exhaled and sat down. A giant sigh of relief floated throughout the Analysis complex. What most didn't see was his expression indicating there *would* be.

He happened to glance toward the doorway. Smiling, Mercado threw him a circled thumb and finger.

Chapter 32

Two dark-suited men wandering through the sixth floor corridors of federal offices wouldn't garner much attention. Unsmiling, bored faces exhibited by Muhamed Dauadi and the Russian were typical of government employees passing by. No difficulty, either, making it into the DHS. In fact, Dauadi thought it ironic: the agency commissioned to secure America's protection lacked anything remotely akin to security. They waltzed through two layers of armed guards without encountering the slightest resistance. His research also revealed the locations of administrative offices, communication and analysis centers, as well as the detention section; even the placements of video cameras.

Marching up to the outer holding room, he displayed a card from the attorney general's office. The Russian flashed a badge identifying him as a U.S. Marshal. Automatic doors slid open.

Two officers manned the booth—a paunchy, middle aged male and a younger woman who pointed to the register on the counter.

Dauadi scribbled signatures in the visitor log.

The inner doors opened, granting them entry to the holding rooms.

He displayed a set of government documents, including seals and names attributed to the attorney general and Justice Department. Unfortunately, the guards wouldn't know fake certificates from USDA food ingredient brochures.

Dauadi spoke without any accent. Maintaining his official persona, he said, "I'm here to take possession of the prisoner Husien Najaif. These documents order his release. He's to be relocated to another facility."

"Okay, okay," said the overweight officer, reaching for a telephone. "But we have orders, too. We've been instructed to notify DHS for anyone wanting to see him. I'll call, and—"

"You disobeying the orders of the Department of Justice? I want the name of your superior. Either bring him out *now*, or I'll have you reprimanded."

Not sure how to reply, the guard looked over at his partner. When she nodded, he said, "Okay, okay. Wait here." He buzzed open the inner doors and disappeared down a hallway. A couple of minutes later he escorted a handcuffed, bewildered looking teenager to the counter. Although confused, to Najaif, the two strangers were just other agents of the government.

Dauadi's black-suited, non-speaking partner placed his beefy hands on the teenager's shoulder. Applying force, he edged him toward the outer corridor.

Noticing the female officer examining the documents, Dauadi quickened his pace and walked closely beside Najaif. The lad, sandwiched between them, now started feeling apprehensive. Their stern expressions set off alarms in his mind. When he tried to back up, two big hands gripping his arms pushed him forward, hard.

"W–where are you taking me?" he asked, faltering.

His escorts didn't reply.

About two yards from an exit staircase, the paunchy guard lumbered toward the trio. "Hey, you forgot to sign out of the visitor log," he said, handing the book to Dauadi. "It's DHS policy."

As Dauadi grabbed the pen affixed to the book, he drilled it into the guard's thick neck. The officer's body shook. He gasped and clutched at his fatty neck. Inserted with enough force that the top of the pen hid behind rolls of skin, it dug in deeper until it was yanked out. A stream of blood spiraled across the wall. More of a squeal than a scream flowing between his lips, the officer tried to grip the Somali's shoulder for balance, but didn't have the strength. Dauadi withdrew his gun from his waistband. He shoved it between the man's ribs and fired. Even with a silencer, the retort boomed down the hallway.

Najaif looked on, horror reflected on his face. Only the Russian holding him kept him from collapsing.

The guard toppled to the floor like a carcass of beef, his legs kicking out into space. His partner dashed from behind the counter. A second shot pierced her clavicle. In detention, jailers did not carry weapons or wear protective body armor. She clutched her chest and bounced backward against the inner steel door. Coughing up blood, she dropped, knees first, to the floor.

Dauadi and the Russian dragged the teen to the corridor exit. Using the elevator wasn't an option. It would take too long, and if passengers were aboard, coupled with Najaif's desperation, the situation could've turned deadly.

Just as they scurried behind the fire door and reached the staircase, the female officer managed to press the security alarm, then sunk, unconscious, to the ground. The shrill siren blasted away at eardrums. For fire and rescue purposes, the doors remained unlocked.

Najaif's body recoiled in horror, then he froze. Despite him being close-shaven, shorthaired, and wearing a business suit, Dauadi's trademark earring finally identified him to the teen.

***

Agents and staff members flew out of their offices, horrified to find the dead jailers. Art and Consuela, followed by Reeves and Curbside, guns drawn, dashed into the hallway. Consuela darted past the detention security doors and checked the cells, in disbelief to find Najaif's cell wide open. Even with everybody yelling, voices couldn't drown out the ear-splitting siren.

McLaughlin and Quintal rushed into the hallway.

"What the hell happened?" the director shouted. "What's going on here? Somebody turn off that damn alarm."

Curbside stepped over the female officer's body and switched it off while Aylesha brought out her cell phone and pressed the security code for the entire federal building.

"Husien Najaif is missing," Mercado said, holstering her side arm as she returned to her partners.

Reeves and Curbside checked for the pulses of the two guards; they just shook their heads, knowing both were dead.

McLaughlin exploded. "What the fuck are you talking about? Missing? You've gotta be kidding…this is a secure section."

"I just…don't get it. I'm as mystified as you are, Walter."

His face was red as the flesh of a grapefruit. He and Quintal exchanged looks…not out of concern for the officers; rather, that the Somali teenager might say what had happened to him.

"Aren't you in charge of security?" he yelled at her. "How could somebody just walk in here and snatch a prisoner?"

"It figures…Mexicans…you can't trust them," Quintal said.

"What the hell did you say?" Mercado snarled.

"Do you want me to repeat it?" Art stepped between them when Mercado balled up her fists.

"We'll check the tapes," Curbside said in an attempt to cool down his team leader. "They're bound to show who breached security."

"Do it," McLaughlin ordered. "Move. Get busy." He glowered at Mercado, and then he and Quintal sauntered down the hallway.

"Dan, Aylesha, collect the videos," Mercado said. "Art, what have you got?"

"These documents I found on the counter. They're from the Department of Justice, ordering that Husien Najaif be released into its custody."

172

She flipped through the pages. On closer examination, she picked out a number of grammatical errors, as though a person with limited English ability had typed it out. She swore in Spanish as she shook the papers. "Look at the names…the signatures. Signed by the assistant attorney general. Like hell. I know him, and this isn't his name."

"The visitor log," Art added, gingerly picking up the bloodstained book. "Last entries. Phony as the release order."

"Unfortunately, they fooled the officers. Damn, why didn't they contact us before…?"

***

Downstairs, Dauadi, the Russian, and Najaif were three of dozens of people scurrying about on the main floor. Security personnel and several police officers, interspersed among the crowd, did their best to keep vigilance. Two suits with a handcuffed prisoner didn't warrant much attention.

As they approached the exit, a deputy sheriff manning the security kiosk confronted the trio. Shaking, Najaif was too scared to say anything.

Almost shoving his fake government ID in the cop's face, Dauadi explained that they had orders to relocate a terrorist suspect to a maximum-security center.

The deputy mulled it over and waved them on. Because of the throngs of people on the front steps, he lost sight of which direction they headed before disappearing.

Seconds later, Art and Consuela raced through the lobby. None of the security officers they checked with reported anything suspicious. Within a few minutes of searching they knew the hunt was futile, and returned to the sixth level.

***

Dauadi spent the next hour driving around Los Angeles. Some streets he traveled twice. Some areas he would slow, as if looking for a particular place. He'd enter a freeway, only to exit a few miles ahead, then retrace his previous tracks. His passengers weren't interested. One, still in handcuffs and trembling non-stop, uttered an occasional question. The driver remained tight-lipped, occasionally gazing back to eye his prisoner. Still burned in Najaif's memory was that just days ago he was thrown into a car and physically abused. This trip was different. He knew who'd snatched him from the jail.

A mammoth structure appeared on the horizon. Dauadi sped into the large parking lot adjoining Dodger Stadium, gunning the motor as he wheeled around in circles. Not another vehicle or person was visible anywhere, just an old Dodger game program cart wheeling on the light breeze. Pulling over, Dauadi jumped out and opened the rear passenger door. The Russian pushed the frightened teen out next to Dauadi, who took his arm and strolled about thirty feet from the Mercedes.

For the first time, Najaif, stammering, managed to speak. "M– Muhamed, why are we here?"Dauadi placed a hand on the boy's shoulder. "Stop shaking, Brother. You have nothing to fear. No one can hurt you. You are free from the infidels."

"Have I not done what you wanted of me, and attacked at the heart of corrupt America as you taught me?"

The Russian strolled around his side.

"Yes. But you betrayed the Brotherhood. The Prophet Allah has cast you to hell." That was the cue.

A nylon cord wound around the youth's neck. Eyes bulging, legs quivering, he almost bit through his tongue as the cord tightened until his feet kicked out in a wild frenzy. Nothing could hold him up, and he slid to the pavement.

The Russian loosened the rope when the boy's movements ended.

Together Dauadi and the Russian started heading to the Mercedes. Stopping part way there, Dauadi pulled a thick envelope out of his suit breast pocket and handed it to his partner.

Tearing it apart revealed a bundle of U.S. $100 bills, which his associate never got to count; nor did he spot the .45 automatic rising toward his head. A bullet fired at close range pierced his left eye. The retort echoed across the empty lot.

Dauadi reclaimed the envelope and returned to his car. Before driving off, he placed a short, two-toned green blanket with black threads lining its edges on the ground, knelt down facing east, and prayed.

***

Analysts at DHS were relieved that the color and clarity surfaced as they pored over three videotapes from the detention center. Every inch of the tapes was scrutinized and inspected frame by frame on fast speed and slow speed, paused, forwarded, and rewound. Flanked by Mercado's unit members, they studied the figures again and again until they could almost memorize features displayed on three split TV monitors. Initial reels showed the two guards stationed inside the lock up. A view of the corridor revealed two men in suits approaching, some form of identification flashed, and distinct blue government papers handed over, followed by the confrontation, signing the register, and Husien Najaif being taken past the security doors. Gasps broke the silence when the live images of the officers being shot flashed on the screen. Enhancing zoomed in on the faces of the phony government duet. Agents rubbed shoulders as they all bent forward, their universal puzzled looks wondering who the men were. All agreed the hulky guy could've been Eastern European, or Russian. The thinner, Middle Eastern or African man posed the problem.

174

Art suggested performing a face recognition analysis with pictures of known terrorist suspects in computer databases. Five minutes of flashing the faces of multiple nationalities went by without a match. Then up popped the Somali brotherhood recruiter, Muhamed Dauadi. Indicators on the screen examined features of the shorthaired, clean-shaven man to his original picture. The words "Match Found" flashed over both revolving Dauadi photographs. The two comparisons clicked together into one picture when two screens displayed the familiar earring. Art and Consuela shook their heads, speechless, wondering how the hell he and the Russian had breached security and invaded the secure DHS detention section. And, just yards from the offices, they had succeeded in kidnapping a prisoner. What kind of man were they dealing with? What point was there to counter-terrorism when he could thumb his nose right under them?

A woman handed Mercado a note.

"What is it?" asked Art, seeing her glum expression.

"You and Tony, get over to Dodger Stadium. Husien Najaif...." She crumbled the paper. "He's been found dead. Go. Police are waiting."

Before the elevator closed on the agents, Art's last image of his partner was her right fist clenched, tapping the side of her hand against her chin.

Later, he identified the Somali teenager's body. He didn't want to sympathize with Najaif's death—after all, he belonged to a militant group who pursued martyrdom, yet had died for his association. Whoever strangled him had used such force it almost severed the boy's neck. Muhamed Dauadi was a killer, but he didn't possess the physical strength to cause that much damage. The ox in the black suit, with a hole in his head where his left eye used to be, had to have been the one who choked Najaif.

A cop gave Art the large man's wallet. As he speculated, cards and a driver's license indicated the guy was Russian, likely hired by the Jihadi Brotherhood. It wasn't difficult to figure out what occurred. The teen died in retaliation for giving up the safe house in South Pasadena. Russian mobsters were often hired as assassins, paid in U.S. dollars, of course, most often astronomical sums. After the grisly attack, Dauadi had cleaned house by executing the executioner.

He picked up the .45 shell casing with a pen and handed it over to one of the forensic technicians. As Agent Curbside wrapped up his note taking, Art wondered if Najaif had any next-of-kin in the U.S. The last known whereabouts of most of the young Somalis who died for the Brotherhood was frequently the address of their family, who either never reported their sons missing or were too afraid to contact the authorities until it was too late, often when FBI agents showed up and told them their children had been arrested for terrorist conspiracy.

Chapter 33

Following the Ford's voice-activated GPS, Art exited the 10 East Interstate in Alhambra and swung a right on the second street, passing Asian mall after mall, stores, shops, and restaurants, all of which appeared affluent and thriving. Heading south for about a mile, its final instruction said to make a left and proceed a quarter mile. The three streets he passed all contained the prefix Vista, followed by the Spanish names *Norte'*, *Camino, and Del Sol*, followed by streets named after trees, such as Spruce and Ponderosa. After parking behind a Dodge Caliber, he locked his firearm in the glove box. For no particular reason, he checked the dashboard clock to the time on his wristwatch—twenty-two minutes shy of eight p.m. In khakis and a light shirt, minus the confining body armor, and except for the odd ping in his back, he felt as though his body had taken a reprieve from its aches and pains. The three OTC pills taken before leaving Santa Monica had kicked in.

Low cut evergreens ringed the one story bungalow. One side of the lawn had escaped withering from the daytime heat. A row of blooming marigolds lined the short sidewalk. Assorted trimmed and flourishing rose bushes bordered a neighboring home. Reddish and pink geraniums lifted their petals to the last rays of the fading sun. More grew alongside the house, as well as in containers on the front porch. A flotilla of petals lay scattered on the landing. From the outside the house appeared in good shape, looked after. He estimated the place was about thirty or forty years old and similar to surrounding homes, its front doors and windows were fortified behind iron bars and railings.

Consuela must've seen him coming up the pebble-covered walkway. Smiling, she greeted him and accepted a bottle of wine. Her hair, pulled back and tied with a red bow, complemented her low-necked, knee-length summer dress. Tear-shaped earrings gleamed from the reflection of two table lamps. He thought she looked dazzling. "Glad you made it," she said, cupping his elbow and leading him to the living room.

While not upscale, the interior's beige walls, its several scroll-framed mirrors, and leather and oak furnishings, radiated comfort. Surprised, he didn't notice an abundance of Mexican styled artifacts or fixtures. The majority of photographs and paintings depicted more of a Latino influence. Next to the dining room, a desk and a computer equipment table were swamped in notepaper, pads, and assorted gadgets. Two semi-large pictures graced the desk; one a family group, the other a beautiful teenaged Consuela.

She bade him to take a seat; a two cushion smaller sofa was the closest, and he plopped down, resting one leg over the other. He heard glasses being filled in the kitchen, and a musical score from *The Soul of Spain* performed by the 101 Orchestra playing in the background. Melodic and stirring, strings and horns blended together to capture sounds of pure Mexico and historical Spain.

A couple of minutes later, a beaming Consuela offered him a wine glass. "It's one of your favorites, Art. Chardonnay. Mild, light, not too dry. I know a lot about you."

"What should I know about you?" he asked as she sat beside him.

"Don't you ever stop questioning people?" she replied. She raised her glass. "*Salud.*"

"*Shalom.*"

Laughing, she clinked his glass, and they sipped.

"There isn't much, really. Hardly anyone claims to be born in Los Angeles. I was. Except for the odd out of state stint for work, I've been here pretty much all of my life. Hey. No chatting about work."

"Agreed." He took a second sip. "I think you've had more than your share of—" He stopped. He didn't want to start off the evening by mentioning subjects that she'd rather leave alone.

"Well, if you hadn't looked after my ass, I don't think we would be…" A tinge of pink appeared on her caramel skin. She rested her glass on a stand. "Ahh. I can smell the Ceviche. You'd better be hungry; there's lots."

"Oh…yeah." His nostrils picked up the scent of an unfamiliar marinated fish.

"Bring your wine. You can help me serve."

In the kitchen, the scent of roasted vegetables and the aroma of herbs intensified. He almost expressed an "ah" himself. He watched her mixing bowls and stirring the contents of simmering pans on the stove. How relaxed and satisfied she looked. Why a new man didn't sweep this marvelous woman off her feet was beyond him. True, the first husband turned out to be a dickhead, but man, would she make some guy happy.

"Come here," she beamed, handing him a wooden spoon. "Stir this pan…not so rough. You want the flavors oozing, not barging out. I know you love pastas, but you'll change your mind tonight. These are authentic Mexican recipes, not the stuff served along Olympic Boulevard."

Unreal, he grinned, stunned by her personality and effervescence away from the rigors of her job.

"Light the candles, okay? Then you can refill our glasses. There's a carafe by the coffee maker."

Within minutes, Consuela sat to his left and uncovered several white, royal red trimmed bowls, releasing aromas that drifted around the table. Eggshell blue walls in the dining room contained more Hispanic themed paintings. She leaned over and dimmed the light switch for the overhead chandelier. Combined with the soft glow of two small candles inside butterfly shaped crystal holders, under different circumstances, this would've provided a romantic setting.

Although she closed her eyes for a few seconds in prayer, she didn't ask Art to follow suit.

"Don't look so puzzled; I'll explain what we're eating." She scooped out a salad mixture of Romaine and dark green lettuce leaves topped with red onion, sliced olives, and mango wedges. "Anyway, here's to our friendship and success down every pathway we meet."

He noted that she referred to them as friends.

"*El gusto es mio'*," he said, raising his glass with hers. "So…explain."

"Well, our soup is an avocado broth—*aguacate*—with a pinch of tequila to heighten your appetite. Its actual name is too complicated to pronounce. Our main meal, or comida, is ceviche, traditional Mexican seafood. It's not raw, so don't get your—" She sealed her lips, then carried on "They're cooked fillets, citrus marinated, with shrimp, tuna, and mackerel pieces; as you see, it's served in cocktail cups along with tostados and tomatoes. Come on, try it."

He swallowed and smiled.

"Well?"

"Great. What makes it so tasty?"

"Mexicans use many herbs and spices. Like Azafran. It's much milder than the real Spanish variety, more famous for its color rather than strong flavor. And achiote—pronounced ach-hi-ote—a paste mixed with oregano and orange juice for the sauce."

He raised his glass to complement her cooking.

During the next hour, they chatted and joked about their university days, traveling, and any subject, which provoked bouts of laughter. She was fascinated with how he described his hometown, Vancouver, British Columbia…a cosmopolitan city much like San Francisco and Seattle, Washington. She possessed a sharp knowledge of politics and current events, critiquing rather than criticizing. It was no accident that neither one mentioned the day's jailbreak. In fact, both made it a point to stay away from anything remotely touching their jobs.

Without her encouragement, he devoured a second helping, then waved her off.

Wine flowed freely. Another bottle came out, this time a medium dry Cabernet Sauvignon, which resulted in gusts of laughter when he broke the cork and she tried to insert a finger into the bottleneck to retrieve it. Fed, full, and cheerful, they returned to the living room. Now and then she would mention some facets of her service at DHS, choosing words carefully when she commented about a case, previous or current. The latter, he observed, made her hesitate or circumvent it completely.

He didn't intend for her to respond that way; if it provided a chance to let off steam by talking to a fellow agent, so be it. At the same time, he downplayed some of his adventures with the Mossad in the West Bank. She'd encountered too much violence in the past week to be subjected to more violent images.

Soon, both sat shoulder to shoulder on the sofa. A Mexican radio station provided a backdrop of contemporary tunes. Once in a while, she'd hum along with a melody, or translate a few lines.

It's crazy, he found himself thinking, and fighting off feelings for her. Intelligent, attractive, sassy and sexy, who wouldn't want to crush her in his arms? It was the warmth of the wine…the atmosphere…that he felt enveloping him, shaking loose his self-control. And when she wasn't actually speaking, those big, dark eyes spoke volumes.

She played with the strands of her hair, twirled fingers over the back of his knuckles, and tapped his wrists. Licking her tongue over her red lips, she chuckled and whispered, "That song…it's a Spanish version of 'When a Man Loves a Woman.' Nice, isn't it?" Their eyes locked. As their wine glasses went to the coffee table, their faces inched closer together. No doubt both felt the lull of the music taking hold of their senses.

***

McLaughlin downed his Vodka Collins. Carefully checking that nobody heard him, he leaned toward his drinking partner. "Najaif's dead. No one knows that we've —"

"Then stop worrying," Quintal said, rolling the Scotch around in his glass. He brushed some dust from his left shoe. "Whoever killed him did us a favor."

A woman in an alcove swayed to The Beatles song, "Yesterday," that she'd selected in a jukebox. She sashayed over to her boyfriend, trying to coax him up to dance. A middle-aged couple nearby nursed their drinks, both disinterested in either the lounge or themselves. The bartender chatted with a guy in a fleece top. One ceiling light flickered, and the neon bulbs marking the letter "D" on the Bud Light sign were missing.

"Yeah, so what's the worry?"

"You should be worried about Dodek. I don't like the prick. He's always snooping around, butting in, taking over."

The director pushed his glass aside.

"How long are you gonna keep him here?"

McLaughlin explained that Dodek was there on a special arrangement between the DHS and Canada's National Security Service, ostensibly to look for the Canadian terrorist leader, Saleh Ali Nabhat Saleh. He agreed that Dodek was a troublemaker. After another round of drinks arrived at their table, he added, "I'll think of something." He dug his finger into the tabletop for emphasis. "I still want that fuck Dauadi."

"You and me both." Hollow laughter drifted from Quintal's mouth, then he took a long swig of Scotch. "Yeah. I'd like to get rid of Dodek before he messes things up."

"Let me work on it."

***

Her fingertips softly touched Art's wrist. The response was extraordinarily enchanting.

"Consuela." Pronouncing her name meant forming his lips like a kiss.

"Yes?"

Her voice jarred him. *God, don't let her read my mind. And stop me from going any further.* He wanted to take her in his arms…did he ever. She wouldn't resist. She was offering herself. *Kiss her. Kiss her.* Her dark eyes closed. Both, now a hair's breadth apart, joined their mouths. The touch of her lips became intoxicating, and he pressed his mouth into hers harder. She accepted the firm touches without pulling away.

But he did. "Uh, I…."

She drew back a bit, yet kept her mouth near his, as though their next kiss would take them past the flashpoint.

"Where do you want this to go?" she whispered.

That startled him, and he edged back. "I didn't think we'd —"

"That we'd feel something for each other?" She added space between them by shifting closer to the edge of the sofa. "I think you do."

"I won't deny it. I'd be lying if I said no. You're a beautiful woman, Connie. I'm sorry if you think I was coming on to you."

"You have nothing to apologize for, Art, especially your feelings. God, I'm not a mixed up teenager. I'm a woman who, when she likes a man, would go out of her way to please him. If it meant passionately, I —"

He placed a finger over her lips, and laughed. "You don't have to say it."

"That ring means a lot to you, doesn't it? I think you're a man who wouldn't cross the line. And you couldn't live with yourself if you did;

181

that's a quality a woman would love. Come on, let's drink to, to…whatever."

They raised their glasses, smiled, and clinked.

As he lowered his glass, she noticed the time on his watch. "You know, the date on the calendar is gonna change in a few minutes. We both have to work tomorrow, early."

Her statement brought everything back to reality. In particular, how quickly they could've gone from dinner to bed partners.

Maybe they were both glad the spark evaporated. Agents were advised not to fraternize with one another. A close relationship in any work environment could present problems; in their line of work it could spell disaster.

Art rose and sighed. "I'd better go. Thanks for a great evening."

"You've got a long trip back. And if you haven't kept track, you just started your fourth glass." Her fingers formed a steeple under her chin. "You're welcome to stay overnight, if you want."

Nothing she said surprised him anymore. "Uh, I don't think that's a…."

"Suit yourself."

For once, he was glad she didn't insist.

At the door, both stood looking at each other with that "what if" expression. She leaned against the door and kissed his cheek. "Good night, Agent Dodek."

"See you tomorrow." He didn't say anything else as the door closed, signaling an end to a fantastic evening with a fabulous woman. He stood on the stoop for a moment, picturing her inside leaning against the door.

Pebbles on the walkway crunched under his feet as he hopped into the Focus. A light shone in the bedroom. He bobbed his head up and down and smiled. It soon vanished, and he realized he hadn't called Lynda tonight.

Once in a while car lights glimmering in the opposite direction shone on his ring as he steered with his left hand. Over twenty years of marriage he'd never strayed or slept with another woman. He'd known other agents who crossed the line. Some paid a terrific price: broken marriages, crumbling families, forced reassignment, even loss of jobs.

Sure, he'd tasted temptation. Being overseas for long periods without wives or girlfriends could cause thoughts of sampling local female companionship. Most places where he'd served were in the Middle East, where even accompanying an unattached woman was considered akin to adultery, and agents were forbidden to date or engage in extra-marital relations. But the first time in his career he was teamed up with a female partner, it had to be Consuela Mercado.

Chapter 34

First thing the following morning Art and DHS agent Lamborghini wrapped up their report on the crime scene at Dodger Stadium. Najaif's identity they knew; who the Russian was remained unknown. His IDs were all forgeries, nothing turned up on face recognition systems in their files, and no match was found in the National Fingerprint Data Bank. They theorized that Dauadi had kidnapped the teen to shut him up, the Russian carried out the murder, and then Dauadi had shot him. Assumptions, perhaps, but locating the Somali American became harder than ever. The change in appearance favored him, also.

For the time being, DHS headquarters in Washington, D.C., decided not to provide the media with an altered photograph. Having an agent browse mosques for any sign of him also was scrapped. Scouring local religious sites catering to Somali Americans wasn't possible, either. Homeland security possessed no one capable of passing himself off as Somali. However, the FBI maintained checks of young men from Minneapolis and back East who had recently returned from Africa and the Middle East after long absences; from Pakistan, in particular, as new recruits often flew back to the United States via Kenya and Egypt, thinking that traveling from those countries wouldn't arouse suspicion. Wrong: Kenya and Egypt shared Intel with the CIA…maybe not always as reliably as the State Department hoped. The FBI could keep track of them secretly once they set foot on American soil. Yet these wanna-be militants were adept at maintaining low profiles. Common among them all was that they were single, young, usually unemployed, frequent worshippers at mosques, and likely to live together in groups of three to four in rented apartments. Their main choice of leisure activity was gathering in Persian teashops.

Consuela and Art strolled by one another outside the communications center. Last night's close encounter hadn't caused a ripple. As she passed, she playfully clutched his ass and laughed, grabbed the report from his hands, and headed for the director's office. Also in her hands was a revamped security system proposal for the detention area. Determined not to engage in another shouting match with McLaughlin — as long as Quintal didn't ingratiate her with his contempt for minorities — her boss would go along with the changes. After all, preventing a repeat of yesterday's jailbreak and shooting was key to her summation. Then it was up to him to convince Washington bureaucrats to pay for the renovations.

***

Art watched her step into the corridor. As usual, the way she moved, always cat-like, was sensuous.

He returned to a desk and hit the command prompt on a lap top computer. His closest co-workers were two cubicles away. Quintal must've been nearby; the scent of burnt coffee wafted through his nose. It still puzzled him how a guy with a vigilante attitude worked for the CIA, and he intended to dig up the truth.

Clicking open a few government online websites, using keystrokes and access codes, Art managed to locate the Pentagon's classified Internal Military Records site. With tricks he had learned from Ham Parnham, the National Security Unit's forensic analyst, he entered a sequence of configurations that bypassed Defense Department passwords and restricted zones. Browsing in the U.S. Army Special Ops site, he tapped and worked his way to Quintal's Army Ranger personnel file, which included standard enlistment data (West Point); personal information (divorced twice); deployments and missions (Bosnia, Columbia, Iraq, Afghanistan); citations (Purple Heart, Bronze star); and highest rank attained (Lt. Colonel). He got an eyeful when Quintal's military profile emerged under the U.S. Army Military Codes Of Misconduct document file.

Infractions:

— Assaulting superior officer
— Unreasonable punishment of enlistees under his command
— Improper and malicious sexual harassment of junior female officer
— Mistreatment of enemy combatants
— Unwarranted and fatal shooting of six Iraqi civilians
— Cover up of botched military mission due to lack of improper Intelligence

Findings of Court Martial

— Guilty on all charges

— Demotion; Dishonorable Discharge; forfeiture of all military benefits.

Disposition

— Fifty-two months imprisonment (less time served), nineteen months.

Art jerked back, then reread some of the excerpts. The episode they'd had at Patches. Shit, Quintal was a ticking time bomb. Clicking his way through classified sites, he hacked into the Central Intelligence Agency database. Intel, previous and current investigations, top secret communiqués, people of interest files, and confidential State Department reports he skipped over, targeting personnel files of CIA officers, overseas and home. Hundreds of names and personal data flew by, none of which piqued his curiosity. Time and time again he entered search engines for the name Mack Quintal, using information from his military records. Cross-referencing, name splitting, reverse coding, the screen continued to spit out "No Employment Data." He rubbed his eyes and tapped the same keys.

Backtracking his route through U.S. Army and U.S. Intelligence Foreign Service sites—erasing sensitive access keystrokes—it didn't surprise him that Quintal had turned up as a non-entity.

Who the hell is he? He claimed to know CIA Officer Lucky de' Angelo in Pakistan.

How? Director McLaughlin raved about his foreign service. True, some of the offshore information he disclosed at the first meeting had sounded legitimate.

What now? Share the information? With whom?

After deleting "History Today," he used a sequence of Parnham's numeric codes and wiped from memory any evidence of computer intrusion. Just as he shut down, his eye picked up a shadow to the left.

"That better be Intel business you're working on," exclaimed Quintal, approaching the desk.

"Uh–huh," Art said, and walked out of the processing center.

***

Quintal swung the laptop around, rebooted the machine, and went straight to Recovery. When nothing popped up, he hit the Recycle bin, then Network Places, and History Today. Clean. Not a sign of files opened or terminated. Scowling, he slammed the cover down and tossed it aside. Fire-shooting eyes rolled throughout the communications center. The message was clear to those feeling the heat: no one was gonna undermine or screw him around.

185

Chapter 35

Just before noon, Mercado flagged down Dodek. She was all business as she leafed through a thick folder marked Classified: Brothers of Somali Jihad Investigation. Once again she unfolded papers related to Ali Tariq and Husien Najaif. Medical reports stated that both men bore electrical burns to the chest and marks of severe bondage to their wrists, pre-mortem. Although inconclusive, the M.E. noted the possibility of torture prior to death.

An extra bombshell, she told him, was that the bullets that killed the two jail guards and the Russian were fired from the same .45 caliber gun. That pinpointed Dauadi, which they had already presumed. Then she brought out documents from the FBI and Department of Alcohol, Tobacco and Firearms (A.T.F). Search records indicated that the firearms used by the Somali militants the prior week—in particular, the AK-47s—were smuggled into the United States by the Russian mob, originating in Marseille, France, shipped to New York, and then transported to Los Angeles. At this time, agents were tracing manifests and tracking individuals who might have received the weapons. The trouble was, two shipments of ammunition and components for IEDs were missing. Compounding the search, smugglers didn't pre-register shipments, contents, or carriers with Customs. After 9-11, the U.S. had initiated a Customs process overseas by pre-inspecting American bound goods. In this case it didn't happen. It was no secret that the Russians infiltrated foreign shippers. Collusion with a U.S. enforcement agency, though not inconceivable, was hard for the Homeland Security agents to digest.

Attention returned to the Somali prisoners. If medical findings surmised that physical abuse contributed to their wounds—and they were recent—who administered them?

He wondered whether to disclose his experience with Quintal at Patches. And the non-existent CIA file. He trusted her. As Unit supervisor, she, not he, would have to inform Director McLaughlin. The way events kept unfolding around the DHS office he decided to hold it back for the time being.

Agent Dan Curbside, fastening his armored vest, emerged from the communications room, joined them, and announced, "Intel at the Los Alamitos Naval Depot contacted us to report three unknown dark-skinned civilians sighted conducting possible illegal recon. They've requested our assistance."

"I'm expected at an emergency planning meeting with Walter in a few minutes," Mercado said. "Tony and Aylesha are on surveillance. You and Art investigate." She noted the big question in their eyes, and added, "Yes, as I've been ordered, Quintal will be notified. Lot of good it'll do. Keep me advised."

Fifteen minutes later the two agents, Curbside driving, were southbound on the 110 South Freeway. From there they transitioned to the 405 and headed south, then exited west toward Los Alamitos.

This location contained storage depots; Quanset sheds storing machinery, ship chandlery, naval offices, oil bunkers and gasoline tanks, building materials, welding and fabricating shops, and provisions for small to medium size dock yard repairs, as well as housing active naval reservists and dozens of civilian workers. Its nearby neighbor, the Long Beach Naval Air Station, served as home to larger naval craft, including fully servable transports, a medical ship, coast guard ancillary vessels, and homeport for repair and maintenance facilities for F-18 Navy Fighter jets, Hellcats, and rocket-equipped helicopters. Hundreds of navy personnel and civilians also worked on site providing logistical and advanced technology installations for testing rocket propulsion systems.

With the Queen Mary passenger ship, now a tourist attraction, anchored off shore, it wasn't unusual to watch destroyers, cruisers, and aircraft carriers entering the harbor, as well as cruise ships docking at San Pedro Harbor, loading supplies and passengers for the trip south to the Mexican Riviera.

At the Los Alamitos entrance, Curbside and his passenger flashed their IDs to armed Marine guards. Eight-foot chain link fences with thick interwoven mesh strips angled around the yard. Cameras, sensor lights affixed to concrete posts, and notices in large print on yellow backgrounds signified Department of Navy Restricted Area, No Trespassing. Two dog handlers and their German shepherds ringed the GMC Yukon sniffing for suspicious contraband. One guard strolled around the vehicle with a hand-held explosive material detector. Finally, while unnecessary, a young master corporal saluted the agents and gave the order for the gate to rise. At that moment the thunderous roar of a fuel tanker swooping skyward above the inlet reverberated and shook the ground with the force of a freight train.

A Jeep with two marines led the Yukon past a row of makeshift trailers. Fork trucks hauling crates chugged by at the first roundabout, revealing nearby endless lines of LNG storage tanks, criss-crossing interconnected stainless steel pipes, and corrosive-proof wrapped flow tubes. Exhaust outlets at the top of the smokestacks shot out plumes of bluish smoke through mesh-covered smoke deflectors. Even with the currents from the inlet pushing the breeze out to the ocean, gas fumes drifted downward among the tanks. Every few seconds a pungent odor invaded the nostrils, explaining why some workers near the storage silo wore facemasks.

Art and his driver exchanged glances. A terrorist with the right equipment and explosive materials could set off a gas-fueled inferno, not only destroying the base and sending noxious fumes over Los Alamitos and Long Beach, but poisoning the air over Los Angeles County for days. Fatalities would be high for those inhaling the deadly gases.

At the next yard intersection, a Jeep and its marine camouflage-uniformed occupant drove up alongside and stopped the Yukon. Stripes on the collars of his shirt showed his NCO rank as Sergeant First Class; a nametag read R. Canaski. An M-16A carbine was clamped to the dashboard.

Rolling down a window, Art nodded and accepted photographic printouts of three men, possibly African-American but of unknown foreign nationality, snapping pictures. None of the photos revealed clear images of their faces.

The marine pointed eastward, and handed Art a map of the naval yard and dry docks, indicating roads and secondary lanes leading to marshes and sand bogs. Red highlighted circles indicated perimeters around the base where gates were located. A couple, Art observed, jutted out beyond naval property to trails, grasslands, and a roadway skirting by oil derricks.

Great, lots of ground to search, he mused. Ample cover for an ambush.

Chapter 36

Roaring away, the agents followed a series of roads, then a winding gravel road fenced in on both sides. Tires bumped and the SUV shook as they drove over sections where recent heavy mobile tracked vehicles had created an uneven gravel bed. Curbside kept his speed to about 15-20 mph. The truck's suspension jerked and bounced over ruts. Strands of faded oak grass fluttered; piles of sun-dried tree branches, some roped together, lay scattered near rows of hogweed and yellow-antlered clusters atop climbing nightingale plants sprouting red, egg-shaped berries.

A mile and half had passed since they left the main yard, and desolation was already creating a sense of foreboding. The growing silence also made them edgier. Still, no visible evidence had been found that someone had ventured this far out around the flatlands. The first gate loomed, situated on an earth-worn berm. Before getting out of the truck, the agents did a mental observation of their surroundings—sufficient clearance for backing up the truck, their top priority. Once outside, they estimated the distance to the next gate. Structures from Los Alamitos peered over the horizon.

Hands over their holsters, they approached the wire fence. Some sections sagged or were bent, but not forced apart. To their amazement, posted on a nearby maple tree was a No Hunting sign. With the sparse edible vegetation, it was doubtful any wildlife flocked there. Odd, too, was the fact that there wasn't one Department of Defense camera in sight.

Art picked up a branch and tossed it at the wire mesh. They were on the Defense Department side and he expected the fence to be electrified; it wasn't.

They decided to separate and scout both ends of the fence. They knew it was risky…two of them against three unknown subjects who may be armed. But there was just too much ground to cover…as much as five hundred feet between gates. Both carried rapid response cell phones in case of trouble.

Curbside wandered eastward alongside the higher part of several sandbars. In the opposite direction, Art strolled on a flatter surface of mixed sand and rocks. Footsteps kicked up dust. Perhaps not surprising this far from the base, few foot or boot prints showed up in the sand.

He rolled his eyes toward mounds of tall sagebrush and wheat grass, ideal hiding places for someone watching him, waiting to pick him off.

Wind from the inlet tossed leaves around like shredded paper. Grayer clouds inland formed along the distant tree lines. Idle, rusted oil derricks about a half-mile north stood abandoned, their steel frames bent over like phalanges.

His ears listened to every sound — from rustling leaves swaying in the wind to the cackling of seagulls. He discovered that the pathway on this side ended. Corroded concrete pylons and broken sections of cement barriers lay stacked nearby. Dry sand beds littered with twigs, rocks, and some floating gross, hardened yellow liquid glob covered parts of a shallow lake. Further, past an empty stream, years ago truckloads of dirt must've been dug up and redistributed over acres of drifting sand. If the EPA saw this place, they would blow a gasket. Everything in this quagmire resembled an environmental disaster.

Returning to the gate, he spotted his partner's figure rising as it neared its starting point. He waved an all-clear sign to Curbside. Expecting him to do the same, the agent kept his arms down. Minutes later, as he approached the SUV, Art thought it odd that Curbside's gait slowed, but paid little attention.

"Nothing on this side," Art said.

No acknowledgement.

"Notice anything?"

No reply again.

About forty feet from Art, Curbside halted, one arm hanging down, and his right arm curved over his abdomen. An unwavering gaze stayed aimed at Art's face.

What's with him? he wondered, baffled by his behavior. *Is he not alone?* He tried to pick up every sound, focusing on any strange movement of the willowy straw grass shifting sand from the ridge. Standing near the front of the Yukon, he slid his hand over his Glock.

Curbside advanced another ten feet, then tapped his right side.

That's when Art noticed the agent's empty holster, and he felt uneasy. *Okay, Dan, you've got company. Where the hell are they?* He rolled his eyes both right and left. He did it again.

His partner moved his eyes leftward.

Gripping his gun butt, his left hand brushing his thigh, he extended his forefinger toward Curbside, then followed with two fingers.

Two fingers responded.

Moving about half a foot forward, he waved his hand straight down.

Curbside followed the direction and hit the ground on all fours.

With lightning reflexes, Art pulled up his weapon and fired just above the berm. The bullet bounced off a boulder and skimmed across a mound of rocks. Seagulls bolted and flew a hundred feet into the sky.

A head peered over the sand hill. A figure stood up and aimed a hand-held machine gun pistol at Art.

Oh no you don't, asshole. He crouched down and fired, hitting the man above the sternum. As the dark skinned gunman slinked to his knees, another figure emerged holding a silver-plated revolver. This guy fired, but the bullet struck the chrome step rail on the Yukon.

Curbside jumped up as the man cocked the handgun. Using his weight and beefy arms, he pounced and threw him frontward onto the sandbar, clasping one hand around the assailant's neck while trying to disarm him with the other hand. Their combined weight sunk both of them about a half-foot into the unstable, soft sand.

The gun exploded under the man's ribs. He groaned and tried to slide the gun out from underneath his bleeding stomach. Lack of strength and his wound prevented him from raising the gun. His finger slid off the trigger, and with a final gasp, his eyes closed.

Curbside rose, dusting sand, dirt, and blood drops off his vest.

"What the hell happened back there?" asked Art, checking on the assailant he'd shot. He figured both men were Somalis—more of Dauadi's recruits—and barely out of their teens.

"Back there," the agent said, pointing at the gate. "Shit, I never heard them. Suddenly I've got a pistol digging into my back." He returned to the second body and retrieved his .45 from underneath the man's shirt. "Fuck, Dodek…I'm glad you caught on."

"The report said three men were observed surveying the yard. Where's the third?"

Curbside shrugged, holstering his sidearm. "Just these guys surprised me."

Tossing the men's weapons on the back seat, the two agents hopped into the SUV. This time Art had the wheel. It took a couple of tight turns to back up on the narrow road, but with sand shooting out from the tires, he peeled down the sandy, gravel lane.

Curbside punched in the numbers for the DHS unit on his cell phone. Aylesha, taking the call, heard what had happened. He added that they would continue their search.

Art and Curbside lowered their eyes at one another when they heard her say that after she and Tony had returned to the Unit, McLaughlin refused to send them to the depot for backup.

Chapter 37

Reaching the base, they drove around makeshift trailers and aluminum roof covered buildings. Sailors in fatigues, plus civilians dressed in denim work outfits, passed by. With the number of storage facilities and their contents, both commented that security personnel were noticeably minimal.

Sergeant Canaski drove up and flagged them down. Informed about the shootings, he activated his shoulder-held microphone and ordered a detail to check out the insurgents.

Art hopped out and Curbside took over. Again, the agents headed different directions. If the other Somali was still on the base, he figured the militant would be wandering amid the buildings, hoping no one neared the LNG storage tanks. The roadways between structures were wide enough for vehicles and larger transport trucks. As he walked toward the first row, he had to scurry out of the way of a low bed trailer truck carrying horizontal sections of steel plates for a ship's lower hull, plus a never-ending parade of Navy blue pickup trucks and forklifts hauling engine shafts and electrical equipment.

Even though personnel noticed his side arm and flak jacket, most went about their business without as much as a second glance.

This is nuts, he mused. He didn't even know who he was searching for. Still, he maintained caution whenever he spotted an African-American worker. One of them could be the third naval yard intruder. No way was he going to get taken hostage.

A message from Curbside advised nothing was out of the ordinary while driving around the outer section of the depot.

That's when he recollected what McLaughlin said…no backup. The director could be hard-nosed and stubborn at times, but he'd never deny a request for additional agents. In fact, he'd insist upon it. This wasn't his doing. The denial smacked of Mack Quintal's influence. For a guy who saw action overseas, sufficient personnel should've been foremost for a patrol to flush out combatants.

Fifteen minutes into his search, Art stopped and wiped his brow. Hazy skies radiated down, which deflected heat off the aluminum-sided Quanset buildings.

Agents were trained to look for the unusual, to be skeptical of what appeared out of place, but also of what gave the appearance of being too casual or too clean. Each agent had his or her method of picking out variances; like built-in radar, it jumped off the screen, and they reacted, took care of it. Someone's normal movement could be a tip-off. Facial expressions, for example, could be hard to discern, or instantly obvious that something was amiss when in a tight situation. An FBI psychological terror analyst once remarked, "Look for what is right; you'll know when to deal with what is wrong." In Israel, when Art and David Tivi, his Mossad instructor, patrolled the West Bank for suspected Palestinian terrorists, it was drilled into him that a person's sudden change in direction, their method of walking, the choice of clothes, their shifting positions, moving quickly then slowing down amongst crowds of people, often signaled a potential threat.

Those characteristics you noticed; non-obvious traits were harder to detect, such as a person trying to blend in when everybody else acted differently; the deadpan expression of a motorist as he approached a checkpoint; a passenger who obeyed a driver's instructions too eagerly on a crowded bus; or attracting emergency personnel by faking an illness. Far too often, these were young Arabs prepared to die for their ideological beliefs, spurred on by committing suicide, and with the largest number of innocent bystanders killed as their goal.

Art had taken out his share of would-be terrorists. The ones you missed, however…those were the ones that haunted you. If only you could have saved…that group of shoppers at an outdoor market; the military patrol of just graduated police cadets; those school kids at an all-girl's school; or people lining up for hours waiting to vote.

Here on this naval maintenance yard, nothing perked his curiosity enough to be concerned. But he'd discovered on earlier counter-terrorist assignments that any error in judgment could be fatal.

Long blasts of horns throughout the yard indicated break time. Trucks stopped, and workers put down their tools and dispersed to various areas and buildings; some lit up cigarettes, or grabbed soft drinks from dispensing machines located throughout the depot. With the fading sounds of lumbering cranes and the banging of steel, the base became too quiet too soon. In fact, the silence felt weird.

At the next crossroad, he entered the fenced-in gas storage facility. The scent of liquefied gas made him wince. Passing a forty-foot high tank, he tripped over a half rolled up brown hose. Nearby he heard the hissing of a machine. Then, on the opposite side of the tank, kneeling below a steel walkway, he saw a worker in navy fatigues using an acetylene torch to cut away a 4" x 6" section of plate at its base. Bluish-yellow flames licked at the metal, and orange sparks flew across the scaffolding.

Shit, he sighed, *what the hell are you doing?* One miss-flying spark and it could cut into the tank's surface lining and take out most of Los Alamitos. What troubled him, though, was the guy working through a break.

Art approached the stairs about a yard from the welder. Following the trail of the hoses to a generator and acetylene tank, he kicked off the on switch. In seconds, the whirring machine stopped and the flame from the torch dribbled out.

The welder turned toward the generator and lifted his goggles, resting them on his forehead. A black asbestos shawl was draped around his denim jacket. Thick non-flammable gloves reached to his mid arm. He hadn't seen Art yet.

But the agent noticed him. Short cut dark hair, brown eyes, black features.

"Isn't that risky, cutting so close to liquid gas?" he asked, climbing the stairs.

Dark eyes stared. No reply.

Perhaps from instinct, Art studied the welder's body language and peered closely at the cowhide protective apron. Mixed in with countless burns on the material were some red spots.

"Could you step aside from your equipment, and come down to the ground?"

Still staring, the man slowly rose to his feet, still gripping the torch. His other hand held the spark lighter. Beside his feet stood a smaller back-up footpad operated generator. He just stood there motionless on the landing.

"Come down here," Art said forcefully, his hand atop his Glock. He placed a foot on the first stair. "I'm an agent with the Department of Homeland Security." Within fifteen seconds he repeated the order to leave the worksite.

The sinewy-framed welder removed the glasses and dropped them on the landing.

From his experience dealing with Somalis, he deduced that the man wasn't African-American. Keeping his gaze connected to the guy's eyes, he climbed to the second step.

That's when he spotted the earring. And that's when an icicle ripped through his side.

He backed up, returned to the pavement, and gripped his sidearm. *What are those dark eyes thinking?* he wondered. Was he aware that he'd been recognized?

With the hand holding the torch, the Somali Brotherhood taskmaster yanked at the spare hose attached to the footpad mechanism, and struck the lighter against the nozzle. Within three terrifying seconds, the torch spewed out a foot-long finger of flame. For another second, he didn't move. Then he stretched out his arm, and pivoted on one foot, screwing open the valve wheel, which released an even thicker flame.

He shot the streaking flame straight toward Art's face.

Jumping back, Art missed the flickering, hissing flare-up by inches, but felt the searing heat near his eyes. Now he withdrew his Glock. The guy was nuts, waving a flaming torch around mere feet from a gas tank.

Maybe not. If the agent foolishly pulled the trigger, the bullet would rupture the LNG tank and both would be vaporized in the ensuing explosion. He couldn't chance it, despite being a crack shot.

He had to disarm a guy with a flame-spitting acetylene weapon. Yeah, right. From the man who killed infidels for sport? Thinking didn't help. Standing there looking stupid didn't, either. He couldn't run up the stairs and charge; the flying, flaming nozzle could strike the storage bin.

Art pointed his Glock at the welder. "I'm ordering you to drop that torch and come down. Do it. Now." Then he moved further back.

Stepping toward the landing edge, his hand lowering the nozzle, Dauadi maintained his eye-to-eye stare. The agent's gruff voice and the pistol were no threat. He moved slowly down to the second step. As soon as he reached the ground, he threw up his arm and directed the flame toward Art's face.

The heat forced him to blink repeatedly. His gun hand lowered, and he drew himself sideways and grabbed at the hose. Goddamn, it was hot. He kept pulling. Again he used his foot to switch off the generator. The bluish-white flame diminished. Multi-colored stars still whirling in front of his eyes from the flash, he craned his neck to the side. That sent a pain shooting through his neck muscles, all the way down to his spine.

The Somali attacked. Jumping atop Art, he wound the tubing around his neck. The smell of welding flux and the gaseous mixture of acetylene and burnt leather of the apron made Art gag. Twice, tubing and hose became as dangerous a weapon as the torch. First, the hot surface bit into his skin. Second, the gas hose and tubing tangled around his neck. As both men crashed to the ground, Art tried to slide his fingers between the man's chest and his upper body, except the materials dug tighter. Although Dauadi was pounds lighter, because of Art's momentary disorientation, he kept the agent from raising the Glock.

Leaning backward, Dauadi edged the nozzle end downward. Despite being turned off, it still dripped flame. Those dark eyes radiated hate, and they spelled m-u-r-d-e-r.

Wild, insane thoughts rambled through Art's brain. Where was Dan Curbside? He couldn't even reach for his cell phone to alert his partner. But that wasn't his concern at the moment. Keeping the dribbling gas away from his eyes was. Gritting his teeth, he began rolling sideways in an attempt to extricate himself from Dauadi. It succeeded somewhat, as he managed to free one leg. But the Somali had the advantage of strength of a man gone wild and inched the nozzle closer.

"No you don't," Art said, grimacing, and swung his leg upward, kneeing his assailant.

Again. Harder. It helped in lessening Dauadi's hold. Still grasping at the hose, Art's gun hand blocked the nozzle, sending the dripping gas to the pavement. Better the ground blackened than his face.

The snapping hoses knocked over the gas tanks used for welding. One tipped and fell on Dauadi's well-worn Nikes.

That movement enabled Art to at least rise to his knees. It also provided some much needed loosening of the tubing digging into his neck. He was able to see more of the bloodspots on the leather apron, which looked too recent to have been immersed between grooves in the material.

Startled, the Somali started to get up and slammed a gloved hand against Art's temple.

Ouch. It didn't daze him, but it smarted. He managed to draw in the tubing and used it to whack Dauadi across the cheek. *Now you hurt, you bastard*, he sneered. The gun was still in his other hand, but he was reluctant to shoot. From this haphazard angle, the bullet may have hit Dauadi, or he could miss-aim and the bullet would strike one of the tanks.

A gloved hand went to grab the Glock. For once something worked in his favor. The rough texture covering the fingers slid down the barrel. Dauadi started shaking the glove off his hand.

That was all the distraction that Art needed. He jammed the point of his gun into the only place on the man's torso not shielded by the heavy apron — the side of the ribs.

Gotcha', asshole, he grinned as Dauadi squirmed in pain.

Yet he lurched to his feet and kicked out at Art, who now was on his butt. All this time only hate-filled eyes stared and glared; not a word slipped from the contorting lips.

Art pivoted to the right as the Nike whooshed by his head. If only he could get the Somali to face opposite the storage tanks. One shot to the bastard's head would end this fracas.

As hard as he could, he gripped his hand around Dauadi's ankle and twisted, upsetting him backward. Now he jumped up, and the men were square with one another. The gun wasn't necessary, so he holstered it.

196

Like two boxers ready to spar, both lowered themselves into karate-like stances. "Let's see what you've got," Art sneered, darting back and forth.

"Infidel." That was the first word out of his mouth. "I don't need a gun to kill you." Art expected an Arabic accent; there was none. And it was the first time he'd heard the rasping cold voice of the militant.

He should've paid attention to Dauadi's hands, which were both free of the gloves, as the metal tip of the acetylene nozzle swung at Art's head. Pivoting sideways, it missed, but brushed against his shoulder. There was enough slack of the hose for him to grab, and he yanked it toward him. Besides unbalancing Dauadi, the heavy apron also acted to slow his movements. It didn't impede Dauadi, though. He retaliated with a kick that made contact to Art's right thigh, and followed up with a swift open-handed whack on the agent's cheek.

Art turned, leaned inward, and pile-dived a fist alongside the Somali's neck. Without flinching, Dauadi crashed into him. Both gripped each other's shoulders. Dauadi broke free first, and then pressed one hand under Art's chin. The other hand smacked across his forehead.

Art tried to keep his blows above the leather apron—hitting the protected torso would've been futile. Each time he landed a blow, the Somali rained back at least two strikes. Simultaneous jabs broke and bruised raw skin, chipped cheekbones. The last one cut his lower lip. But there was no time to be concerned about blood dripping down his cheek. Despite the apron, Dauadi's thin frame gave him lightning fast reflexes. A mix of fists and open hands pummeled each other. And some of them stung.

Swinging out too quickly, Art twisted and felt the muscles in his spine prick nerves like hot needles. Dauadi pounced and knocked him against one of the railings surrounding the storage tank. Gritting his teeth from the pain, he swung back and sent a knuckle sandwich hard into Dauadi's right cheek. It must have hurt, as his opponent squeezed both eyes shut. Art's right arm felt as though arthritic pain knifed right through his skin.

The horn to indicate the break was over should've sounded by now. Maybe the workers wouldn't try to intervene, but the crowd might make Dauadi decide to flee.

Never once did the Somali lower his eyes from Art's; he seemed to enjoy witnessing the agent's reaction whenever a blow hit home.

Jostling back and forth, they continued grappling with one another. Art managed to lock his arms around the man's neck. In an instant, he sensed that the ground moved as his body flew a hundred and eighty degrees in the air. Partly bracing for the fall, he hung onto Dauadi's neck and both crashed over the railing onto the ground. He was just grateful that he didn't land on his back.

Like snarling lions, both clenched together and banged and slammed fists into each other's faces, rapid blows. Not a spare inch was spared. Dust from the pavement covered their clothes.

When one strike dazed Art, the Somali ripped off his non-flammable vest and swung it against his head. Then Dauadi rose straight up and bolted between two Quanset buildings.

It took about half a minute for Art to shake off a bout of dizziness as he climbed to his feet. He could see the Somali running toward another fuel tank. He also spotted a cell-phone like device lying on the ground. One hand on his back, he bent over and picked it up. It wasn't just your ordinary mobile phone. Right away he eyed the multicolored row of colored light buttons and short electrical wires dangling from a crevice at the bottom.

Shit, he swore, that's why Dauadi was cutting open a section of the plate around the LNG tank...to install an IED. Shoving it in his pocket, he quickened his step and headed for where he believed Dauadi would run to—the base exit.

Just then the horn blasted, and he had to be below one attached to a pole. He batted his ear and darted down a driveway. In seconds, workers poured out of buildings. Some noticed him running; some never gave it a thought.

He pressed the single button on his phone that would alert Curbside that his partner required assistance. All he heard was static, then a loud uneven ringing. *Goddamn electronics never work when you need them the most.*

Rumbling close by caught his ears. Work vehicles starting up, he figured.

As he cut between a trailer and a pipe shop, grinding wheels became louder. *Holy shit.* When he looked up he wheeled to the side as a yellow and black striped forklift, with its tongs set at mid level height, chugged straight for him. Behind him was a tall pile of aluminum sheets. The trailer was to his right. Adding to feeling fenced in, this particular roadway was much narrower, and had no exit.

Protective steel mesh shielded Muhamed Dauadi, the driver. The same hateful expression encased his face.

Art pulled out the Glock and aimed it at the window of the speeding forklift. Not until he extended it fully outward did he realize the soreness in his muscles ripping through his arm. Using his other hand for a brace, he fired three quick shots. One bounced off a fork, another pierced an upper bar, the third whizzed past the Somali's left shoulder.

198

Four civilian Navy yard workers darted out of the trailer after hearing the shots, then made a hasty retreat back indoors; not because of the charging machine, rather the guy holding the pistol.

Dauadi jerked the gears and lowered the forks. Less than ten feet separated man and machine.

Leaning alongside the aluminum pile, Art fired off two more rounds, this time shooting much higher.

It may have helped. Dauadi's eyes blinked at the muzzle flashes. The gears moaned, then squealed. He jumped out of the cab, leaving the forklift heading for Art's legs.

An out of control forklift, as well as being stuck beside a pile of unstable, separating heavy sheets, made chasing the terrorist next to impossible.

Disregarding the aching pain, Art didn't intend to just stand there. As the two metal forks neared, he grunted, grimaced, and swung his legs up, pushing himself onto the stack of sheets. Not exactly the right choice. Sharp, rough-edged corners almost sliced through his body like a meat slicing machine.

When the driverless forklift smashed against the pile, its tongs slid beneath the one half inch thick sheets, toppling him onto the ground. His head struck the trailer's three-step metal ladder. Like a round of fireworks, multi-colored sparks flashed through his head. The rear wheels of the vehicle jerked upward, and now it bounced like a devil-possessed metal monster. Pallets below crumbled under the surge and weight. Twelve-foot wide aluminum sheets moved and shifted sideways, bumping several of the unsecured plates toward the edge.

Somewhere in the distance the sound of rubber tires on uneven pavement drifted through to his ears.

On the ground, half bent over, wrenching in pain, he stared up as half a dozen rough-edged top-heavy sheets began tumbling over. Muttering something in Hebrew, he slid backward on his ass and rolled twice on the ground as they crashed inches from his shoes. Even when he sat up, the aluminum surfaces seemed to moan. Actually, the grinding sound came from the forklift motor.

With one eye, he spotted the GMC Yukon dashing between rows of buildings. Now standing, though a bit fuzzyheaded, he grinned. "About time, Curbside."

A dozen or so workers surrounded him. One sailor jumped into the cab and switched off the propane-fueled engine—something that he had entirely forgotten about, which could have exploded on impact.

From another crossroad, the Jeep with Sergeant Caniski careened around a corner. Both vehicles entered the intersection at the same time. The Jeep got clipped and turned sideways from the larger truck. The marine bounced about half a foot off the seat, but held onto the steering wheel.

Both drivers hopped out, looked at the Jeep's twisted front bumper, and shrugged their shoulders. Damage to the bigger SUV ranged from a bent chromed bumper to a broken signal light.

"If the FBI and the Marines aren't gonna call their auto agents," Art smirked at the pair examining the damage, "Dauadi is still on the loose."

"You look like shit," his partner said. "Dare I ask?"

"To tell you the truth, I'm not sure. Tell you, though…Dauadi is one tough SOB."

The marine ambled over. "The body of a navy worker, a welder, was found shot to death on base," he reported, eying the shambles of aluminum plates.

"Dauadi's handiwork, no doubt," remarked Curbside.

Art nodded, motioning agreement with his hands.

"Fuck me," the sergeant chuckled. "The DHS and FBI shot it out with terrorists at Los Alamitos."

Chapter 38

An hour later, Art downed a tall glass of water and Tylenol 3 tablets, hoping they would alleviate the pinching in his back. His fellow agents at DHS suggested that he visit an orthopedist about his back pain. Twice he'd bashed the area along his waistline, and he knew the blows caused extreme pressure. *Yeah*, he acknowledged, *soon*.

Next, after two soaked, bloodstained washcloths, he managed to scrub off some of the bruising on his face. After applying a couple of round, shaver-type Band-Aids on his forehead and the corner of his jaw, he strolled into the Analysis center. He opened a laptop and browsed his way to the current file on the Somali Brothers of Jihad. It took a bit of finger flexing—still scraped from the fight—to press down on the keyboard.

His mind wandered back to his hometown of Vancouver, Canada, and the assignment that still reflected in the window of his mind…one of the blackest days of his career. Two AK-47 shooting terrorists outside a suburban sports arena had pinned down him and his National Security Unit partner, Keith Dawson. Although he eventually killed one of the militants, they'd watched helplessly as a young couple was murdered outside the doorway. No matter how much they tried, including taking fire, they were unable to prevent the killings. It shook him to the core. He believed that's why he hadn't hesitated to shoot the wounded Somali gunman the previous week.

Agent Reeves passed by and informed him that the FBI had cancelled their search for Muhamed Dauadi; he managed to sneak off the base somehow. Not surprising. The Somali had a talent for eluding dragnets. Since Art was the only member of the unit to engage the terrorist, Lamborghini peppered him with questions.

"If he's banged up as bad as you," he said, "we've alerted clinics and area hospitals should he decide to seek medical aid."

"Don't count on it," Art said. "He'd never expose himself to people who could report him."

Sitting down, Art began typing in highlights of today's wild adventure. He sighed, rolled his tongue, and attempted to chronicle events in circumstantial order. What a crock of shit, he swore, tearing up the first draft and preparing a second. Then he revised the opening lines and started again. He dismissed his actions as temporary forgetfulness. It better be, he speculated. Out of shape or medically unfit agents weren't allowed in the field. It could also be from the back pain, or the effects of the Tylenol.

Mercado pranced into the room. It was the first time she had seen him since he left that morning. "You look like hell," she smiled, tapping the underside of her chin.

"So everybody's been telling me. Hey, look...it was just like any other terrorist versus agent encounter."

"Well, we're all glad you made it back. Soon as you draft your report, FYI, Walter requests your presence. Don't rush." She stroked his arm and headed to another section of the processing center.

She had done it again. Whether she flirted with him for sport or tested him to see how far she could go, he wished it wasn't so obvious. With Curbside and Lamborghini, she maintained a constant professional relationship. Tony, though, enjoyed playfully bantering with her. And, just like any normal, red-blooded male, who wouldn't welcome a tryst with her? He'd already experienced a situation with her, which spiraled him near the top. He intended to not let it happen again. *Women*, he squinted, noticing her conferring with a systems analyst near Noordine Assad's terminal. *Who can figure them out?* Or, perhaps, with danger emerging over every horizon, acting precocious was her relief marker.

A half hour later, working on the third document, he heard a voice boom over the intercom.

"Agent Dodek, my office...if you don't mind."

He shook his head and printed out the report.

When he entered the director's private office, McLaughlin was sitting down; Mack Quintal stood beside his desk. Quintal gave him one of his cold expressions—lips stretched flat across the face, eyebrows raised closely together.

Dropping the summary on the desk, he stepped back and waited for his boss to speak.

While Consuela called him by his first name, Walter, Art neither referred to him by first name nor the more official Mr. McLaughlin. Even Alistair Burke, Director of the National Security Unit in Canada, for whom Art had worked for over two years, he'd greet by his first name, never as "boss" or "Mister." When he'd first met Walter, he had referred to him with the formal "sir" salutation; since then, too many events had passed to be polite.

"Take a seat, Agent."

"I'll stand." He wasn't being impolite. Sitting down added pressure on his back.

"Up to you." The director buzzed through the report, and then set it down. In an obvious uncongenial voice, he said, "You the man."

Art shrugged. *No, I'm not*, he said to himself, wondering what was coming next. With Quintal present, his gut told him that it wouldn't be pleasant.

"You taking on the Somali Brotherhood single handedly?" asked McLaughlin.

Get to the point, damn it, Art swore under his breath.

"All I hear around here is about your confrontation with Muhamed Dauadi. You appear like you came out of it fairly unscathed. Says in your report that you observed him trying to sabotage a liquid natural gas storage tank. Guess you saved the Southland from another terrorist catastrophe; that I'll give you credit for. The commander of West Coast Naval Operations called to thank DHS for its diligence."

Why was it, Art reckoned, that he sensed being sucked into something?

McLaughlin leaned backward. "You put in a good word for Agent Curbside's assistance. Commendable. That's what I instill in all my operatives…teamwork." He paused, tapping his fingers over a ring binder. "What are you looking so dazed about? What do you want? A medal?"

What Art would've liked was an explanation as to why the director held back sending a back up team to Los Alamitos.

"How'd it feel, Dodek, tangling with that mother-fucker?" Quintal injected.

"Excuse me?"

"You had a firearm," the ex-army ranger said, straightening up, eying Art with the same menacing look as when they were in the Analysis Center. "Why didn't you use it? Getting too soft? Muslims your friends now?"

"Go to hell!" Art exclaimed. "I managed to get off a few rounds. We ended up fighting. And I—"

"I…nothing. You let him get away."

Art was ready to claw the smug look off Quintal's face. "That couldn't be helped."

"Mr. Quintal is right, Dodek," The director added. "Did you let him get away or not?"

"I wasn't in a position to make an arrest."

"I detect sarcasm in your tone," McLaughlin said. "I expect members of this unit to be civil."

He wasn't about to apologize. Shit, no. Not to any of their screwball denunciations.

"That sort of inaction can impact your service in the Unit. I expected better of you," said McLaughlin. "For Christ's sake, since you've been here, it's turned into the Wild West. On top of that, two prisoners — two material witnesses — are dead. What else can you accomplish before the Unit goes all to hell?"

"You seem more concerned about your position."

"What?"

"What's your boss gonna think about your administrative capabilities? Two guards executed. Two prisoners dead. Both of them tortured under your watch."

Quintal exploded. "What? How the fuck would you know?"

"According to the medical report, they —"

"Medical report? What medical report?" McLaughlin shouted, quickly getting to his feet. He and Quintal exchanged glances. "I've never seen anything as to how they died. Ali committed suicide; Najaif was killed by some European hit man."

"Both underwent extreme physical abuse prior to their deaths."

"I suppose that you know who harmed them." The director's face turned reddish.

"I'm sure we'll find out...whoever they were. To me, they're just a level below what those Somalis represented."

"I suppose you're going to take it upon yourself to find out."

Art drew a deep breath. "Give it time...we'll discover which thugs..."

"Then what, Dodek?" asked Quintal. "You gonna fuck up that arrest, too?"

"You know," Art said, starting for the door and squinting at Quintal, "I might be inclined to use deadly force. If we're through, I have work to do."

Quintal was going to interrupt, but McLaughlin waved him off. "Your job, Agent, is to find Dauadi. And if I recall, you're supposed to be looking for Saleh Ali. I suggest you get your ass out of here and start looking. Don't let them escape this time."

Meeting over. About damn time, were Art's thoughts as he departed.

A grin lit up his face as he peered through the frosted glass panel, observing the two men inside obviously having an argument. Big deal, if it was about him.

A few minutes later, he entered the staff lounge for a coffee. Turning around, Mercado, smiling, leaned against the doorframe. He wasn't startled by her sudden presence. Her coy expression, though, caught him off guard, again.

She handed him her cell phone and hit the Memory Replay button. On video, with good audio and picture clarity, he watched the episode in the director's office from just minutes ago. "Don't get your balls in a knot," she said, "but I think you've knocked their buttons out of shape."

"Didn't you provide McLaughlin with the M.E.'s report?"

"How come you didn't give me more info about the prisoners?"

"Are you withholding evidence on me?" both of them asked together.

Consuela broke into laughter, contagious enough that he followed suit. Despite curtailing where they should've ended last night, their hands slowly moved toward one another.

A spontaneous look of "hands off" brought them back to earth.

Damn integrity, he cursed.

Art's BlackBerry beeped. "Agent Art Dodek here." The skin around his eyes crinkled at a familiar voice. He waved at Mercado as she sauntered down the hallway.

"It's my dime, so I'll make this brief," the caller began. "Art, old friend, how you doing?"

"Just fine, Lucky. Thanks for getting back to me this soon."

"You like the DHS job? The Unit has some good people keeping you company."

Art wouldn't disagree. "Most, of them, anyway."

The secure call was coming from Karachi, Pakistan. With a sixteen-hour time difference, Art knew Lucky must've awoken before sunrise to make this call.

Lucky was Art's Intel counterpart when he served in Pakistan with the Canadian Intelligence Service as a junior agent years ago. Though his actual name was Luciano de 'Angelo, everybody called him Lucky. Yet it had no connection to luck. Neither one remembered how the nickname began, but it stuck. Today he headed CIA operations in Karachi. The two men hadn't seen one another since those early days, yet they'd managed to keep in touch over the years. Plus, his information was invaluable when Art required Intel, or the odd personal request. Like under the radar type info.

Art smiled. He could picture his friend doodling or picking favorites for cricket games, Pakistan's national sport. "Well, what did you find out?"

"I know every officer who's worked with me at CIA, abroad or at Langley." His tone, fairly clear, turned serious. And, despite almost a dozen years stationed overseas, his voice still resonated with a Bostonian brogue. "And I remember names. Mack Quintal never worked on any of my watches. You've never heard of him?"

"I didn't say that. Hold on for a minute." Agent Reeves dropped a notebook on Art's desk. "Nobody knows much about him. Personally, I think Director Walter McLaughlin inferred they worked together overseas, including Pakistan. Something doesn't gel. CIA records were a blank." Static interrupted the call. "Hello. Lucky?"

"Yeah. I knew McLaughlin. Not well. Personally, some of us thought he was just working Intel for political gain. Even his superiors were dubious about his investigative methods."

"What about Quintal? His military history is a joke. No wonder the army threw him out of the service. Aside from that, I think his involvement with McLaughlin isn't giving me the whole story. I think he's covering up. Like, why the claim about the CIA experience?"

"Well, I went one step further with your inquiry about Quintal's court martial. My source in DOD got hold of court statements, stuff left off online. That guy in your Unit abused detainees, roughed them up to the point it became torture."

"That was my impression. I won't bore you with the details, Lucky, but he more or less bragged about captured militants being mistreated."

"What are you thinking?"

"I'm not sure. It's kind of complicated here."

Audio decreased again on the line.

"Damn phone service," de 'Angelo said. "If it's office politics, just go with the flow. Otherwise, keep alert. Anyway, don't ask me how he received clearance to join DHS."

"Maybe McLaughlin should answer that."

"Hey, look, old buddy, glad to talk with you, but," he yawned and chuckled, "the roosters aren't even awake over here."

"Okay. Thanks for the info."

"Anytime. So when you coming back to Karachi?" He knew Dodek wouldn't return. The question was meant as a standing joke. "Heads up over there."

"All the time."

After hanging up, Art rolled his tongue around for a few seconds. He stifled a yawn, grabbed a blueberry muffin, and left the lounge.

The first person he passed mere feet from the lunchroom was Quintal, arms crossed, expressionless.

Avoiding eye contact, he bit into his muffin and continued walking. He felt Quintal's eyes seared into the back of his head. Art didn't give a rat's ass whether the jerk overheard the conversation or not.

206

Chapter 39

Everyone in the Unit received a text from McLaughlin to meet in the conference room. Each message ended with the time, down to the exact minute.

By four in the afternoon the members were dragging their asses after spending most of the day mired in communiqués and analyzing intercommunication reports from a number of U.S. and international counter-terrorism agencies. Most contained standard chatter amongst suspicious groups in the Middle East, with nothing pointing toward any imminent threat. Still, from experience, Taliban and al-Qaeda radicals were notorious for sending messages smacking of innuendo and double-speak.

However, the odd one cropped up that would be sent to the CIA for overseas investigation and the FBI for internal scrutinizing. Patterns, similarities in words and places were often clues worth checking, and should never be second-guessed. That's what the terrorists hoped analysts would do...become sidetracked or confused about potential targets.

More worrisome to authorities were e-mails and Twitter messages that indicated knowledge of troop movements and locations of joint allied conferences where top administrators would be gathering. As was all too familiar and tragic, even with extra security, insurgents had penetrated these events, with a high number of civilian casualties their intention. All too often, corrupted officials and individuals who worked for the allied forces provided the information.

Homeland Security also had to sift through hundreds of reports coming in daily about suspicious activities occurring at every level of the American infrastructure...ship terminals, airports, international business branches, and transportation corridors most frequently. No-Fly lists and stricter Visa requirements helped to a degree, as well as stricter security. Yet errors and slip-ups happened. Hours of time consuming surveillance and interviews with suspected individuals often resulted in not just no arrests or charges, but agents deliberately misinformed or constrained by threats of lawsuits of constitutional violations and witnesses who disappeared.

After two hours of non-stop translating and deciphering coded messages from Afghan and Pakistani sources, Noordine's ears were ringing. And, for an unexplained reason, telecommunication exchanges between Taliban militants continued heating up the lines. Nothing definitive or useful to national law enforcement agencies…the majority were the usual chants against Western imperialism, degradation of Muslim lands by NATO soldiers, and diatribes directed at the two Great Satan's: the United States and Israel.

Pinpointing their actual locations was difficult because senders and recipients often used phony IPO addresses and transmitted through non-traceable Third World cell phone outlets. When she identified certain numbers or made connections to names, she would transfer copies to the FBI and Interpol for investigation. During the last series of intercepts her keystrokes picked up something odd on her monitor—communiqués with several overlapping Middle Eastern dialects.

Signaling to Art Dodek across the room, she hit Replay as he approached. The screen displayed the foreign language message, followed by her English translation. First thing, she informed him that the Afghani sender, a person by the name of Safiulla, was unknown. Each version started off with Quaran (Koran) *Hadith* narratives of the Prophet Muhammed's sayings and actions. Expecting Arabic as the principal language, both were surprised when two Northeastern Afghanistan dialects—*Dari* and *Pashto*—emanated from *Hzib-i-Islami*, a rebel faction offshoot of the Taliban. Finding a corresponding match in English became a challenge for Noordine. She inserted another software program in order to break down some characters that had no equivalent letters of the alphabet. Safiulla had gone to extreme lengths in the event someone attempted to translate. Soon she managed to organize specific letters into Arabic, which she spelled out and then transcribed, resulting in the following message:

> "Warriors of Islam take up arms and follow your Lord. In the hour of sunset the traitors have gathered to lay siege to your homes. Go now. Strike your foe. The tongues of your enemies shall be silenced. The men of the shops; the women of the market; the children of the untrue school; the administrator and the soldier. Bless the warriors with the bomb."

Her shoulders sagged as she leaned backward. She drew in a long breath of air and exhaled. Covering her face and rubbing her eyes, she felt drained, exhausted.

Art and Noordine locked eyes. Slowly, shock set in. An imminent attack planned somewhere in Afghanistan...what could they do? Where? Kandahar, the major site for military bases of the NATO forces? Kabul, where most of the country's government officials were located? There were dozens of remote towns and villages in the Peshawar region bordering Pakistan, which were constantly invaded by Taliban insurgents, places that even U.S. and Canadian soldiers were reluctant to patrol. They were astonished that Noordine's vast database of terrorist organizations contained no current Intelligence information from the CIA or FBI about the rebel group named in the text.

She forwarded multiple copies to Intel agencies around the globe, the first to the State Department, which in turn had to pass the information through various channels in Washington before it notified overseas decision makers. Provided the commanders in Afghanistan received the warnings, they were already hamstrung—how did they stop, let alone prepare for, an unknown terrorist attack that may be occurring at that moment?

DHS analysts were cautioned about allowing distressful situations from becoming too personal. No matter how she fought it, her mind swirled at images of the terrorists murdering civilians and school children, adding to the carnage undertaken by fanatics in the name of religion. Fingers shaking, she popped open a water bottle. Some of the liquid splashed onto her top as she drank. Art rested a hand on her shoulder; the gesture was appreciated, but it would take a while before her somber mood wore off.

A female member of the processing center dropped a bundle of videotapes by Noordine's monitor; a note on the top disc read, "Review. Save or Destroy." She didn't have to look at the initials (WM) to know who issued the assignment. The job could wait. Right now, scanning possible disturbing discs was on her to do list.

About ten minutes later, the group, red-eyed and quiet, sauntered into the conference room. McLaughlin and Quintal sat together at the far end. The director had his nose buried in the report of the imminent attack in Afghanistan.

A fresh pot of coffee had just finished brewing. With the exception of Mercado, the others lined up for a late afternoon jolt. They remained quiet as they selected their chairs.

Avoiding Quintal's gaze, Art fixed his eyes on the director. Still stamped in his mind, however, was the peculiar association of McLaughlin and Quintal. A demoted, imprisoned ex-army officer didn't

209

just walk into Homeland Security and get named as number two man for no reason. Lucky De `Angelo had confirmed that Mack Quintal wasn't listed in CIA personnel records. Art intended to investigate further. No damn way he'd accept their alliance as coincidental.

McLaughlin had already started speaking when Mercado tapped his arm. Thoughts evaporated as he leaned back and took his first sip.

"In front of you is the guest list for a State Department gala tonight at the Century Plaza World Hotel. Besides her own Secret Service detail, the secretary has requested that our unit be on hand. Dress code is formal. While there hasn't been any chatter about anybody interrupting the affair or planning overt action, you're in attendance to observe, and keep alert. She's made it clear—you are there to prevent any disruption, not engage in Wild West roughhousing. The LAPD is handling external security; you assist with internal."

"Regarding security, boss," Lamborghini said. "The first line of defense should be before the party gets underway. What measures have been planned to assure those attending are who they're supposed to be?"

Quintal raised his hand. "Every person prior to entering has an invitation card with an embedded chip that will be checked by an electronic reader."

"What about women's purses?" Alyesia inquired. "Shouldn't they be—?"

"Don't even think about it, Reeves," Quintal stated.

"Why are they getting a pass?" Mercado asked.

"Figure it out...protocol," answered McLaughlin. "In any event, you're free to mingle, but discretely. Don't talk to the guests. Any shenanigans from you and the secretary will bite your ass off. Questions?"

The group shrugged their shoulders at what they perceived as obvious. "Quintal will be in charge. You have concerns tonight, check with him first."

For the first time, their eyebrows rose at that announcement.

Art twirled his tongue. *We don't know squat about this guy, and he's gonna oversee the Unit. Besides the gala, we'll keep an eye on him.* Rising, he had a question. "The public is aware of tonight?"

"It's been posted on Washington websites, CNN news," the director said. "We're not anticipating problems. It's up to you people to sniff out trouble. Get yourself tidied up...date night begins at 7:30 p.m. sharp. Dismissed."

Outside the office, Mercado quipped to Art, "What's Quintal gonna wear—an army uniform?"

"He was booted out of the service, remember. Maybe security won't let him in."

"We wish."

***

Leaning against the headboard in his hotel room, Dauadi twirled prayer beads around his hands. A water bottle lay on the bed, two empties scattered on the floor. Nearby, the black suit he'd worn a few days earlier hung sloppily over a chair. The welding gear he had discarded at the Los Alamitos Navy depot. In navy fatigues, he had merely strolled by the security gate without anyone questioning his departure. Some of the bruises on his face had healed. Scrapes and cuts on his hands would fade in time. But what he'd failed to accomplish, sabotaging the gas tanks, lingered in his head. Dauadi swore he would have the advantage, as well as seek revenge against, the infidel Homeland Security agent who had interrupted his mission, if they met again. To him, all Zionists occupying Muslim lands in Palestine should be drowned in the Red sea.

Earlier that day at his mosque he also didn't find any young Somalis who would replace his dead comrades. None of the teens he'd talked to showed the slightest interest in joining the Somali Brotherhood. He had to be careful when he conferred with the imam, who conducted prayers, about potential recruits. While they were close religious brothers with the militants, imams had been known to contact the FBI on hearing that young men agreed—whether voluntarily or when threatened with violence—to become martyrs. The two men at the house in South Pasadena were useless; besides, neither had any insurgent training. He considered traveling to Minneapolis to search for recruits, but abandoned the idea. His father would notify the authorities immediately, and even using public transportation was risky, as his name and picture were posted on every airport No-Fly-List across the country. There were still targets in Los Angeles, some already planned. He needed accomplices, and quickly.

The only person he regarded as his true father, Saleh Ali Nabhat Saleh, wherever he resided, had heard about American agents pursuing and shooting other Jihad Brothers. While Dauadi would've given his life for Saleh, at the same time he often wondered if his mentor would save his life. Many times at the Pakistan training camp allegiances changed, or were bought and sold. Someone holding favor, to a mullah, for example, or warlord of a certain district, would be banished from the inner circle, or assigned a mission with next to impossible chances of coming back alive. Saleh Ali either liked you or hated you. The latter meant a hail of bullets as you departed from your family home. Instead of being a new recruit, you were ordered to suit up in a suicide vest and forced to crash through a military barrier. This action particularly happened to men who strayed from the strict *Wahabi Islam* sect. In some cases, cousins or uncles of Saleh lost limbs as signs to other fellow warriors: never challenge his word.

Dauadi's main concern was staying off Homeland Security and FBI radar, but he was primarily geared to revising logistics and planning better-prepared attacks. He viewed himself as a cut above the average terrorist—trained and fostered by one of the fiercest men in *al-Shabad*—and foresaw the day all Americans would crawl under the terror of the Jihadi Brotherhood. His grandiose world blurred the blunder he had committed. You didn't kill the hand that fed you, such as the Russians who provided your armaments, by murdering a Russian assassin. So what? Russian enforcers were bought and sold everyday. Instead of giving him the money, it could be used toward purchasing weapons.

A TV remote control was about as obscure as the murkiness of his room. Swearing in broken Arabic, he jumped off the bed and switched on the set. Seconds later, a poor quality picture emerged. Fiddling with the buttons underneath the chassis, at first he ignored the ending of a commercial, and then sat down on the crumpled carpet as a local station reported acts of terrorism. His mood changed. Up close he didn't need his glasses. Coal dark eyes watched intently.

***

Before leaving for the gala, the agents heard about an attack late the previous day in the Helmand province region of Afghanistan. As foretold by the rebel group *Hzib-i-Islami*, insurgents raided several remote villages. Combining squads of gunmen with automatic weapons and RPGs and suicide bombers, they executed village elders, regional administrators, and policemen, blew up a girl's high school, and ambushed an international foreign aid organization. The number of fatalities was unknown, but could reach dozens of mostly civilian deaths. Reports filtered out that the terrorists scattered into the mountains before allied troops arrived. Wounded officers claimed that besides Afghan and Pakistani militants, some of the attackers spoke dialects from Yemen, Saudi Arabia, and Egypt, reinforcing NATO assertions that foreign fighters were regularly recruited and financed by the Taliban.

Chapter 40

Department of State Gala, Century City

Limousines disembarked their passengers at the front entrance of the Century Plaza World Hotel, all under the watchful eyes of police officers and security guards hired by the DHS. Although traffic control and protection outside the hotel was essential, cops wore their formal uniforms. No gun-toting SWAT members huddled around doorways to dispel the notion that U.S. authorities had to fortify every state occasion. State Department personnel escorted multi-national diplomats, government officials, politicians, and prominent business people from Western and Eastern Europe, the Middle East, South East Asia, land rivals India and Pakistan, Central and South America, Africa, China, Canada, and the host country, the United States, to a security checkpoint prior to entering a designated ballroom. After guests swiped invitation cards through to an electronic reader, instead of guests emptying pockets, a radar-like ceiling beam pinged. It wasn't an electronic strip-search where scanners could see through clothing; the beam detected only suspicious substances such as powder or metal objects concealed on their bodies, being respectful of their personal dignity and cultural differences, yet necessary to prevent the possibility of a potential threat.

Agents Reeves and Lamborghini and a Secret Service officer observed the security procedures. Throughout the room other agents wound their way around the guests. Their appearance — dark suits and ear buds in contrast with the colorful evening dresses worn by women and majority of the men in tuxedos — singled them out as government agents.

A band of black-tied musicians provided background chamber music, as well as varying musical selections from the different countries. Champagne in flutes, served by white-jacketed staff, was instantly scooped up from trays whenever waiters strolled amongst the guests. For those seeking more traditional spirits, guests could quaff back any drink imaginable or sample West Coast micro-brewed beers and ales, and a wine bar featuring Californian reserves. While various languages and dialects hummed through the ballroom, English and French seemed for the most part the principal languages for conversing. Flags from the representative nations were strung along the walls, with the Stars and Stripes elevated, and the seal of the Department of State affixed to a floor stand centerpiece.

Greeting and mingling with her guests, the secretary, a portly woman in her late fifties, brownish-tinged gray hair curled just below her neck, and wearing a royal blue sequined floor-length evening gown, exchanged small talk in several languages. The occasional official remarked about her accent, which was pure Tennessean. In fact, the woman who once ran for vice-president and was now serving her second term as Secretary of State spoke fluent German, French, Spanish, Italian, and various Nordic languages. Besides her holding a long line of government positions, other family members also had significant roles in the current administration, including her husband, the American Ambassador to the United Nations, plus an aunt who served on the United States Supreme Court.

Close by, yet discretely positioned, two Secret Service agents ringed her at forty-five-degree angles.

Red, white, and blue adorned tables displaying hors d'oeuvres were busy places. Servers doled out selections of American cheeses, Pacific Northwest oysters and shell fish, Atlantic cod and smoked salmon, duck pâté, succulent sauces, collections of special Californian and Hispanic appetizers, breads, buns, crackers and half a dozen different dips, endless trays of vegetables and mixed salads, beer battered sausage rolls, and assorted cold cuts, plus crepes and wine flavored sherbets. Popular egg-size strawberries from the fields of Oxnard in nearby Ventura County and Modesto in Central California drenched in chocolate sauce accentuated plates stacked with blueberries, melon, and cantaloupe wedges.

Hobnobbing with the dignitaries and pitching Los Angeles as the place to relocate or establish branches and subsidiaries, as well as utilize their infrastructure and high tech research and development ingenuity, the mayor sucked air with anyone who listened. Chief operating officers, presidents, and industrial giants in aerospace, shipping and transportation, auto assembling, and clean energy resources touted Southern California to consul generals and trade commissioners. The governor of California, who couldn't be there, sent his state trade representative, who listed tax incentives. Not mentioned was that California, which was suffering one of its worst recessions, needed jobs and extra tax resources. Chinese delegates more than likely calculated the already billions of dollars in loans outstanding. Once in a while an ambassador, upset at a neighboring country for an issue long forgotten, engaged in a heated discussion with his counterpart.

As the evening progressed, the Unit found themselves growing restless. Watching dignitaries drink and stuff themselves wasn't their standard assignment. Bets were on, and at least one in the Unit promised to check tomorrow whether black tie affairs were in their agent's manual.

Nothing in particular stood out. None of the guests illustrated anything suspicious; no one got out of hand. It was up to security, not them, if a person appeared belligerent toward anybody. Yet they remained observant. Words weren't flowing, but body language did as they passed one another, wondering why they were chosen. At least one time or another, they all circumvented Quintal whenever he approached. A few minutes later they noticed him, wine goblet in hand, brown-nosing the secretary. What would her reaction be if she discovered Quintal had served time and lied about his service in the Central Intelligence Agency?

Art and Consuela relaxed near a post. In a dark pant suit and crisp white shirt, her hair done up in a bun, she could've been a member of a wedding party. Even with light makeup, she looked radiant. And she was not unnoticed…often Art caught male guests observing her every move.

Art had to lower his eyes a bit when a freckle-faced fellow with reddish hair sauntered over and enquired if Art was Jewish. Upon hearing yes, the man, who identified himself as the Israeli ambassador, spouted off several words in Yiddish. Some of it Art understood, said *shalom* a couple of times, and made a polite get-away with his partner. She smiled and adjusted his necktie. Dressing formally he did not like.

Nearby, Dan Curbside and a Secret Service agent gabbed. From their easy-going chatter, the two men likely knew one another.

Just then a senior police officer whispered something into Lamborghini's ear near the ballroom doorway. A serious faced Tony Lamborghini nodded and joined the two agents. Ten minutes prior the LAPD had found a limo blocking the entrance to a garage three blocks from the hotel. Forcing open the doors they found a body slumped over in the rear, its throat slit. No identification was discovered, but the police believed the man was from a Mediterranean or Middle Eastern country. Art's skin color turned off white.

Mercado jarred her head backward, grasping the information with an expression that he hadn't seen on her face before.

His hand automatically felt alongside the Glock beneath his suit coat.

Eyes browsed throughout the crowd. Training told them to focus on someone who didn't stand out. With over a hundred guests, scores of servers and staff workers, getting pricked by a needle in a haystack would've been easier.

215

Apprehensively, they searched for the secretary, lost somewhere in the throng.

Chapter 41

Mercado noticed her about a minute later chatting with a couple from the African delegation. Regardless of their own personal agenda, Quintal had to be apprised, and quickly. Finding him winding his way through a group of foreign ministers, she inhaled deeply and tapped his shoulder. When informed, there was no reaction from the ex-army officer. And when she told him that she and Art would advise the secretary and her bodyguards, his lips tightened and eyes rolled. No junior agent would talk to a cabinet secretary, as far as he was concerned.

Of all places for him to have a snit, she sighed.

To stave off a public disagreement, she suggested that as Unit supervisor, and a female, it was best for her to report the development. Without waiting for him to respond, she calmly approached the secretary. Art grinned and walked alongside about a yard away.

"Madame Secretary," she said, standing a foot away and interrupting her conversation with a young couple. "May I please speak with you?"

"Of course. Please excuse me, Mr. Ambassador."

The two women moved toward an occupied table.

"And you are—?"

"Pardon, ma'am. I'm Consuela Mercado, the Unit Supervisor of the Homeland Security detail in support of this evening's event. It's extremely important to let you know something has happened. As of yet not confirmed, we think there's been a security breach."

The secretary gasped after hearing that someone had been slain. "Oh, my God, the poor man. Do you know who he was?"

"The FBI and police are checking. Ma'am, it's possible his murderer used an invitation card to gain entry."

Standing nearby, Art directed Lamborghini and Reeves to close the ballroom door, no one out or in.

One of the secretary's Secret Service agents, a hulk of an African-American with a dark moustache, noticed his boss's worried expression.

"Ma'am?" he inquired, stepping alongside the two women.

217

Within a fraction of a minute after hearing the news, he motioned to his co-agents. Three of them instantly encircled Mercado and the secretary.

Several guests near the group gazed at the sudden movements. Soon a buzz began from other people. The secretary placed her hand on Mercado's arm and whispered. "Ms. Mercado, look around you. If they think something is up, we could have a stampede on our hands. Does anybody else know?"

"No. Only the agents here and the police investigators at the crime scene."

"Good. What are you proposing?" She tilted her head and smiled at people out of earshot.

Mercado changed shoulder locations with her handbag. For this kind of affair, only her P-35, a cell phone, and an extra ear bud would be contained in her purse. Plus, no doubt, spare lipstick, and an eye mascara container.

She motioned for Art to join them. "This is my partner, Art Dodek."

"Madame Secretary," he smiled, nodding. "If there's an intruder, we believe the best course is for you to leave."

A defiant-looking woman crossed her arms. "You're commended for thinking about my safety. However, I won't be intimidated in my own country. Agent Dodek, if I left…which won't happen…what about all my guests? Some would be utterly offended. Right now, mind you, they're the least of my worry. As I said, I will not be chased away." She glanced at the husky agent. "Harvey, what would you do?"

"Whatever you think is best, ma'am."

"I want to carry on as before. Can you not investigate who may have crashed my party?"

"Absolutely," Mercado said confidently, realizing that she had no suspect.

"Splendid. Then I suggest you take care of what you do best. Please check back with me."

Her Secret Service escort followed their boss as she turned and mingled with a group of Japanese businessmen.

Consuela Mercado emitted a low whistle.

"I got an idea," Art said. "You heard the lady…carry on." Stepping backward, he almost squished Quintal's right shoe. "Agent Mercado will give you a heads up." He edged his way through a crowd of Italian businessmen and went to the front desk.

"Thanks a lot," she muttered, with Quintal pressing her for details.

Piled on top were the invitation cards, arranged alphabetically by guest name, title, and country, as well as a tick mark in red ink denoting check-in. In addition, the electronic reader entered a time stamp.

Attendance records confirmed that between 7:30 and 8 p.m., a hundred and five guests had arrived. Three more followed within ten minutes, plus three no-shows; the Romanian charge`d'affaires, the consul general from Uzbekistan, and the secretary general from Nigeria. No big deal. Diplomats were notorious for ignoring invitations.

Sighing, he wondered who was the imposter. The murderer could be any one of the hundred and eight people in the suite. His immediate speculation as to the target centered on the Secretary of State, partly because she often lent vocal opposition against some of America's international foes, and staunchly defended Israel. What about many of the representative countries there tonight? Either they were strong allies of her foreign policies or vociferous critics.

He made some mental calculations. Okay, about ten minutes ago Lamborghini had announced the limo found at the parking garage. Perhaps five minutes before the police arrived. Another three to four minutes for cops to inform senior officers at the Century Plaza. Average time for walking to the ballroom, five minutes. Add on time they'd discussed the matter with the secretary. Yeah, the guy would've had plenty of time before he infiltrated.

"Aylesha, can you tell who last arrived?"

"Sure. All the attendee names were recorded upon arrival; times entered." She scrolled through the list and hit the cursor on her laptop.

Two women in sleeveless gowns were about to open the suite door. Stepping in front, Lamborghini explained that for the moment guests were advised to remain inside. A Spanish accented voice remarked that was silly; however, both spun around, rejoining the gala.

"This man," Reeves said, pointing to the name.

"Shaalzar. From the Sudan," Art said. "Odd that the U.S. would invite a Sudanese government official,"

"Not government—look again—heavy machinery importer."

"That doesn't make sense. Sudan isn't exactly a champion of human rights. And as far as I know, that country is off limits for buying American goods."

"Well, the secretary invited him."

He surveyed the large assembly of guests. Several African nationals wove their way through the crowd, as well as several Middle Eastern high-ranking officials adorned in their formal garb.

Man-oh-man, the last thing he wanted to do was profile individuals. What else could he think? The intruder could be white, black, dark, anything.

Wake up, Dodek, he said to himself. Any intruder planning to carry out some kind of mission wouldn't want to draw attention.

He scratched his chin. "Aylesha, you and Tony were here all the time when people checked in?"

"Yes we were. Except—"

"Except what"

"Uh…when Tony had to intercept a guy who climbed over the rope stanchion. He was making a fuss about the screening process."

"Somebody could have slipped by you?"

"If we were distracted long enough," gushed Reeves. "Oh, man…that might have been…."

"Or deliberately distracted you. Would you recognize him?"

"Dark, mid height, black suit…I didn't see him long enough before he drifted inside." Her partner, standing a few feet away, snapped his fingers. "One of the staff had to translate for him about the card."

"What was a staff member doing at the check-in?"

Lamborghini shrugged. "What are you thinking?"

Art bit his lip and ambled through the throng, catching up to Mercado and Quintal.

Again, the latter showed disinterest at the news, almost skepticism. His only comment, after downing his Scotch, was "You heard the woman—she's not leaving. Get on with your jobs." With that, he sauntered away from the two sullen-faced agents.

Mercado hissed. If Quintal were one of her agents, not only would she ground him, she'd insist that McLaughlin throw him out of the Unit. It wouldn't happen, and that incensed her.

Now they had a dilemma on their hands.

Art scurried over to Harvey, the secretary's chief agent, who was standing behind his boss, and whispered what had developed.

Harvey, who stood at least half a foot over Art and topped him by sixty to seventy pounds, nodded, measuring in his head how serious the situation could become. Most likely he'd put a guy down with one swing if someone tried to endanger his charge. From his years of experience in the Service, alarm bells sounded in his head and he realized this was no false alarm. Entrenched in his brain was a knack, perhaps a perception, that a situation could change from threatening to risky. He'd feel it in his gut when he scanned a crowd; something, someone generally, made him nervous. Assigned to members of cabinet and two vice-presidents, he'd encountered the overzealous fans who wanted an autograph to the sociopath who demanded an audience, or else. Ninety-nine point nine percent of the incidents were trivial. The remaining small percentage could turn into an ugly situation. Ask him or anyone of hundreds of agents, none would hesitate to give their life.

Art's previous partner with the National Security Unit in Vancouver, Keith Dawson, had served with the Secret Service. In any event, they had to find a delicate way to remove the secretary without causing a problem for her or her guests.

Chapter 42

If the infiltrator had a weapon, Art figured the Unit or the Secret Service agents could take him out with minimum civilian casualties. His heart pounded at the horror inflicted if an IED discharged. How in hell could they stop a lunatic bomber hell bent on committing suicide at a State Department function?

Mercado and her partner approached the secretary, intruding on her discussion of current peace talks with the Israeli and Jordanian ambassadors. It was clear from her disdainful expression that she resented the interruption. Familiar, however, with how her bodyguards increased the ring around her when a potential threat was imminent, she may have sensed danger lurking in the shadows. Still, her annoyance hadn't ebbed.

"Are you sure?" she asked, glancing up at Harvey.

"We think it's serious, ma'am."

"Ms. Mercado...Consuela...what am I supposed to do? Can you picture the ramifications from leaders of the free world if they saw the Secretary of State run like a possum through the Ozarks?" Those who worked for her knew about her stubbornness. She would never cut and run. "Look at my lips...I am not leaving."

"Your bravery is commendable, Madame Secretary," Mercado smiled, admiring her courage, wondering what she'd do if their roles were reversed. The circle of officers and audible voices caught the attention of those around them to the extent that people ceased talking and stared.

Art clasped his hands by his waist. "Would you agree if we disperse your guests in groups?"

"What then, Mr. Dodek—frisk them? Am I not getting through to you people?"

"Ma'am, keeping everybody safe is our only intention."

"No searching my guests. God, how embarrassing."

"It won't happen," Mercado followed.

"If you have something else in mind, Harvey and I will listen."

For the first time tonight she included her chief agent in how they would extricate themselves from a touchy situation; evidently, she respected his opinion.

"Ma'am," asked Art, "do you know most of the people here tonight?"

"Not all. Some I've met or known regarding State business."

"Any one you don't recognize? I mean, anyone that you think doesn't fit?"

Mercado noticed the woman's head turning, and stopped her by moving in the same direction. "You'll have your guests thinking something is amiss if you gaze at everybody. Off the cuff, anyone…?"

"Not really. Harvey, you're the one with the photographic memory."

The agent shifted his eyes for a few seconds, then shook his head no.

Just as Art turned, both of Harvey's large arms shot forward to the secretary.

Stepping quickly toward her, one of the white jacket clad waiters pushed aside two women. A white towel draped over one of his arms, which he extended to his waist.

"Look out," Art hollered, as he opened his suit coat to grab his Glock.

Harvey wheeled and used his size to shield the secretary.

"Freeze! Don't move!" ordered the other Secret Service agents, four guns aiming at the dazed dark skinned server.

One agent tackled the waiter from behind and threw him to the ground. A clunk echoed when the towel hit the floor. With help, they twisted the man's arms to his side.

Mercado and Art encircled the secretary with their arms, their movements so fast that the woman almost lost her balance. They didn't have to say anything to the near panicked expression enveloping her face.

The waiter grimaced and moaned when handcuffs tightened around his wrists.

"Harvey…w–what…?" a flushed secretary asked.

Her chief bodyguard unraveled the cloth. Out dropped a set of cutlery.

Although none of the officers said a word, "Oh, shit," formed over their mouths. A pair of agents whisked the trembling man to the kitchen.

Some of the onlookers oohed, awed, and gasped, while others backed away in pockets.

"Madame Secretary, it's okay," Mercado said.

Rubbing her hands and letting out a long breath, she squinted at the two DHS agents, unimpressed with their actions. "This is why you want me to leave? Dropped cutlery?"

Mercado and Art almost blushed.

"I have guests to meet. Plus, I'm going to eat something. Excuse me. Harvey."

She worked her way through astonished officials and headed for the appetizers. Before he caught up to his boss, Harvey whispered, "You guys did okay."

A Scotch in one hand, Quintal came up alongside the agents, who both made a beeline for the kitchen.

Lamborghini stopped them. "The waiter…he's the guy who showed up at the entrance when the last guest arrived."

"You're sure?" asked Art, exchanging concerned expressions with his team.

"Damned sure. I think that episode was a test to—"

"See how fast we'd react," Mercado finished, and muttered something in Spanish.

Art surveyed the room. "Meanwhile, we've got an infiltrator roaming around."

"Hold on," Mercado said as her phone buzzed in her handbag.

Curbside joined his partners. "Secret Service is gonna release the waiter. There's nothing to keep him in custody."

"Dan, try to get them to hold him longer," Art said, running out of options.

"Noordine, yes, we're still here," Mercado murmured into her cell phone. "We thought we had the real thing. Could've been serious. You heard what? Repeat it again." She held the phone a few inches away for Art to hear.

"Saleh Ali Nabhat Saleh is at the hotel."

Dead silence. Mouths widened, eyes opened to the point of popping.

"Are you sure? Are you sure?" repeated Mercado.

Noordine's voice shook. "Cameras got his picture entering the Century Plaza. We've been online with the Secret Service all evening. Everybody who was invited is on camera. I'm sending you his new photo…and the only picture we have of him from a previous file photo that was matched to a Face Recognition System."

Within seconds the hotel frame appeared on her cell phone, followed by the one known picture of the Somali Brotherhood al-Shabat leader. The agents froze as though an ice covered crevice had opened up below their feet.

From bearded and scruffy looking in a white shawl draped over a *Galabeya*, the traditional Muslim men's long sleeved shirt, to closer trimmed, wearing a dark suit and rounded gray-lensed eyeglasses, all they had to do was focus on his ink-black eyes in the initial image. It felt as though knives scraped down their backs.

This was the man many Holy warriors would follow into hell, if it meant massacring infidels and launching world scale Jihad. The self-appointed mullah worshiped by Muhamed Dauadi. His twisted mind had already caused the loss of countless lives in Southern California.

"Consuela…Connie, are you there?" shouted Noordine.

"We're here." Another round of Spanish expletives sprouted from her mouth.

"Walter's on his way to the hotel. He thinks you should get the Secretary of State out of there before…something happens."

"You don't know this woman."

"Hmm?"

"Thanks, Noordine. We'll look into it." Mercado hung up, and, one by one, eyed each of her partners. "Now what?"

"Let us know what you want to do," Lamborghini offered.

"Connie," Art said, waving his hands, "if you have to pick her up and carry her out of the hotel…."

"You hold back Harvey, then."

From out of nowhere, a shock wave pricked through his head as he recalled the first DHS meeting after arriving in Los Angeles, when Consuela informed the Unit about Saleh Ali. Neither Border Services, Immigration Enforcement, nor U.S. Customs ever showed him as entering the country. Being Canadian, a visitor B-2 Visa wasn't required. He might've slipped through the cracks; it happened. Yet surveillance cameras in front of the hotel picked him out of a hundred and ten guests. Nevertheless, Saleh Ali wasn't the martyr type—he made sure others succeeded or died for his violent ideology. There had to be another person inside the ballroom. Or outside.

Mercado passed bleary-eyed Quintal, who, despite supposedly being in charge tonight, chose Scotch whiskey as his companion. She didn't even bother advising him, instead, whispered details into Harvey's ear.

Without hesitating, she and her agents closed in on the secretary, clutching both her arms. Her plate of appetizers banged to the floor. Before she could object, her feet were off the ground as they escorted her to the door.

Art was waiting for them. Opening the wide doors, he stood in front of the group as they started to leave the ballroom.

Guests behind them began forming at the door, only to be stopped by Lamborghini and Reeves. Holding up their hands, they ignored the protests.

Just as the secretary and her security entourage entered the hallway, the hearts of four people stopped. Standing about ten feet away, two armed SWAT officers confronted them. Helmeted, faces shielded, M-16s at waist level pointing straight ahead, the pair uttered not a word. Both shifted themselves from side to side.

Neither did the astonished agents say anything.

One of the arrangements for tonight's embassy function was that no heavily armed police officers be within sight of the secretary and her guests.

The metallic clicks of the M-16 trigger releases echoed like rockets through the ears of those parked by the door. Assault rifles pivoted upward, aiming straight at the group.

Instinct kicked in as Harvey leaned over the secretary and shoved her to the granite-paneled floor. A muffled scream escaped from her mouth as she struggled under the weight of her senior bodyguard.

"Connie!" Art shouted as he dropped to his knees. "They're not cops."

Art and Consuela whipped out their weapons. Not even ten feet separated them from the gunmen. Who fired first didn't matter, but each round hurtling out of their gun chambers had shoot-to-kill on its point. Because of the thick vests on the gunmen, they shot repeatedly above their chests until their bullets pierced the face shields. One guy instantly went down. The other one staggered and jerked sideways, his carbine firing up at a light fixture, which shattered, raining glass splinters over Harvey's back. Despite the woman squirming underneath him, he wouldn't loosen his grip.

People in front of Reeves and Lamborghini yelled and watched in horror as the second cop's body wilted and dropped to the ground. Gun smoke swirled up to the high ceiling. Some of the insurgents' high-powered shells had ripped into the side of the ballroom door.

Both agents used their combined weights to prevent anyone from leaving. That was until Reeves, gritting her teeth, swayed and sank to her knees. Seeing his partner in distress, Lamborghini knelt down and shook her arm, shocked as blood streamed from her left side.

With no one to block them, terrified men and women loped through the corridors like antelope pursued by cheetahs on the African Savannah.

"Aylesha, damn it, no…!" he yelled.

"T-Tony…I–I can't breathe."

"Take it easy, partner."

She may have looked up at Lamborghini, but her eyes didn't see him.

Art kicked the M-16s aside across the floor.

Mercado whirled around and knelt down beside her colleague. "Tony…what…?" Blood smeared her hand as she tried to turn Aylesha.

Curbside, plus the other Secret Service agents, guns drawn, flew to the doorway. One helped Harvey up. Together they lifted the secretary as gently as they could. She was in stocking feet; her shoes had slipped off

226

when she got knocked to the floor in the frenzy. She still took the time to inquire about her bodyguard's welfare. "Harvey…are you all right?"

"Yes, ma'am," he said, brushing colored glass and pieces of brass trim off his jacket. Before she peered into the hallway, he escorted her back inside the room, intent on not letting his boss observe two bodies lying in the corridor and a wounded federal agent.

Curbside called 911 as Art knelt beside Aylesha.

A gun in his hand instead of his cocktail, Quintal shuffled into the hallway. "I'm in charge here. What happened? Dodek, you…did you shoot those cops?"

"Yeah, except they weren't cops. Write it up. Just get the hell out of our way."

"You and me are gonna talk about your attitude."

Nothing I'd like better, Art promised.

"If you haven't noticed," muttered a disheveled Mercado, "Aylesha has been shot."

"So how is she?" If he had asked what time it was he might've sounded more concerned.

Reeves began wheezing and spitting out blood, yet her eyes showed no sign of pain, despite the large caliber shell that had cut through her flesh. None of the Unit wore bulletproof vests. It wasn't on their security list of priorities for tonight.

"No, don't try to move," her supervisor cautioned, holding her hand. "Medics are on the way." Mercado looked up at Lamborghini. "Tony, what…?"

"We were stopping people from leaving. We heard the shooting, screaming. I didn't know Aylesha was…."

Art patted the agent's shoulder, and clenched his teeth from a twinge of pain burning in his back. Exerting his body when firing had singed another nerve. Everybody was too pre-occupied with his or her injured partner to notice him pressing a hand on his lower back. With no medication in his pocket, he had to suck wind until he got some pills later.

A pair of paramedics quickly arrived and attended to Aylesha. Now she was gasping and twitching.

McLaughlin dashed toward the scene, alarmed at watching one of his unit members being treated for gunshot wounds. He rushed up to the group, followed by a couple of genuine LAPD officers. He also inquired about Saleh Ali.

No news, no sighting, Art related to the director as they stepped aside for a stretcher wheeled in by a second Emergency Response Team.

Spotting Quintal and the Secretary of State engaged in a noisy conversation, McLaughlin insisted that he be apprised of Aylesha's condition, and then strolled into the ballroom. Mercado, examining the bloodstains on her fingers, just hoped he was as interested as he expressed.

***

The secretary, sitting down and gulping a glass of water, and Quintal were engaged in a heated conversation. Voices rang out all around her. In spite of her hair being mussed up and her being shoeless, the glum look on her face matched the ruddy lines creasing her cheeks. She inquired whether any guests were hurt, relieved that everyone survived. She gave a thumbs-up sign to Harvey. In a few seconds, though, she scowled, annoyed that the diplomatic gala she'd hosted had been interrupted.

***

As Aylesha drifted in and out of consciousness, medics peeled off her jacket and cut off most of her shirt. Rolls of gauze and tape were applied to the wound, and a tube was inserted down her throat. Vitals were taken, which numbered into the stratosphere. Without a medical examination, it was difficult to pinpoint which rib had taken the brunt of the bullet, where it entered, or whether it was still inside. They managed to stem the blood flow from under her ribcage, but discovered torn flesh consistent with another bullet wound. This one had pierced her lower abdomen below the pubic bone. If there was any good news, little blood on the floor indicated that none of her arteries had been hit. Moans rolled over her lips, which began turning blue, while her eyelids fluttered uncontrollably. One hand rolled back and forth along the floor, as if she were reaching for something.

A minute later they rushed her outside the hotel to a waiting ambulance. Her partner jumped in beside her just as a paramedic placed an oxygen mask over her face and told him she was going into shock.

***

Art slid the cracked face shields off the two bogus SWAT cops, convinced the pair, barely out of their teens, were Somali. Another officer chalked outlines of the bodies. Art couldn't count how many bullets had struck the pair, but penetration wounds ranged from under their necks to cheeks and upper faces. It really pissed him off that the insurgents could've picked up fake police uniforms at any costume shop or resale props store in

Hollywood.

Mercado holstered her firearm. Unlike how shook up she became after the incident at Encada Engineering, this time her emotions appeared more mechanical. If she did feel anything, no damned way she'd show him. Training told her to fire; that's exactly what she'd done. Whatever motivated his partner to fire without hesitation was her choice and decision, as long as she kept it in perspective, and didn't enjoy it. That was a danger most agents didn't want to experience. If you were incapable of differentiating necessity from satisfaction, you may as well join the other side.

Art Dodek had long ago given up measuring his actions on the firing line, not from hatred of an enemy. That was part of his job, and he carried out lethal force essentially for the safety of others, as well as defense of his own life. At one time he'd had to reason why he would take a life. Not anymore. Justified, necessary, do it. But he never worried about it. God knew that would make him normal. In his world, the only ones who may be normal were those who stayed out of his way.

Saleh Ali still posed a problem. They realized that searching would be next to impossible; he would've dispersed with the crowd, disappearing anywhere in Los Angeles by now. What about the impostor who stole the invitation card? An accomplice? Or was that Saleh Ali?

Recruiting two youths to attack the diplomatic corps and possibly kill the Secretary of State would've reinforced to other Islamic dissidents that the Jihadi Brotherhood could carry out an execution inside America right under mass security. Their deaths were immaterial; after all, dying was more important, especially to demonstrate how weak American Intelligence performed. The greater the deed, the more followers and worshipers flocked to its leaders. Muhamed Dauadi remained unchecked. Saleh Ali, presumably, had meandered unnoticed, mere feet from one of the highest-ranking cabinet secretaries in the federal government. Only one thing would be bothering him: they'd missed.

Art lost sight of the director in the corridor filled with Secret Service agents and a ring of police officers.

Three hours later the Unit crowded around the surgeon at Mercy General Hospital. The lounge was full of other people anxiously waiting for word on their family members.

Lamborghini looked like hell. Little wonder. His eyes were reddened, and lines burrowed into his forehead. Bloodstains matted on his suit coat. Like most law enforcement partnerships, they had become not only dependent but attached, until they knew each other inside and out. Nothing rankled an agent more than having their partner go down.

He jumped off a chair when he spotted his colleagues sprinting down the corridor. Surrounding him with questions, he muttered that he hadn't seen Aylesha since she was admitted into the ER. They'd had to chase him out, he reported.

The doctor, on the short side, a slim beard coming to a point under his chin, and, at most, in his early thirties, removed his cap. His blue scrubs were wrinkled and sweaty. He asked the first question, which hit the group like a cannonball. "Is Aylesha Reeves married?"

"What are you talking about?" Mercado winced.

"First, let me assure you that your associate will be okay. Surgery went well. There's still some internal bleeding; the healing process should minimize any danger. We removed the bullet from her third rib. Bone fragments made the extraction difficult. Her other wound was more serious…it destroyed her fallopian tubes. Unfortunately, the damage is permanent, meaning she'll never bear another child."

"Another child? Aylesha was never married. Are you saying that she was pregnant?"

He looked at Consuela and said, "We couldn't save her fetus. If you weren't aware, she was approximately into her nineteenth week."

Shaking her head, Mercado asked, "Does she know yet?"

"She's not awake. We have her heavily sedated in ICU."

Noordine, a bouquet of yellow and white mums in her hands, sighed. She expressed a few words in her mother tongue about Aylesha's medical condition, along the lines of, "God speed your recovery."

"She's bound to recover," the doctor added. "I'd recommend you pray for your partner. Rest is what she needs. And she's under excellent care. Stop by tomorrow, please. If you want, call my office in the morning. I'm Doctor Haleem as-Sabur."

Everyone thanked the doctor, and tried to digest the news. Aylesha never kept secrets from her female partners. They all knew that after her CIA fiancé dumped her, she never married.

While they waited for the elevator, Lamborghini asked Art, "How did you know the Somalis weren't cops? You just had a split second to react."

"You didn't notice? SWAT officers in blue jeans; no LAPD shoulder patches."

"Well, I bet the secretary was relieved you noticed," Noordine said.

Art glanced back as the surgeon disappeared behind sliding doors. He had to grin at his surname. In Arabic it loosely meant "the patient." Or, in its literal text, one who has learned to become patient.

Unfortunately, patience was never one of Art's virtues. Tonight was no exception. While he shared similar distress with that of his partners over Aylesha Reeves, he focused on Saleh Ali and the Secretary of State. Not content with murdering civilians or law enforcement officers, the Brotherhood had come close to assassinating a high-ranking federal cabinet secretary.

The agents remained silent as they rode down to the main floor. Mercado, however, picked up on his frustrated expression. No inquiry necessary…she felt the same way, as well as deeply concerned about the shooting of a unit member.

Chapter 43

It was after one the next morning when Art arrived at his apartment. Tired, still upset at Aylesha's shooting and Saleh Ali vanishing, he chucked off his vest. Unbuckling his holster, he had his first chance to see how many bullets he had fired. One bullet remained in the chamber, one in the clip. Shit, he hit both of the Somalis seven times, plus whatever Consuela blasted off. It could've waited till he arose in the morning; instead, he slammed in a new magazine, tossed his holster on a chair, and raided the refrigerator, downing almost half a pitcher of orange juice.

Minutes later in the bathroom, he ripped off his clothes and jumped into the shower. For a solid minute he allowed the steamy water to splash down over his body. The smell of gun smoke had permeated his skin. Lynda would be infuriated when she smelled gunpowder on his clothes. The inevitable argument ensued; leave NSU before you get hurt, or worse, and take a job at the national security headquarters in Ottawa, Canada's capitol, which he refused to do.

Oh, shit, he cursed, *I didn't call her tonight. No sense phoning now.* His previous calls hadn't gone over well, anyway.

The shrill ringing of the telephone sliced through his ears. Grabbing a towel, he picked up after the fifth ring. His voice didn't sound welcoming, perhaps because he knew it wasn't Lynda. "Hello. You'd better have a damn good reason for — "

"Don't get your shorts in a knot, Dodek," chided his partner.

"Don't you ever go to bed?"

"Depends if I have someone to go to bed with."

He wasn't in the mood to be amused, but sensed her half-hearted joke was a way to wear off her frustration. "Well…?"

"I called the hospital. They said Aylesha came out of her anesthetic. She'll be doped up for a while." Her voice started cracking, brought on by the strain of one of her own suffering from gunshot injuries.

"Logical. She took two shells. Bad news about her pregnancy."

"Yes. Noordine and I certainly never knew. I'm going to Mercy General before checking into the unit. I'd like to be there when she finds out, you know, about…. Anyway, she's gonna need a hand to hold."

"Sure, okay." He stifled a yawn by pressing the towel against his mouth.

"That was close tonight, the ruckus with the secretary."

Odd choice of words she used to describe a near assassination, he thought, breathing away from the phone. "Yeah, it was. How are you doing, Connie?"

"We did what we had to. That's all that matters. God, think of the paperwork we must fill out for the bureaus." She meant the FBI and the Secret Service, who wanted reports from the agents involved in a fatal takedown. "You'd better get to bed. Another big day tomorrow."

"Grab some sleep yourself."

"Yeah, yeah."

He visualized her stretching. "If Aylesha is awake, let her know we're all rooting for her."

"Thanks, she'll appreciate it. *Buenos noches*." She disconnected her end.

Art put his pill bottle on the night table. Sooner or later he'd pop the bottle open. Drying his legs, he gazed at the phone. In a way, he wished that Consuela had stayed on the line. No talking shop, no DHS bullshit…just two people who had too many emotional cords.

Early in the morning, atop the main reception desk at Homeland Security, staff and Unit members found a huge bouquet of chrysanthemums, carnations, and American red roses in a vase wrapped in sheer plastic. A note pinned to the front read:

To the Unit
With Gratitude
I won't ever doubt you again.
Whitney Mitchell, Secretary of State.

The card had the official seal of the United States State Department. Everybody also learned that a bouquet and card were delivered to Agent Aylesha Reeves.

These tokens of appreciation were unfortunately set aside when Consuela informed the Unit that Aylesha found out about her unborn child. Its effect, she added, may not strike her completely until the morphine injected into her wore off.

Today Consuela wore a black cowl neck sweater dress with dark stockings. No matter which dress style she chose, when her auburn hair danced along her shoulders, you couldn't take your eyes off her.

The first piece of business started with information on the two youths disguised as cops. Both were Somali-American citizens. However, Yemeni passports found in their belongings indicated they just returned to the United States the day before. Transcripts from family members in Newark, New Jersey, reported them missing seven months ago. There was no Intel follow-up. In fact, not only were their information files lost or misplaced, the Central Intelligence Agency North African division had failed to investigate the youths' whereabouts.

Tony Lamborghini wandered in late; nobody said a word. Even McLaughlin, who demanded on time from his agents, decided not to make a fuss. But, like the others, he still requested a full report of the hotel incident from all members.

While the U.S. and the international media recounted the attempted assassination of the Secretary of State, there was not a blip from any terrorist organization claiming that it was behind the plot. DHS surmised there must've been a Somali Brotherhood connection. For an organization that regularly bragged about its bravado to strike anywhere, they remained strangely silent. That didn't cancel out any new terrorist wave, not by any stretch...not with Muhamed Dauadi and Saleh Ali Nabhat Saleh roaming around Los Angeles. Did Saleh come to the U.S. to orchestrate Century Plaza personally, or bring new plans for his unstable protégé? Was the secretary the third target of the prophecy related to the June tenth Islamic celebrations, after the military contractor bombings? Agents knew better than to assume. With little to go on at the moment, it made their analysis that much more difficult.

The National Security Administration and Central Intelligence Agency clogged Homeland Security computers with communications from the Middle East. Ordinarily, they would be searching for messages with cross-references to groups, factions, or elements of the Taliban and al-Qaeda. Most statements had domestic ramifications for Homeland Security analysts. The Brothers of Somali Jihad, while sharing common goals of defeating the Great Satan, created their own communiqués with their own brand of ultra-extremist overtures, chose their own targets, planned and prepared for them, selected the weapons, and carried out the mission. From what had occurred, while their methods were crude, the results were devastating.

The DHS unit had no one on third base, and they were still battling zero.

Chapter 44

Something else that morning diverted attention from analysis-gathering information.

Noordine Assad joined her colleagues. She preferred loose fitting pant suits to dresses; her choice today, a light emerald shade with butterflies embroidered over the flaps of the side pockets.

A grim Noordine took her supervisor aside. In her hands she held two videotapes. Art watched Consuela's reaction, and it wasn't pleasant. Both women huddled for a couple more minutes, and then motioned him over. His eyebrows bounced like fluttering sagebrush when they brought him into the discussion. Noordine kept pointing to the tapes, insisting that her partners view them at once.

The translator-analyst said, "Last night when you were all covering the Century Plaza World Hotel gala, I spent some time editing and deleting video tracks. I came across some serious stuff."

"There's a machine," Mercado said, pointing across the room.

"Uh, no. Not here in the Analyst Center. There's nobody in the conference room…let's use that one."

They followed her down the corridor. Noordine was already setting up a VCR when they entered. There was something on her face, which indicated this had to be reviewed at once.

Taking their seats, they waited for Noordine to press the Play button.

"This is the first tape," she explained, still standing. "Recording time, shortly after 10 p.m. The date is in the lower right corner."

No graininess, no inferior picture quality, this tape clearly showed Walter McLaughlin entering the outer hallway adjacent to the detention area, then walking through the open security door to the guards' station. While there was no sound, he was directing the two guards to open the cellblock. Within a minute, Tariq, who was arrested at Dream Girls, walked out in handcuffs, and was handed over to the director. Both McLaughlin and Tariq then left.

The VCR went to Stop, then Fast Forward.

Noordine waved her forefinger. "Now it's after 11:30 p.m. Watch."

McLaughlin was escorting the Somali prisoner back to the detention center. Tariq was limping, and his face looked contorted; he was obviously in pain, his orange jump suit and T-shirt torn. A guard had to hold him up to keep him from falling. The director walked away.

"Next morning, you know what happened...Tariq was found hanging in his cell."

"What happened to the prisoner *before* he committed suicide?" Art asked, thinking back to the medical report.

Mercado uncrossed her legs and leaned forward. "What's Walter doing in the cell block at that time of night? And the prisoner looks like shit."

Noordine ejected the tape and inserted the second one, starting at the point where she had it set for Play. "Watch. The date should ring a bell. It's the evening after all the terrible explosions at the B of A tower. Connie, I think you know what's coming."

Again, the director entered the secured detention area. This sequence showed him waiting. The Somali teenager, Husien Najaif, handcuffed and bewildered looking, was brought outside and handed over to McLaughlin.

"Look closely at the boy's temple. I'll zoom in and stop. The only abrasion he has is a bump from when Tony hit him with his firearm." She resumed Play at the next editing sequence.

"The kid sure didn't go for a late night burger and Coke," Art said, peering at the teen's condition as he was returned to detention.

Najaif was almost falling over; without assistance he'd have collapsed. His clothes were also messed up.

Mercado uttered a comment, which would have consequences later on. "He looks like he's had the shock of his life."

"Should I replay them?" asked Noordine.

"No. Is there more?"

"I'm afraid so," her voice dropped. "The next patch is actually from two separate evenings, the same nights Mr. McLaughlin accompanies the prisoners. Have a look." In less than a minute the VCR whirred until it stopped and began playing. "This footage, you can tell, is from our parking garage surveillance cameras."

The two agents had never fixated on a tape as much as this one. On two different nights the director was shown first placing Tariq in the van, shackling his legs and tying a mask on his head, then a repeat on the second night with Najaif being shackled and a hood thrown over the teen's head.

"Turn it off…we've seen enough," Mercado scowled. "Where the hell does Walter take the prisoners? Art, is that what you were trying to tell me a while ago — that you suspected they were abused?"

"Yeah, guess I was." His mind shot back to Quintal at Patches.

"What are you thinking?"

"Uh, just what we've viewed."

"Noordine," Mercado asked. "Have you shown these tapes to anyone else?"

"No one. I wanted you both to see them before…. What should I do?"

"You have a place to hide them?"

The analyst nodded. "In my desk there's a secure drawer."

"Good. Keep them there for now. I don't want anyone else to view them, let alone know about them, for the time being. Thanks for bringing this to our attention."

"What about Mr. McLaughlin? Shouldn't we —?"

"Let us handle him. Come on, Dodek. We have work to do."

***

Somebody else also viewed the tapes. Standing outside the half open door Quintal clenched his lips together, then jaunted down the hallway as Consuela and Art headed to the exit.

Chapter 45

"I don't give a shit that it's nine in the morning," Quintal boomed when he stormed into McLaughlin's office. "We gotta talk. You're coming with me. I need a drink."

The director didn't take kindly to being bossed around, but said, "I have a bottle in my private room; we'll talk there."

"No. Anywhere else except this building."

"What's got you riled up? Dodek flexing his muscles on you again?"

"Get up, Walter. We're leaving. By the other way so we don't pass the communication center or the reception foyer." Quintal was already into the hallway as McLaughlin grabbed his suit coat.

Next to the private office, a corridor led to a set of unused rooms, which sometimes housed boxes of files. McLaughlin used this as an occasional private exit. Furniture, what there was of it, had long ago been taken to other offices. Since the lights worked off a main panel switch for the sixth floor main offices, overhead fluorescent lights remained on. A second doorway ran kitty corner to the main elevators. No one behind the large glass doors leading to the DHS center would have seen them leaving. As well, only downstairs from the lobby to the front doors would there be any cameras or security guards, who would've hardly given a glance as the DHS managing boss departed with Quintal.

Los Angeles Street had no shortage of restaurants and lounges. One that McLaughlin frequented was three buildings down from the next corner. If it had a name, nobody knew it...just the address on the door, a beer ad on one side, a whiskey name on the other. The place was old...smelly old. Furnishings must've come with the bar when it first opened years ago. Chairs squeaked on the frayed linoleum floor. Cushions on semi-circled booths had slits or threads hanging. Whatever atmosphere this place wanted to allude to wasn't clear, either. Newer functional sports bars were the rage, so there were big-screen television sets, more substantial food choices, umpteen varieties of brews and drinks, games such as shuffleboard, darts, and pool. Part of the place looked like a nightclub. Someone had tried L.A. sports themes, although you'd never know which sport it represented. Half the photographs lining a wall were of bartenders and staff from long ago, retired or dead. If anything modern was what a casual drinker expected, this watering hole didn't have it. The most recent photographs were of a former mayor who'd lost a civic election over ten years ago. Perhaps it was his notoriety that attracted the faithful. Apparently, he was greasing cronies' hands with taxpayer dollars...like all politicians, deny any wrongdoing, and blame it on your underlings. Except the district attorney had come down hard on him after the election...fines, mostly. It was rumored some wanna-be gangster had pocketed the bulk of the cash. Anyway, perhaps the guy was a regular; city hall wasn't that far away.

All types headed there regardless of the time of day. Morning made no difference. Patrons were comprised of attorneys, private and government office workers, and managers unable to cope without a couple of stiff drinks in their gut. Males outnumbered women six to one. Two bored women in black skirts guzzled as many martinis as the bartender plied them with.

No wonder McLaughlin favored a no-name bar; none of his staff would've set foot there. The old guy who tended bar acknowledged him and went on mixing drinks.

The two men found a booth as far back from the entrance as they could find. Quintal ordered the drinks. Two Cutty Sarks, crushed ice for his glass. When the drinks arrived, Quintal stuffed a twenty into the waitress's side pocket. Without a murmur, she sauntered to a nearby table. He downed half his Scotch. Burping, he said, "Mercado and Dodek have tapes of you in the garage."

"Big deal. So what?"

"Do Tariq and Najaif ring a bell, Walter?"

"The Somali prisoners. Yeah, so?"

"When I worked in Special Ops and Intel I would've made sure my movements were clandestine...not for the whole fucking world to view. Didn't you think somebody sooner or later would see the contents?"

"Mack, you never worked for any Intel agency. You and me may have operated together when I was a section manager for the CIA in Pakistan. You know damn well we worked behind the scenes, but we got results. And what the hell are you talking about?"

"The video tapes."

"Me in the garage? What else? Make sense, okay."

Quintal downed the rest of his Cutty Sark, and held up the empty glass for the waitress to notice. "You and those fucking Somali insurgents in the DHS car park, outside the cells."

Rubbing his lips together, McLaughlin shook the ice cubes in his glass. He rested one elbow on the table. "Yeah, how else do you think I got them to the warehouses for you to work over?"

"Well, aren't you quick on the draw to lay the blame on me."

"Am I talking to the wall? Mack, get to the point."

"You're on Candid Camera escorting those two into your van and escorting back two beat-up looking prisoners. Is that enough of a point?"

McLaughlin stared at his partner. Maybe the booze had affected his mental ability. Only now was he connecting dots. "You said Consuela and Dodek have seen them. When?"

"Before I walked into your office. What the fuck does it matter when they saw them? They viewed them. Dodek's an asshole, but he's not dumb. I told you, he's always snooping around. Then there's your Mexican supervisor, Ms. Know-it-all bitch."

"What about Consuela?" He sipped immediately as the second round appeared.

"They're probably hatching a plan to use those tapes against you."

"Like hell. Where are they?"

"In Noordine's desk."

"Who else has seen them?"

"Only your translator, Dodek, and Mercado. Don't just sit there, Walter. You better think of something. You're not as innocent as you think you are. You got me to mishandle prisoners—just as we did in Pakistan—and I did when you authorized me to. Maybe over there, who gave a shit about torturing terrorists? Just be damn glad Tariq and Najaif are dead."

"I didn't kill them…we didn't kill them. They did us a favor by dying."

"Yeah, right." Quintal pounded the table, shaking the glasses toward the edge.

McLaughlin had to hold the table steady.

"When word gets out, the FBI is gonna start snooping around. What the hell do you think they'll do when they see the videos? What a goddamn mess. You're supposed to be searching for that prick Dauadi and Saleh Allah, whatever you call him. That's the main reason you brought me on board…spark the fuck out of the prisoners to disclose where Dauadi is. Mind you, there's nobody that I would like to string up more than Dauadi. Of course, it'd be on your order."

"Back off, Quintal. Don't you go holier-than-thou on me all of a sudden."

Their loud voices drew glances from some of the other patrons.

"Fuck you, Walter. I already spent over a year at Leavenworth. I sure as hell won't set foot in any federal prison again. If you —"

The cell phone in McLaughlin's breast pocket beeped. He checked the message, surprised that it was from Noordine, but didn't answer. He sipped slowly on his Scotch. "Mack, I can take care of Mercado. And for the tapes, leave that to me." He leaned back and shot a quick stare at Quintal. "I'll leave Dodek to you."

Quintal curled the glass in his hands. "Finally you're talking like the director you're supposed to be." The lines on his nose reddened. He grabbed a long breath as he felt the Scotch drop to the bottom of his stomach.

"Knock it off. I have to get back to work. You watch yourself."

"Like I'll be watching you."

Both men slid out from the booth. Quintal paid the rest of the bill as they were leaving. They separated about half a block from the federal building. Before heading back, McLaughlin lit up a cigarette and puffed until the end glowed red, and stomped on it at the curb. He stopped at a newspaper kiosk and bought a package of breath mints.

As he ascended the stairs to the federal building, he couldn't stop a muffled, "Fuck you, Quintal" from slipping over his lips.

Chapter 46

An hour later, Art and Consuela were seated at desks opposite one another reviewing notes on the Somali Brotherhood investigation. Once in a while they glanced over but didn't speak.

Her mind was still pre-occupied with Aylesha and that the Unit had temporarily lost an agent, and a damn good one. The purpose of the Unit was to keep two teams and herself as supervisor. With Dodek on loan from Canada they could still function, provided that some potential danger didn't arise that affected their current number. The last time she ran into Lamborghini he was still shook up over his partner. For now she'd assigned him light administrative duties. Still, she expected him to be a crack agent when called upon. That applied to all members'…compassion, definitely; alertness and readiness, always.

With each minute passing, Art noticed her waning interest in reports. Although not going overboard emotionally after watching the videos, it must've struck a sour chord with her. How she could keep her emotions in check was beyond him. If somebody from his Canadian National Security Unit pulled a similar stunt, he'd have exploded and marched the guy off to jail, if it went that far.

Sitting for long periods made him uncomfortable. Nerve endings along the spine continued to plague his back. He stood, grimaced, placing one hand forward on the desk and the other pressing along his lower back.

Consuela narrowed her eyes. "Back still bothering you? Don't think I haven't noticed. You screwed it up when I fell on you, didn't you?"

"Actually when I was trying to get you down, when I hit the landing. Must've jarred a disc."

"What are you taking?"

"Some OTC extra strength pills."

"They won't cut the pain. I can give you some Oxycocet painkillers."

"You don't seem to be a woman who would take such a strong drug."

241

"I don't."

"How would you obtain prescription-only drugs?"

"You think I can't?"

He didn't doubt her for a moment. Surprising him went out the window days after they became partners. Legal or bordering on the illegal, no doubt she'd produce whatever he wanted.

He smiled as he slowly resumed sitting. "Uh, no thanks. They're too addictive. When I'm in the field I don't want some drug messing up my judgment."

"Suit yourself."

She was about to turn aside when he added, "Does anyone else in the Unit know?"

"Probably. Listen, I already have one agent laid up. If we're in a firefight, the last thing I need is my partner trudging off in pain from health problems. I want a partner who's with me all the way."

"It won't happen." He gave her a reassuring look just as a nerve struck home again.

Mercado stood and stretched her arms. "Anyway, it's a good time as any to hit Walter about the tapes. Boss or not, I think he owes the Unit an explanation."

"You know him. How do you think he's gonna react?"

"What's he gonna do—deny that's him on camera hanging onto two sorry-looking prisoners?"

He leaned back a bit. Her red-hot Latina eyes seared the air between their two desks—she was hell-bent on making this her mission.

At about this time McLaughlin walked over to Noordine's workstation. "Noordine, there's two disks on my desk that require translating. Guys in Analysis are waiting."

"All right. But I'm piecing together text messages from —"

"Now please. Use my computer. I've already entered your clearance code."

"Yes, sir." She did her best to steer clear of his eyes, worried that he'd notice her nervousness. Pressing Save on her monitor she slipped on her high heels and left the room.

For about a moment the director stood in front of her desk, then reached into his pocket and brought out a small black zippered wallet.

Chapter 47

Dodek and Mercado strolled the main area of the communications center. Banks of monitors displayed live feeds emanating from world trouble spots, with the focus on the Middle Eastern regions of Iraq, Afghanistan, Israel, Syria, Libya, Iran, Pakistan, and Yemen with its expanding militancy, and the Sudan, which had divided itself into two separate countries. Two satellite images centered on sections in Somalia controlled by the vicious al-Shabbad organization from which many Somali-Americans inherited their hatred for America. The bulk of these transmissions were sent through classified CIA lines. American spy agencies depended on these feeds twenty-fours a day, three hundred sixty-five days a year.

Connected as well was the massive communication and watchdog nerve center for the West Coast, all under the directorate of the Department of Homeland Security. Extensive security coverage spread out from the cruise ship harbor in San Pedro, the ports of Long Beach to the large installations of gas, oil, and electrical facilities dotted throughout the Southland. Since its inception the Unit had been carrying on covert and occasional open counter-terrorist operations against foreign intruders and homegrown radicals. The Somali Brotherhood continued to be the most dominant and dead center on the Unit's radar.

Noordine was back at her workstation. The translation her boss wanted had taken only minutes. In fact, most of the wording had previously been done. When the agents neared her desk she opened the locked drawer and gingerly handed the tapes to Mercado as though they were classified presidential black boxes.

"I know you mean well," she said. "Something terrible happened to those young men. It makes me sick to think that Mr. McLaughlin was…is involved. After all, he's my boss. Your boss, too, Connie." Her eyes lowered as she fiddled with her fingers on her lap.

"Don't confuse loyalty with conspiracy. I never imagined either that we'd be...." She didn't finish her sentence, as if she found it hard to think that McLaughlin may have contributed to the prisoner's injuries.

"What happens next?" asked Noordine.

Mercado shook the videotapes and took a long breath. She wasn't too thrilled about this, either. McLaughlin had handpicked her as supervisor of the Unit. While disagreements and arguments were rampant between them, with the exception of adding Quintal to the team, she believed that his allegiance to the Department of Homeland Security was genuine. As Unit leader it was up to her deciding a course of action after he issued the assignment.

She cleared her throat. "What's next? Truthfully I don't know. This is no longer a DHS problem. Guess we'd have to notify the authorities."

By alert authorities she meant the FBI.

Mercado turned to her partner. "Come on, say something."

"Let's get it over with," he replied as a vote of confidence. What he added might've surprised her, but she wouldn't have disagreed. "If he's involved in a conspiracy, then he deserves to get his ass burned."

His rash statement bothered Noordine even more. Swiveling her chair, she faced her monitors to prevent them from seeing her glum expression. A few seconds later when she swung around the agents were gone.

Without knocking Mercado swung open the door to the director's private office.

He dropped a file folder and rose. "Doesn't knock first mean anything to you? And what's *he* doing here?"

"Skip the formalities," she said. "We have information on the two Somali prisoners."

Both agents planted their feet in front of his desk.

Mercado made it obvious about the tapes in her hand by holding them in his direction, thinking that he'd comment about their contents. His answer wasn't what she expected.

"Like what? They're dead. I've closed their DHS investigations."

"You may want to reopen it. This information confirms that an individual at DHS contributed to their deaths." She paused, thinking that he'd make the honorable gesture of volunteering his responsibility. She considered tapping into his ego. Instead, she dove straight to the point. "We long suspected the two were abused. You read the M.O. report; '...signs of torture clearly visible....' The person we suspect is on these tapes. Would you like to comment, Walter?"

The game had gone on long enough. He sliced his hand through the air. "Absolutely not. And I don't like your attitude. I don't appreciate your insinuating that I had anything to do with…. You forgetting they were terrorists?"

"Who said I was accusing you of anything? Is that what we should be discussing?"

"You watch your attitude, Agent Mercado."

Art pointed to the VCR atop a TV monitor on a three-shelf stand diagonal to the desk. "Show him, Connie."

McLaughlin returned to his seat, loosened his necktie, and watched Mercado set up the machine, inserting the first tape.

Crossing her arms with the remote control resting over her left wrist, she pressed the Play button. A second before the screen lit up she pivoted toward her boss.

With a stern expression still coating his face he waited for the audio and picture to appear.

Seconds shot by. Another minute. Into the third minute all three stared at a snowy blue screen. The only sound in the room was the hissing of static and Mercado's heavy breathing.

She shook the remote, stopped the machine, and then resumed Play. It didn't make a difference.

"Fast forward," Art suggested.

She hit the button. Nothing appeared. No sound. No video.

McLaughlin leaned forward. "Well? Something wrong with the tape?"

"I-I don't understand," she murmured, letting the fast forward go straight to the end of the tape.

Art and Consuela exchanged looks that bordered on "what the hell goes?"

"I'll try the other one," she said, miffed, and ejected the first tape.

Once again she hit Play for the video which contained footage of the teenager Najaif. She clamped her teeth together. Just like a couch-quarterback subconsciously making a winning touchdown, her shoulders rose in anticipation of the big play. Except it didn't happen. Seconds floated into minutes at the blue-glowing blank screen.

Now Art took the remote and redid the set up and replay. Absolutely nothing. He withdrew the tape and handed it to Mercado. A dumbfounded look crawled over her face. Not of embarrassment, of being made a fool.

"You look troubled," McLaughlin said. "What was it you were saying? Oh yeah, 'someone in DHS having a hand at electrocuting those boys.' Did you see anything?"

Art exploded. "You're responsible for the security of detainees. Your actions on those videos confirmed that you had a hand in their being tortured." He came around the desk, his fists clenched and lips curled. "You denying it?"

"Denying what? I didn't see any —"

"We saw you dragging those boys back to detention," Mercado shouted. "And, Walter, I never mentioned electrocution. But you did."

Art leaned in close to McLaughlin's shoulder.

"Get away from me, Dodek. Both of you...get outta my office. I'm the director of this unit. Where do you get off accusing me of torturing prisoners?"

"Admit it, Walter," Mercado said forcefully.

"You might not have pulled the switch," Art said, "but you had a partner. Who was it? Your buddy Quintal...did he do your dirty work?"

"What did you do to the tapes?" Mercado asked, her eyes livid, slamming the video boxes down on his desk.

"Mercado, you're grounded!" he exclaimed, rising. "And, as far as I'm concerned, Dodek, your assignment here is over. I'm calling your boss and —"

"Be sure to tell him why," Art smirked.

"Get the fuck outta my office, both of you." His cheeks reddened. Saliva dribbled over his lips. "I'm notifying the Secretary of Homeland Security."

Mercado picked up the tapes and led her partner to the door. "Don't think this is over, Walter," she said as they departed, banging the door shut.

The first person she headed for was Noordine.

***

Sliding open the second exit door to the director's office, a steely-eyed Quintal stared at McLaughlin. He formed a fist, pounding the side of his hand on his chin until the skin on his knuckles whitened. No words flowed from his mouth, yet the long breath he exhaled said volumes.

***

The translator noticed the furious look on her colleagues' faces.

Before she could speak, Mercado asked, "Noordine, the tapes are blanks."

"That's impossible. We watched them."

"Were they always locked in your drawer?"

"Yes. I have the key." She slid open a desk drawer and pointed to a key ring. "What happened?"

"Sabotaged, that's what happened." She spun around, throwing her hands skyward, and let loose a few Spanish expletives. "Ohhh, I could strangle someone."

A staff member wandered up to Mercado and gave her a one-page print out. After a quick review, she looked up at Art and exclaimed, "Holy shit!"

Chapter 48

Mercado spun her head and handed the paper to Art. "Can you believe it?" Her question sounded more like a statement.

"If this is true, we'd better move."

The note had McLaughlin's signature.

"She's going nowhere," a voice boomed from behind. Quintal had a look on his face as though he were the boss and Mercado just an underling to order around. Although required while on duty, he wore no badge or photo ID card affixed to his green polo shirt. And he was the only Unit member who never carried a firearm. "You heard the director...she's grounded. And I'm reinforcing his order. Dodek gets the call. Alone."

"Field operations always call for two agents," she protested. "Who the hell knows what will happen?"

"Not this time. You're doing surveillance. You can handle that, can't you, Dodek?"

"Hold on," Mercado said. "Tony's unavailable at the moment. But if I'm out, Curbside can accompany Art. You know damn well that the Unit sends one agent each from the FBI and DHS."

Quintal gave her a defiant stare. "He's on another job. Dodek goes by himself."

"I'm the Unit supervisor. It's up to me to assign whose —"

"Not anymore. I don't need a Mexican screwing up any more missions."

"Watch your damn mouth," snarled Art.

Mercado eyes blazed. She balled her fingers into a fist and raised her hand in a striking motion. "Quintal, you're a piece of shit. I'm gonna shove your tongue up your ass."

Quintal laughed.

Stepping closer to his partner, Art flexed his fingers. "You have a line of people lining up to kick your butt."

Eyes widening, Noordine slunk back in her chair, looking worried that the three of them might go beyond arguing.

"Don't tempt me, Dodek." Quintal snatched the print away from Mercado and slid it behind Art's bulletproof vest. "You've been given an assignment — move."

Art could feel his heart pounding and diaphragm shaking. The domino effect caused a brief spasm that snaked into his back. Half turning, he said, "I'll keep in touch, Connie. If you want to go a couple rounds with dickhead, be my guest."

Mercado smiled, watching him disappear around a hallway. Quintal sauntered away.

Not until he started up the Crown Victoria in the garage did Art read the entire note.

> *From the desk of Los Angeles DHS Unit Director Walter McLaughlin*
> *Clearance Authorization Order C/W – VE35880*
> *Read as Follows:*
> *FBI reports sighting of suspect Saleh Ali Nabhat Saleh, alleged mastermind of The Somali Jihad Brotherhood (DHS case #20114500). Homeland Security Surveillance urgently recommended.*
> *Investigation assigned to Agent Art Dodek.*
> *Information below.*
>
> *By order of Walter McLaughlin, Director*

After memorizing the Intel info described in the order, Art backed up and wheeled his way through three exit lanes, past the DHS kiosk, which scanned and captured the plate number, up a ramp, and onto the street. As soon as the scanner picked up an ID number for a vehicle belonging to the DHS, a chip system similar to Low-Jack installed in the bottom left windshield corner kicked in which could trace the car's movements, such as monitoring direction and speed. Even when he set the GPS for the destination, Homeland Security computers could track his route. This system provided a safety net in the event that the field agent required assistance or had an emergency. A voice could interrupt route directions and inquire whether help was needed.

Making a right at the first corner, he worked his way over to the far lane.

Several thoughts bunched up at once in his head. He sorted through the important ones, trying to put together their importance. The confrontation with McLaughlin over the tapes; the smug look as the

249

director deflected any blame to prisoner abuse; Consuela grounded; and that jerk Quintal ordering them around. Staring quickly at the paper lying on the passenger seat, he pondered for a few seconds, thinking how the FBI was able to sight Saleh Ali this soon after he breached security at the Century Plaza, and the attempted assassination of Secretary of State Mitchell.

If it led to apprehending the Brotherhood leader, he'd do all within his power to get him into a federal prison.

A mile ahead, while taking his turn for going west on a one-way street, a fifth thought rolled in his head. Since the brawl at the naval depot, Muhamed Dauadi, it seemed, had slid from radar. The question was what to make of his absence. Was he running out of ideas or preparing another attack? Art knew better than to assume anything, especially with that lunatic terrorist on the loose.

***

A diesel-chugging transit bus pulled out from a stop and inched behind the Ford. With his left mirror obscured, he didn't notice the dark GMC Yukon two-car lengths back.

Chapter 49

Once Art hit the Number 10 West Santa Monica Freeway he picked up speed and managed to maintain fifty-five by using the second and third lanes. He had entered his destination before leaving downtown Los Angeles—an area near LAX. Soon he transferred to the 405 Southbound San Diego Freeway. Heavier traffic reduced his speed a bit. The voice activated GPS indicated the distance and advised him to exit Century Boulevard.

Checking his left mirror he noticed a dark SUV trailing an eighth of a mile behind in the third lane. He thought it looked familiar, but then, over half the SUVs in Southern California must've been black. And he wanted to keep his focus on Saleh Ali.

The print out consisted of three sections: suspect's whereabouts, instructions for surveillance, and apprehension procedure, if necessary. On his own, that's how McLaughlin described the assignment. For an agent who depended on details, something else on the page hadn't caught his eye.

Easing into the Century Boulevard exit lane, he crept behind other vehicles waiting for the right hand signal. Shuttle vans, delivery trucks, and airport buses up front made for a long wait until he entered the main road that led to the airport. Hotels, stores, office buildings, couriers, freight distributors, airline corporate offices, and strip mall-type shops lined both sides of the street. Large billboards showcased travel destinations to virtually anywhere in the U.S. or overseas, as well as scores of hotels in Las Vegas featuring big name entertainers.

The guidance system instructed him to turn right on the fourth street straight ahead. Every few seconds the Ford vibrated as jets roared down the nearby runways.

Right before his turn he passed a building with neon-lighted signs flashing Live Nude Girls and Triple XXX Rated Videos. He grinned. Guess some guys wanted to get their jollies before traveling. This road led to shuttle bus-parking garages; further ahead, truck depots and industrial structures.

A few seconds later the GPS announced that he had arrived at his destination. Pulling over to the curb, he gave the buildings around him a long gaze, yet was a little puzzled about this location.

With his attention focused on his surroundings he didn't notice the SUV, which stopped at the end of the block.

Art shifted into park and withdrew his cell phone. Pressing down three numbers on the number pad, within seconds he heard a familiar voice answer.

"Art, we have your location on the board."

"What gives, Connie?"

"Remain where you are."

"And do what? Is Saleh Ali at this location or not?" A bunker oil trailer truck passing by shook the Crown Victoria. Shuttle vans and vehicles passed him almost non-stop.

"Keep your shorts on," she chuckled. "Tony managed to dig up some new Intel on Ali Saleh." There was a five second pause, the sound of pages being handled, and a muffled voice in the background, as if someone was trying to attract her attention.

"Connie...talk to me."

"Hold on. I'm sorting through.... Noordine and Tony are with me. Tony, at least let me have them in numerical order."

"Will you get on with it?"

"I'm not a robot." This time her voice had a tinge of sarcasm, no doubt from stress.

"Connie...."

"Okay, ready. Listen. I had Noordine pull up the photograph of Saleh at the hotel."

"Damn luck, huh? In the same room with us and we couldn't find him."

"Don't remind me. Anyway, she also acquired his Canadian passport information, which had his previous picture in it, and was issued under his full regular name. The current one expired long ago; no renewal applied for. Stamp arrival-departure endorsements are only in and out of Kenya, Somalia, and Pakistan. Since he's a citizen of Canada he doesn't get stamped entering the U.S."

"I know that. Only holders of Visas are tagged, and I-94 Arrival cards issued."

"Right. But if he entered our country, he'd still undergo customs and immigration inspection and turn in a U.S. Customs card dated day of travel. There's not one entry, not one date listed in the USC data bank. We figured all along that he snuck into the U.S. — which happens every day in this country to bypass being identified—or had help. Well, the former is what we discovered. Okay, Tony, your turn. Art, Tony's gonna send you info on your phone. Read 'em and weep."

"Read, yes. Weep, no. I might swear, though." Putting Consuela on hold, he skipped over a couple of buttons and pressed the button for an incoming text. "Okay, it's starting."

With his entire focus on the screen he hadn't realized the SUV had inched several feet closer.

***

Art had an inkling that Ali Saleh used the method described by Lamborghini.

The Somali Brotherhood leader entered border posts along rural areas of Montana and Minnesota where there were neither immigration manned checkpoints nor Border Services agents for one-on-one personal inspection of international travelers. These Ports of Entry (P.O.E.'s) usually consisted of a hut with a camera, and forms for self-declaration and identification. No one prevented you from crossing the border even if you disregarded the personal ID check.

Someone, or Ali Saleh himself, would drive up to the border. Even with a video camera that occasionally wasn't activated, he'd just walk across and hop into a waiting car.

It appeared he preferred two unmanned crossings. One, a town traversing Whitetail, Saskatchewan, along the Montana border; another further east at a Manitoba/Minnesota crossing. Also, DHS and the FBI knew he periodically flew to the Midwest for recruitment drives of young Somali-Americans, whisked them to Pakistan for terrorist training, and sent them back to the U.S. as insurgents. Intel had already confirmed that Minneapolis was the top market for new recruits. Muhamed Dauadi, his logistics man, was from Minneapolis.

Ali Saleh wasn't stupid. Flying on domestic flights neither passports nor international travel documents were required. Since his regular name was on the TSA no-fly list, all he needed was forged documents, a driver's license being the standard ID card in the U.S. No doubt that's how he flew to Los Angeles, where he'd planned to assassinate the Secretary of State.

***

Art reconnected to Consuela. "Okay, got it all. Thanks, Tony. Hey, how's Aylesha?"

"Improving. Thanks for asking."

"You bet. Connie, you still there?" He turned the A/C back on.

"Yes...Agent Dodek. I'm not going anywhere."

"Connie, if the FBI located Ali Saleh, why aren't they following him? Aren't they supposed to keep him under surveillance?"

"Yes, they are. That's why you were sent."

"Then why the hell isn't there a team over here?"

"They can't join you unless Walter gives the order. He hasn't, or he won't."

"Can't you pressure him?"

"He refused, period," she shouted into the phone.

"Because we accused him of torturing the Somalis?"

"It wouldn't surprise me. You've been on solo missions before; I'm sure you have."

"Sure. After pre-Intel briefings. Something's not right, Connie. I have the feeling I've been sent out to the wolves." *Sent? More like fed to the wolves.* "What about Curbside? Besides Aylesha, he's your FBI point man. Put him in a car."

A pause, then, "I don't know where he is."

"You're the damn supervisor. Don't you know where Dan is?"

Mercado understood his frustration. "Didn't you hear Quintal say Dan was on a case? Except, I hate to say it…I don't have a clue. No one will tell me. So you're on your own for a while."

"Great." Art shifted his torso so that he faced one of the cold air duct fans below the dashboard. From the rearview mirror he noticed that the SUV was parked down the road. "Great," he repeated, knowing that he was under DHS orders, no matter how much he balked.

"Art, I'll get back to you."

"You do that." He hadn't intended to end their conversation with a terse tone in his voice.

For a moment Art thought about Lynda in Vancouver, who he hadn't talked to for a few days. Even if she ended the last call with a not so welcome voice, he missed her, and promised to call her as soon as possible.

Chapter 50

The here and now brought Art back to Walter McLaughlin. The man was hard to figure out. At times he shone with pride with his loyalty to the Unit. Alternatively, he'd act with total disinterest. What pissed Art off the most was the director's deflecting responsibility onto others. By others, it meant Consuela Mercado, his team supervisor, who took the hit, unwarranted criticism, and an employer-employee situation that tested which one would be first to tell the other to shove it.

As director of the Los Angeles unit, he'd established the one-each DHS member along with an FBI agent for joint field operations, with another backup team ready at a moment's notice. It was a strict requirement, which the secretary approved when the Unit was created. *He's either disregarding or thumbing his nose at department policy.*

Art smelled the aroma of Scotch all over these department infractions. McLaughlin could be stiff-necked and stubborn, but he didn't have the *cajones* to defy Washington. He adhered to government procedure, and wouldn't go outside the box unless pressured. Mack Quintal possessed that type of pressure. Since the day he arrived he'd just about taken control of the Unit. If he could manipulate McLaughlin into neglecting his own team members, anything was possible. This was what plagued Art. Ordered to stake out parking garages with no prior intelligence and minus a fellow agent, not only was it out of department policy, he couldn't dispel the notion that McLaughlin and Quintal wanted him out of the office.

***

Add to the mix that McLaughlin desperately sought the position of assistant secretary in Washington. Colleagues in the department had leaked that his name remained in the top-ten replacement candidate long list. By the end of the year it would be reduced to five, then narrowed to three on the short list. The current assistant secretary's tenure ended early next year. He had connections in the department. Every bureaucrat and senior civil servant did. You couldn't survive or advance your career without connections. McLaughlin figured he'd served long enough in low-level positions. He'd fought long and hard; it was time he received the recognition that he considered way overdue. Satisfied with nothing less, he'd exchange his L.A. desk nameplate for one that read Assistant Secretary of Homeland Security, come hell or high water.

What could railroad acquiring the number two-job in the department? Government snoop dogs that would meticulously check his background. Because he served as a CIA officer in Pakistan it would be thorough, and he had good reason to want certain events to remain secret.

While over there he'd befriended numerous unsavory characters, many of which would have shocked his superiors, let alone made them doubtful of his patriotism. Anything transacted in Pakistan amounted to collusion with corrupted government officials, under the table cash deals with businesses, associations with crooked Pakistani Intelligence officers, the occasional Taliban narco distributor, and the Russian mafia, who were into the illegal arms trade and money laundering. Some of their illicit cash ended up in his pocket for bribes with Pakistani ministry officers. Plus actions that would've gotten him booted out of the Central Intelligence Agency. Whoever he hooked up with, whatever he did, he'd swear it was for counter-terrorism and protecting American interests. To make matters worse was his knowledge of prisoner abuse in Pakistani and Afghanistan jails, along with his actually approving the torture of detainees with his accomplice, Mack Quintal. Coupled with Art and Consuela uncovering personal involvement with the torture of two Somalis, he'd be lucky if he weren't posted to some Third World country, opening doors for U.S. Consulate staff.

Washington had dozens of dirty secrets, cover-ups for which politicians would pay thousands to keep people quiet...and the media, who would pull teeth to unearth the next big scandal. The director made sure nobody knew about his past or present. At any cost, even if it meant placing members of the unit in jeopardizing situations.

***

Uneasiness increased the longer Art sat outside the parking garage. He had expected updates from Consuela by now. Nothing changed, except the rising temperature. Every ten minutes he closed the windows and switched on the air conditioning, otherwise he'd be soaked in sweat. Shuttle vans, buses, and private vehicles continued to pass by, along with the parade of flatbed trailer trucks hauling giant refrigeration units and heavy machinery components, no doubt headed to LAX for loading onto cargo planes.

"Come on, Connie," he muttered, flipping over the phone in his hand.

Two shrill rings cut through the whir of the A/C fans. Pulling up the cover on his cell phone, he looked in stunned silence at the name on the screen.

"Dodek, wake up," Quintal said in a not-so-friendly tone. "Level 4 or 5, garage on your right. Check 'em out."

"Who? What for?"

"Suspected terrorist activity. Check it out. Copy."

"Yeah, yeah. Details."

"What do you want…instructions? Check the fucking place." Quintal disconnected.

Art shook his head then keyed the ignition to start. Before moving, he pressed three numbers on his phone keyboard.

"Hello, Art. What's up?" Mercado came on with a cheerful voice.

"The heat, that's what." He pulled at his shirt collar. The tight vest also increased warmth over his upper body. "Quintal called, wants me to take a look on specific levels of the garage next to me. Know anything? He gave no details."

Mercado knew he meant Intel info. "No. There's nothing new to report. Quintal's not even in the office. Take a look, but keep me in the loop."

"Copy." Closing the cover, he eased the Ford toward the entrance. A machine dispensed a time-in ticket, which he laid on the dashboard. After the gate rose, he removed his sunglasses and followed the parking lot directional arrows around a curve up to the second floor.

Seconds behind, the driver of the SUV reached out for a receipt then drove toward the ramp.

Chapter 51

Each subsequent floor had Level Full signs posted; vehicles were parked wall to wall.

As Art climbed, the more he wondered what Quintal meant by "Suspected terrorist activity." No other assignment had felt this weird. Zero Intel, no substantiated threat, unknown target...and a parking garage seemed an unlikely place for an attack. Terrorists chose targets that were intended as messages, where catastrophic damage and high human death rates resulted. Destroying parked automobiles lacked any thing of political substance.

Something else buzzed in his brain. Although Mercado was with Art when Quintal ordered him to the garage, she had no idea about the purpose of the mission. The same was true with Curbside...no contact, no knowledge of what case he was supposed to be investigating. As unit leader, it was her duty to arrange teams, assignments, instructions, and, if needed, issue special tactical orders. DHS required her to keep records of agent movements in the event they had to testify at the trial of an alleged terrorist. Agents had to cover their asses, too, for arrests, detaining and interrogating militants, writing up reports, taking witness statements. No entity mandated everything be written, itemized, summarized, and recorded more than the government.

Furthermore, Quintal, and not McLaughlin, seemed to be directing agents' operations.

Each subsequent parking level was full. In all there were seven floors plus rooftop parking. Vehicles exited from the far side of the structure; brakes squealed as they wound around the steep curves. Once in a while a van would drive by picking up customers.

Ascending floors also flooded his mind with recollections of climbing staircases at the Bank of America tower, painful reminders he hoped wouldn't repeat themselves.

Between the third and fourth levels he stopped beside a pole. From this angle he had no view if someone came up behind him. Tapping the gas pedal, he proceeded upward.

Art withdrew his Glock while steering with his left hand. At the top of level four he halted again, and then began driving down lanes between rows of parked cars. All was quiet…no vehicles departing or signs of other drivers. In his line of work, you never doubted anything. Yet he started doubting whether this was an emergency as Quintal advised.

Two minutes later he reached the fifth floor. Gripping his weapon and coasting around the five-mile range, he tensed up as he peered between spaces of each vehicle where someone could be hiding.

He came to a stop near the sixth row of cars and shifted into Park. With his free hand he pressed the three-number sequence to Mercado's direct line.

He spoke in a low voice. "Connie, nothing sighted."

"I had a feeling you wouldn't. Why don't you turn —?"

The sound of a crack vibrated through her phone. A bullet slammed through the left side of the rear window, whizzed by Art's head, and ripped into the sun visor.

"Art…what was that? Art?"

Without glancing back he leaned over the passenger seat and crawled out, down to the pavement. He rolled along the right side and knelt down near the front grill.

"H–Hello, Art! Are you there? Talk to me."

Art whispered into his BlackBerry, "Someone took a shot at me." He raised his Glock up to his chest.

"Are you okay?"

"Yeah. If I knew where the bastard was I'd return fire."

"Now you know why we operate in pairs. Think it was a militant?"

"Right now, I don't give a shit who he is. I'm gonna find him."

"Watch yourself, partner. Call me ASAP…please."

Pocketing the phone, Art slid toward the right rear tire and peered quickly at the back window. He surmised the bullet was a .22 caliber, as just a small hole with tiny glass splinters dropped onto the back ledge.

Silence in situations like this always bothered him. At least you had an opportunity to detect somebody's movements.

Come on, he said to himself. *Make some noise. Show me where you are. Take another shot at me.*

No vehicles came up the ramp. Not even someone picking up a car or the shadow of a figure that could be lurking nearby.

If an insurgent had fired the shot, a small handgun seemed odd. Terrorists relied on bigger, more powerful weapons, such as semi-automatic rifles or large caliber automatic pistols. And they didn't travel alone.

He thought about running down the ramp, which would've been foolish; he'd be wide open as a target. An idea entered his mind...the old "let's flush him out" trick. Better than just sitting on his ass. Since he'd pulled over on a level portion of a lane, he aimed down near the curve of a pillar. He jumped to his feet and fired a round at the post. Cement particles flew out onto the ground. The bullet reverberated throughout the fifth floor.

Shifting backward, he looked up at the concave mirror attached to each ceiling corner of a ramp, meant to view who may be driving toward you. It also provided a clear line of vision to the previous ramp.

Parked facing upward, he stared wide-eyed at the dark SUV, which had sat behind him outside the garage, except this time there was no driver.

Just as he began to straighten up, he heard the crack of another gunshot, with this bullet shattering a side window of a Dodge Caravan parked about ten feet away on his right. Who the hell? he swore, ducking down. Since this shot passed to his right side, the shooter had to be located opposite where he was standing, and relatively close by.

He dropped almost to his knees and headed toward the lane from where he presumed the bullet emanated. Crouching lower, his finger tight around his trigger, he began a systematic vehicle-by-vehicle low body search for the gunman. Though he felt confident that his Glock would offer better shooting capability than a .22, he still used caution as he made his way to the next car. What he hoped for, however, was that no customer decided to drive down the ramp.

About midway down the lane he heard a bumping sound, then quickened footsteps.

Coming around a Cadillac Escalade, he held his firearm close beside his knee and followed the sound. He stopped and knelt down, peering under the side chassis of the SUV. There they were; he glimpsed a dusty pair of men's brown shoes. With his entire focus on the gunman, he hadn't connected a dot about the person on the other side.

With only one chance for surprise, he snuck around to the rear and then crashed down on the guy in a sandy colored golf jacket.

The man grunted as Art increased his grip and added pressure to hold him down.

"Let me go...get off of me," the man in the brown shoes exclaimed.

Art pinned his arms behind his back, squeezing tight enough that the gun he was holding should've dropped to the pavement. Except, there wasn't anything in his hands.

Relaxing his grip, he pulled on the man's left shoulder, forcing him to turn sideways, ignoring every other feature on his face except for the severe rosacea on the nose.

He holstered his Glock and stood up, moving to the side, which allowed the man to resume standing. Every muscle in his face tightened. He clenched a fist and shouted, "What the fuck are you doing here?"

"Dodek, you are a nut case," Quintal said, dusting off his clothes. "We're supposed to work together...there you go and jump me. What's with you?"

Unapologetic, Art rolled his tongue. "I asked you, what are you doing here? Some joker's been taking shots at me." While talking, he glimpsed at Quintal's jacket pockets. A small .22 could be stuffed in one.

"You think I shot at you? Fuck me, Dodek, you on drugs or what?"

Art wasn't about to let up his suspicious nature. "Were you following me?"

"In a way, yeah. After you left DHS, since no teams were available, I decided to act as your partner. I heard the gunfire, took evasive action, and then you pile drive me." He paused, a stoic expression enveloping his face. He broke into a quick smile seconds later, adding, "Did you see the shooter?"

"Not...really." *What an understatement*, he thought, when he had his suspicions. "Well, if it's one of the insurgents, let's look for him. There could be others."

Still debating whether to allow Quintal the benefit of the doubt, Art asked, "Why did you send me here? Look around you. What interest are cars to terrorists? Something else I—"

"You read the notice from McLaughlin. There was Intel that terrorist activity could occur."

"Elaborate."

Quintal lost his smile. "I don't have any docs with me right now. I don't like you questioning my integrity."

Integrity? Is that what you call it? Art scoffed to himself. "Why wasn't Dan sent out as my backup?"

"Goddamn it, Dodek. What's with you? What's with all the questions? Which, by the way, since I outrank you, you don't have the right to ask."

Now it's about outranking. This keeps getting wilder.

"We sent Curbside out for an investigation, if it's any of your business."

"Odd, Consuela had no record of Dan being out on assignment, nor had he called in with his location."

"Maybe she forgot. You know how hostile she got when Walter grounded her. Don't you know by now Mexicans aren't reliable?"

261

Lunging forward, his eyes livid, Art grabbed the lapels of Quintal's jacket. "You got a problem with Consuela because she's Hispanic?"

"Let go," he glowered. "Or...."

"Or what?"

The driver of a shuttle van honked at the pair blocking the lane.

Art released his grip, but kept a clenched fist by his side. He moved back about a foot.

"You keep this attitude up, you're gonna find yourself under a review board. I can have you booted out of the Unit so fast your head will spin."

"Like fuck you can."

Quintal smirked, and pulled a cell phone from his pants pocket. "Doubt it? One call to McLaughlin...you're gone."

"I'll phone for you."

Quintal thumbed the phone then shoved it back into his pocket. "You're still on assignment. You were given an order to secure the garage. Do it." Wheeling around, he started toward a drive through lane. Without turning, he grunted, "How the fuck...? I can't figure out how the hell you were asked to join DHS."

"I don't know how McLaughlin brought you in—you have no Intelligence experience."

This was the first time Art referred to his questionable association with the Central Intelligence Agency.

A loud "Fucking watch out" echoed around a pillar as Quintal stepped down the ramp.

Art shouted back, knowing Quintal heard him. "You got a .22 pistol on you?"

His cell phone beeped. On the screen in bold letters, "*Art...urgent, pick up.*"

Chapter 52

Art dashed back to the Crown Victoria. Shifting into Drive he screeched down the next lane and headed for the exit. He pressed the phone against his ear. "Talk to me, Connie. Tell me something."

"Did you find out who shot at you?" Her voice sounded low-pitched, as though she were inside a tunnel.

"I'll tell you later. Your message said urgent. What...what?"

"Where are you? There are pictures I want to transmit to you."

He noticed the urgency in her voice. "On my way out of the garage." One hand holding the phone, the other steering as he rounded a curve, a Ford F250 blasted its horn seconds before the two would've collided. He swerved and sped by, ignoring the driver swearing at him. Each level down he braked hard to also avoid scraping the posts.

"What's the noise in the background?" he asked. "Sounds like —"

"I'm on the south bound Santa Monica Freeway. Tony's with me."

"Huh? I thought you were busted."

"I'll tell you later. Watch your screen."

Just about clearing the last level, pictures began popping up. Eyes shot toward the exit gate as he glared at the screen. Two still photos came into view. He had to halt at the gate, otherwise he would've smashed through it. Waving his DHS badge at the startled cashier, he hollered for her to raise the barrier. It took a few seconds before she activated the automatic gate, then he careened onto the roadway, narrowly missing a tractor-trailer truck as he darted over to the right side of the road. He couldn't concentrate on driving and viewing pictures at the same time; braking, he rubbed the tires alongside the curb.

He hardly heard Mercado speaking when she inquired if he'd seen the photos. Using buttons on his phone he hit Replay, and gawked for a few seconds. The first was a clean-shaven Muhamed Dauadi surrounded by a group of unknown individuals. Since the shot only showed above the shoulders he couldn't tell what was happening around Dauadi. When he flicked to the second, a long breath flew out of his mouth. It was Saleh Ali Nabhat Saleh in a similar background

"Tell me you're not shocked?' asked Consuela over the phone. "Tony, there's your transition lane to the 405 — "

"Where are they? With the crowds it looks like they're in a line of some kind."

"They are. Art, they're at the Northwest Airline terminal at the Los Angeles Airport." She thought her announcement would surprise him; it didn't. "I'm on another phone…damn, I almost dropped your line. I'm on the phone with Northwest Airlines. You're the closest to LAX, Art. Get over there, but wait for Tony and me. Don't go in alone. That's an order, Agent Dodek."

"What about back up?"

"Tony is talking to the LAPD, arranging for port police to meet you. I'll be there as — we're swinging onto the 405 — wait for us. I'll update their movements. Wow, Tony, that was close…. Honk your horn at the prick."

The call ended. Art pulled away from the curb and roared up the road. In a minute he'd be back onto Century Boulevard and minutes from the airport.

Time to ponder what happened in the parking garage. Quintal's word over his, but how the hell did the guy show up so damn quick? At DHS he'd never seen Quintal with a gun belt. For an ex-Special Operations soldier, he wouldn't have used a small caliber gun — Special Ops fired Sauer handguns, which were more powerful and more lethal.

Regardless whether he'd overdone his welcome with the DHS, or might find himself back in Canada, he still had a personal score to settle with Quintal. Art Dodek wasn't the type to leave anything undone, or anyone not answerable for his or her actions.

Two blocks ahead he roared through an intersection on a yellow light.

His phone vibrated on the passenger seat.

"Art, they're buying tickets," Mercado said. "Paid cash for a Minneapolis bound flight at 2:50 p.m., and also inquired about connecting to an international flight in Europe…Frankfurt, Germany, destination, Nairobi, Kenya."

"They don't like Los Angeles hospitality any longer?" he asked, noticing the first directional signs for LAX.

"That's less than an hour from now. Both purchased tickets by presenting Canadian driver's licenses for identification. Neither checked in luggage. And under different names, using your city, Vancouver, as addresses. Tony, pass that guy."

Smart move, Art sighed, one hundred percent sure they'd used phony documents. Also, flying on U.S. domestic flights, Canadians weren't required to produce passports for proof of citizenship—no doubt forgeries, anyway—until prior to boarding in Minneapolis for the international travel segment.

Since the State Departments of both the United States and Canada prohibited their citizens from travelling to Somalia, once inside Kenya Saleh Ali and Dauadi would either catch a chartered flight or be smuggled into Somalia, then head for Taliban safe-haven encampments in Pakistan.

The urgency in her voice intensified. He didn't expect her next sentence to amplify as it did, but he knew how determined she became once something was within her reach. "I have had it, Art. They've fucked us around long enough. They are not gonna leave the airport."

He wanted to say, "That's the girl," but kept it to himself. "Okay, I'm approaching the ramp for Departures…and I'm stuck in a traffic jam."

"All right," she sighed. "We're half a mile from Manchester. See you soon."

"Copy," he acknowledged.

While his adrenalin surged from being minutes away from the two Somali Jihadi Brotherhood leaders, a dose of reality flashed in his mind: the crowded airport terminal filled with civilians and two desperate terrorists.

Chapter 53

Northwest Airlines Terminal, Los Angeles International Airport

Weaving his way past never-ending buses, vans, cars, taxis, and trucks all vying for a space to offload or pick up passengers, Art noticed Northwest just ahead. Approaching the curb was like playing chicken with automobiles swerving and worming their way through to unloading curbs.

LAX International Airport trailed O'Hare in Chicago and Hartsfield in Atlanta in passenger numbers. About every ten seconds aircraft lifted off from two runways, plus jets arrived on other designated runways. It felt and sounded like sonic booms exploding on the approaches to the terminals.

Easing his way in was futile; it took aggressive nerves to work his way over. Once parked, he jumped out and waved to three airport police officers standing by the main entrance. He identified himself as an agent of Homeland Security, and explained that an FBI Agent and the DHS Unit supervisor were on the way. A sergeant mentioned that they were advised about Saleh Ali and Muhamed Dauadi being inside the terminal. As they stood near the sliding doors, Art withdrew his cell phone and flashed their photos to the officers. Prevalent on everybody's mind was that once they entered, to eliminate panic among staff and passengers, unless warranted by a life-threatening situation, firearms were to be kept holstered.

A siren and flashing red-blue lights atop a GMC van caught their attention. Double parking, Mercado and Lamborghini hopped out and joined Art and the three cops.

People mingling around the curb and approaching the terminal gawked but went on with their business. The sight of law enforcement officers was no big deal. Mercado huddled with Art. First, he mentioned that Quintal showing up at the parking garage after Art being shot at had to be more than a coincidence. She nodded. Yeah, Quintal was a jerk. But would he shoot at a member of the Unit? She knew that he resented Art's influence. Would he be mad enough to kill him? With what had been hitting the Unit all this month, nothing surprised them anymore.

Her cell phone vibrated in her shoulder bag. "Oh, shit," she said when the caller's name appeared on the screen. She showed Art before acknowledging the call. "What is it?"

"What the hell do you think you're doing?" shouted the infuriated DHS director. "You were ordered to stand down. Get back here. That's an order, or this time I will take your goddamn badge away for good."

"Ali Saleh and Dauadi are inside LAX. We're...I'm...not going anywhere. Tony and Art are with me, plus the LAPD."

"Damn you, Mercado. You've depleted the home base of agents. There are no other agents here in case of—"

"Bring Dan in from wherever you or Quintal sent him. We have a flashpoint situation here and we're gonna take care of it."

A few second pause, then, "You and Dodek are relieved of your duty. That's final.

Don't you dare defy my orders again! Did you hear me?"

"Copy that." Mercado closed her phone, and turned to her colleagues. "In less than fifteen minutes they'll be boarding. I think it's time to go in."

The first place they headed to was the Northwest ticket counter and cornered one of the ticket agents. To alleviate unnecessary alarm, when Art and Consuela showed their DHS identification, they advised that the Department of Homeland Security were concerned about two passengers on the 2:50 p.m. Minneapolis bound flight...in particular, the two men who paid cash for their tickets. The Northwest employee concurred that the photos from their cell phones matched the two men who appeared at her counter.

The agent swiveled her computer to the side. Bringing up the flight information, she pointed to the passenger manifest. She remembered, she alluded, mainly because of the older man's demanding that a Frankfurt outbound departure to Nairobi would be available if they reserved seats in Minneapolis. She tried to tell them that seats would be held if they pre-booked at LAX. Both men refused. They just wanted to ensure that the flight connection could be reserved overseas as well as the exact departure time. Neither one flinched at the higher costs of tickets. Both paid cash for the Minneapolis one-way flight.

"Didn't this seem peculiar to you," asked Mercado, "that they paid cash and inquired about only one flight to just one specific destination?"

The agent shook her head no and explained that some customers booked at the very last minute, adding they presented valid ID, and, yes, their names weren't on the TSA no-fly list.

"What about the Automatic Face Recognition System?" Art asked. "It would've signaled that they're a fly risk, and you'd alert security."

The system was down in the entire airline terminal, he heard, and shook his head. Staff had to rely on personal recognition. And she added that while it was unusual for neither one to check in luggage, it was a non-stop domestic flight and each one had a tote bag for carry on.

Art looked at his watch. "They could be anywhere in the terminal."

The agent mentioned they would've cleared security by now, and were probably waiting near the boarding gate.

Mercado rubbed her chin, and wrote down the names used to purchase tickets. "Can you delay the flight?"

She picked up her telephone and spoke with someone at the departure gate. Hanging up, she returned to her station to assist other customers, who by now were expressing their displeasure about the delay.

Art glanced back at the three cops who stood a few feet apart on both sides of the line. Police officers patrolling the terminal were a common sight. He also noticed a pair of deputy sheriffs strolling past an adjoining ticket counter. Three armed DHS agents in flak jackets, however, would cause a few stares, and be instantly noticeable to Saleh Ali and Dauadi, thus eroding any type of surprise. Plus, Dauadi would recognize Art from the Los Alamitos naval depot.

A male ticket agent emerged from behind the luggage belt.

Art and Consuela flashed looks.

Interrupting the ticket agents again, who were about their height, they told them to remove their Northwest Airline blazers. Although a bit tight, slipping into the jackets concealed the vests and side arms.

That left Lamborghini, whose vest with big yellow DHS letters on the back would've stood out like neon letters, without a blazer. Mercado instructed him to mingle with crowds of passengers, but maintain vigilance.

Motioning for the officers to follow, everybody turned to the left and headed to an escalator.

At least a hundred passengers were lined up at the security corridors for pre-flight inspection. Mercado weaved through the roped lines, returning a few minutes later with a shake of her head. The pair had already cleared; they had to be somewhere near their gate.

With the airport police officers, the agents bypassed security and checked the large departure board ahead of them, which indicated NW

Flight 603 to Minneapolis was on time for departure, about fifteen minutes from now.

When they neared the gate area, the agent was already calling some of the final row numbers, but she had been advised the departure would be delayed. The cops sauntered along the walkway past stores, gift shops, and fast food restaurants. Art and Consuela found a corner close by a lounge almost opposite the rows of chairs and the departure doors. Plenty of men were strolling around, several of whom were of Middle Eastern descent, but not their guys. Once Saleh Ali and Dauadi boarded it would be difficult, and perhaps dangerous, for the crew and passengers. No one wanted a plane cabin turned into a shooting gallery.

While Art remained beside a post, Mercado wandered over to the counter, her hands covered by her handbag. Discretely pushing her badge to the opening, she handed the young woman the notepaper with names scribbled on it, and attached it to a clipboard. To waiting passengers, in the NW blazer she looked like one of the airline employees. Then she edged back to the left side of the counter, allotting her a clear view of anyone coming forward.

The young woman clicked on a microphone. "Your attention, please. Would Flight 603 passengers Mahmoud Jaballah, Seat 21E, and Zacharia el-Kaei, Seat 27C, please come to the counter?"

The sergeant moved to the front area while his partners walked between the last rows of the crowded waiting room. Lamborghini, reading an airline magazine, sauntered to a partition, which linked to another departure lounge.

Now Art perked up, affixing his gaze first to his partner and then the counter. His breathing increased, his heart pounded. Apprehending Dauadi wasn't just a thought at this moment…rather, a mission, and a commitment that his killing days were over; not forgetting as well that he'd be coming face to face with the Somali Brotherhood mastermind.

Dozens of voices buzzed throughout the waiting section, but no one advanced.

Mercado nodded to the attendant.

"Passengers Mahmoud Jaballah and Zacharia el-Kaei, please approach the counter for flight information. And…. Ladies and gentlemen…." Her voice faltered nervously. "We may expect a delay for departure."

Both Art and Consuela picked up the change in her tone.

And so would two men expert at noting differences in people's behavior.

A dark-skinned young man in a windbreaker, jeans, and a ball cap rose, sunglasses perched over his eyes, glanced around, looking both left and right, then behind him. He caught sight of the police officers, and an eye noted Agent Lamborghini across the corridor.

Art couldn't pick out to whom the man lowered his eyes. Would it be Saleh Ali?

"We have been advised that Flight 603 is being delayed because of an alleged security risk," the airline agent said.

Both Art and Consuela exchanged disbelieving glances. The last thing they wanted to hear was someone mentioning a security problem.

Even though she stood a few feet from the woman, Mercado couldn't blow her cover and enable Dauadi's avenue of escape. Just looking around at the waiting passengers had caused a stir, which intensified by the minute. There were people already on board the plane, as well as those being cleared for boarding.

The man in the ball cap gazed out toward the corridor. Nothing in his demeanor suggested that he had been spooked. Nothing unusual either about the clothes he wore; twenty to thirty percent of the male passengers near the gate dressed alike.

Then Art fixated on the man's left ear. He had no doubt now who stood about fifty feet away. Idiot, he mused, you should've removed your earring. As his partner glanced to the rear, Art made a tiny shift of his head, letting her know the guy in the ball cap and sunglasses was their quarry.

Chapter 54

Another dilemma surfaced. Fine, go grab him. Even if X-ray machines revealed no weapon in his carry on, they had no idea if he was armed. Dauadi never went anywhere without packing his .45 automatic.

Dauadi paced in front of the person seated before him. The other man's shoulders twitched, comprehending that both were being observed. Then Dauadi shifted his carryon bag toward his chest and slowly inserted his hand.

Mercado straightened up, her lips closed tight, eyes riveted to Dauadi. Sliding back the bottom of her blazer, she inched her fingers closer to her P-35.

The sergeant and his two partners observed the slight changes in body movements. One by one, they walked between aisles of chairs. The Hispanic officer sauntered to the end of the second row nearest the suspects.

No, don't approach them, Mercado shouted in her mind.

Art noticed as well. He just couldn't stand there. Trying to move closer without signaling to Dauadi that he was about to be apprehended equaled stalking a deer without it bolting.

Agent Lamborghini also understood the necessity now of discreetly forging across the corridor. He dropped the magazine and headed into the waiting area. His disadvantage was that he couldn't move his hand toward his side arm without the Somali catching the motion.

The police and agents were within striking distance; great, if there weren't so many people around them. No one had really seen Saleh Ali. Passengers in seats behind him had blocked his view, and he had not stirred. Was he waiting for his protégé to make a move? Indicate an avenue of escape? Prior to today, Dauadi had instructed the insurgents to either carry out his orders or die to evade capture. This must've been a mind-bending situation for a Somali who depended on others. Saleh Ali had never participated in direct attacks, only the planning. Even in the

Taliban-held remote towns in Pakistan and Afghanistan, others carried out raids or executed those he wanted killed.

Although the agents found themselves at a standstill, they hoped the pair was sweating it out; everywhere, eyes were piercing at them, and they must be realizing they were enclosed in a box, close to being apprehended.

Dauadi still had his hand in his carryon bag. Straightening up, he turned and took three paces to his left. Now he faced the departure counter. Who was he staring at? Mercado wearing the Northwest Airline blazer? The nervous airline employee?

Three women walked up to the counter. Even from Art's position he heard them inquire about the delay. One, leaning over the ledge, obscured some of Mercado's view of Dauadi and the person still seated. He nodded at Lamborghini, who started down a middle aisle.

Dauadi watched the agent as he halted beside the sixth row. Glancing quickly, he saw that the police officers had decreased their distance, and were getting closer to his row. To everyone's surprise, he waved over the sergeant.

Mercado shifted her position to the front of the counter, her hand pressed against her side arm.

Art also stepped away from the partition and crossed the floor. No sense keeping his face hidden anymore, he and Dauadi were going to meet again.

When the cop stopped, Dauadi leaned forward, as though saying a few words to the officer, rotated his body sideways, grabbed the Taser from his belt, and pushed him over two chairs, knocking a couple of women to the floor. The sudden movement confused the nearest officer. Before he could pull out his firearm, 20,000 volts of wire-thin electricity overpowered him, sending him crashing against a row of chairs.

Dauadi possessed incredible speed and reaction. In a split second he slid out the cop's gun, wheeled around, and fired almost point blank at the young Hispanic police officer. Unlike some of the Somali's inexperienced shooters, Dauadi's aim was accurate.

Not all airport cops wore protective vests; he was one of the unlucky ones. The bullet pierced the pocket right under the badge, hitting him squarely in the heart region. The cop likely didn't even realize he'd been hit until he collapsed, then watched as blood poured over his hands.

People screamed and jumped off their chairs. In the packed departure room, most stumbled over other passengers or fell to the floor. In the confusion, a group of stampeding men bowled over the third officer.

Mercado darted around the counter and hollered at the employee and three women to hit the ground. She fished out her P-35 and released the trigger lock. The counter had provided some protection. Now she lost whatever it had provided, placing her right in the open.

Art and Lamborghini, guns drawn, rushed to the aisles, but were slowed down and hindered from firing by fleeing passengers.

"Saleh Ali, my Lord, I shall protect you," Dauadi shouted, dropping to his knees, shooting toward the counter. The first bullet chipped off a piece of fiberglass and drilled into the frame of the desktop computer; the second blasted the microphone right off the ledge.

Lamborghini figured he had a clear shot. But when he extended his arm, backs of the chairs hid the kneeling Somali.

Almost screaming at the top of his lungs, Dauadi yelled out, "*Jihadi Salfah...Jihadi Salfah!*" the name of the violent terrorist organization in Mogadishu that vowed to turn all non al-Shabbad Arab states into one fanatical Islamic homeland.

Mercado crouched, raised her gun, then lowered it and fired in Dauadi's direction. The shell skimming along the floor near him didn't faze him. With coal-dark eyes under the sunglasses and teeth clenched together, he returned fire, which startled her for a few seconds.

Jumping over a row of seats, Art, incensed that someone—a terrorist—would shoot at his partner, had less than two seconds to aim and let off a round. His bullet slammed into a chair, just feet from the back of Saleh Ali.

The Taliban-trained Dauadi had no fear of crossfire. In fact, the agents, not he, were disadvantaged. Years of experience shooting it out with militias in the rugged mountains of Afghanistan had taught him to recognize an enemy's weaknesses. Here was no different.

Rising slightly, with the agility of a cat, he managed to grab the service pistol from the dying officer.

Now Lamborghini had no one blocking his view. Two rounds sailed a foot over the large window ledge and bounced off the thick glass, which faced the runway, parked airplanes, ground crews, and mobile equipment vehicles.

Surprisingly, all this time Saleh Ali, the recruiter of militants and martyrs, had remained almost motionless. Yelling passengers and flying shells hadn't sent him into shockwaves. Yet he and his number one son continued to exchange glances.

Cleared of civilians, the agents approached closer to the seating area. Trying to contain their composure in the midst of a firefight wasn't on the menu when they'd arrived minutes ago, or now when confronting the two major Brotherhood members.

As Art crept along the chairs his eyes widened at what he had hoped not to see. Crouched behind an adjoining chair a foot from Saleh Ali and lying underneath another a foot away were two young women too frightened to move. He couldn't yell at them to crawl away. Yet a stray bullet could've struck either one of them.

Another shot sailed close to Mercado; this time she sunk to the floor. Whatever the reason, she seemed to be the principal target.

Art rose. Gun hand extended, he hollered, "Hey...Muhamed," as a way to divert gunfire away from Consuela.

The Somali leaned over the chair. It took mere seconds for the Somali to recognize the DHS agent he had fought with at Los Alamitos. What registered in his head may be unknown, but recalling that day and staring at him for a second time seemed to send his hate meter skyrocketing.

And for the first time, Saleh Ali, sliding down on his chair, glanced over to where he heard Art's voice. All he really looked at was the glint of gun metal from the Glock 9 pistol. Wearing the same suit and smoky-lensed sunglasses from the function at the Century Plaza, he appeared more gaunt, almost frail, and even shorter than the subject in his photos.

The other agents closing in on them didn't register much concern.

Was he thinking that his position as Somali Jihad brotherhood leader—once consul to Osama bin Laden's inner circle—made him invincible? By brainwashing scores of gullible Somali-Americans, he brought death and destruction into the laps of Americans, proving he could attack with impunity. History would record his name, and show that he never cowered before the infidels.

Saleh Ali tugged on Dauadi's windbreaker. Both men stared at one another, contented smiles breaking across their faces. Dauadi faced a decision unlike no other. Perhaps long ago in the hills of Afghanistan mentor and protégé had somehow made a pact should a no-win situation arise.

Sounds of shuffling echoed on the tiled floor across from the departure lounge. Four deputy sheriffs in flak jackets and carrying M-16A carbines took positions between the rear aisles.

Only the roar of a jet plane departing broke through the dead silence at the Northwest gate area.

Pistols and rifles were on the verge of firing.

It was doubtful Dauadi's quickness could work in his favor. Now the way the two men looked at one another, it was as if father and son were preparing for some monumental event.

Chapter 55

Homeland Security agents and the deputy sheriffs moved closer. Most now had unobstructed lines of fire.

Dauadi crouched lower, his attention focused near his feet. Then he hopped up, dragging a young woman who had taken refuge under the chairs with him as he rose. He clutched her throat with one arm and shoved the officer's pistol against her ear. The more she screamed the tighter he added pressure around her neck. Just muffled cries and spurts of coughing now emerged from her throat.

"Oh shit," muttered Art, at the second hostage-taking situation he'd encountered this month. No one saw this coming. No one had spotted the woman lying under the chairs.

The first person to approach the pair was Mercado. Firearm extended straightforward, she inched away from the counter. "Muhamed, put the gun down. You don't want to do this. Let the girl go."

He moved backward toward the window. Even outnumbered, Dauadi showed no emotion, other than that he was determined to shoot somebody…whether it was his hostage, an agent, a cop, or a waiting passenger, to him it made no difference. Just like the Beverly Hills massacre, the carnage at UCLA, or the innocent people at the Bank of America and the December 26th mass murder at the courthouse, it was death tolls that enthralled him. Fear—cold, deadly fear, from his hands—that's what mattered. And attacking more American institutions. He believed these acts, with Saleh Ali's blessing, would one day place him at the leadership of the Brotherhood in Somalia, and as a tribal leader in the inner circle of the Taliban. The people with guns pointed at him weren't going to change anything.

Stopping about ten feet away, Art, the Glock still positioned outward, waved his left hand sideways. "Is her life not worth saving? No one else has to be hurt."

"Keep away…keep back. I can snuff out her life."

Sweat was sliding down his cheeks. Despite how unpredictable he could be, his gun hand remained rock steady. Eyes strayed quickly between Dodek and Mercado, then back and forth to Saleh Ali.

Art and Consuela exchanged quick glances. She was the closest to Dauadi and his hostage. At Encada Engineering she'd found an opening and shot the fake armored guard. Here she had no clear sight line. She couldn't risk striking the woman.

"There's no Jihad brotherhood to protect you, Muhamed," Art said through thin, taut lips. "Look around you. You're alone. Put your damn gun down...now."

Dauadi gazed to his right at Mercado. "Infidel woman...put your gun away...go home."

"Brave, aren't you, you son of a bitch?" she said. "Hiding behind a woman."

Art, figuring another tactic might work, edged forward another half foot. "Saleh Ali, tell him it's over."

The brotherhood leader, staying partially hidden, disregarded the order.

"You *don't* talk to him," Dauadi shouted vehemently. "He is a prophet of Allah." All of a sudden, he spouted off a verse (*Sura 3*) from the Koran, "Say to the unbelievers: You shall be overthrown, and mustered in to Gehenna—an evil cradling."

"The Koran," Art followed, "also states, '...whosoever murders his neighbor, his brother, shall be cast out, and he who has sinned against the truth of Islam, and the Prophet, shall be deemed as unworthy to enter the kingdom of heaven."

"No...no." He lowered the gun, moving it just below the girl's shoulder blades, stepped back, and fired. The bullet streaked through her breastbone, ripping through organs and emerging between her breasts, then slammed into the metal frame of a chair ten feet away.

She let out a blood-curdling scream and crumbled into his arms. Blood spurted to the floor and saturated his windbreaker. Dauadi held onto her limp body. Continuing to use it as a shield, he dared anyone to retaliate. Still no panic surfaced from Dauadi.

By this time other deputies had arrived and pushed passengers out in the corridor into the stores and told them to fall to the ground. Rage exploded from everyone witnessing his horrific act. Trigger fingers could barely hold back the urge to shoot.

Then Dauadi turned to Saleh Ali. For the first time, tears welled in the young man's eyes.

The Brotherhood leader stood, clutching the gun hand of his protégé. Both men stared pensively at one another. To those watching the scene seemed surreal, like father and son exchanging silent admiration with one another.

Dauadi relaxed his hold of the young woman, ignoring her lifeless body as it slid to the floor.

Consuela and Art now had a clear view of the pair, yet they loosened their fingers around their triggers, letting the scene play out. But with any threatening movement they were prepared to respond with deadly accuracy. At present this was their only countermeasure.

Pressing his hand tighter on Dauadi's wrist, Saleh Ali closed his eyes and shouted, "*Eid al-Adah*," the Arabic phrase for the Day of Sacrifice, the same expression that the Brotherhood had chosen for the June tenth bombings at the Bank of America.

Dauadi placed his free hand over the man's hand and drew him closer. In a hardly recognizable voice he screamed out in his Somali dialect a phrase similar to that of the Arabic Day for Sacrifice, "*Chiidwayneey.*"

Then he pulled the trigger of his .45 and fired three times, all bullets smashing into the chest of Saleh Ali. No pained expression coated the face of the brotherhood leader as he slumped to the floor.

From the other side of the waiting room, Tony Lamborghini loped over a chair and fired over Dauadi's head. Again the bullet bounced off the thick window glass.

***

Dauadi released the hand of his mentor. He had made the decision with Saleh Ali's blessing. He knew that if Saleh Ali was captured, even if he was as thick-skinned and resilient as his number two man, the FBI would've interrogated him for hours, using intimidation and deprivation to force him to reveal names of other Somali-American insurgents. The CIA would grill him for names of Taliban terrorists in Pakistan, their secret training camps, locations of terrorist leaders, and where caches of munitions and bomb making materials in Peshawar were concealed. Also, websites, e-mail addresses, contact telephone numbers here and in the Middle East, and most importantly, plans and dates for future terrorist attacks in the United States. Once the CIA analyzed the Intel, then the U.S. military would strike back with missiles and unmanned drones. This information had to be protected at all costs, including the killing of the mastermind who kept it all in his head. Despite their close relationship, personal trust, and hatred of all things American, Dauadi wasn't privy to important, high ranking names within the Taliban and al-Qaeda terrorist organizations. Conversely, since he'd trained at camps in Pakistan and Afghanistan, participated in deadly attacks against allied forces, and carried out innumerable raids, which killed scores of civilians in his homeland of Somalia and other Middle Eastern regions, those

277

governments would demand his extradition from the United States to face their brand of punishment for war crimes. Except, however, the U.S. would definitely try him on its soil for killing American citizens. In addition, he had many contacts across the country. The FBI, Homeland Security, and the National Security Administration would relentlessly hunt down those conspirators—dead or alive.

***

"It's over, Muhamed," Art exclaimed, rushing forward. This time he intended to fire.

The cell phone beeped inside Mercado's handbag, which she ignored. At a time like this she had no intention of talking to anyone. It stopped after the fifth ring. Her boss, no doubt, ranting that she contravened the order to stand down.

On her haunches, she moved to the front of the counter and, in a raised voice, shouted, "Dauadi, drop your weapon…hit the floor. Drop it or we will shoot. This is your last warning."

***

Normal men may have obliged with her command. Enough firepower surrounded him that could've blown him into another terminal. However, he didn't see himself as a regular human being…rather, the deliverer of death and destruction. That's what he had been groomed for…trained to fight as a master explosives specialist; a mass murderer, who turned any weapon against the American establishment into a killing device. He didn't take orders from infidels; he ordered them killed. Whether orchestrated by Saleh Ali or on his own initiative, he struck with abnormal ferocity, and vanished like a reed sinking under water.

Boxed in? Not the way he speculated. This was merely another challenge.

***

Mercado wanted to lower the odds. She fired off a round, which sailed over his head. "Next shot, I won't miss," she growled, and meant it.

Tilting her head sideways, her mind picked up his next movement, and she wasn't going to let it happen.

Chapter 56

Mercado guessed right. Her instinct kicked in at exactly what she figured the Somali would do.

Inch by inch, second by second, Dauadi pressed his back and slid against the glass window toward the gate doorway.

Art noticed as well. He could've exchanged a glance with his partner, but he didn't want to remove his gun sight, not even for a second. Then he heard her voice boom out, "Close the doorway," she hollered at the desk attendant. "Lock it!"

The woman had her fingers on the automatic door closer. Her hand shook nervously.

"Do it!" Mercado screamed. "And hit the deck."

The woman hit the button. The door slid shut, locking itself as the attendant, tears blurring her mascara, dropped to her knees by the side of the counter.

Mercado slowly rose, her P-35 aimed straight at his forehead.

Dauadi stopped, gazed around, but kept his gun at chest level, his frantic mind calculating which person he intended to shoot first, second, or third. Who, didn't matter. He swung his arm to the right and now stood face to face with the female DHS agent. He ditched his sunglasses. With his black eyes filled with hate, he squeezed the trigger.

"Dauadi...remember the shipyard?" It was Art who asked the question, standing five feet to the right.

The Somali's lips parted, coated by drops of saliva. "You want to kill me?" he blurted, turning toward Art, aiming at him less than four feet away.

Everybody in the terminal—law enforcement officers, passengers hiding in the stores and down the corridors——froze as though they'd been encased in a river of ice. Heavy breathing, as if blasted through wall-to-wall air conditioners, intensified from every square foot of the room.

Art, in a crouching motion, responded with a deadpan answer. "I'd rather not, scumbag." Without a second's hesitation he fired, hitting

Dauadi's left leg. Then, as he rose, he sent another round, this one into the right upper thigh.

Dauadi flinched and jerked sideways, frantically trying to reason in his mind that he was in pain.

"I want you alive," Art said, closing in, his Glock 9 millimeter still extended. A third shot exploded, this one ripping through the upper arm of the hand clutching the gun, forcing it downward.

Pain aside, for the first time fear reflected in Dauadi's eyes. Tears welled up around the corners of his eyelids. Wincing, rocking back and forth, he glanced at blood flowing from his limbs, and fell against the bottom window ledge. The sudden crash released the tight grip on his gun, but it still remained partly upward. Those bullets hit parts of his body that should've produced cries of anguish, if not agonizing screams. His lips weren't clamped shut; how he withheld from screaming was astounding. But he hurt.

Cheeks flushed, his eyes blinked rapidly, perspiration beaded down his face, and his jaw made weird gnashing movements. Half a minute later, his gun hand drooped to his side, yet he still clutched it as though it was his most prized possession.

"Y-you shot an unarmed man!" he cried out, pain searing through his entire body. "You shot...an unarmed man."

Stepping forward, Art pressed the gun barrel against Dauadi's left temple. "Whine all you want, asshole. Nobody gives a shit." There was no compassion in his expression. Firing point-blank didn't bother him. He compressed his finger tighter around the trigger of his Glock, neither concerned what may happen to a human head at this close range nor worried that the single bullet would mean instant death. With his right foot, he struck the man's foot, sending the leg twisting downward. In one swift motion, Dauadi collapsed to the floor.

Without the strength to raise his weapon, Dauadi stared coldly at the agent, waiting for the final deathblow. "A-Allah...send me to Heaven. He wishes it."

Art stared into his eyes, a minute seconds away from complying with Dauadi's wish. Tightening his finger around the trigger he tapped the gun barrel against the temple, hard enough that its steel point cut through the skin and drew blood.

Mercado and Lamborghini circled the pair. Neither uttered a word, but sensed the cold determination in their partner's eyes that he was about to fire off another bullet.

"Allah Bakbar," Dauadi sobbed. "You...you shall hear the cry of all my brothers until you are wiped off the face of the earth."

"Me included? I want you to remember my name before you join all your lunatic brothers in hell. It's Dodek. Yeah, I'm Jewish."

Art could feel the tightness in his finger intensifying on the metal trigger. Nerves hadn't even entered his mind. In fact, he had gone beyond feeling anything. Muhamed Dauadi represented everything that he hated. Why shouldn't he destroy this fiend, as he had destroyed the lives of countless innocent people? Nor did he feel an ounce of sympathy for him as he writhed around like a wounded animal. All he could visualize in his mind was a scene of a long time friend, who less than a year ago had betrayed him and paid the ultimate price. Was this any different? Both adhered to a cult that viewed Westerners as infidels, heathens, unworthy of breathing the same air. Both shared the conviction that theirs was the true religion of God. Except theirs pursued a path of intolerance, misguided by wanton extremism. Just one more bullet, and in an instant he'd snuff out the life of a fanatic who placed absolutely no value on human life.

Besides Dauadi staring at Art's riveted eyes and squinting at the almost blood-red lines in the agent's cocked trigger finger, other persons in the room noticed a man's imminent death was mere seconds away. Some of the onlookers drew in their stomachs, holding back from breathing as they anticipated the crack of a bullet.

Somewhere within the seating area he heard a soft voice, at first unsure whom it belonged to. Bit by bit his brain picked up someone talking to him close by, the words going from murmuring to a loud monotone. The voice became familiar, yet the rock-hard staring continued.

"Art, let it go, you've done enough," Mercado said quietly.

Almost at attention now, he avoided turning toward his partner.

"Come on, Art. Lower your weapon. No one will think less of you."

His hand remained straight down at the Somali's head.

The level of her voice increased. "Agent Dodek...listen to me. Not one of us cares if he lives or dies. What concerns you...us...is that we swore to uphold the laws of our country, not break them. That's where we differ from that piece of shit."

Reducing his grip and lowering the Glock, with his other hand he squeezed just below where his first bullet had pierced the arm, increased the pressure on an artery, until finally, Dauadi screamed and slid across the window ledge. Blood squirted out of the wound, smattering onto the window, and down the side of his leg.

"Art...stop," whispered Mercado, placing a gentle hand on his shoulder as she stood next to the sobbing terrorist. "You'll just get your balls in a knot. I wouldn't blame you if you wanted to kick the shit out of the asshole. God knows we'd all enjoy drilling him. Let it go. He's done."

He slowly turned his head toward his partner.

"Dauadi wants you to kill him. If you do, he believes that he'll die as a martyr. Don't give it to him. Want to make him suffer? Rob him of his martyrdom."

Nodding, he removed his hand. Before walking away, he wiped the blood off his fingers on to Dauadi's jacket. Glancing quickly at the body of Saleh Ali Nabhat Saleh, Art rolled his tongue over his teeth. Without giving it a thought, he stepped over the body of the Somali brotherhood leader and holstered his weapon. When he stared down at the dead woman, he swore under his breath. He slid off the Northwest Airline jacket. For a few seconds he gazed at planes parked outside on the tarmac.

"The only place he's going to is inside the rubber-room of a prison," she said.

Lamborghini gave him a look of confidence, reiterating Mercado's rhetoric, and said, "Aylesha will be glad to hear we've apprehended Dauadi." The agent knelt down and removed the gun from Dauadi's hand. Another cop knelt down and helped the Tasered sergeant get to his feet.

"Let's go outside for some air, Art," Mercado said. "We both could use a breather."

He nodded, and, amid the rush of other law enforcement officers racing to the front row terminal seats, allowed her to clasp his elbow as they headed down the corridor.

The cell phone in her purse buzzed.

"If that's Walter again, I'll — Hello."

"Consuela, it's Dan."

She squeezed her phone. "Dan, where the hell are you? I couldn't reach you."

"My phone was turned off. Someone screwed up my line to prevent a signal. I'm on the 210 Foothill Freeway. Even my GPS is off-line. I'm looking for an exit to a freeway back to Los Angeles. Would you believe Quintal sent me up to Claremont to check out something suspicious? A damn goose-chase if you ask me."

"Quintal, huh?" Mercado recalled that "suspicious activity" were the words that Art used parked outside the parking garage.

Both grabbed deep breaths as they exited. Scores of passengers had been cordoned off behind police lines. Buses, autos, and vans were backed up all the way down the ramp, preventing them from approaching the main causeway to the terminals.

Art didn't hear the conversation, but got the drift from her expression.

"What's happened?" asked Curbside. "Who's with you? Where the hell are you?"

"At LAX, Northwest Airlines Terminal," said Consuela. "Art and Tony are with me. Ready for some news? I'll let Art clue you in." She handed the phone to Art, and, for the first time today, he smiled.

"Yeah, hi, Dan. You've been had."

"Say what?"

"Tell you later."

Four LAPD cars, two paramedic units, and an ambulance, sirens shrieking, roared up the airport causeway.

Cuffing his ear, Art hid behind a post to block some of the noise. "Don't even ask right now," he shouted into the cell phone. "Saleh Ali Nabhat Saleh is dead, gunned down by Muhamed Dauadi."

"What…in hell are you talking about? When?"

"Five minutes ago. Dauadi is under arrest. A bit banged up, but we have the prick in custody! Uh–huh. I think Consuela wants you back downtown ASAP. Yeah…see you soon." He returned to the curb and handed the phone over to Mercado. They jumped clear of emergency personnel rushing into the terminal.

A second call followed. When the monitor revealed that it came from Walter McLaughlin, he shoved the phone into her purse.

Both broke out laughing when they noticed that their DHS vehicles had been ticketed by the airport traffic police for double parking, as well as violating the no parking by-law. Despite the official seals of the United States Department of Homeland Security clearly visible above the windshield VIN stickers, the agents became victims of rigid airport enforcement.

Six armed LAPD officers surrounded Dauadi as medics wheeled his stretcher outside. Strapped down, sniveling, and sobbing incoherently, Art and Consuela turned their backs on him.

Chapter 57

It took over ten minutes for Art and Consuela to circumvent their way through the traffic bottleneck on the LAX causeway created by the closure of the Northwest Airline terminal. Eventually they reached Century Boulevard and soon entered the left turn lane for the 405 Northbound Santa Monica Freeway. Up ahead, they'd transit onto the Number 10 West for the trip back to downtown. Overhead skies turned hazy; another hot afternoon loomed in Los Angeles.

Mercado, in the lead vehicle, called Art. After he clicked on his BlackBerry, she asked, "Are you okay?"

"Why wouldn't I be? Is it important that you know?"

"Well...." She hadn't expected him to answer that way. Not wanting to make it sound like a leading question, she rephrased. "Have you had enough for one day?"

"Have you?"

While he didn't answer as she thought he would, she knew his mind would be full of events which both of them had experienced the past few weeks. "You broke the back of the Brotherhood."

"Thanks to everybody in the Unit."

"You did okay, Art. Any one of us in the same situation...well, let's say, we'd have to take it one step at a time. No, wait. You had every right to act as you did. Who am I to say I'd not be close to losing it?"

"I didn't think you—you think I lost it back there?"

"Now you're putting words in my mouth." She jarred the GMC Yukon to a stop when a shuttle bus tried to edge its way past her at a traffic light. "I think you showed what bravery is all about."

"What's brave about wanting to kill someone?"

"Man, are you difficult to talk to."

After a pause of five seconds, he said, "I owe you, Connie."

"Oh, come on. You don't. Thank God, there's the freeway. Art, I'd like to know...tell me, what is on your mind at this very minute? No smart-ass answer, okay?"

The reply was immediate. "Who shot at me in the parking structure. And the in your face meeting with Quintal. What about you? McLaughlin's gonna chew your ass for taking off."

"No doubt. Doesn't faze me. If I recall, that's not the only bones left on the plate." She increased her speed as she wheeled over to the third lane. "If we get separated on the way back...."

"See you." Art turned off his phone. Within minutes, as traffic volume built up the nearer to downtown, he soon lost sight of her SUV. Checking his mirrors, he signaled to the left, waited until a transport truck passed, then changed over to the next lane. Once joining the traffic flow, he gave a quick eye check through the rear view mirror at the small bullet hole that penetrated the back window of the Crown Victoria.

His thoughts wandered back to what Consuela said. Was I that close to losing it? To shooting Dauadi to death? Self-defense, that'd be different. Shooting the wounded Somali insurgent at the B/A tower, yes, that was warranted. Factually, he didn't give a rat's ass if Dauadi had died of blood poisoning in the passenger waiting room. After all, he was a wanted terrorist, a mass murderer who would've still gone on killing. God knows how many other innocent people.

Picture this, though: a federal agent—a foreign one no less—kills an unarmed criminal. That's how the liberal media would portray his action. No matter what horrific crimes were committed, they'd eat it up, castigating an out-of-control counter-terrorist agent as a wing nut. "Jail his goddamn ass," they'd demand in their editorials. And, "Homeland Security hires shoot-first, ask-questions-later agents. Let the agents do the dirty work, but don't get your fingers dirty," that's how the press perceived those who carried out the war on terrorists. *Well, shit*, he mused, *it's a dirty business; it gets messy, and blood flows. Just don't let it be our side.*

Art wasn't undermining his actions earlier, nor excusing any of them. Firing that fourth bullet at Mohamed Dauadi, damn right it would've pushed him over the edge. With his free hand off the steering wheel, he clenched his fist until the knuckles turned bright red. If this was all a game, who the hell wins? He shook his head from side to side, realizing that hadn't Consuela intervened, he might as well have turned the gun on himself—he was that close to permanently losing it.

Another thought sprung into in his mind. McLaughlin and Quintal. What side of the terrorist war were they on?

Transitioning from the freeway to a surface street in downtown Los Angeles wasn't exactly the easiest thing about driving there when you figured every driver in the city was heading the same way as you. Crawling was more like it. To pass the time he switched on the car radio, fiddling the station lever over until static gave way to a clear signal. Art checked the time on the dashboard, then on his watch. Sighing, he hadn't

285

realized how long it had been since he left the Unit that morning. After a traffic reporter finished with her Sig Alert, the news announcer reported on the shoot-outs at LAX. "Shoot-outs?" he muttered back at the radio. *What about telling your listeners that an innocent young woman, in the right place at the wrong time, lost her life by being shot by a deranged terrorist?*

Within three to four minutes he spotted the federal building. All the way back he hadn't caught up to Consuela's SUV. When he pulled the Ford into his parking space number 23A, Mercado, arms crossed, leaning against the structure leading to the DHS elevator, waved and smiled.

As Art climbed out, he picked up the director's printout off the passenger seat and stuffed it into his back pants pocket. Approaching her by the doorway, Mercado, never the one to flinch from making statements you'd rather not hear, murmured,

"Hurry up…I can't hold it in any longer."

Returning to the sixth floor DHS offices, Art first made a stop at the ordnance section. After any agent discharged a firearm while in the field, replenishing spent bullets was a must. A quarter or half empty clip could result in dire circumstances should it be necessary to fire the next time out. As well, reloading required date, time, and amount to be recorded. Each agent of the Unit had a log, which listed their usage, caliber of ammunition, and type of firearm. A master ordnance-keeper, most times a retired police officer hired by Homeland Security, would stow the information in a locked box denoting the agent's name.

After jotting down his information, as he was about to head outside the steel and wire-meshed room, he noticed the log books for Mercado, Curbside, Lamborghini, and Reeves were sitting atop a counter, figuring that the keeper would place them in their appropriate containers. Only Director McLaughlin hadn't been provided with a government-issued weapon. It was well known, nonetheless, that he kept two registered guns, one in the glove box of his van and a snub-nosed .38 revolver locked in his office.

That left Quintal. While Art hadn't seen the ex-army colonel carry a gun in any of the offices, Quintal had free access to any weapon he chose. A former army Special Forces commander, he would've also been a specialist with small arms.

Despite the circuit TV camera attached to the overhead doorframe, Art unlocked the box next to that of his partners. When he left, he had shoved a fully loaded .9-millimeter bullet clip into his Glock, plus two spare clips into a pouch pocket on his vest.

Minutes later, Tony and Consuela told him that Mohamed Dauadi was under FBI guard in a downtown hospital—location undisclosed to the media or public—and after he was patched up would be transferred to a federal maximum detention center. They doubted they'd have to face him again until some future court date. Next time, too, tighter security would ensure that there was no chance for him to escape. There wasn't a big discussion about the takedown, nor was it viewed as mission accomplished...just as another terrorist captured. None of the agents talked about the episode at LAX, except that another family would be heartbroken because of the death of their daughter at the Northwest Airline departure lounge.

Something else struck the agents as unusual, however—not being summoned by their boss to immediately turn in their reports, which he constantly insisted upon, and him not lambasting Mercado for taking off after he strictly barred her from leaving.

Overlooked or not, Art and Consuela had some unfinished business to take care of.

About an hour later, Dan Curbside arrived back at the Unit, pissed off that he was sent out to the Valley with no specific plan or valid counter-terrorist subject for investigation. The director could be hard to read sometimes, he mused, but this seemed over the top.

Mercado darted past McLaughlin's secretary, knocked on his inner office door, and, without waiting for an invitation to enter, preceded Art into the room.

"Did I ask you into my office?" he asked dismissively. Leaning forward, he shut down his laptop. A stack of CD's near his right elbow toppled over. The flushed face was far from welcoming.

Mercado, pressing her hands on her hips, started to speak when she noticed Quintal standing on the far side of the room with his standard cold reaction and touch of scorn expression. One arm hung loose to his side, while his other hand dug deep in a side pocket of his khaki pants.

"What do you want...have more ridiculous charges against me?" The director's voice couldn't have sounded more resentful. "You two are lucky I haven't reported you to Phillipson," referring to the name of the Homeland Security assistant secretary, the man whom McLaughlin intended to succeed next year. "When I want to see you, I'll buzz. Now get out."

Mercado pulled up an armchair, pushed herself close to the desk, and crossed her legs, peering straight into his eyes. "I have no intention of leaving." When he started to rise, she said, "Walter, sit down."

Lips curling, McLaughlin plopped back into his large plush chair. "Watch your tongue, Agent Mercado. You don't know how close you are to being on the way out of the Unit. Especially since you were forbidden to leave. I don't care what transpired at the airport."

She increased her staring. Long before she and Art returned from LAX, he would've received information from other law enforcement agencies about Saleh Ali Nabhat Saleh and Mohamed Dauadi. Plus accounts from Lamborghini, the only agent he'd conferred with when everybody reported in.

"I want to discuss two assignments you sent my crew out to," she said, being careful how she crafted her statement. "Neither one is remotely logical, and I think were done with malice in mind."

"What the hell are you talking about?"

Just then, Quintal drew closer to the desk. "Mercado, you're already in deep shit. You want to add being sued for slander? I'm ordering you to shut your mouth."

"I'm not talking to you," she said, "and you don't order nothing."

Quintal scratched the redness on his rosacea-scarred nose, and was about to speak.

"Make another ethnic slur," Art said, "you'll regret it." After Quintal resumed his earlier post, Art added, "Don't leave...you and me aren't done yet."

"Are you criticizing the way I operate the Unit?" McLaughlin asked Mercado. "I happen to be in charge here...not you. How I assign agents to the field is my business."

"Says you, Walter. All right, no more pussyfooting. Let's stop with the pretense. I'll start with Dan. Sending him almost out to the San Bernardino Mountains was designed to keep him away from the team. Think not? To top it off, you had all his communication devices deliberately cut off. Why? So as to prevent contact between Dan and I." She took a short breath, and then went on. "Art took a bullet in a parking garage...that topic we're gonna discuss in a minute. I wanted Dan or Tony to join Art as back up. That's the standard requirement when agents go into ops. Your 'suspicious activity' you dreamed up was a pretense to put him in a dangerous situation."

"Careful, Mercado, about what you're insinuating." Shifting sideways, McLaughlin slid a pencil along his desk, snapping it in half near one of his two telephones. A sudden pink tinge darkened his cheeks. "You already accused me of inappropriate action against a detainee, which you can't prove ever occurred; now you're castigating me for how I run this department. Who put you up to this? Ah, yes, Dodek. Always ready to fuel the fire. I had misgivings about bringing him here. I should've guessed—"

"You should've guessed your lamebrain scheme would come to light?" injected Art, moving up to the desk. He pulled a folded notepaper out of his pocket. Smoothing it out, he dropped it in front of McLaughlin, who brushed it aside. "Look at it. Look familiar? It's your print order, where you assigned me to check a certain parking garage near LAX."

"It's a standard order for a field operation, so what?"

"When did you obtain Intel that something suspicious needed Unit investigation? In particular about Saleh Ali?"

The director tightened the corners of his mouth. "Earlier this morning. It warranted checking."

"And you selected me?"

"Yes, you, Dodek. You were available. Remember, your partner was grounded. Curbside was already in the field. Lamborghini was still messed up over Aylesha's accident."

"Without a back-up partner," Mercado said, "is highly irregular. Dan could've gone. Only you made sure he wasn't around."

McLaughlin stood and glanced over at Quintal, lowered his gaze, and walked end to end along his desk.

"Only there was no terrorist activity, as you never had Intel about Saleh Ali," Art said, letting out a deep breath, adding, "and without a partner, I'd be an easy target."

"Mercado's almost talked herself out of a job, now you're coming up with more shit."

"Think so? Consuela and I were in your office just before you handed me the assignment. Look at your print out."

"I don't have to. I prepared a basic field-op order; you were ordered to follow up."

Art smoothed the print out and waved it, face up, under McLaughlin's chin. "Check the date...*boss*. A day and a half before the call came, you had printed it. And it came from your printer. Convenient, huh. There was no report from the FBI about Saleh Ali at the time you assigned me—not until Noordine actually received notice about him and Dauadi today at the airport. In my book, you threw me to the wolves."

"You're way out of line, Dodek," Quintal barked, throwing his hand into the air.

"Says who? Now let's turn our attention to you...Walter's CIA consultant. Or should I say, his phony CIA connection. Except, you were never a member of the Central Intelligence Agency. The Unit would sure be interested in why you were kicked out of the army. Allegiance to your country...honor as an officer of the United States military...? Bullshit. You used your connection to McLaughlin for your insane firebrand form of justice. Should I tell the Unit why you were court-martialed?"

Art spotted Quintal's eyes tensing up, and the clenched fist aiming for his head. Pushing out his right forearm, he blocked the hand, pivoted sideward, extended an elbow, and clouted Quintal over the left temple, sending him awkwardly against the desk.

Mercado jumped off her chair and moved about a yard from her partner.

"Come at me again," Art snarled, his arms raised in karate motion. "I'll finish what I should've done long ago."

"You're fucking crazy, Dodek," Quintal shouted, shaking his head to lessen the stinging in his ear. "McLaughlin, you gonna stand by and let this fucker — ?"

"I wouldn't say too much right now, Walter," Mercado said.

McLaughlin pressed his hands on the top off his desk. He could've said plenty. Instead, he chose to remain silent.

Art relaxed his stance and said, "At the parking garage, someone put a bullet through the car window. A .22. To send a message? Must've disappointed you, Quintal, that you missed."

"I don't know what the fuck you're talking about. You are nuts!" Stress added to a person suffering from rosacea; it certainly affected Quintal. Thickness and redness of the face, patches of bumps on his nose, even on his chin and forehead, increased. Ugly purple veins protruded en masse.

"You have a .22 pistol," Art continued. "A check in ordnance could confirm a spent bullet. Real coincidence, wasn't it, you showing up right after."

"Dodek, stop it," McLaughlin said loudly. "You're inferring that a member of my unit took a shot at you."

"One of us isn't a member of the Unit," Art shouted back.

Quintal lunged at Art, shoving him up to the wall. "You think you can accuse me...?" He clutched Art's neck and dug a thumb into his skin next to the Adam's apple. Then he ploughed a clenched fist below the left eye, stunning Art momentarily.

Recovering, Art shoved the former soldier to the opposite side, braced his shoulders, and sent a hard swipe with the edge of his hand against Quintal's jaw. This sapped the strength of his holding on, and a weak arm dropped to the side. Art grabbed his shirt, spun him around, and brought up his fist, aiming it straight to the temple.

"Touch him again, Dodek," McLaughlin hollered, "and I'll have you brought up on federal assault charges." Although he wouldn't risk separating them for fear of a wayward punch, he certainly could press a charge against the Canadian agent. This time the tone of his voice carried authority.

Art loosened his grip and pushed Quintal onto the chair, which Mercado had vacated. Flexing his fingers, he swallowed a breath of air and stepped a foot backward. The chance of a federal charge wasn't the reason he let go. Quintal wasn't worth it.

"Both of you get out," McLaughlin ordered as he checked on his dazed partner. "I'll deal with you later, Mercado."

The two agents didn't hesitate and started for the door.

Mercado stopped, wheeled around, and let fall a set of documents that she'd been holding onto. As they floated down to the desk, she said, "You might want to read the excerpts from the M.E. again, like, where it states both Tariq and Najaif conclusively showed signs of torture administered to their bodies pre-mortem."

"Get out, damn you!"

They left, banging the door shut behind them. Ranting and swearing behind the door bounced off their ears. A startled secretary watched the pair disappear down the corridor.

Chapter 58

Art wasn't even sure what time it was when he sat down at his desk near the Central Processing section. Noordine and another analyst three desks away were conferring over a set of computers…more than likely an Arabic e-mail intercept, which she'd translate. Long, black hair draped over the shoulders of her off-white shirt. As usual, she had kicked off her high heels. Yet, in her stocking feet, she seemed taller than what he remembered.

Twice, since he left McLaughlin and Quintal stewing about the events about an hour ago, his wristwatch had slowed. Perhaps slamming his hand on Quintal's jaw had jarred some mechanical components. His eyes were sore and tired. It took a full thirty seconds when he glanced up at the world time clocks to zero in on the Los Angeles West Coast time, 4:43:18 p.m. Stale gun smoke residue from earlier today still clung to his right shirt cuff. Determined to forget about the airport incident, he meditated for a couple of minutes, something that he rarely did anymore. Nothing significant popped up. Then he realized he hadn't spoken with Lynda for several nights. As soon as he got back to the apartment tonight and showered, he promised he'd call her. Mentally, he began listing certain words he would say. That idea didn't last long.

Right now, there was DHS business to finish. He completed today's field operation report, reviewing only the first three of six pages on the computer monitor, noticing a few spelling mistakes, which he ignored, but fixed an obvious typographical error. After printing it out, he signed and dated the block on the lower right corner, stapled the pages together, and dropped it on his desk. The director could read it later, he figured, wondering whether his days at DHS were numbered. Following the second hand on the L.A. time clock with one eye closed, he straightened up. Underneath his left eye he felt a small bruise forming where Quintal had scored his only hit. For all the brouhaha that Quintal made out about his toughness, it surprised him that he could be restrained so effortlessly. He expected greater resistance; it never came.

Even if Art's assumption about him firing off the .22 was circumstantial, it sure shook the hell out of Quintal. In one way, he wished he'd seen him sneaking up behind the Ford—going beyond a slap and one punch would've been a lot more forceful, and worth the consequences, such as a written reprimand in his file, or suspension.

As he rose, another tinge of pain shot through his lower back. He drew in a breath until the pain subsided. *Shit*, he mumbled, he had left the pill bottle in the Focus.

Heading out of the section, McLaughlin cornered him in the hallway.

Art just wanted to pass, go on his way. This was the last person who he wanted to talk to. But he noticed something in the director's eyes, a lets-talk-like-father-and-son look, and he stopped. Art had nothing to add. In fact, he expected Homeland Security to follow up with its own internal investigation about the Unit's handling of Saleh Ali and Mohamed Dauadi, among other issues, which assuredly would lead to them questioning McLaughlin. And Quintal.

"Give me a minute of your time…please," the director said in a non-antagonistic voice.

Art nodded. A brittle feeling still lingered between them. *Let's hear what you want to say*, he said to himself, but not without some reservation.

They walked down to the end of the corridor, made a slight right turn, and stopped.

There were no offices at this end; no doubt he preferred no one listening. McLaughlin loosened his tie. Sweat stains were evident on his white shirt from nerves going viral in his office. "You're a newcomer to the Unit, Dodek. You have to understand that things are done differently here than what you are used to in your National Security organization in Canada."

"Did Quintal ask you to talk to me?" Art asked suspiciously.

"No, not at all. Mack is down the street nursing a Scotch. You made him angry as hell."

If this discussion concerned Quintal he wasn't interested, and he started to leave.

"No, wait, let me finish. In spite of what you think of me, how I run the Unit, I'm on the same team as you. Counterterrorism is a dangerous business. People get hurt. People get killed sometimes. Other times people misinterpret what we're up against. I don't want to argue with you— we've had enough animosity, wouldn't you agree?" He didn't wait for Art to reply. "Mercado and you, especially you, make a big thing about prisoner abuse. You still can't implicate me. There's nothing you can do anyway. For years there's been covert operations where some prisoners— terrorists, militants, insurgents, freaking killers—have been roughed up on our soil. Think I'm gonna deny it? Think my government is gonna

293

deny it? Those liberal asses from the media like nothing better than to smear the people who put their lives on the line.

"Just because some Jihadi religious extremist gets his ass kicked in. We're at war, Dodek. Crazies from the Middle East, fanatics, want to annihilate us. Why shouldn't we have the right to strike first? You think I've conspired to torture prisoners. I'd rather be thumped for that as opposed to letting them destroy us. Intelligence works best when we get the upper hand. How many people have you roughed up? Killed? You have no compunction to hold back. You of all guys, I doubt you'd hesitate using any means to save your own."

The last sentence riled Art, the inference about his Jewish heritage. He shook his head and said, "We rely on Intel. Agreed. Torturing them is gonna help? The only ones who it helps are the same militants you're chasing, the ones you call fanatics. It just piles up more grievances, more hatred for the West, which results in more terrorist attacks. I agree there are some sob sisters out there who flip out every time a detainee is manhandled by us, but crawls away in denial when some fanatic blows up a school, a marketplace, inside a mosque filled with their own people. Non-typical methods have succeeded where violence fails—counter-intelligence, disrupting their leadership, cutting off funding, destabilizing their rank and file, blockading their supply routes, confiscating weapons, munitions, bomb making materials. Convicting terrorists with stiffer sentences. Show fanatics that our justice is absolute, not always for retribution."

"Where in hell did you pick up such idealistic bullshit? What we've accomplished in this country, by whatever means used, might...will...prevent another 9-11."

"I won't disagree. Around the world since then many potential terrorist attacks have been prevented. The ones who are intercepted and caught outnumber the numbers of suicide bombers that do succeed. And it's due to damn good intelligence by people working around the clock that work their butts off and risk their lives and won't stop until they've reigned in the worst of the bad that want to hurt us. I just think that a person responsible for the security of your homeland hasn't the right to act out your own brand of justice. Walter, somehow you've confused violence with justice. You may think you're helping your country; it just isn't so. And how you got mixed up with that nutcase Quintal...from what I've seen, you've been brought down to his twisted level. The man is a coward. And a risk to your...our...fight against terrorism. Do you really believe he'd risk his ass for you, take a fall for you? He's a liability that's gonna fuck you up sooner than later."

Whatever the director might've thought about his connection with Quintal, he refrained from commenting. Instead, he referred to Art

Dodek's involvement at the NSU. "Although I was skeptical about bringing you here, Alistair Burke reassured me that you'd be a team player, anxious to add not only your experience but your optimism to go along with the way in which we conduct intelligence. Truthfully, Dodek, I expected more from you, not your slamming the DHS or being a shit-disturber. I should've realized when he wrote in your file that you tend to go ape, you weren't a fit with the Unit."

Art shrugged his shoulders.

McLaughlin stepped back, his eyebrows pulled together, and the corners of his mouth lifted and lowered. Pointing a finger at Art, he said, "You may be out of the Unit sooner than you think."

"Whatever. Regardless where I'm assigned, I follow orders, occasionally unpopular ones. Isn't that what you were mandated to do?"

Lips stretched flat across the face into a thin line, the director scowled and turned, walking at a fast pace toward the administrative offices. With a quick turnaround, he muttered, "You of all people know the whole thing is bullshit. It's a game. The politicians play it everyday. Us? We're handed the ball. Except, it's wet and slippery. How many touchdowns have you fumbled?"

Art just shook his head. Whatever demons had infiltrated McLaughlin's mind were his to deal with. He wasn't without his own issues. Damn, there were plenty. His past was full of problems, the present continued to plague him; what loomed on the horizon, he didn't want to ponder.

What pissed Art was the knowledge that McLaughlin even considered sending him out on a mission that didn't exist, with the intention of causing Art serious bodily harm. Would he be capable of such an act? The director disliked Dodek intensely for always questioning his authority, operation tactics, and accusing him of prisoner abuse. The man was power hungry, yeah, but that wouldn't send him over the edge. Perhaps the director didn't participate in their actual mistreatment; however, he was no less guilty.

Enter Quintal. With deliberate conniving, he'd found the mountain edge to send him over. Since he watched the tapes of McLaughlin removing Tariq and Najaif from detention, it had occurred to him that Quintal had a mean streak bad enough that torturing them would've been for his own gratification, not just for interrogation purposes.

Art had his share of individuals feigning their support for all things patriotic, and then betraying those who they entrusted. Having a hand in eliminating such a person wouldn't have held him back at all.

Around six o'clock, Mercado and other members of the Unit invited Art to join them for a drink. Not for a victory celebration—Saleh Ali and Muhamed Dauadi left a sour taste in everybody's mouth—just a get-together to share their comradeship. Within walking distance of the federal building they found a lounge near Union Station. The place was packed with office workers and both uniformed and civilian-dressed cops, deputies, and officers from the immigration services, along with scores of people from various government agencies.

The group's selection of spirits couldn't have been any stranger. Naturally, Art ordered a glass of Californian Chardonnay; Mercado, a bottle of *Dos Equis* beer; Curbside, who maintained a regimen of weight training, chose a Coors Light; Lamborghini surprised his partners by ordering a vodka martini. Laughter erupted when Noordine ordered a Shirley Temple plus a jigger of Gordon's Dry Gin. Aylesha received their first toast with a hearty "get well" shout and round of applause.

All four TV monitors were tuned to a L.A. Dodgers game that was about to start. The fans at Dodger Stadium quieted down for the singing of the national anthem, and just as the last verse blared out, Consuela jumped up, raising her bottle to the ceiling. The others rose in unison.

Near the end of the last stanza, in one loud voice they roared *"for the land of the free and the home of the brave."*

Taking a break from the noise, Art strolled outside. Heat from the early evening that radiated up from the pavement made it uncomfortable to stand on the sidewalk. He took refuge alongside the building. A parking lot divided the lounge from a two-story commercial complex. Besides, there was something he wanted to do. Whisking out his cell phone, he pressed down a recall digit for a number in Vancouver.

After three rings, he clicked off before the answering machine came on. Then he thumbed down a second set of numbers, plus an extension code.

"Lynda Dodek speaking. May I help you?"

"Hi, Lyndie."

Brief silence, then, "Oh…it's you." At first her voice had sounded energetic, cheerful, before it lapsed into a flatter tone. "The stories from Los Angeles…whenever I hear about a terrorist incident, I stop and think, *you're* right in the middle of it; you wouldn't have it any other way."

"Did you throw out your welcome mat? I called to —"

"No need to be sarcastic. I do worry about you. Are you coming home? Or do you and your Mexican partner have other plans?"

"Now who's being sarcastic?"

"Your partners at NSU called the other day, wondering when you're coming back."

"Could be soon. Just a few areas to wrap up. How have you been?"

"Doing all right." Muffled voices and a telephone ringing sounded in her real estate office. "You'll let me know when you're leaving, won't you?"

"Certainly. I can hardly wait."

Another pause on her end. "We have to talk, Art, about your—"

"My job? We've done that. What more is there to talk about?"

"I'm serious. I do have to leave. Right after dinner I have an open house. Take care, okay?"

"Sure. You, too." He was about to add something when he heard her voice trail off, and her line fell silent. Going back inside, he waved at his fellow agents engaged in conversation. With Lynda's words fading in his mind, a couple of minutes passed before he joined back in.

Chapter 59

Santa Monica

A couple of minutes before 8 p.m. Art turned off from Ocean Boulevard, down one block, and swung a right toward his apartment driveway. Letting loose with the members of the Unit had allowed him to drive from downtown to Santa Monica in a fairly cheerful mood. Just like his comrades with the Canadian National Security Unit, he'd developed a close relationship with the Unit…become friends quickly, fathomed which way his partner was coming from. Perhaps it was reliance on one another, backing each other up when a situation became messy; talking sense into each other when they were too stubborn to see the forest for the trees; and without a second's hesitation, placing their lives before their fellow team members. Regardless of how long he remained in Los Angeles, he'd carry good memories about the Unit.

As he faced the underground parking garage, the clicker to raise the gate wouldn't activate. Aiming it mid-level and depressing more forcefully, a second and third try also failed. Then the Ford Focus shuddered and stalled in drive. Shifting back to park, he slid the ignition key to off then switched back on. Nothing. Not even the whirring of a weak engine, which might've suggested a dead battery. None of the panel lights or accessory electrical components in the vehicle worked, either, as he fiddled with some of the buttons and levers. *Shit*, he mumbled to himself, *now what?*

He withdrew his BlackBerry, flipped up the cover, and stared at the blank screen. Hitting the keypad with his thumb and forefinger resulted in all programs malfunctioning. Half a minute later only the numbers, extensions, and pre-set codes from a memory card entered from his Canadian National Security organization illuminated, plus a few personal numbers. A little aggravated, he began pushing the Los Angeles FBI and DHS pre-sets, which Noordine had coordinated into his phone on his first day at the Unit. *It figures*, he muttered, when "Access Cancelled" appeared.

The person who he wanted to contact was Consuela; it wouldn't happen now. Walking around the parking lot he heard a car horn, and glanced sideways to check its nearness. His eyebrows arched and lips parted when a black Ford Crown Victoria, big white letters on its doors signifying Department of Homeland Security, drew up alongside. Consuela Mercado waved at him through the open window on her passenger side. At the wheel was the agent who had handed him the keys to the Focus at LAX.

Art stopped, watching Mercado, a broad smile across her face as she walked over and said, "I've never seen you at a loss for words, partner. Feel like you're outside looking in?"

"What gives? The car, my phone...."

"Don't get your balls in a knot. Hasn't it dawned on you everything's been disabled?"

"It was beginning to occur to me." He stood beside her. The driver in the Ford nodded.

"Your assignment with the DHS is finished," she said.

"McLaughlin didn't lose any time, did he?"

She moved to the left so now they were standing face to face. "He's cleaning house.

You happen to be the first. Guess what? I'm suspended. He actually suspended me. Know how? On my cell phone...he texted me the news."

"So, what happens next?"

"I'll fight it."

Not surprising she affirmed her position to oppose her suspension. Feisty, strong-willed from the get-go, Mercado wouldn't lose any time setting up her defense. Subject to a formal hearing, as a member of the Homeland Security Department, she'd be entitled for a lawyer to represent her, *pro bono*, and no loss of pay while off duty.

"I hear you and Walter exchanged a few heated words about the Unit."

"Not the Unit, per say, but his tactics. You know he's in way over his head."

"You will never get a consensus on what happens in America and how to deal with the trouble it faces every day. After September 11, everybody expected the government to be transparent about its fight against terrorism. Well, Iraq and Afghanistan changed all that. We've encountered an enemy we've never fought before. Our tactics had to change to match and overtake theirs. Thank God we have the Intelligence organizations in this country to combat a handful of crazed religious fanatics. Look what's happened since you arrived—deadly shoot-outs, terrible loss of lives, terrorists attacking. I'll be truthful; I've never had such a fight on my hands. To say we should've done more...or we've stretched ourselves too far over the line...well, maybe one day we'll figure it out."

Art nodded and crossed his arms. Until today, Mercado had hardly uttered anything close to a political viewpoint. But he'd never heard a person express herself so sincerely. There were all sorts of things he could've mentioned. His country had its own war with militants. To succeed at all, he knew it would take the coordination and determination of the international community, and to stop much of the apathy of those who stuck their heads in the sand.

He unfolded his arms. A sudden breeze lifted her dark hair over her forehead. She made no effort to hold it down. Each time he would look toward her he would gaze for a few seconds, lower his eyes, and then return to meet them again. As always, though, her intense eyes peered at him as if she could see right through him.

Mercado moved over to a pillar next to the garage. Art followed, stopping at a hedge of shoulder-high cedars.

"You know, Art, some of us will miss you when you're gone. Then there's those who can't get rid of you fast enough." Her eyebrows pulled together, as though she were thinking of how to say the right thing. "Many people owe their lives to you."

He started to shrug off her statement, but she tapped his arm.

"I'll miss you, Agent Dodek. I'm proud to have had you stand in as my partner."

"Ditto, Connie," he smiled. He raised his hand, waved his thumb behind him. "If I can't get into the garage...what about my stuff in the apartment?"

"Everything's in the trunk of my car," she chuckled.

"You people sure move fast, don't you? Was this happening when we were at the lounge?"

"You know I can't disclose confidential info. Tell me...." she began in a serious tone. "Would you have killed Muhamed Dauadi? Be honest."

"What do you think?"

"That's something you have to ask yourself. Anyway, you're leaving no baggage behind."

"Forgetting Quintal?"

"Forget the bastard."

"I won't forget that when he took a shot at me, it was for real."

"Uh-huh. Let it go." Stepping closer, she placed a hand on his shoulder and hugged him. Then she kissed his left cheek. "Did you ever wonder what might've happened that night at my place?"

Far from feeling embarrassed, he pressed himself closer for a few seconds, and stepped back.

His silence left her question unanswered. She let it go at that.

Both came out from behind the cedars and approached the Crown Victoria.

"Take off your vest; its U.S. government property, and your badge," she said.

The uncomfortable vest he wouldn't miss, but regardless of whose badge he wore, it felt like part of him was missing.

After tossing the items onto the rear passenger seat, Mercado pulled a small folder from her inside shirt pocket. Still in her DHS vest, she had to struggle with the envelope before she placed it in his hand.

At first, Art couldn't make out the contents until he noticed it was an airline-boarding pass for a one-way flight to Vancouver, Canada. He folded the envelope and shoved it into a side pocket.

"Get in, Art. We'll drive you to the airport."

Day or night, freeway traffic and the bottleneck on the ramp leading to the terminal added to the length of time it should've taken from Santa Monica to LAX. Both Art and Consuela remained silent all the way over. Perhaps everything that could've been said had been said. Sometimes when your mind is doing the talking, thoughts get mixed up. True, he'd miss the camaraderie of Mercado and the other agents of the Unit. Going home. The overwhelming tension that he'd felt when his finger ached from squeezing the trigger on the gun he held against Dauadi's temple. The crummy attitudes that McLaughlin and Quintal had toward the Unit. For all that had happened this month, maybe it was better that he left before he took it all too seriously.

At the terminal, he retrieved his garment bag and one carry-on piece. He stood beside the passenger door, quiet, reflective, as Mercado gazed up at him. When she spoke, it didn't surprise him a bit when she whispered, "Look me up next time you visit L.A. Now go home to your wife." Just as the driver eased off the brake, she exclaimed, "FYI: Noordine made backup tapes. They're in my safety deposit box."

No time to respond, not that he wanted to; he watched the Ford speed up the airport causeway.

Art joined dozens of people heading to the terminal entrance. Fortunately, with his National Security identification he would avoid the long wait at the check-in counter.

***

He didn't notice the fast moving surreptitious figure in a beige golf jacket mount the curb. Less than thirty feet separated them.

A perfect situation loomed. Art had his back to the roadway. The man with the red veins on his nose was almost unnoticeable amongst the crowd. No one saw the .22 pistol with the homemade 4" metal silencer when he slid it out of his right jacket pocket, hugging it tight by his side. Just as the automatic doors opened, he brought up the gun mid level to his chest. At this distance, the experienced Special Ops soldier couldn't miss. One shot to the back of the head, that's all he needed.

Surrounded by a throng of arriving passengers, no one observed his hand rising. Even the gun's velocity at this distance would be shrouded by the noise of vehicles.

Eyes narrowed. Lips tightened. There was no abundance of Cutty Sark in his system to fortify his action…just cold, hard revenge. Art was in the sightline as he squeezed the trigger.

Except, at that split second, his finger loosened.

The man with rosacea lowered his head as his quarry disappeared inside. Despite his many years in the military, he felt the sickening feeling of defeat surging through his stomach.

Now he wanted that Scotch. Maybe by the third or fourth glass he might ask himself why he withheld from killing Dodek.

***

Because Art had a permit to carry a firearm, which he now covered by slipping on a light jacket, security allowed him entry through a passage where U.S. air marshals were issued their specific seating arrangements. Depending on flight and destination, one may sit in First Class, while the other occupied a seat in coach. On this particular flight, he wasn't assigned a seat until he checked in at the gate, port side, 21A. He handed the garment bag over to the attendant and threw the strap of his carry-on bag over his shoulder. *Damn it,* he muttered. The sudden movement sparked a nerve in his lower back. He promised himself that he'd visit a chiropractor as soon as he returned to Vancouver. He would let the guy walk all over his back, if that would ease the muscle spasms.

Twenty minutes before boarding, he bought a medium sized coffee at Starbucks, topped it up with two creamers, strolled into a nearby store, bypassed all the souvenirs, gift items, rows of Los Angeles sportswear, and browsed at many of the international newspapers. Practically whichever front page he viewed there were either pictures or articles about the current stalemate in Afghanistan or the aftermath of the latest Taliban attacks against allied forces and civilians. One article he read through: U.S worried about the increasing violence of the al-Shabad brigade in Somalia, and its export of militants.

Returning to the corridor he glanced for a moment at the boarding gate and front row chairs opposite the windows looking out to the runways. Sipping his coffee, he scanned the passengers, recalling the chilling episode at the Northwest Airline waiting room. That was then, this was now.

Art walked over to a bank of telephones, taking the one at the end, and looked up a number from one of the attached phone directories. Resting the cup on a shelf, he inserted the required coins for a local number, and then pressed the numbers on the keypad.

"Los Angeles Times news bureau," a voice answered.

"Your White House reporter, please."

Within fifteen seconds a man answered. "Joel Ritzier speaking."

"You should ask the White House about the Department of Homeland Security covering up the fact that they're torturing prisoners in Los Angeles."

"What? Who is this?"

Art hung up the phone. Give a news tip to a reporter, especially about a political cover up, he's going to dig until he unearths the next big White House scandal.

As he passed a lounge, some patrons were standing below one of the wall mounted TV sets. The bartender increased the volume to enhance the audio. Breaking news in big red letters flashed along the bottom of the screen. A local news reporter, a notepad in one hand and a microphone close to her mouth, stood in front of the Los Angeles federal building. The entire street was ringed with police cars and a multitude of uniformed and civilian dressed law enforcement officers. He leaned over a railing to catch the sound of the reporter's voice amongst the crackle of airline address systems and the noisy, crowded corridor.

"Although news is sketchy at this time," she said, as sirens blared in the background, "the FBI has confirmed that the body of a man found dead on the sixth floor was that of the West Coast director of Homeland Security. Authorities won't confirm, but it's believed a staff member found him in his private office. Anonymous sources say he died of a gunshot wound to the head. All police will say is that's too early in their investigation to pinpoint cause of death."

The gate attendant announced the first boarding call.

Several passengers rose and proceeded to form a line near the departure counter. Waiting for row number, he found a seat beside a middle-aged East African couple. The woman, wearing a full-length black chador and hijab headscarf, smiled, and then resumed twirling her Tasbeeh prayer beads.

THE END

About the Author

R. J. Hepner chases history and current events like a NASCAR racing driver. Ancient Egypt, the Persian Empire, and the Roman/Greco period are his favorite pursuits. Through these mediums he draws inspiration for creating a series of Intel thrillers. A dual U.S. & Canadian citizen, he resides in the Okanagan Valley in Northeastern British Columbia with his wife, Marion. Previous occupations included working as a ship chandler salesman, iron shop finisher, shipyard store man, and at a regional Hyundai auto distribution center. He owned and managed two consulting businesses in Newport Beach, California and Vancouver, B. C. During this time he wrote business plans and proposals for Asian entrepreneurs and investors.

Made in the USA
Charleston, SC
20 November 2014